A Lake Mistletoe Collection

SEASON ONE

BY
PENELOPE GERHARDT

A LAKE MISTLETOE COLLECTION. SEASON ONE.

First edition. July 16, 2024.

Copyright © 2024 Penelope Gerhardt.

ISBN: 978-0473719951

Written by Penelope Gerhardt.

Dear reader, please be aware that this tale contains strong language and detailed descriptions of sexual acts.

For anyone who loves a sweet shot of steam...

especially at Christmas time.

ABOUT THE AUTHOR
SEXY. SWEET. FUN.

My books bring together the perfect blend of sweet and steamy, with characters that leap off the page.
They feature relatable heroines and swoony heroes, along with happy endings *wink wink* guaranteed to leave a smile on your face. Life should never be boring, and neither should books.
Come along with me and enjoy the love, laughs, and lives of my colorful cast of characters.
They're tasty. Cross my heart.

xx PG xx

The Christmas Crush

BOOK ONE
SEAN AND LEXIE

1

Lexie

As soon as I see that big green sign dusted with fresh snow, I know I'm home, and not just because it reads "Welcome to Lake Mistletoe." I've been staring down at concrete and cabs from a cramped twelfth story apartment for so long that I've almost forgotten what peaceful feels like.

A row of snowy pines lines either side of the main street, and the storefronts darkened by the late evening, come alive with the twinkling Christmas lights strung from their eaves. I take a deep breath and pull my jacket collar a little tighter around my neck as I take it all in. In the distance, I can see my old high school on the hill and make out the black and white banner of the Mistletoe Magpies flapping in the chilled wind.

I'm immediately transported back to the days I walked those halls, telling my friends what an amazing life I was going to have after graduation, that I'd be in art exhibitions all over the world, and thinking there was nothing more important than me and Jack being crowned prom king and queen. Things were a lot easier back then, that's for sure.

Mom looks back at me, her blonde hair tucked under a cute pink knitted hat. She smiles. "I've got your room all set up, just like you left it. Gosh, it'll be nice having you home, Lexie."

I smile back, and I wish I didn't have to force it so much. "I'm excited too. I would have stayed in a motel but… "

"Don't be silly, Lexie," Dad adds to the conversation. "No point wasting money when you have a perfectly good bedroom at home."

"You couldn't have timed it better," Mom says. "I could use your help with the Christmas party. Your father and I will get to show off both our girls."

"Polly might give you a little attitude to start," Dad says. "She's used to having free rein at the house. But I'm sure she'll come right after a couple of days. She's high maintenance. Gets it from her mother."

He nudges mom with a wink and she laughs, playfully slapping his arm.

I roll my eyes. Right. The cat. It took about five minutes for Mom to decide the house was far too quiet with me gone. The result of her empty nest syndrome is Polly, the fluffiest, snuggliest, bitchiest Persian cat you'll ever meet, and apparently the trade-off for free room and board was sharing my space with the puffball my parents affectionately nickname 'Lexie's little sister'.

Just before we exit the main street, with its lamplights wrapped in green ribbons and bows, I glimpse a building I remember as Deena's, a cozy family-style restaurant where everyone went for their birthday. But it looks shut down. Newspaper blocks out the windows, and the old neon sign is gone, replaced with much classier gold-etched signage showcasing the building's new name, Talley's.

"Oh my gosh, what happened to Deena's?" I ask, genuinely unsettled. That place was a part of my childhood after all, even if the mashed potatoes tasted like lumpy glue.

"Oh yeah," Mom says, looking over her shoulder and out the window as we drive by. "Deena retired and moved to Pine Point to live with her son. It's being renovated by the new owner. Opens on Wednesday night, I believe."

I look at the sign again before we drive so far it's only a gold blur in the distance. Talley's. Why does that sound so familiar? Before I have time to ask more questions about the destroyed memories of my youth, Dad pulls into the driveway of our two-story craftsman house and hits the brakes just before he smacks into the garage door. Mom and I lunge forward then grunt when our seatbelts yank us back. Dad's driving is definitely not passenger friendly. At least some things haven't changed.

I gaze out the window and admire the light show Dad has put on this year. Twinkling white lights delicately trace the roofline, like a pathway to the stars, and the eaves are strung with blinking garlands of vibrant red and green. His trusty vintage reindeer display takes center stage on the snowy lawn, towing Santa in his sleigh, though Santa has seen better years. I remember how bright the red of his suit was when I was a kid, and it makes me a little sad to see how time has faded it.

I climb out of the car and amble to the back, but Dad is already there with the trunk open, heaving out my suitcases. He puts two on the drive then pants, with his hands on his hips, as he eyes up the other pair.

"Geez, Lexie, are you moving back home?" he teases.

I laugh uncomfortably. "I haven't decided what I'm wearing to Tom and Sophie's wedding, so I brought a few options."

"You'll look beautiful no matter what you wear, sweetheart," Dad says, and I'm in such need of an ego boost I inhale his words, even though I'm sure every father says that to his daughter.

I hope there's something in one of those suitcases that looks decent. I would have liked to get something new on such a special occasion, but my bank balance vehemently disagreed. Then there was the matter of finding something that still fits. I've put on a couple of pounds. I didn't notice, but Jack brought it to my attention over dinner one night, and now I can't unsee the additional width in my hips and thighs.

I hear a creak and worry that it's Dad's back, but then I glimpse warm light spilling onto the porch of the next-door neighbor's house and a figure standing at the front door.

"Is that you, Sean? Couldn't bother you for a hand, could I?" Dad called. "Looks as if my eldest child has brought everything but the kitchen sink."

I frown. Great. A cat jibe. Wait. Who's Sean?

"No problem, Stan," a deep, rumbling voice calls from across the driveway.

I can hear him jogging over, his boots squelching in the snow, and his breath turns to smoke in the air. When he arrives, I can't help staring at his face. He's got the bluest eyes I've ever seen, like the sky over the lake in the summer, making any other shade of blue seem ordinary. The cold evening frosts the tips of his tousled brown hair, the streetlights catching glimpses of gold, and he's wearing a loose red sweater that hangs off his broad shoulders. As he bends over to pick up one of my suitcases, I can't help but enjoy how his black jeans tighten around his firm backside. I redirect my attention to his face when he stands up, and cough to clear my throat.

"Hi. I'm Lexie."

In the corner of my eye I see Dad's jaw drop, and I don't think he's looked this embarrassed since I crashed my first car into the flower box outside the grocers. I guess bad driving runs in the family.

"Lexie. This is Sean. You know Sean."

I look at him again, which is far from a chore. How did his eyes get bluer in two minutes? He gives a half smile and I feel a wobble in my knees. No. I definitely don't know Sean. I would remember Sean.

"I'm sorry," I say awkwardly through my teeth. "Have we met?"

Sean reaches behind his head and rubs the back of his neck as he lets out a breath. "Yeah. We used to be pretty close." He glances at the house next door. "Still are actually."

I look at the Talley house. They've been our neighbors forever. I'm pretty sure they bought their house the same week my parents bought theirs. I remember when I was a kid my window looked straight across into their son's bedroom. He was in a band, I think. I'd hear his tuba at all hours, and I don't know how many times I caught him watching me. He would play it off, act as if he was cleaning his blinds or checking the weather. One time he just flat out ducked. I guess it was cute. Poor guy. He didn't have many friends, but seemed nice enough. He was always sweet to me. What was his name?

My eyes widen. "Sean," I mumble.

He inhales. "That's me."

"Sean Talley," I repeat as it all sinks in. "Like Talley's, the new restaurant in town?"

He nods. "One and the same."

My head jerks with disbelief. "You own that?"

He looks at me, and it feels like he's looking into my soul. "I do."

"Sean has become quite the restaurateur," Dad chimes in. "It's very impressive."

I manage to pull myself free from the gravity of his gaze and clear my throat again. "That's great, Sean. Congratulations. I'm so sorry, I... I didn't recognize you."

He smiles. "I've gotten taller, I guess."

And hunkier. And fucking hotter.

I gulp as I obsess over the stubble on his Adam's apple. "Yeah. That must be it."

"You can just put that on the porch, Sean," Dad interrupts as he drags my suitcase through the snow.

"Yes, sir," Sean replies.

He moves closer to me and my stomach knots.

"Excuse me," he chuckles, gesturing to the snow-sprinkled cobbled path that I'm blocking.

I laugh a little louder than I mean to, then step aside. "Shanks."

He cocks an eyebrow, and when I realize what I said, I wonder how long it will take to dig a hole in the snow and bury myself. "I was going to say sorry, but I thought about saying thanks, and then it just came out... ."

"... As shanks. No. I get it." He chuckles and my heart backflips. "Well, shanks to you too."

Sean walks past me and I catch a hint of some leathery cologne and discover the back of him is just as appealing as the front. I follow him up the stairs where he sits my suitcase next to the porch swing, with far less fuss and grunting than Dad. He turns to look at me and I still can't believe this is Sean Talley from next door. I go to speak, but he beats me to it.

"So, how's Jack?"

I suddenly catch myself as if I was falling out a window, or jumping from one.

"Jack's great," I reply without missing a beat. "He really wanted to come, but he's so busy with work. He just picked up a big celebrity client, which is amazing for his brand."

"Wow. A celebrity," Sean says, and I can tell by his tone that's he's just being polite. "Anyone I might know?"

"Do you watch 90 Day Fiancé?" I ask.

He puffs his cheeks, then exhales. "Can't say I do."

I can feel my cheeks redden, and I bite my lip like an idiot. "Then probably not."

An awkward silence sprouts between us.

"Dinner," Dad blurts, and I've never been so grateful for him shouting out a random noun. "You should come over for dinner tomorrow night," he finishes. "We can have a proper catch up. Maybe this time Lexie will remember your name."

He frowns at me. I really don't need him jumping on the humiliation bandwagon.

Sean chuckles politely. "Sounds great. See you then." He dips his chin at me and smiles. "Welcome home, Lexie."

I've heard my name before, but not the way he says it. It makes the tiny hairs on the back of my neck stand on end. He slips past me on the stairs. His shoulder grazes mine and I catch that scent again, and suddenly he's gone far too soon.

"Geez, Lexie. Are you serious?" Dad frowns.

"What, it was just a shoulder touch," I snap.

Dad raises an eyebrow. "You don't remember, Sean at all? You lived next door to the boy since you were a kid. You saw him every day."

"Dad, in my defense," I scoff, "he did not look like that when we were in high school. His hair was long, and he had glasses and he always wore that fugly denim jacket."

Dad rolls his eyes, which is justifiable. I literally just described the plot of every nineties' movie where the nerdy girl takes off her glasses, puts on a red dress and is suddenly the hottest babe in the school.

"This is exactly why I love Polly more," he sighs. His expression is stern for a moment, then he breaks into a laugh, leans down, and pecks me on the forehead while I glower. "Come on. Let's get these bags of rocks upstairs. Then I can tell your mother all about that embarrassing exchange."

"Dad," I whine.

"What? It was painful. I thought I was going to vomit."

He continues laughing until we're both inside and I close the door.

2

Sean

When Tom and Sophie set their date for a Christmas wedding, I knew that meant Lexie would eventually be back in town, but that still didn't prepare me for seeing her again. She's just as stunning as I remember. She's grown out her sun-kissed blonde hair. It's not the cute little bob she used to have, but I like this more. It took all my strength not to brush the stray strands behind her ears when she was talking, or get lost in the million shades of green within her eyes. And I don't know how she's done it, but the curves she's pulling off should be criminal. I didn't think about her body in high school. I was too busy obsessing over the way she laughed and the beauty spot near her right eye. But now she has this amazing fullness to her hips, and that ass... I didn't think it was possible for her to get hotter.

I guess I'm a little surprised she didn't recognize me, or maybe that just confirms what I'd figured in high school. I was invisible to her. Especially with Jack around. But things are different now, and if her reaction is anything to go by, I might not be invisible anymore.

My phone rings and flashes Blake's number. I answer, even though I'm dreading what he's about to say.

"Why the fuck did you hang up on me? Did someone die?"

"No. Stan needed my help," I reply. There's a silence and I can practically hear the smug grin on his face.

"Was Lexie there?"

I exhale and lean my shoulder into the closed door. "Yeah. She was."

"And?" Blake pushes.

"And she's still beautiful," I say. "But..."

"But what?"

"She didn't recognize me."

"Like, not at all?"

"Nope."

"Geez, it's not like you've had plastic surgery," Blake laughs. "That must make you feel like shit."

"Yeah. Thanks for reminding me," I chuckle.

"Who cares about Lexie Moore," Blake says. "Her and Jack are practically married. Maybe you can stop obsessing over her long enough to meet someone else at the wedding. You know what they say. The best way to get over a girl is to get under a bridesmaid."

"I'm almost positive that's not what they say," I grin.

"Oh. Maybe that's just what I say then."

I decide I've endured enough of Blake's words of wisdom for the night. "Hey, I can't hang out tomorrow night. The Moore's have invited me to dinner."

"You pussy," I hear him tease just before I end the call.

If you had told me five years ago that I'd be friends with Blake Ward one day, I would have told you to jump in the lake. If I was invisible to Lexie, then I was non-existent to Blake and the other Magpies. But that's the thing about high school. It ends, and when I opened up my first restaurant in South Hills, I needed a PR bulldog to get her off the ground. Hiring Blake was the straightforward part. Digging through the layers of douche-baggery to find an actual decent human being, now that was the challenge. But when we figured out we had things in common, like playing hockey and making money, we got along just fine.

It was even Blake who suggested I try out for the local club team. I may never have been a Magpie, but now I get to play left wing for the Mayhem, and I've made some great friends, and Blake's more than just my PR guy now. We're partners in my latest venture. But I'm almost positive he's just there to drink scotch and look cool.

Alone with my thoughts, I realize how quiet the house is now. Seeing Lexie again reminds me of when she was the girl next door and my parents still lived here. When they decided to move somewhere warmer after years of freezing their asses off every winter, buying the house from them was a no-brainer. They offered to rent it to me first, but I'd already made enough from my South Hills restaurant for the down payment and, at least if I bought it they'd have cash to make a new start with.

They live in Macaroy Beach now. Dad is beet red ninety percent of the time, and Mom's happy as long as she gets to drink margaritas in the sun year round. Mom keeps nagging me to not just visit next time, to sell this place and move out there with them. But that's the last thing I want to do.

I switch off the lights and head upstairs, taking my time with each creaky step. Considering I take old things and make them new for a living, you'd think I would have fixed this staircase by now, and the leaky bathroom faucet, and the temperamental heat pump. But then it wouldn't be home, would it? I reach the landing and carry on to the room I had when I was a kid. I'm not sentimental enough to still bunk down in my good old single bed, and I was quick to take the double bedroom with the balcony and bath when my parents moved out. But my old room still has its charms.

As I linger in the dark, a light flicks on at the Moore house next door, in the room that faces this one. Doors open and close, and bags get flung from one side of the room to the other, until Lexie walks by the window. She looks like she's run a half marathon but, in her defense, those bags weighed a ton. She looks around her old room, picking up a trophy and smiling as memories of the good old days rush back to her. She returns it to the shelf, then wanders to the mirror, taking herself in, seeing herself as I saw her every day. Then she wrestles off her coat, tosses it onto the bed, and slowly unbuttons her shirt.

Apparently, even after living in the city, Lexie still doesn't remember to close her damned curtains. Her skin is flawless, and the more I imagine how it would feel under my fingertips, the harder I get. As she slips the last button, her blouse falls open and my dick presses hard against my jeans when I catch sight of her gorgeous full breasts and pink lace bra.

I exhale before I turn my back on the most beautiful girl I've ever seen and close the door. My phone vibrates in my pocket and I'm grateful for the distraction. As if on cue, Mom has sent a pic of her and Dad's latest eternal sunshine adventure. Jet-skiing. Dad looks terrified, and Mom's probably had enough margaritas not to care. She follows up with a message. "Wish you were here."

If only I felt the same.

I love Lake Mistletoe, the hockey, the snow, the people, and this house. Especially the view from my old bedroom. Shit. I'm instantly reminded of

Lexie and her perfect breasts. Maybe I should have stayed a little longer, waited until she got down to her panties. And just like that, I'm hard again. I walk into my room, reach over my head to pull off my sweater, then toss it onto my parent's velvet wingback armchair in the corner. I've updated a lot of the furniture in the house, but that scarlet vintage chair is a classic. It stays. I kick off my black boots and drop onto the bed, staring at the ceiling with my hands clasped behind my head.

Just because I was too much of a gentleman to stick around and watch Lexie undress, doesn't mean I can't pretend, right? I close my eyes and she's right there in front of me, her blonde hair resting on her soft shoulders, her skin bare and creamy and close enough to touch. Her bra straps slip off easily and those magnificent, heavy breasts are on display for me to enjoy, her pink nipples standing on end. I lick my lips as I imagine flicking my tongue over those gorgeous buds and hearing Lexie moan softly into my hair. I'm so hard now I'm almost busting out of my jeans.

I take my right hand away from the back of my head and drift it over my pecs and down my abdomen until I find my belt. In my dreams I take Lexie's nipple into my mouth, softly sucking and licking before pinching it lightly between my teeth. She groans and grips my hair at the roots as I trail my fingers along her inner thigh, her heat beckoning me to touch her between her legs. I do not deny her, cupping her little pussy in the palm of my hand, her dampness seeping through her white panties. Her scent is intoxicating.

I fumble with the notches until my belt slips off and I hurry to release my throbbing cock from the confines of my jeans. It springs out eagerly and I take it firmly in my hand, stroking softly at first, from the base and along the shaft, rolling my thumb over my head. When I close my eyes, I'm palming the soft mound between Lexie's legs, kneading at her clit while I tongue her rock hard nipple. Pre-cum dribbles from my head and I'm quick to rub it over my cock. With the extra moisture, I stroke harder while I slide Lexie's panties to the side and slip a finger between her slick folds. She's soaking wet, and the noises she's making and the way she tugs at my hair make me want to blow my load right there.

I stroke even harder, choking my cock up and down, feeling it thicken and throb in my hand. In my dream, my fingers are moving just as fast, sliding in and out of Lexie's center, her muscles tightening as her body quivers. Fuck. I can't hold it. She feels so good. I grip the base of my cock and with one last stroke, ropes of cum erupt from my throbbing head. I shake, and my shoulders jerk as the exquisite release sends shocks through my entire body. I inhale deeply as the last of my seed drips onto my jeans and I lie there spent.

That was good, but it makes me want Lexie even more than I did before. I've loved that girl since high school, and I want to show her I'm not the same kid I was back then. But, once again, I have to compete with Jack. I guess hoping she would break up with him eventually isn't working out so well for me. This will have to do for now. The euphoria of blowing my load passes, and I'm reminded of the cum painting my favorite jeans. Probably a good idea to throw them in the machine before hitting the sack.

3

Lexie

My phone vibrates vigorously on the nightstand and blasts Thank U, Next by Ariana Grande at max volume. I bolt upright and clumsily fumble about, trying to grab a hold of it. After knocking over the lamp and spilling my glass of water, I finally grab the squirmy sucker and mash buttons until it shuts up. My back is aching thanks to the hundred-year-old mattress underneath me, and a hot soak in my parents' tub sounds like a fitting remedy. I might as well have a hose and a bucket in my shoe box apartment in the city.

My phone blares again, and I get ready to button mash once more, then I realize it's ringing. Jack's name pops up on the screen and I feel an anxious squirm in my stomach. I put the phone face down on the nightstand as if that will magically make him disappear, and prepare for my bath. The water is so hot I feel like I'm boiling in my skin, and it's absolutely amazing. I'm lucky if I get ten minutes of hot water from the shower in my apartment, and if Jack gets in ahead of me, it's barely five. The bubbles sit at my chin and I stare down at my toes peeking out by the faucet. There's a slow rhythmic drip that has me hypnotized, and the steady sensation sends a shiver over my skin. I close my eyes and shuffle, the warm rolling water finding its way to my crevice. My core tightens and I exhale, my fingertips brushing over my nipple, peeking through the bubbles.

It should be Jack that I see when my eyes are closed, but it's not. It's Sean Talley. The quiet kid from next door who always peeped at me through my window. A smile tugs at the corner of my mouth. I guess I could have closed the curtains if I was really that bothered. It wasn't like I didn't know he was there. It made me feel kind of powerful, being so desired. Jack had the power in our relationship, and I always felt like I was the one doing more of everything. Pleasing more, chasing more, loving more, wanting more. Sometimes I got the feeling that he wouldn't notice if one day I wasn't there.

I hear my phone ring again, and it breaks me from my moment of bliss. It's probably Jack, and it looks as if he's noticing now. Problem is I don't know what to do with that. Especially with Sean from next door taking up so much room in my head. Sean seems so different, yet comfortingly the same. I cringe, thinking about last night and not recognizing him straight away. But back then, Jack was my universe, and when something shines that brightly, it's hard to notice anything else. What an idiot I was.

"Lexie. Sophie and Charlotte are downstairs," Mom says, tapping at the bathroom door.

I cast aside whatever I was planning to do in this tub, pull the plug and clamber out, fishing a towel off the rack and drying off while I listen to the water squelch down the drain. I dash into my room with my towel tied under my arms and throw open one of my suitcases, and when I look up, I realize my curtains are wide open. I'm startled at first, quickly reaching out to close them, but then I pause and strain my eyes across the distance to Sean's bedroom. It doesn't look like he's in there, but I can make out a tuba, old band posters and hockey pennants pinned to the wall. The room's a time capsule, just like mine. No way he's still sleeping in there. I'm tempted to drop my towel, just to see if it brings him out of hiding. Why not? I grin and untuck the towel from under my arms. It falls to the ground in a heap. I stand there for a moment, basking in the aura of my cheekiness as I ruffle my hair at the roots and run a hand along my collarbone.

Suddenly, the door flies open and Sophie bursts into laughter. "Lexie, what the hell?"

I drop to my knees and grab the towel, pulling it back up with me when I stand. "Me what the hell? How about you what the hell? Ever heard of knocking?"

"I didn't expect you to be up here parading around fully nude. What are you doing, filming an OnlyFans or something?" Sophie looks past me to my window with its open curtains.

"Oh my god, you know that's Sean Talley's house right? What if he saw you?" She walks past me, grabs the curtains by their edges, and yanks them shut.

"Yeah. What if," I mumble.

My words catch Sophie's ears and she grins. "Oh. You've seen Sean lately then?"

I nod. "I suppose. He's ah... taller."

Sophie's grin stretches wider, and she crosses her arms over her chest. "Taller. Sure."

We stare at each other for a second and I can see Sophie trying to pry details out of me with her mind.

"Can I get dressed?" I ask, gesturing to the door.

"Fine," Sophie replies. "But we're talking more about this."

She shuts the door as she leaves and I rummage through my suitcase, deciding on a pair of black leggings and an oversized emerald sweatshirt. Sophie doesn't need to worry. I have no issues with Sean being the topic of further conversations.

As I jog down the stairs, I twist my blonde hair into a bun and secure it with a scrunchie. Mom has set out coffee and fruit cake, and Sophie and Charlotte sit at the table nibbling while scrolling through their phones with their elbows on the table. It's another time warp, seeing them sitting there like they did in high school, waiting to catch a ride with me and Jack.

But Sophie is a kindergarten teacher now, and doesn't straighten her hair anymore. It's a wild, gorgeous tangle of honeyed waves and she wears a lot less makeup. Big black eyes and deep red lips were her trademark back in the day. Now she's more muted and prefers the natural look. I wish I was that brave. If I don't leave the house in full makeup, Jack loses his shit.

Then there's Charlotte, a real tomboy at heart and a hell of a hockey player. She could have gone pro if she wanted, so you would never guess that she's an interior designer now. But as soon as the working day is done, she's out of her silk pantsuit and heels and into track pants and an oversized hoodie, and normally on her way to the rink to give the guys a run for their money.

I take a seat at the table and Mom puts a full cup of coffee down in front of me. "Two sugars."

I nod approvingly and take a sip. It hits my nerves like a lightning bolt and I shudder. "That's the stuff."

"So," Sophie begins. "Sean Talley. Where do we start?"

Charlotte looks up from her phone, her ears pricking and her interest piqued.

I frown. "You could have told me he's gorgeous now." I glance at Mom. "All of you. And why didn't you say anything about him being the one who bought Deena's?"

Mom shrugs as she unloads the dishwasher. "It didn't cross my mind. He's just Sean who lives next door. He's just very successful and handsome now, I suppose."

"Care to elaborate?" I ask.

Sophie leans on the table, excited to get started. She knows everybody's business. "You remember how he used to work at the grocer's every day after school and on weekends?"

I didn't, but I nod to keep the conversation going.

"Well, he saved every penny of that. Then after graduation, he goes to college in Middleton and gets a business degree, and when he comes back to Mistletoe, he's buffed, ridiculously hot and owns a restaurant in South Hills. He has like two or three now, and he just bought Deena's."

"Where are his parents?" I ask.

"Moved to the beach," Mom replies. "I hear he helped them retire early." She narrows her eyes at me. "Sounds nice."

I frown. "Maybe your favorite will do a better job than me?" I tip my chin at the pug-faced fluffball ferociously licking itself on the windowsill.

"Don't you listen to her, Polly," Mom says consolingly.

But that cat really couldn't give a shit.

"He owns that house," Charlotte adds. "Not bad for someone who barely said two words in high school. He's Lake Mistletoe's golden boy now. Hangs out with the biggest loser in town, unfortunately, but just because he's rich doesn't mean he has taste."

I cock an inquiring eyebrow, and Charlotte responds reluctantly. "Blake."

Sophie rolls her eyes. "Don't get her started, Lexie."

Charlotte raises her hands placatingly. "Sophie, I love you, and I can't wait to be your bridesmaid, but your brother is a man whore."

"Still?" I add. "He must have slept with the whole town by now."

"And then some," Charlotte says. "I think he's halfway through Pine Point. Not to mention he lives to make my life a living hell. I was bidding on this gorgeous grandfather clock for a house I'm decorating. Absolutely stunning and the dealer assured me that no one else was interested. So I mention at one of Sophie's dinner parties I'm in love with this clock and the auction closes tomorrow, and Blake is there. He feels the need to tell me what a complete waste of money it is, and then when Sophie shows off their new guest room I decorated, he calls it basic!"

I keep nodding, knowing Charlotte will get to the point eventually, while Sophie leans against her hand with the vacant stare of someone who has heard this story a thousand times.

"So, anyway, I jump online the next day, expecting an email congratulating my winning bid, but what do I get instead? Sorry, Miss Powell. You have been outbid, and the auction is now closed." She closes her eyes, puts her pincered fingers to her lips, and draws out a deep breath. "Guess who won my clock?"

I try not to laugh. It doesn't take a genius to figure it out. "Blake?"

"Fucking Blake," Charlotte confirms. "And it's not even on display. Ask Sophie. She's not seen it at his townhouse. Why is he constantly making my life miserable? Probably because he knows I can shoot a puck ten times faster than him." She takes another breath, shrugging the tension from her shoulders as she calms. She looks at me curiously. "What were we talking about?"

"I forget," I say, sipping at my coffee.

Charlotte picks up a piece of fruitcake and takes a massive bite. "Oh hey, how's Jack?" she muffles with a full open mouth.

A breath gets stuck in my throat and I wonder if anyone notices when I gulp. "Jack's fine. He couldn't come out. Just so busy with work."

I feel Sophie's stare pressing down on me, as if she knows something's not right.

"That's good," she says slowly, narrowing her eyes. "How long until he puts a ring on that finger?"

I knew it wouldn't take long before Sophie noticed the absence of a ring. She asks every time we talk, as if it's a forgone conclusion that Jack and I will end up married. I used to think so too.

"Don't waste your time, Sophie," Mom groans as she leans against the sink and throws a tea towel over her shoulder. "Getting details out of her is like trying to get blood from a stone. Be quicker just to call Jack."

"Please don't," I sigh, slurping back the rest of my coffee. "Like I said, he's really busy."

Sophie, Charlotte and Mom all ease up on the topic, thank god.

"I'm going to the store to pick up some things for dinner. Want to come along for some lunch? My treat?" Mom asks.

Zero effort is required to talk me into a free meal these days. I turn to the girls. "Hungry?"

Charlotte glances at her phone, then shoves the remaining cake into her mouth. "Nope. I'm already late. Having a couch delivered in twenty minutes." She stands, leans over the table and slaps a crumbly kiss on my cheek. "I'll catch up with you later. It's so good to have you home, and now we get to be Christmas bridesmaids together." She looks over her shoulder at Sophie. "I even hear the bride is going to let us wear sneakers instead of heels."

Sophie rolls her eyes. "For the millionth time. No sneakers."

"I'll wear her down. Just watch." Charlotte winks as she dashes out the door.

"Don't let the cat out!" Mom screeches. Polly is strictly an indoor cat and if you value your life, make sure you don't forget.

Sophie releases a deep breath, as if her headache has magically vanished.

"Everything okay?" I ask.

"Why did I choose a Christmas wedding?" she sighs as she rubs her temples.

"I was about to ask the same thing," I reply.

"There's just so much going on with the venue and the catering, and everything costs twice as much in December, and it's so cold, but I thought it would be romantic, you know? It's mine and Tom's favorite time of year."

I offer a comforting smile. "I'm sure everything will be perfect, plus I'm here now."

"Yes, and I need you more than ever. Between the wedding dramas and what's happening at the arts center, my brain is fried."

"What's happening at the arts center?" I ask, my eyebrows narrowing. When our under-funded arts program got removed from the high school curriculum, the arts center down at the community hall became my second home. I've loved to paint since I was old enough to hold a brush, and what I could no longer get at school I learned from artists who volunteered their time to kids like me who wanted nothing more than to fill the world with color and beauty.

Mrs. Coral was a retired teacher, and Mr. Simmons was an accountant who sculpted in his spare time, and they opened my eyes to where my talent could take me. But not long after I moved to the city with Jack instead of going to art school, I found out Mrs. Coral had passed away and Mr. Simmons moved to live with his son overseas.

Sophie took over running the center, which is a totally unpaid gig, scheduling the classes and finding the volunteers. She's an art kid like me, and she wanted to make sure all Lake Mistletoe kids had somewhere to express themselves. But I imagine between her teaching and a Christmas wedding, she doesn't have much time to spare.

She notices the worry in my voice, and her chin drops. "It's not good, Lexie. There's just not enough help or money to keep the doors open. We struggle to make rent every month, and times are tough."

"Surely there's something that can be done. Charities? Fundraising?"

Sophie shrugs. "I just don't have the time, Lex. I chase kindergarteners around eight hours a day. The rest of the time, I'm planning this wedding or trying to get some sleep."

"Of course," I say. I reach over the table and clutch my friend's hand. "I should have been here to help. That place was my passion. It shouldn't have become just your responsibility. But I'm here now."

Sophie exhales. "I'm glad. I've missed you. But you might be too late. I'm sorry." Her phone beeps and she releases another heavy breath. "That's Tom. We're looking at napkins. Again. I'll talk to you later, okay?"

I smile and nod as she walks out the door. I can't believe things have gotten so bad. I feel my phone vibrate in my pocket. I pull it out just enough to read the name. Jack. I send it straight to voice mail. Hopefully, a little free lunch will help me solve that problem as well.

4

Sean

Is a tie too dressy for dinner at the neighbor's house? I glare at myself in the mirror, tugging at the navy fabric strangling me. I hook my finger underneath and tug it loose, then run a frustrated hand over my hair. Should I brush this? Slick it back like Blake does sometimes? Shit. It's just dinner, man. Why am I bothering trying to impress her? She has a boyfriend. I'm the last thing on her mind. Yeah. Screw the tie. Backup jeans and sweater it is.

I stopped by Daisy's bakery this afternoon and picked up a sponge cake. She assured me it was Lexie's favorite, and even substituted strawberry jam for plum, which Lexie likes better. I've got the cake box in my hands and I take one last look at myself in the mirror and, even though I'm trying to keep my shit together, I still can't get out of my head the way she moaned in my silly fantasy.

When my cock twitches, I head out the door, hoping the cold will snap some sense into me so I don't show up hard at the Moore's house. I jog up the stairs and take a deep breath before I tap on the front door, and when Lexie opens it all the noise in the world fades away.

"Hi," she says. Her smile is warm and welcoming, but when she bites her bottom lip, I can see she's just as nervous as I am.

"Hey," I say back. I hold out the cake box. "Dessert?"

Her eyes widen, and her excitement chases away my nerves. "Did Daisy make this?" She peeks inside the box like it's Christmas morning. Anyone would think it's a diamond ring, not a cake, with how excited she is. It's so adorable and all I want to do is kiss her.

I nod. "Yep. Fresh today. It has ah, plum jam."

Her jaw falls open, and I work overtime not to stare at her full glossy lips.

"How did you know I love plum jam?" she asks.

I shrug. "Lucky guess."

She snaps the box closed and takes it from me, then steps aside. "Well, what are you waiting for? Come in?" The nerves are gone now, and there's a cheekiness to her tone that has my cock twitching again.

I walk inside and immediately smell the pot roast Beth is making, as well as the cinnamon candle burning on the coffee table and the fresh pine Christmas tree in the living room. I've never really been inside the Moore house, not long enough to pay attention to the details. Usually, if Stan needs my help, it's in the garage, or I'm in and out helping Beth with her groceries. It's nice in here, cozy, with a big fluffy couch covered with festive throw pillows and chunky-knit blankets. The lights on the tree twinkle red, gold and green, and it doesn't take long to figure out the fuzzy pink stocking hanging over the fireplace is Lexie's. That's always been her favorite color.

She catches me nosing about and leans her head against the garland-dressed door frame. She smells like flowers.

"See anything interesting?"

I gesture to the Christmas stocking. "Aren't you a little old to still have one of those?"

"You're never too old to believe in Santa, Sean."

She tilts her head slightly, and I get lost in her jade eyes. I'm about to ask her if she's been a good girl this year but, thankfully, Stan interrupts us.

He slaps my back. "About time we got you over for dinner. We need to do this more often. You should come to the Christmas party as well. It's just some old friends and work colleagues, but you're more than welcome."

"He's a very busy man, Stan," Beth sighs, a red tartan oven mitt on each hand. "How are things looking for your grand opening?"

I nod and wander to the island in the kitchen, taking a seat on a stool. "Great. I've got you guys a table in the VIP area, and a nice Barolo on the house."

Beth claps her oven mitts and giggles, and now I see where Lexie gets her zing. She freezes when a notion hits her. "It wouldn't be too much trouble to get an extra seat for Lexie, would it?" she asks.

I look over at Lexie still leaning in that doorway, her blonde hair framing her face, her loose, low-cut shirt giving me a hint of what I imagined last night. "No trouble at all."

Lexie smiles and joins us in the kitchen. "I've never been to a restaurant opening."

"Really? Not even in the city? I'm sure you and Jack get invited to a bunch of things like that. Especially if he has so many high-profile clients," Stan says, and there's this suspicious, low tone in his voice.

Lexie hears it too, and she shuffles uncomfortably, grabbing at a strand of golden hair and twisting it around her finger. "Of course, I mean yeah. But those are expensive, classy restaurants." She stares wide-eyed at me when she realizes she has insinuated Talley's is the opposite. "Wait, I didn't mean it like that." She cups her face in her hands. "Shit. I'm sorry."

I shrug and it off and try to comfort her with a smile. "No, I get it. Those restaurants are on a different level. But my brand is all about the sort of fine dining you'd expect to find in the city, but with the charm and character of a small-town eatery. Somewhere you can feel at home." Her hands fall away as her embarrassment dissipates, and I couldn't be happier to see her face again. "Well, at home with a six-hundred-dollar bottle of wine and imported king crab," I add.

Stan and Beth laugh, but Lexie and I just look at each other a little longer, and I can feel there's something there. Some energy or connection, and definitely heat. But maybe I'm just imagining it.

"Dinner's ready," Beth announces, carefully transporting the pot roast to the green-dressed table.

I take my seat, impressed by the pretty poinsettia center piece and ivory dishes etched with a swirly gold pattern. I really need to decorate my place better for Christmas. Maybe Charlotte can help. Lexie sits across from me and when she flaps out her napkin I catch another glimpse of gorgeous cleavage. Stan stands up and takes hold of a giant carving knife. I swiftly look anywhere else, deciding it's a bad life choice to get caught staring at his daughter's chest while he's wielding a sharp object.

He pierces the pot roast with a fork, then slices away at the slab of meat, which is perfectly pink in the middle. Beth notices the coloring and gives a sigh of relief.

"So," she starts, handing me a bowl of mashed potatoes. "What other projects are you working on, Sean?"

I take the bowl and scoop myself a serving. "A few things here and there, but enough about me. I'd like to hear what Lexie has been up to."

She looks up from the green beans. "Me? Nothing really. Same old same old."

"Lexie's working in retail, right princess?" Stan says as he slices.

Beth nods, answering for her. "A makeup counter."

I'm stunned and I lean back in the chair. "You're not painting?"

Lexie looks just as startled by my comment and her eyes glaze over. "You remember I paint?"

My chest rises with my breath. "Of course. You were always at the arts center, in all the exhibitions. Didn't you even get your work assessed by a curator?"

Lexie nods and I can see the genuine joy in her eyes. "Yes, I did." Then her smile slips away. "Sophie told me today that the arts center could be closing. I'm trying to figure out a way to keep it open, but I don't even know where to start."

"You're resourceful, with a creative mind. I'm sure you'll think of something amazing," I say. Her cheeks flush, which is the desired effect. I'd be this good to her every day if she'd let me. "Honestly, I thought you'd be off to some fancy art school as soon as we graduated."

Stan serves us each a few thick slices of the roast. "You're not the only one," he mumbles, but it's clear enough for everyone to hear.

Lexie's mouth falls into a straight line. "It wasn't a good time. We prioritized Get Jacked with Jack."

I have to bite my tongue to keep from laughing. That's what he called it?

"It's been five years, Lexie," Beth adds to the passive aggressive grilling. "Maybe it's time for Jack to prioritize what you want now? Especially if his business is doing as well as you say."

Stan serves himself last, then takes a seat. "Right. 90 Day Fiancé money can't be too shabby. I'm sure Jack can hold down the fort while you go back to school. Get your degree."

"Seems only fair," Beth says.

"Yes. Only fair," Stan adds.

Beth collects some beans on her fork, holds them to her mouth, then pauses. "And is he ever planning on proposing?"

I can see that's about all Lexie can take. She pushes her chair out from the table and stamps to her feet, dropping her napkin over her plate.

"Really? How long have you guys been saving the inquisition? And was Sean coming over for dinner a requirement, or just something special to add to the embarrassment?"

Stan and Beth exchange heavy looks, but I can't tell if either of them regrets what they said.

"Sit down, Lexie, and have some dinner. We'll talk about something else," is Stan's peace offering.

"We just want you to be happy, Lexie," Beth adds. "Please. Sit down."

"No, I need some air," Lexie snaps, turning on her heels. She storms to the front door, throws it open, then slams it just as hard behind her.

Beth gives an awkward frown. "Sorry about that, Sean. We probably shouldn't have had that discussion now, with you here."

"It needed to be said," says Stan. "But yes, the timing wasn't the best."

"She's just not herself anymore," Beth says. "Not since she moved away with Jack. It's been almost impossible to get her back to visit. She's working so much in the city. I don't think she even paints any more."

Stan grumbles. "I worry Jack isn't taking care of my little girl like he promised." He stabs his beef. "I shouldn't have spoken to her like that."

Beth folds her hand over his wrist. "We're just concerned, dear. When she comes back in, we'll apologize and get this all sorted."

I can hear them talking, but I'm not listening. All I care about is that my girl is upset and freezing outside without a jacket. I push roughly away from the table and the chair leg scrapes against the floor.

"Excuse me," I say, my tone gruff, and I head straight for the door. I don't bother thinking of a polite excuse for why I'm leaving. I just have to get to Lexie. Now.

5

Lexie

Shit, it's cold. I didn't really think this through. Storming out seemed like the right thing to do at the time. Why didn't I grab a jacket? Same old Lexie, lots of good ideas, but zero sense. I can't go back in. How lame would that look? I bury my chilled face in my hands. And right in front of Sean, too. What a perfect night this turned out to be.

The door behind me opens and I'm about ready to tell Mom or Dad to leave me alone, but it's Sean. He's taking off his red zip-up jacket, and when his Henley rides up I glimpse a streak of light brown hair trailing from his belly button to the waistband of his jeans.

"Are you okay?" he asks.

I nod as my teeth chatter. "Oh, sure. Slightly humiliated, but nothing that ten years of therapy won't fix."

Sean laughs lightly, and the sound is comforting.

"Come here," he says.

He doesn't ask if I want the jacket, he just wraps it around my shoulders, paying special attention to the collar, making sure it's snug around my neck. His thumbs graze my throat and suddenly I'm not sure if it's just the crisp Lake Mistletoe evening that's sending shivers through every nerve in my body. Sean's hand moves to my face, his thumb wiping the icy dew from my cheek while his fingertips trace my jawline. His touch is soft, but assured, and from the way he's looking at me, I can tell he knows exactly what he's doing.

"Do you want to go back inside?" he asks.

I shake my head.

"Well, you can't just stand out here all night," he states. He looks upward, his tongue rolling in his cheek as he ponders. He turns back to me. "They're lighting up the tree at the lake tonight. We could go there... together."

A lump gets caught in this throat as he pushes the words out, and it's the first sign of nerves I've seen from him.

I smile. "That sounds nice."

His eyes widen as if he's surprised I said yes. He smooths out his hair, dampened by the frosty night, and gestures toward the porch. "Let's go."

His hand leaves my face and next thing I know he's laced his fingers with mine as he leads me down the stairs and across the driveway to the black pickup parked outside his house. He opens the door silently, and when I put my foot on the step to climb in, I feel his hands grip my waist from behind. He lifts me gently, but the feeling of his thumbs kneading my hips gives me tingles. I sit and wait for him to come around the driver's side. It's ridiculously clean in here and smells brand new. He finally arrives, starts the engine, and the truck rumbles to life.

A swirl of excitement runs havoc in my belly. "I've not been to the lake in forever," I say.

"Some things are just as beautiful as ever. Doesn't matter how long since you've seen them," he says, looking straight at me.

I raise an eyebrow. "Sean Talley. Are you flirting with me?"

He stifles a grin. "Me? Nah," he scoffs. "Just making conversation."

I look at his face in the moonlight and suddenly I'm ashamed I didn't recognize him. It's Sean. The same Sean I've lived next to my whole life. I was too blinded by Jack to see anything else back then, but after a couple of days in Lake Mistletoe, that glare is finally fading.

Sean reverses out of his driveway, and we take off down the road, the streetlights glowing bright as stars against the vast night sky, while the snow falls in an ivory veil. We talk the entire drive about what everyone is doing now. About Tom and Sophie's insane decision to have a Christmas wedding, and how the event has brought out the crazy in all our friends. Not once does he ask about the city, or Jack, or why I turned down a huge scholarship to color-match foundation fifty hours a week. Instead, he wants to know what makes me laugh; the last movie I watched; if I had to be a giraffe or a zebra, which would I pick and why? The conversation is funny, and easy, and I can't remember the last time someone was interested in what I had to say. And the answer was giraffe. I like their spots.

As we approach the frozen lake, my eyes are drawn to the colossal artificial Christmas tree standing proudly at the center. The sheer size of it catches me off guard, and the familiar glow of the twinkling lights welcomes me back to a world I once knew, while reminding me of what I've missed.

The ice is alive with people. Some skate like they're born on the stuff, others try not to end up flat on their faces. As soon as I'm out of the truck, the aroma of roasted chestnuts and hot cocoa are like a wintertime hug, and I see and feel first-hand that Sean is absolutely right. Lake Mistletoe is still so beautiful, no matter how long I've been gone.

Amongst the snow-dusted pines there's a grandstand, and I notice a band is setting up. I instantly recognize their black and white uniforms.

"It's the Magpies' band," I say excitedly. "We should go watch."

Sean's jaw clenches. "I don't know. Don't you want to skate? Maybe get something to eat? We didn't get to touch that pot roast."

I tug on his sleeve. "Didn't you used to be in the band? Come on!"

Sean reluctantly follows me, and we arrive just as the teens prepare to play, finding ourselves a spot within the huddled group of spectators, bathed in the warm lights that circle the grandstand. But before a single note sounds, the conductor locks eyes with Sean, and holds up his hand for the band to wait. A wide smile spreads across his face, while in the meantime Sean shrinks behind me.

"You can't hide from me that easily, Mr. Talley," the conductor chuckles. "I've got a tuba here with your name on it."

Sean keeps his chin against his chest and waves away the attention, but the conductor is not taking no for an answer, and soon the crowd joins in. They clap and cheer his name, encouraging him to get on stage, and I soon realize that everyone in town seems to know Sean Talley.

"Go on, they want you up there!" I say, pinching his arm.

Sean shakes his head vehemently. "I'm not great in front of lots of people."

A young girl on stage with her own tuba tries to catch his attention. "Please, Mr. Talley!" she calls.

I make my eyes as big, and wide and watery as possible, taking a leaf out of Polly the cat's book. "Please, Mr. Talley?"

He frowns and lets out a heavy breath. "Fine."

Sean strolls to the grandstand accompanied by roaring applause, and takes up an unmanned tuba at the back of the band, and no one is happier than the girl beside him. The conductor raises his arms then pauses, and with one flourished sweep of his hands, music fills the air. As they play Hark! The Herald Angels Sing, my chest fills with a peaceful warmth I've not felt for so long. A peace that comes with finding your way home.

When the song ends, finishing on a long, booming note from Sean's tuba, the crowd applauds once more when the teens... and Sean... take a grateful bow. The kids put down their instruments and huddle around him. You'd think he was a teacher, the way they seem so familiar with him. I walk to the edge of the grandstand, stopping beside the conductor as he packs away his sheets of music.

"That was beautiful," I say. "I used to go to Mistletoe High. It's so good to see the band still going strong."

The conductor frowns. "Not if the school board had their way. The way they're shutting things down, music would end up just like the art program. Luckily, there are good people in this world like Sean."

I glance over at him, and he smiles back at me while the teens continue to bombard him.

"They seem pretty taken with him," I laugh lightly. "I guess they really like the way he plays the tuba."

The conductor chuckles. "Yes, indeed. Sean's good, but they also want him to know how grateful they are. I mean, he's the one who paid for all their instruments."

My eyes widen. "He did?"

The conductor nods. "That was the school board's first excuse, a way to shut down the music program. No room in the budget for instruments. So Sean bought them."

I look back at Sean, and find him still smiling at me.

"Are you two... together?" the conductor asks.

"No," I say, and I feel my cheeks flush. "We're just friends."

"Well, Sean is a good friend to have. It was nice to meet you.". The conductor clips his briefcase shut and props it under his arm. "Alright, give

Mr. Talley some room to breathe, will you? Let's pack up these instruments. Chop, chop."

Sean wanders over to me, scratching the back of his neck as I give him a mini standing ovation.

"You still play then?" I ask.

Sean shrugs. "I didn't choose the tuba life. The tuba life chose me."

I nod my head toward the conductor, hurrying the kids along. "I hear you're the savior of the music department?"

Sean sighs. "Mr. Collins likes to make a much bigger deal of it than it really is."

"It is a big deal," I say. "Those kids are lucky that you care."

"Giving is what it's all about, right?" Sean says.

The icy wind nips at my neck and I shiver, but Sean is quick to pull the zip of his jacket higher so it's right under my neck.

"You've been in the city too long. You need to re-acclimatize to how cold it can get here."

"That would mean sticking around a little longer," I say.

Sean digs his hands into the pockets of his jeans. "I like the sound of that."

I laugh, which isn't easy with my teeth chattering.

"Come on," he says, rubbing my arms to keep me warm. "Let me get you home."

I nod as he guides me back to the truck, but there's a reluctance to my step and it's not just because I'm in no hurry to see my parents. I could happily freeze to death beneath the glow of the giant Christmas tree, as long as Sean was standing beside me.

6

Sean

I'm supposed to be sleeping, but my head is full of Lexie, like always. The difference is I'm not just the kid next door anymore. She sees me. I see her. We see each other. She's only been back a couple of days and I'm trying my best not to screw it up. I'd give anything for a chance to see where this could go. But that would mean her staying beyond her parent's party, beyond the wedding, beyond Christmas. But there's another problem. He's about six-three, even though he brags to be six-four, lives in the city, runs a successful personal training business and gets to wake up next to the most beautiful girl in the world.

Being with Lexie is all I've ever wanted. Her mind, her soul, her body, but she has to want me the same way. That can't happen if she's still with Jack, and I don't want her to cheat. Not only does the very word 'cheat' make me sick, but that would also mean sharing her. Something I'm not willing to do. I want Lexie to be all mine, to be my girl. I'm used to waiting. I'd wait forever if that's what it took. I just wish forever wasn't taking so long.

When my phone starts ringing, I'm already wide awake. I check the number. Unknown. But I answer anyway in case it's a supplier. I don't want to miss something with the restaurant opening so close.

"Sean speaking."

"Sean, it's me. Lexie. Sorry, I got your number from Mom."

I bolt upright in bed, smoothing out my hair even though she's not here to see.

"Lexie. Good morning. What's up?"

"I've got a massive favor to ask," she says. "Apparently, Mom and Dad's party will be a complete disaster if they don't have a Sweet Honey ham. Dad's at work and Mom's stuck across town, so she asked if I could pick it up. I don't suppose you want to drive me?"

"I will absolutely drive you," I reply, already out of bed and trying to pull my jeans on with the phone to my ear. "I'll meet you outside in ten."

"Great. Thank you," she says, and the soft rasp of her voice isn't helping my morning wood.

She ends the call and I toss my phone away as I hop around on one leg, eventually winning the battle with my jeans. I throw on a green sweater and head downstairs and when I open my front door, she's standing right there, still wearing my red jacket.

Lexie notices me looking. "You don't mind, do you? It's actually really comfy."

My heart races in my chest as I imagine her smell around the collar and the fabric against her skin. "No. I don't mind at all."

I walk her to my truck and hold the door open, doing my best not to let my eyes linger on her backside when she climbs in. I jog around to the driver's side and as soon as I'm in with the engine running, she's twirling the dial on the radio. When Taylor Swift hums through the speakers, Lexie loses her mind.

"This is Lover!" she shrieks. "Oh my god, do you remember this? They played it at our graduation dance."

I give an uncomfortable laugh. "I didn't actually go to that. I worked at the grocery store instead."

"Oh," she replies.

"I saw the photos, though," I say quickly, to ease the awkwardness. "You and Jack looked like you had a great time. King and Queen, right?"

Her cheeriness wilts as she turns down the volume and sinks into the leather seat. "Yeah. Something like that. It gets a little less magical when I remember him asking how much I ate that day, right before we went up on stage."

My jaw clenches. "What?"

"Then he suggested that I should have gone up a dress size, but you know, it's too late now." Lexie shakes her head wearily. "Good times."

I grip the steering wheel so tight my knuckles turn white. Am I allowed to call him an asshole out loud, or am I just supposed to listen to this absolute bullshit? Maybe Lexie's just venting, maybe all she needs is a friend right now. But I'm just trying to get the image of me beating the living shit out of Jack out of my head so I can see straight.

"Wolsey's," she says. "That's where the ham is."

I'm still seeing red, but now she's changed the subject. Just drive, Sean. Just drive.

"No problem," I say, reversing down the driveway, then stepping on the gas. "Did you smooth things over with your mom and dad after the other night, then?"

Lexie nods. "They apologized. They're just worried. I don't come back as often as I should. I'm surprised they haven't given Polly my room by now."

"They love that cat," I sigh. "A package got delivered to my place by mistake, so I came over to drop it off, and when I opened the front door, Beth threw the remote control at me and screamed, DON'T LET THE CAT OUT!"

"No outdoor fun for Polly," Lexie laughs lightly, and I can see her smile returning. I remind myself to not bring Jack up again. It always seems to make her sad.

We stop in at Wolsey's and fight our way through the Christmas rush to the deli section for Beth's precious ham, weaving around carts and screaming toddlers while Silent Night crackles over the speakers. With the package secured, we head back to the truck and, for a guy who hates errands, I could do this all day. Lexie getting in and out of my truck as we drive around Lake Mistletoe feels so normal. The kind of boring shit couples do. I'm just a hand touch away from holding her purse in Home Depot while she picks out paint samples.

As we head home, our old high school grows close in the distance and Lexie leans onto the dash for a closer look.

"Let's go there," she says.

I furrow my brow. "The school? Why?"

"Just drive," she says. "And park around the back."

I take a deep breath and do as she asks. I'm curious as well as nervous about what she has planned, but I'll never turn down the opportunity to spend more time with her. I pull into the rear parking lot, and Lexie directs me toward the back of the gym.

"How do you remember all of this?" I ask.

"I could tell you, but then I'd have to kill you," she grins, and call me crazy, but the mischievous glint in her eye has my heart racing.

I pull around the back and Lexie tells me to stop beside a dumpster. She opens the door and jumps out, then flaps her arms impatiently at me to hurry up and join her. Once I'm out of the truck, I catch up with her at the double doors of the gym.

"Back entrance," she states.

"Surely it's locked," I say.

Lexie pulls on the handle and the doors click open with ease. "Some things never change," she sighs. She pokes her head inside and peeks around, but the gym is empty and silent. Even the shutters are closed, so it's practically pitch black in there.

Lexie reaches back and grabs ahold of my hand and it takes all the restraint I have not to pull her into my arms. She drags me into the gym, right to the center of the basketball court, and looks up at me.

"What are we doing here?" I ask.

She grips both my hands, her fingers hooking around mine. "Imagine this place with big white streamers, a balloon arch and DJ Snowstorm in the corner and that was pretty much the graduation dance."

I nod as I look around. "Good to know."

She tightens her grip around my fingers and before I realize what's happening, she's pulling me closer, her hands slowly sliding up my arms to encircle my neck. The warmth of her touch on my skin sends a rush through my veins.

"What are you doing?" I try not to stutter, but it's hard when she's looking at me with those endless green eyes.

"What, have you never danced with a girl? Put your hands around my waist," she giggles as she bites her bottom lip.

I keep steady as I grasp the smooth curves of her hips. There's nervous anticipation at first, but it's not long before she feels like home in my hands. I gently pull her closer until her breasts press to my chest and her head rests on my shoulder, and just when I think I've died and gone to heaven, she sings in the croakiest, most off-key voice I've ever heard, and it's spellbinding.

"Can I go where you go? Can we always be this close forever and ever?"

I close my eyes, the sweet scent of her hair filling my head. "So this is what I missed out on, huh?"

She draws circles on my nape. "This is what we both missed out on."

Lexie's words fill me with a heat that burns like the sun. I'd pull her closer if I could, until we melted into each other.

"Sean," she says into my shoulder. "I need to tell you something."

"You can tell me anything," I reply.

"It's about Jack. We're not together anymore."

My stomach churns, and I don't know whether to be happy for myself or sad for Lexie. I gulp. "Oh. Are you okay?"

She exhales. "I don't want to go into the details. But I wanted you to know."

"Thanks for telling me," I reply, and I'd crawl across the desert if it meant I could hold her every day.

"What are you doing tonight?" she murmurs as our bodies sway.

I take a while not only to remember what my plans are but also how to form sentences. "Practice," I manage. "I've got hockey practice."

"Can I come?" she asks.

I want to tell her she can do anything she fucking wants, as long as she never lets go of me. But I just say, "Yes."

7

Lexie

We arrive at the arena. Bright spotlights illuminate the signage announcing games every Friday night and a banner flaps in the evening wind, emblazoned with a white leopard in a red hockey helmet and the words MAYHEM slashed across its face.

A scattering of cars and trucks fill the snow-covered parking lot and I'm a little nervous about who might be inside. A lot of these guys were friends with Jack in high school, although he's fallen out of touch with them. He's made new friends in the city. A collection of losers and asshats if you ask me. Still, I don't know how they'll react when they see me walking in with Sean.

Like a gentleman, Sean jumps out and jogs around to my door. He pulls it open and offers his hand, and I step down onto the snow with a squelch.

From the back seat, Sean grabs a bag with a hockey stick poking out. We head to the arena and he pushes open the heavy door for me. I can hear ragged laughter and deep voices, and as I approach the rink I make out a group of men in red jerseys, passing a puck between them while they talk. When the door closes behind us with a bang, they fall silent and I'm immediately the center of attention.

"Holy shit. Is that Lexie Moore?"

I recognize that voice. It's Charlotte's favorite person and future brother-in-law, Blake, and he doesn't waste any time speed skating toward me. He slams his skates into the boards and grips the rail. Blake's almost offensively handsome, and he knows it, with waves of sandy-blond hair and warm brown eyes, not to mention a jawline so sharp you could cut your teeth on it. It's a shame he ruins it by being such a prick.

Sean takes a seat on the bench, retrieving his skates from his bag as he kicks off his boots.

"I didn't realize we were bringing dates," Blake jibes at him. "I would have brought one myself."

"Just the one?" I ask, raising an eyebrow.

Blake sighs and puts his hand on his chest. "Don't hate the player, Lexie. Hate the game."

I roll my eyes, and I'm relieved when Tom pulls up and shoves Blake aside. The Christmas groom, Tom, is sweet, the absolute opposite of Blake. He has shaggy brown hair, the same shade as his sister Charlotte, and a bushy dark beard that Sophie has complained about on more than one occasion. He leans over the rail and kisses my cheek and I get what she means when his scruff scratches my skin.

"Lexie, if I knew you were coming, I would have brought Sophie."

"It was last minute. We'll catch up later," I say.

"Okay," Tom exhales. "But don't go talking up Jack too much." He pinches a tiny space between his thumb and finger. "I'm this close to getting her down the aisle."

I force a little laugh. We joke around a lot about the crush Sophie had on Jack. I mean, she wasn't the only one. I feel like most of our high school relationship consisted of me beating off his legions of adoring fans with his hockey stick, while also keeping him convinced that, out of everybody in Lake Mistletoe, I was the only one for him. No wonder I remember being so exhausted back then.

"I still think she can do better," Blake says.

Tom frowns. "You think I'm looking forward to having you as a brother-in-law?"

I know Charlotte isn't, I think to myself. The math sounds complicated if you don't know them, but Tom is Charlotte's brother, and he is marrying Sophie, who is Blake's sister. That's the problem with small towns. You either marry each other, or end up related by marriage to half the population. It makes for very overcrowded Thanksgivings.

As if he's reading my mind, Tom continues. "And can you maybe give my sister a break?"

Blake rolls his eyes. "Is she still going on about that fucking clock?"

"You didn't even like the clock," I add.

Blake scoffs. "I guess she is."

He skates off, and I don't envy the Christmas lunches to come for the soon-to-be-combined Powell and Ward households. One of them is going to take to that family tree with an axe.

"I'll tell Sophie you said hi," Tom says, before he's off too, joining the guys in the middle of the rink.

I feel a wall of warmth behind me and I smell Sean's leathery musk before I see him.

"Is it nice catching up with everyone?" he asks. He's pulled a thick red jersey over his Henley, and grips his droopy fringe at the roots to keep it out of his eyes.

"Yeah. Some things never change. But I like that," I reply.

He nods. "Me too. That's why I love this town. Especially now that you're back."

I gulp and his eyes widen, as if he didn't mean to say it. But I'm so glad he did. I want to respond, but he makes a hasty exit toward the gate and is on the ice before I can part my lips.

"Make yourself comfortable," he calls. "There is coffee and tea in the shed. Help yourself."

He's gone again before I can reply. I bite my lip, wondering if I'm reading the situation right, or if I'm just naïve like Jack says. Maybe Sean is only being friendly. He was always sweet to me, so no reason to think this is anything different. But I'm not so clueless that I can't tell when a man is looking at my chest across a dinner table, or checking me out in the corner of his eye when he's reversing his truck. And the way he held me when we were dancing... there are some things that can't be faked.

I can't be wrong about this, can I?

I wander over to the shed and make myself a hot cup of coffee to pass the time, then take a seat in the bleachers and zip up Sean's jacket with my free hand. It's warm, well-worn and smells like him, and I feel perfectly content as I sip and watch him skate.

There's something about this game that is just so freaking sexy and instantly makes any guy who plays ten times more attractive. But as I watch Sean scrape his skates across the ice, his damp hair curtaining his eyes whenever he leans down to line up the puck, I'm almost certain that even without the hockey stick in his hands, I want him. But how long do I wait until he makes a move?

8

Sean

Especially now that you're here. What the fuck, man! Blake is right, you are a pussy. I take my frustration out on the puck, smacking it hard with my stick whenever I get the chance. The guys notice too, ducking and diving whenever I slam it their way. In the corner of my eye, I see Lexie watching me from the stands and I'm doing my best not to look straight at her.

I know it sounds strange, but I've been in love with Lexie since high school. How do you love someone who barely spoke to you? By taking the time to see the little things that everyone else misses as they go about their busy lives. The way she laughs, the crinkles in her smile, the kindness she shows others when she thinks no one is watching, and the pain she suffers when she thinks she's crying alone.

Yes, she's beautiful, but so are flowers and trees and sunsets. I love what's beneath all that, the glow that radiates from her soul, a soul my own is drawn to, as if it has found its mate. I didn't need to know everything about Lexie back then to know my heart craved her, just as much as it does now.

But that's a lot to tell her. I don't want to freak her out. Instead, I can show her, and maybe along the way, her soul will find a likeness in mine as well, and if Jack's out of the picture, this could finally be the moment I've been waiting for. The opportunity to shoot my shot. But even after years of scenarios and what ifs, I'm terrified of fucking it all up.

After I've whacked the shit out of a puck and shoved my teammates into the walls for an hour, practice wraps up. Tom needs to get away quick. Sophie's waiting on him to finalize the seating arrangements. Blake's next. Hot date, no doubt, and by the time our goalie Big Henry heads out, it's just me and Finn. He's scrolling through his phone, checking messages and emails as usual. I thought I was ambitious, but then I got to know Finn. He's a venue manager, and a useful friend to have if an upscale place like the Northwellian is where you pictured your dream wedding. It's a beautiful old hotel that sits right on Chestnut Hill and looks over the lake. Under a powdering of fresh snow and twinkling lights, I imagine it looks pretty beautiful. Finn got Tom and Sophie their preferred date for half the price.

He looks stressed, and I'm still trying to figure out what to say to Lexie, so I start up a conversation to stall for some time.

"You doing alright?"

He glances up at me from his phone. "Anyone would think I was the one getting married. Sophie's insisting on using Daisy as her caterer, but she's impossible to work with. She won't confirm start times, or give me a menu. She keeps saying she wants the cake brought in on a floating cloud, but Tom and Sophie don't have the budget for something like that, and how am I supposed to get a floating cloud built before the wedding day?" He grumbles under his breath. "I can't stand the woman."

I give a comforting shrug. "She makes a delicious cake, though. Made a special plum sponge for me."

Finn shakes his head, unconvinced, then halts his scrolling when something on his Instagram feed catches his eye. He squints and zooms in, and now he's got me curious.

"What?" I ask.

He glances over at Lexie in the stands, then back to me, and shows me his phone screen.

"Who's that with Jack?"

I look at the picture. It's Jack at a bar holding a beer, wearing a white V-neck shirt so tight it's cringe-worthy, and he's got his big tattooed arms wrapped around a petite girl with sheet-thin black hair.

"It's not Lexie," I say. "Maybe they're just friends."

Almost on cue, Finn flicks to the next photo, and Jack's tongue appears to be pretty deep down his friend's throat.

"When was that taken?" I ask.

Finn checks. "Just posted. Did Lexie say anything? Did she and Jack break up?"

I nod. "She told me tonight they weren't together. I guess these are the details she didn't want to talk about." My heart thumps hard in my chest. "I gotta go," I say, yanking off my gloves and skating over to the gate.

"Yeah. I figured," is Finn's reply as he smirks and skates in the opposite direction.

I almost crash straight through the gate, but I throw it open at the last second and stumble in. My gloves are off and now I'm pulling my jersey over my head, all the while getting closer and closer to where Lexie is sitting, staring straight at me.

"That was great," Lexie says, sipping at her coffee. "Do we go out for milkshakes now? Are your parents driving us?"

I give half a laugh. She's funny and adorable, and I could happily talk to her for hours in the easy way that we do, but I'm focused on finding out what the photo means. I don't know how to say it calmly, so I just flat out ask. "What happened between you and Jack?"

She's like a deer in the headlights. "I don't want to talk about it."

I drop onto the bench in front of her and swipe my hair back from my forehead. "I know, but... Finn just showed me a photo on Insta."

She stares into her coffee cup, and I can see tears welling behind her eyes. "You saw Jewel?"

Fuck. Way to go, Sean. You're desperate not to fuck things up, but you upset her anyway because you can't be chill for five seconds. "Sorry. It's none of my business."

Lexie looks at me and puts her hand on top of mine. Her hand is warm, and I can't help but gently slide my thumb along her palm. "No. It's alright. I've been keeping it a secret for far too long. It's time to tell the truth. I tried to buy a new dress for the wedding. That's when I found out about the money." She closes her eyes, trying to work through her thoughts. "It was gone. All of it. Everything I saved, everything I worked twelve-hour shifts for. Apparently, his gym equipment was getting repossessed if he didn't pay the finance company."

"I thought his business was doing well," I say. Her face sinks into a sadness I can't stand, and it's obvious she's been carrying a burden these last couple of days. "There's no 90 Day Fiancé money?"

She shakes her head. "Jack has only one client. Jewel." Her voice stumbles over the name. "I popped into his studio a couple of weeks ago to sort our travel plans for Tom and Sophie's wedding, but he was far too busy screwing Jewel on the weight bench I paid for. So... yeah."

"Lexie. I'm so sorry."

The idea that anyone could not treat Lexie with care and respect blindsides me. As far as I'm concerned, Jack was the luckiest son of a bitch in the entire universe, but the way he can throw away something so precious also makes him the stupidest. I wish I could take her hurt away. I wish I could make this easier for her. I wish I could drive my truck to the city and break Jack's face with one of his dumbbells.

"It's not your fault," she laughs softly, trying to lift the tone of the conversation, but I can see how much she's hurting.

I squeeze her knee. "He's a piece of shit, Lexie, and he never deserved you."

She catches a tear before it escapes her eye and sniffs away any lingering sadness. "Do you mind taking me home?" she asks. "I'm really tired."

I nod. "Of course." I pull off my skates, throw my boots on, and pack my bag, then I take Lexie's hand and we head for the truck. I open the door and guide her inside, loving how her hips feel as I lift her into the cab. When I dump my bag in the back and climb into the driver's seat, she's staring out the window, her hands trembling on her lap. I start the engine and turn on the heat, but I wish I could be the one to keep Lexie warm.

All I want to do is hold her in my arms and watch the world go by. I should be happy that Jack's out of the picture, but there's no joy in seeing Lexie so sad.

The drive home is silent. Lexie isn't talking and I'm not going to make her, but I'll be right here if or when she needs me. I pull into my driveway and turn off the engine. Lexie isn't moving, still staring out the window. I'll sit here as long as she wants.

"I was embarrassed," she mutters, her voice so low I can barely make out the words. "That's why I didn't tell anyone. I left my family and my home, I gave up my dreams to be with him and what does he do? Takes my money and cheats on me. I don't even know if Jewel was the only one."

Lexie bursts into tears and I can't stand it. I slide across the seat and take her in my arms. She cries harder into my shoulder, and I stroke her hair and the small of her back to comfort her.

"It's okay. I'm here," I breathe in her ear. "For whatever you need. I'm here."

The tears quieten, and she pulls from the embrace to look me in the eye. The moonlight dances upon her porcelain skin, the jade of her eyes dappled with the gloss of her tears. She's so beautiful and I want her so badly.

"You've always been here," she says, "haven't you?"

"Yes," I whisper, "and I always will be."

9

Lexie

The hunger in his eyes is so intense, but he's holding back I can feel it. He wants me to make the first move, to let him know it's alright for him to want me so badly. I sweep his hair away from his eyes and gaze into flawless blue pools you could drown in if you weren't careful. I exhale. He wants me to be in control. To relieve him of this agony.

"Do you want to kiss me?" I ask.

He gives a deep growl. "Yes."

"Then kiss me," I whisper.

I close my eyes and part my lips as he pulls me closer against him. He grips the back of my neck, directing my mouth to his. His first kiss is long and deep and he's inhaling me, the sound of his heavy breathing causing my core to tighten. I reach out and find his chest, trailing my fingers over his pecs and down until I find the hard muscles of his abdomen. My hands search out the warmth of his skin, slipping under his shirt, and he shivers when he feels my touch. I run my thumb over the trail of hair that starts below his belly button, then disappears beneath his belt while my fingers explore his toned stomach.

He kisses me again, harder this time, then again and again, each kiss deeper, as if he's devouring me. He keeps his grip on the back of my neck while his other hand traces along my collarbone. His head tips down, and he breaks his kiss long enough to glimpse at my chest.

"Do you want to touch me?" I ask him.

He nods. "Yes."

"Then touch me," I whisper.

His finger slides away from my collarbone and trails down my cleavage until he reaches the zip. He pulls me into his kiss again while he unzips me from his jacket and eases the sleeves off my shoulders. My nipples are already hard and tender by the time he slides his hand under the back of my shirt and unhooks my bra with an effortless finesse. He closes his hand around my breast, tenderly kneading the flesh, and when his thumb rolls over my nipple, I gasp. I feel my panties dampen and a burning heat swells between my legs. Sean grasps my hair and pulls my head back, exposing my quivering throat. He drags his hard kisses down my chin to my neck, where he lingers at my shoulder, his kisses intensifying.

My body trembles and my eyes roll back in my head as I grip him by the waist. He lifts my shirt, my breasts even more tender in response to the cold, but it's not long before he takes my nipple into his mouth. His tongue masterfully encircles the stiff bud as he licks and sucks and I groan when an electric sensation surges over my center. His kisses trail across my chest to give attention to my other nipple, spoiling it with the same excruciating bliss, and with the way he's lapping hungrily at my breasts, I'm curious to see how expertly his tongue works in other places.

My hands move from his waist to the crotch of his jeans, where I feel his thick mass pushing against the denim fabric. He pulses at my touch and I work at getting his zip undone, eager to free his cock. But Sean stops me, wrapping his hand around mine and shaking his head.

"Let me take care of you," he says.

I bite my lip. "But..."

He grips my hand tighter. His eyes are stern, his face set. "Let me take care of you. Please."

I shiver at the tone of his rumbling voice. I'm so turned on that I temporarily forget how words work, so I just nod. With my permission, Sean swings me around so my back is against the passenger door and he lifts my legs onto the seat. He leans over me and slides his hands down my sides, pausing at my hips to knead my skin and I love the pleased groans he makes as he explores me.

He hooks the waistband of my leggings and inches them down to my knees, his piercing gaze never abandoning me, not even for a second. I expect him to the pull my leggings all the way off, so I'm surprised when it's only my right leg he undresses, the one on the edge of the seat, the other side he leaves the leggings at my knee.

Sean scooches down the bench seat as far as he can and I giggle as he stares, hypnotized by the sight of my pink panties. I can feel how wet I am, so I can only imagine how soaked they must look from where he's sitting.

"You are so beautiful, Lexie," he says. He moves my bare leg off the edge of the seat, splaying it wide while he puts my other leg over his shoulder. I gulp, my stomach fluttering with anticipation as I watch his head disappear between my legs. His nose brushes against the fabric, nudging at my clit. I lean back on my elbows, watching his head bob up and down as he laps at the gusset of my panties, skimming his skilled muscle against my yearning folds.

I groan. It feels amazing, but the teasing is agony. I don't want him to stop, but I also want him to rip off my underwear and eat the fuck out of my pussy. Then I remember I'm the one in control.

"Sean," I murmur, my core tightening.

He lifts his head and all I can see are his blue eyes looking up at me from between my legs.

"Do you want to eat my pussy?"

I feel his tongue licking greedily at the pesky fabric that's keeping him from my clit as he nods.

I bite the tip of my finger, and I can't believe what I'm about to say. "Eat it, then."

Sean needs no further encouragement. He noses at my clit one last time before I feel his tongue searching for an entrance. He finds a way through the side, near my inner thigh, and the tip of his skilled muscle skims my aching center. I groan as I run my hand through his hair, gripping it at the roots every time he licks me. He's teasing me, and I roll my hips, pushing myself into his mouth, eager for him to shove that amazing tongue deep between my folds.

Sean knows what I want, but he wants me to feel in charge, and when I grab the crotch of my panties and pull them aside, I've never felt more powerful. I roll my hips again, and just the thought of his tongue lapping at me has me close to orgasm.

I hear Sean growl as he buries his head between my legs, gripping the thigh that's over his shoulder while he pushes my other leg wider so he has me completely on display for him. His stiff tongue follows the curves of my folds and it's not long before I demand more from him, my entrance desperate to be filled. His tongue rolls firmly over my tingling bud and I mewl.

"Sean. Do you want to fuck me?"

He lifts his head from between my legs and drags his forearm over his mouth. "I'm not going to fuck you tonight, Lexie," he says sternly. "But I am going to make you cum. Hard."

He runs his fingers up my thigh, his nails lightly scraping my goose pimpled skin until he finds my clit. He presses his thumb, then rubs up and down, and sweeping circles. It feels amazing. Sean looks down as I writhe and grind against his thumb and I watch as he opens his mouth, allowing a glob of spit to drip onto my swollen clit.

"Oh fuck," I scream, as he rubs harder.

Sean reaches up and takes my breast in his hand, kneading my flesh and pinching my nipple between his fingers. At the same time his thumb is working my clit, I feel two fingers slide down my dripping wet crevice and he eases them deep inside me with one firm push until I swallow him up to his knuckles.

"Fuck," I scream again, digging my nails into the leather seat.

He thrusts his fingers inside me and I push against him with my hips, forcing his digits deeper.

"Oh yes," he groans. "My good girl likes that, doesn't she?"

I dig my nails deeper into the leather. "Mhmmm," I whimper.

"Is my girl going to cum for me?" he asks.

"Mhmmm."

His fingers dip harder and faster and deeper inside me, and my clit feels like it's on fire and about to explode like a ticking bomb.

"Cum for me, Lexie."

It's not a request. It's a demand.

The deep tone of his voice sends me over the edge and my body stiffens, my hips thrusting one last time against his hand and writhing as I cum in exquisite, aching waves. My muscles tighten around his fingers, and he squeezes my breast hard. Slowly he withdraws his fingers, and through glazed, half-closed eyes I watch him put them in his mouth and suck them dry. The breath he exhales is guttural and I can see he is savoring the taste.

"Mmmm," he sighs blissfully. "I knew your pussy would taste delicious."

My cheeks redden. I pull myself upright and fumble with my leggings. It doesn't help that I feel numb below the waist.

"Let me help," Sean says.

I attempt to shrug away the offer, but he's already beside me, slipping my breasts into my bra and fastening it as swiftly as he unhooked it.

"You're good at that," I say, straightening out my shirt. I blush. "Among other things."

He drops his chin with a glow of bashfulness, then rolls his shoulders and gestures towards his house. "It's early. Did you want to come inside? I put together a pretty good charcuterie board, too."

I nod. "Sure."

A smile blooms on his lips and grows until it's almost ear to ear. "Great."

Sean jumps out the driver's side and jogs around to my door. He pulls it open, and when I swing my feet around onto the step, he takes me by the waist and lifts me down to him, dragging his nose through my cleavage and along my neck. I hear him inhale my hair before he sets me on the ground.

Sean takes my hand, lacing his fingers with mine, and I can't help but notice how perfectly they fit together. He walks me across the snow and up the stairs to the porch, then holds the door open for me. Once we're inside, he's as good as his word, and after a few minutes, he appears from the kitchen with two glasses of wine and a wooden board dressed with cheeses, olives, crackers, and an assortment of salamis. He puts the board on the table and I can see him trying to draw my attention to the pepperoni flowers.

"Impressed?" he asks.

"Oh yeah," I reply. "Not often you find a man who can origami cold cuts."

"Damn right," he says with a wink, popping an olive into the air and catching it in his mouth.

Sean flicks on the TV and lays back on the couch, his eyes set on mine, and he's reclined for only ten seconds before he lunges forward, scoops my face into his hand and kisses me with more passion than I ever felt from Jack.

When his tongue has finished exploring my mouth, he holds my face against his. "Do you want to stay the night?" he asks.

His words send my stomach into raucous flutters, and I graze my lips against his bristled cheek. "I don't want to be anywhere else," I reply.

10

Sean

My girl fell asleep in my arms. I breathed her in all night, slipped my hands under her shirt just to feel her smooth, warm skin, and let my fingers roam over every luscious, full curve of her perfect body. I've never been rock hard for twelve hours straight, but at sunrise, when my eyes flicker open, the first thing I feel is my swollen cock pressing against my jeans. I wince and pull at my crotch, trying to make some room for the big guy, but all it does is thicken, filling out the pant leg.

I can't help but think the best way to get rid of this thing is to bury myself in Lexie and make love to her until we cum together. I lick my lips, and run a hand along my denim-encased shaft before looking across the couch. But Lexie is gone.

I take a moment to gather my senses, giving my face a tap and rubbing my eyes until they focus. I look around the living room and glance over my shoulder at the kitchen. "Lexie? Are you there?"

There's only silence in reply. I stretch my arms behind my head and yawn, scratching my chest before groaning and rocking to my feet.

"Lexie," I call again, staggering to the bottom of the stairs and leaning on the post. I forget the damn thing is a wobbly, code violation and stumble when it leans with me, but I catch myself before I face-plant onto the floor.

I steady and grip the railing, towing myself upstairs a step at a time, grateful for the relief as my hard-on retreats. I cross the landing to my old bedroom, making straight for the window. The curtains are open as always. I never close them. When I look across the snowy yard to the house next door, I find Lexie looking straight back at me. Her clothes are disheveled, her hair is a mess of ruffled blonde waves. To be honest, she looks like a truck's hit her, and she's never been sexier.

I wave, and she waves back. "Good morning," I mouth, and she looks away coyly, her cheeks bright red. "Dinner tonight?"

She points to her ear and shrugs. Right. She can't hear you, idiot. I glance around the room, my eyes locking on a pad and paper on the bedside table. I hold my hand out to her, gesturing to wait while I sprint across the room, stubbing my toe on my tuba in the process.

"Fuck my life," I shout, swiping the pad and paper and hopping back to the window. I bite off the pen cap and begin writing. When I'm done, I hold the message up to the window.

Dinner tonight?

Lexie squints her eyes to make out my chicken scratch, then smiles before disappearing out of sight, returning with her own pen and paper.

Christmas Party.

Of course. How could I forget? I throw aside the paper and write a new message. I hold it up.

See you there?

She nods.

I write a new message. I had a great time last night.

She reads the note and puts her hand against her chest. I watch her mouth. "Me too," she mouths.

She leans forward and presses her lips against the window, and my heart thumps hard against my ribcage. Then she giggles and waves, and then she's gone. I claw at my left peck. I've never felt like this before. Lexie's been the love of my life since high school. I've dreamed of her, longed for her, yearned for her, imagined what it would feel like to hold her in my arms and taste her in my mouth, but nothing could have prepared me for the euphoria that came with having her. Nothing else mattered last night in my truck, with the windows steamed and her hands in my hair. She opened up for me, gave me everything she had, and I savored every drop.

Lexie means everything to me. More than success, more than money, more than breaking the left wing scoring record. With Jack gone, there's a chance she could actually be mine, and I'm taking it. One night is not enough. I want to marry her. I want to have children with her and, Jesus Christ, I want to make love to her and take my time doing it. I want her body to be so spent from cumming over and over that she begs me to stop, but only when she can't take another inch of me will I let her rest in my arms.

Lexie will never know what a broken heart feels like ever again and, I swear to God, if anyone tries to hurt her, if Jack comes crawling back, I'll snap my hockey stick over his fucking throat.

It takes me a good while to get out of my head. I go to the gym for a bit and push my limits on the weights. Blake spots for me, and I can tell there's something on his mind.

My muscles strain under the weight of the bar, sweat pouring from my forehead while my thighs spasm. With a final grunt, I grit my teeth and push, and the bar snaps into the rack. My arms fall like dead weights at my side and my shoulders are little more than aching lumps of tissue, but the endorphins are a temporary reprieve from my thoughts. The worrisome expression on Blake's face is a downer, though.

"What is it?" I pant. "Nervous about the restaurant opening?"

Blake scoffs. "When am I ever nervous? No. It's nothing,"

He lies much better to those poor girls than he does to me. I sit up on the bench, grabbing my towel from beside my foot and wiping the thick sweat from the back of my neck. "Spit it out."

He leans into the rack. "Jack called me this morning."

I don't react at first, but slowly my teeth start to grind. "What did he want?"

"What do you think? He was asking about Lexie. Did you know they broke up?"

"Finn showed me some pictures last night of Jack and another girl. I asked her about it and she broke down, told me everything, everything that piece of shit did to her."

Blake is still friends with Jack, so I know I'm putting him in an awkward situation, but I couldn't care less. I don't expect him to pick sides, but if he's going to bring Jack up, he can deal with me shit-talking the asshole.

"He wants her back. He asked me to talk to her, says she's not answering his calls."

I throw my towel over my shoulder, not looking at him. "And why are you telling me this?"

"Just figured you would want to know before you start thinking too seriously about Lexie. It's no secret that you're in love with her."

Now I glance at him. "Bit too late for that."

Blake cocks an eyebrow. "What. You banged her? Bullshit."

I shake my head, and I don't like the way he talks about Lexie like she's one of the randoms he hooks up with. "No. But something happened, and I want to see where it goes."

Blake exhales. "She's been with Jack since high school, man. They've got history. I know this is something you've wanted for a long time, but maybe she's just rebounding with you."

I snap to my feet and I'm immediately in Blake's face, my chest heaving with rugged breaths. "What did you say?"

Blake takes a step back and holds his hands up like white flags. "I didn't say anything, bro. I'm just stating the facts. Jack is headed to Lake Mistletoe. He told me himself, and he wants to take Lexie back with him."

"When?" I snarl.

"Soon," Blake replies.

I take a breath and try to soothe the blood racing like firewater through my veins. So much for coming to the gym to relax. I'm trying to stop myself from throwing a dumbbell through the window. I take a step back from Blake and unclench my fists. He nods appreciatively.

"Geez, I thought we were going to throw down for a second," he chuckles. He puffs his chest out. "I would have kicked your ass, of course."

I smirk and snort a laugh. "Yeah. Sure you would."

He grips my shoulder. "What are you going to do?"

I ponder, rolling ideas over in my mind, but I already know. "I'm going to protect Lexie."

"From Jack?" Blake asks.

"From anyone who tries to hurt her. Not while I'm around. Not while I'm breathing."

Blake drops his chin and shakes his head. "Well shit. I guess I'll have to make sure I'm there to save your ass when Jack lays you out."

"Oh, really?" I scoff. "You're taking my side?"

"Yeah," Blake says, folding his arms over his chest. "Jack's always been a bit of a prick. He deserves whatever he's got coming to him."

I shove Blake's shoulder, and he understands I mean it as a thank you.

"How about we stop throwing our dicks around and get ready for our grand opening?" Blake says. "I didn't finger bang the editor of Northern

Fine Dining for nothing. You better give her something amazing to write about."

"Did you really have to finger bang her?" I frown.

"I never have to finger bang anyone. What can I say? I love what I do, and I do what I love." Blake grins.

I roll my eyes. Of all the douchebags to have in my corner, I'm glad it's this one.

11

Lexie

I wasn't planning on leaving Sean's place as early as I did. I could have happily laid in his arms for the whole day if that was an option. But Mom made it very clear that I would be disinherited if I wasn't in the kitchen bright and early to help get ready for the party. It'll be just my luck that the only thing I inherit is Polly. That will be her final revenge on me.

I wasn't sure if Sean would come looking for me when he woke up. I didn't know if last night was anything more for him than going down on a girl in a truck. But when I watched him walk into his old room and come straight to the window, it answered the question my heart has been asking since I said shanks to him in my driveway. I'm falling for Sean Talley.

As if she can tell my mind is all over the place, Mom tosses me a bag of potatoes and a peeler. "Once those are done, you get on the sweet potatoes," she says sternly.

When it comes to the Moore Christmas party, Mom is the captain, and Dad is her first mate. I've missed the last couple, but I still carry enough trauma from my youth to know that today is going to be the worst. I just keep telling myself that once I've peeled and scrubbed and baked my fingers to the bone, I'll be rewarded with a massive glass of wine.

She's got Dad on decorating duty, and they've decided on red and gold this year. Dad's hanging garlands from every archway and stringing them with gorgeous, glittery baubles. He's wrapped the staircase with gold ribbon and changed out the cushion covers and rugs to red. Even my fluffy pink stocking got the boot because it didn't match the color scheme. There is nothing more important to them than this party and it being absolutely perfect. Even Polly plays second fiddle today. Mom's not stopped to pat her in almost twenty minutes.

We're now in the afternoon, and the place smells amazing. Besides the fig and cinnamon candle Mom's burning, which cost as much as my rent in the city, the brie bites and fruit cake flood the house with waves of buttery, spicy scents. Mom's gone all out this year with her presentation ideas, including a large candy cane made of interchanging tomato and mozzarella slices, and a pesto pizza shaped like a Christmas tree.

Of course, the centerpiece for the evening is the succulent Sweet Honey ham cut into perfect, thin slices and served on a bed of cloves and cranberries. I place the prosciutto wrapped asparagus on the table and unleash a long held breath. Time for my wine.

"I'm going to get changed, darling," Mom says as she unties her 'Kiss Me, I'm Mrs Claus' apron. "Guests should arrive in an hour."

I've poured an offensively tall glass of red wine and sprawled myself over the couch. Dad sits down beside me and matches my exhausted energy.

"Expecting a good turnout?" I ask.

He stretches his arms and yawns like a bear. "The usuals. Friends from town, people from work. But it's always a great night."

"Sean's coming," I say. "You said he could, right?"

Dad nods. "Of course. I like Sean." He narrows his eyes on me. "Do you like of Sean?"

I try to hide my blushing cheeks behind my enormous glass of wine. "Would that be okay?"

"That depends," Dad sighs. "Is that asshole Jack still in the picture?"

I'm taken aback. Dad's never exactly loved Jack, but he's said nothing bad about him either.

"No. He's not," I reply, interested in what his response will be.

Dad simply nods. "Good. Well then, I suppose it is okay that you like Sean." A smile cracks his straight lips, and he leans over, kissing my forehead. "I just want my girls to be happy."

I roll my eyes. "Seriously?"

"At least I don't have to worry about your sister's man troubles. The most intimate relationship she has is with squeaky mouse." Dad reaches under the couch and retrieves a fuzzy gray toy mouse. He gives it a squeeze, and it spits out a high-pitched squeak. "Pol, Pol. Squeaky mouse!" When he tosses it across the room, the cat loses her fucking mind, doing a full somersault as she skids across the wooden floor and pounces on top of it.

By early evening, guests start arriving. But there's only one face I'm trying to find in the crowd and when Sean shows up, my heart soars into the stratosphere. It's hard to meet his eyes at first. I still can't believe what happened in his truck and what he brought out in me. But he doesn't seem to be as shy.

Sean takes my hand and says nothing, leading me through the clusters of cocktail-wielding guests until we're concealed behind a wall. Then he cups my face and kisses me so desperately he must have been waiting for this moment all day. Just the franticness of his breath is enough to stir heat between my legs, and I clutch at his waist as I allow his mouth to devour me.

"I couldn't stop thinking about you all day," he whispers. "When do I get to have you again?"

My heart races and I gulp. "As soon as this party is done, I'm yours."

He shakes his head. Our eyes locked in a magnetic gaze. "That's too long."

He kisses me again, and his hands find their way under my shirt. The tingling between my legs intensifies, and unless the world falls apart right now, I'm going to let him do whatever he wants to me.

"Lexie, are you here?"

I recognize Mom's voice and Sean pulls away from me, wiping his lips on the back of his hand as he tries to steady his breathing. When Mom comes around the corner, she eyes us up and down with a suspicious gaze.

"Oh hello, Sean. How are you?"

"Great," he coughs. "The party looks fantastic."

She bows appreciatively. "Yes, but it's all a little much for Polly. Lexie, would you mind taking her upstairs? I think all the people are scaring her."

I roll my eyes. I'd much rather get my clothes ripped off by the hot neighbor than babysit that damned cat. But Mom gives me that look, which means it's not a question.

"Want to keep me company?" I ask Sean.

He nods immediately and follows me into the living room to collect Polly. Mom's not wrong, she's definitely in a shitty mood, batting at the decorations, and scratching the ankles of anyone who gets too close to her. Even when I scoop her up, she gives me a fuzzy slap across the cheek.

"Come on you," I grumble, spitting out her white fur that somehow always finds its way into my mouth. By the time we get upstairs, she has gone into full bitch mode, contorting her plump body left and right, and I can barely keep hold of her. Suddenly, she lets out a ragged hiss and takes one good swipe at me. She twists free from my hands just as the bathroom door opens and Lottie, the local mechanic, staggers out waving her hand in front of her nose.

"Oh, hey Lexie," she says warmly. "I heard you were back in town for Christmas. How are you?"

I peek around Lottie and watch Polly dart into the bathroom.

"I'm fine," I reply.

She narrows her eyes as she takes in Sean and me side by side and waggles her finger. "What's happening here then?"

We catch each other's gaze and glow red in unison.

"Just... reconnecting," I reply.

Lottie smiles, the lines around her mouth riding up her cheeks. "Well, Merry Christmas to that. It's like when I get a car in and can't get it to run. But once I put the right wires together... bingo."

Sean nods. "Couldn't have said it better myself."

"Sorry to cut you off, Lottie," I say, gesturing to the bathroom. "But I'm on cat sitting duty."

"No problem, hon. You'll have to excuse the smell. It's my fault for eating too many brie bites when I know I got the lactose intolerance. I had to crack a window in there."

My eyes bulge. "What did you say?"

"Just a smidge," Lottie adds. "Maybe I'll see you later."

She passes Sean and me, rubbing her stomach as she goes, and as soon as she disappears down the stairs, I run into that bathroom. The first thing I notice is Lottie wasn't kidding. The brie bites did not agree with her at all. But the second load of bad news, but not much worse than the smell, is that the window is open and Polly is gone.

I brace my hands on either side of the door frame. "Fuck my life!"

"Should we tell Beth and Stan?" Sean asks.

I shake my head frantically. "Mom waits all year for this party. This will completely ruin her night, plus it'll be all my fault. No, we have to find Polly ourselves."

"Well, what are we standing around for then?" Sean says with an urgency that matches my own. "Let's haul ass."

Sean's already halfway down the stairs before I can blink, and I hurry to keep pace with him. I grab my coat from the rack as I head out the door, slipping out before Mom can see. Sean and I head around the back of the house and stand below the second story bathroom window. Luckily Polly is incredibly overfed, so the marks she's left in the snow during her escape are like potholes.

My eyes track her trail, leading behind the row of houses on the street and toward the elementary school just a block away. I grab Sean by his sweater. "This way!"

We trudge through the snow and I'm flip-flopping between rage and worry, more for myself than Polly, if I'm being honest. If I lose that cat, my parents are going to be so pissed.

Sean scratches the back of his head, and I can see that he has a dictionary's worth of words on the edge of his tongue that he's trying to get out.

I smile. "Something on your mind?"

He lets out a deep breath. "So, about last night?"

I nod and gulp as knots tighten in my stomach while I wait on what he's going to say next.

"I want you to know it was the best night of my life, and I'd love to do it again."

The knots ease. "Me too. Not just the truck stuff... you know... ."

A grin slips across Sean's mouth, and he digs his hands into his pockets.

"I mean, the truck stuff was nice..."

Now he's looking anywhere but in my eyes as his cheeks turn bright red.

"I mean really nice," I continue, and I'm not sure why I'm still talking. "What I mean is..."

Sean takes me by my waist and pulls me to his lips, and I can't remember what I was about to say.

"I meant the truck stuff too," he whispers, his deep voice rumbling in my ears. "But I liked everything else just as much."

A warmth tingles at my core as he eagerly grasps at my hips, his eyes glaze over and he's staring at my mouth like he's already imagining what he wants to do with it. I feel him thickening against my hip, and I'm sure there's a reason we're out in the cold instead of naked in his bed. Then I see a white ball of fluff leap into baby Jesus's cot.

"Hey bitch! I see you!" I yell.

I pull free of Sean, running toward the nativity scene set up on the front lawn of the elementary school. I hate to leave him there with that gorgeous problem growing in his trousers but, unfortunately, this is a matter of life and death.

I'm panting by the time I reach Joseph and Mary huddled over the cot, and when I peer inside, I'm appalled by what I see. It's like when two cartoon characters fight, and it's just a swirling ball of dust, arms and legs as they tumble, except I'm looking at a swirl of white and ginger fur, and I can't figure out where Polly ends and the humpy tomcat begins. It's made especially uncomfortable when the ginger stud taking Polly for a ride makes direct eye contact with me.

"Wow. Do Mom and Dad know their youngest daughter is a common tramp?" I ask. "And on top of baby Jesus, of all things."

My commentary makes little impact on their activities, in fact, they keep going. I screw up my face and rock the cot. "Okay. Fun's over. Let's go."

The tomcat leaps off Polly and scurries into the night. I shake my head as I watch him leave. "Typical man." I reach into the cot and scoop Polly into my arms. "If you don't tell, I won't tell," I say to her, before firmly tucking her under my arm.

"You found her!" Sean cheers with a slow clap. "What was she doing?"

"Observing the birth of Jesus," I reply.

"Okay...," Sean says, "shall we head back to the house?"

I nod as he leads the way. I lift Polly and whisper in her ear. "You're no better than me. Remember that."

12

Sean

With the cat safely returned and Beth and Stan none the wiser, Lexie and I spent the rest of the evening restraining ourselves. She looked so beautiful, and the way her red dress clung to her hips had me in a constant state of stiffness. When the guests started to leave, I got hopeful we could finally be alone together. That was until Beth almost fell off the porch when waving goodbye after a few too many gingerbread gins and, with Stan snoring his head off in the recliner, Lexie felt it best that we call it a night. That walk back to my house was the hardest thing I've had to do. But I'm in this for the long run. There'll be a lifetime of nights with Lexie, and I can't wait.

When I wake up the next day, I decide to take her out. Daisy James, our town baker who made the amazing plum sponge, is running a cooking class at the arts center. They're good friends, and I don't think Lexie has had the chance to catch up with her yet. I'm up and dressed and out the door in a flash.

When I knock, Lexie greets me at her front door with her hair in tangles and her eyes are half open.

"Morning," she yawns with coffee cup in hand. "What's going on?"

"I want to take you somewhere," I say. "Are you up for it?"

A surge of energy brings a warm glow to her cheeks, and she nods. "Let me get dressed."

She's out the door with me in under an hour in a tight pair of jeans, a jacket and a red beanie, her dark-blonde hair falling over her shoulder in soft waves.

"How's your mom?" I ask as I drive.

Lexie shakes her head. "It's the one day a year she goes all out, and with the state she was in when I left her, she'll have a hangover until next year's party."

I take a breath. "Do you think you'll be here to take care of her again when that happens?"

Lexie smiles at me. "Would you like that?"

I lock her in my gaze. "Lexie, you know I would."

She exhales. "But it feels like I've achieved nothing. You and my friends, you've all got these careers, these futures ahead of you. What have I done? Coming back to Lake Mistletoe would feel like I've failed at making it on my own."

"There are no failures, Lexie," I say as I take a corner onto the main street. "Just lessons, and you've still got so much left inside you to give. So why not give it back to the people who love and appreciate you?"

I pull into the parking lot, and Lexie looks up. "The arts center?"

I nod. "Daisy is running a cooking class, which means the possibility of a free breakfast."

"Lake Mistletoe's resident philanthropist needs to score himself a free breakfast?"

I unlock my seatbelt. "How else am I going to afford all those damned trumpets?" She laughs, and the sound soothes me. "I'm serious," I continue. "They're really expensive."

We head inside, past the bulletin board with a schedule of all the free classes being held this week. This place doesn't work without everyone volunteering their time. There are cooking classes, home repair, you can even learn how to fix your carburetor with Lottie on a Thursday afternoon. After Daisy's class, an art class with a painter from Pine Point catches Lexie's attention on the roster.

"Did you want to stick around for that?" I ask.

"I know this guy," she says. "He's really good."

I furrow my brow. "So are you."

Lexie shakes her head and drops her chin. "I used to think I was. But now whenever I look at a canvas, my mind goes blank."

"Maybe you just need some inspiration," I suggest.

Lexie links arms with me and nuzzles into my shoulder. "Maybe I do."

We walk through the corridor, dodging a group of kids sprinting from what looks like a pottery class, their arms bundled with misshapen bowls and vases. We arrive at the kitchen and see Daisy standing behind a counter at the front of the room, calling instructions to a dozen people standing at the ready with mixing bowls and wooden spoons.

"It's not just kids anymore?" Lexie asks.

I shake my head. "They run classes here for all ages now. This is actually where I learned to make my salami flowers."

Lexie laughs. "Well, say no more."

I tap on the glass and Daisy excitedly waves us inside.

"It's so good to see you," Daisy says, wrapping her arms around Lexie. "It's been so long."

Lexie nods. "Too long. Thanks for the plum sponge, by the way. Delicious as always."

Daisy grins at Sean. "A custom order placed almost a month ago."

"Is that right?" Lexie giggles, and I wonder if client privacy laws apply to bakers.

"Excited for the wedding?" Daisy asks. "God, have you seen the bridesmaid's dresses? Sophie fell in love with ruffled necklines last spring and she's just run with it."

"Not yet," Lexie replies. "She seems pretty stressed."

Daisy nods. "Between the wedding and work and running this place, she's lost the fucking plot. But no one else has stepped up to take over. I can do the odd class, but I've got the bakery to run, not to mention I'm catering the wedding."

"That's amazing!" Lexie gushes.

Daisy's bottom lip clenches between her teeth. "Amazing is one word for it, sure. Terrifying is another. But I'm sure everything will be fine."

There's a cough from the students, and we turn to find them waiting on Daisy's next instruction. "Anyway, we need to finish this shortbread. How about brunch tomorrow with Lola?"

Lexie nods. "Sounds great."

We leave the kitchen and as soon as we've stepped outside, Lexie's phone blares what I think is Ariana Grande.

Lexie answers, "Hello." The voice on the other end sounds frantic, and Lexie isn't getting a word in, instead just throwing out a yep or okay when she gets the chance. Then her eyes widen. "Are you serious? No, I can't. There's no one else?"

I'm hanging on every word here. "Is everything okay?"

Lexie ends the call and gulps. "That was Sophie. The painter from Pine Point is stuck in a snowstorm. She asked if I could take the class."

I take her by the shoulders. "That's great!"

Lexie shakes her head vehemently. "It's the opposite of great. I can't teach an art class."

"What are you talking about?" I chuckle. "You're an artist!"

Lexie frowns. "I'm a girl who paints sometimes. I'm not an artist."

My jaw clenches. That sounds like something she's been told by someone who enjoyed bringing her down to make themselves feel better. It's becoming clear to me that Jack has done some real damage to my girl's self esteem.

A group of folks of all ages pour through the front doors and one of them, a young girl, makes a beeline for me and Lexie. "You wouldn't know when the painting class is starting, would you?"

I squeeze Lexie's hand and offer her a warm smile. "Right now."

"Great!" the girl says, returning to tell the others.

Lexie grits her teeth and slaps my chest and I chuckle lightly as I rub the spot.

"What! Can you just trust in yourself for five minutes and show everyone what I see when I look at you? A beautiful, talented... ," I exhale a deep breath, "sexy woman."

Lexie frowns, pinching the bottom of my sweater in her fingers and giving it a tug. "I'm not showing them anything remotely sexy," she says, "but I suppose I can teach them how to paint a winter landscape."

I nod and kiss her cheek. "While you're doing that, I'll try to talk Daisy into some pancakes."

Lexie walks to an empty classroom and opens the door. "I guess we're painting," she announces, and the excited group file in.

I stand outside the window and watch as Lexie goes from nervous to assured in five minutes. She starts by referencing her own canvas, explaining the brush strokes and color choices for her snowy scene. But it's not long before she's gliding around the room, leaning over shoulders and offering advice to those eager to receive it. Lexie looks like she was made for this, and the way she glows as her confidence blooms is intoxicating.

As much as I love seeing her come into her own, her mind and her heart making me swoon with every step she takes, the fullness of her hips and dangerous sweeping curve of her ass have me thinking far simpler, more carnal things. I'm champing at the bit, waiting for the next time I get to taste her.

13

Lexie

I feel the best I have in years. After spending yesterday afternoon at the arts center, I find myself basking in the afterglow of inspiration. As the last strokes of paint splashed on the canvases and the students left with smiles of accomplishment, a wave of rejuvenation washed over me, and I feel as if something has reignited the fading flame of my creativity. No. Not something. Someone. Sean. It's been so long since someone believed in me and put me first. It's becoming just as addictive as his lips.

Lola and Daisy arrive at 10am for brunch. I open the door dressed in a cute little scarlet twin-set and jeans and put on a carefree smile. I get the feeling everyone in town knows about the time Sean and I have been spending together. My parents, the guys at the rink, and Daisy seeing us at the arts center doesn't help. But I'm not sure I'm ready for it to be common knowledge. It's so new and exciting, and it's something I want to keep just for us. But in a town the size of Lake Mistletoe, that'll only last for so long.

"Morning," I say when I greet Lola and Daisy at the door.

Lola stares down her perfectly contoured nose at me, tapping her manicured finger on her chin. "Have you had sex recently?"

I gasp, glancing over my shoulder to make sure my parents pottering about in the kitchen didn't hear.

"What the heck?" I hiss, joining her on the porch and closing the door behind me.

"Is Jack here?" Lola continues.

Daisy grins mischievously from behind her. "I don't think it's Jack,"

I shoot Daisy a silencing scowl. "No. Jack's not here."

Lola laughs. "Lexie, you're totally glowing. Like someone turned on a light inside you. Trust me, I'm very good with auras."

Maybe she is, because that's a pretty good guess. "Take me to breakfast and I'll tell you all about it," I say.

Lola rubs her hands together excitedly. "Well, let's get a move on."

Lola's got the cutest little pale lemon Mini Cooper with fluffy cream seat covers and a custom glitter-ball gear stick. She's blasting K-Pop as she zooms through the snow-laden streets, the fuzzy rabbit hanging from her rear-view mirror swishing from side to side whenever she takes a corner.

"And that's where I work!" she announces. "Everyone wave to Hangry Henry!"

She sends out a few short, sharp toots of her horn as we pass Purr-fect Health veterinary clinic. A massive hunk of a guy wearing a white coat and cradling a bunny looks away from the woman he's speaking with on the sidewalk, turning his attention to Lola with her head out the window.

"Morning, Henry!" she squeals. "See you tomorrow! Don't forget to water the Monstera!" She ducks back inside and smiles. "That's my boss, Henry. When I asked for the morning off to have brunch, he gave me the whole day! He's such a sweetheart."

I recognize him from the ice rink, and I remember hearing Mom talk about the new vet in town who Polly absolutely adores. "Then why do you call him Hangry?" I ask curiously.

"Oh, that's my little nickname for him. Everyone thinks he's so grumpy, but he just works so much he never has time to have a proper meal. He's always sending me out for cans of Red Bull, or ordering in from the Mexican place around the corner. If he just ate a vegetable once in a while, I think people would see how lovely he can be. I've started grating carrots into his nachos when he's not looking."

I remember Mom mentioning he's engaged. "His fiancée probably thinks he's lovely," I say.

Daisy shakes her head. "Not anymore. Henry got dumped."

Lola nods. "I heard he didn't go to a karaoke bar on her birthday because he had concerns about the cleanliness of the microphones. He's a bit of a germaphobe."

"But he has no problem stopping a puck going a hundred miles an hour every Friday night," says Daisy, laughing.

"I don't think they were right for each other, anyway," Lola sighs. She never went to any of his games, and she was always kind of bitchy when she called the clinic, and I'm sure there's more to the karaoke story." A grin tugs at the corner of her mouth. "Like that time, I had a really really bad cold, and he brought me homemade chicken soup. A grumpy person doesn't do that."

"But you're the only person he treats that way?" I ask.

Lola shrugs. "I guess. I'm not sure."

I glance over my shoulder at Daisy in the back seat, and she grins. "Well, could Hangry Henry possibly have the hots for you, Lola?"

Lola bursts into knee slapping laughter. "Lexie! Of course not! We're just friends."

I look at Daisy again and find her shaking her head in silence, confirming my suspicions. "If you say so," I sigh.

Lola showers us with cutesy stories about Henry for the next ten minutes. By the time she pulls into the Lakeside Cafe, I have secondhand emotional whiplash. We walk inside the quaint little cabin-style establishment, taking a seat at a table by an enormous window that overlooks the lake and the giant Christmas tree, surrounded by snow dusted pines.

Lola at last takes a break from talking about Hangry Henry when she's presented with a menu, and if I had to put my hand on a bible and tell a judge exactly how Lola feels about Henry, I think he or she would be shit out of luck. I don't think even Lola knows.

The server checks on us a few minutes later, but I already decided on my order in the car. "Coffee with two sugars and milk, and scrambled eggs on toast, please."

He nods and takes the menu, then turns to Daisy.

"Let's do a full breakfast and a banana smoothie," she says decisively.

Last is Lola, and I can tell by the overstimulated twitch in her eye that her order is going to be as complicated as her feelings for Henry. The server stands patiently, picking at a loose thread in his black apron and a smile beams on his face when Lola shuts her menu and looks up at him.

"Tap water, with a squeeze of lemon and a slice of lime on the side and a GoGo Cranberry juice in the box with the straw. Don't put it in a cup, please. And then a bagel smothered in cream cheese."

"Smothered?" he repeats.

Lola nods. "Think of it more like cream cheese with a touch of bagel, if that helps." He takes her menu and smiles politely, and I can tell it really didn't help at all. "Now," she starts, catching her reflection in the steel napkin dispenser and fixing a stray hair, "who were you mounted by?"

I glare at her to keep it down, but Lola has never cared about what anyone else thinks. "There was no mounting, but there was definite sexual activity," I reply.

"But not with Jack?" Lola asks.

I gulp and shake my head. "We broke up."

"Was it the Instagram skank?" Daisy asks with a frown.

My heart aches for a second, like it's been stabbed with a butter knife. "You know about that?"

"It's getting around," Daisy says.

"Great," I mutter, fidgeting with the condiments to ease my anxiety.

"Fuck, Jack!" Daisy snaps.

Lola rolls her eyes. "Language, Daze."

I laugh. "You don't like fuck, but mount is okay?"

Lola frowns. "Lots of things get mounted, Lexie. TVs, horses, antlers. There's only a couple of things that get F'd, in the traditional sense."

Daisy tries to keep a straight face. "Right... in the traditional sense."

"Anyway," Lola groans. "I agree with what Daisy said. Good riddance. So if it wasn't Jack, then who was it?"

I exchange knowing looks with Daisy, who's grinning like a Cheshire cat. I scrunch up my face and look at Lola through one half-open eye. "Sean."

Her eyes bulge. "Yum! Not exactly the boy next door anymore, is he?" she giggles.

"But he is," I reply, the memory of his waves of soft, brown hair bobbing up and down between my legs sending shivers through my center. "That's what's so wonderful about him. He treats me like I'm this precious thing, like I'm perfect. He makes me feel like I'm enough, just the way I am."

Daisy leans back in her chair. "He's a smart guy."

My stomach knots and my hands are suddenly trembling around the salt shaker. I split my gaze between the pair of them. "I really like him."

Lola reaches out and puts her hand on top of mine to steady it. "That's great, Lexie. You deserve it."

I needed to hear that. Sometimes it can be a simple thing to forget.

"So does that mean you're moving back to Lake Mistletoe?" Daisy asks excitedly. "We'll all be back together again." Her eyes widen. "We can make our own softball team."

"Don't buy the uniforms yet," I say, scratching an invisible itch at the back of my head.

"But why?" Lola whines.

Daisy nods in agreement. "If it's over with Jack and you want to start something with Sean, it makes sense to move home."

They're right. But can it really be that easy? As I've been growing more fond of Sean, I've wondered what would happen if I stayed in Lake Mistletoe. Would I move in with him, get engaged, start a family, live next door to my parents for the rest of my life? It sounded small, like an old button sitting in my hand. The city was big and endless and I could be anyone there. But instead I almost faded into nothing. Somewhere along the way I stopped being Lexie and just became Jack's girlfriend. Until Sean reminded me that the person I am and things I want are just as important. "You're right. Everything I need is right here."

"Emotionally, absolutely... but we should probably get your shit back," Daisy says.

Lola nods. "Road trip."

I laugh and a warmth fills my chest, like I'm finally comfortable in my skin. "It's just clothes, really. I guess my paints are at the apartment, but I'm pretty sure I have art stuff in my parent's basement."

"I'm glad you're still painting," Daisy says. "I have that landscape of the lake you did. You better get famous soon. My retirement fund is relying on that painting."

"It's been hard to find inspiration lately," I say. "I was exhausted, working double shifts to keep the lights on at Jack's business. But the paintings I've managed to finish I've sold online. One collector has bought quite a few of them, actually." I smile blossoms across my lips. "I went to the arts center yesterday. Now all I want to do is lock myself in a room and paint for hours."

"There's this cute little shop near the clinic. It has big beautiful windows and a skylight. It's been empty for a while. Could be the perfect place for a studio," Lola says. Her eyes widen like a Disney princess. "We could have breakfast and lunch together every day."

"A spot on the softball team and a permanent food buddy? This just keeps getting better and better," I reply.

Lola and Daisy laugh as the server returns with a tray in the crook of his arm. He places the plates of food on the table, followed by the drinks.

"Why two?" I ask, as Lola receives her double drink order.

"Oh," Lola says, surprised, as if it were blatantly obvious. She points to the water. "This is for hydration." Then to the GoGo Cranberry juice. "This is for yumminess."

"Of course," I say, and it actually makes sense if you understand Lola's logic.

I bury my fork in the fluffy mound of scrambled eggs, scoop up a portion, and sweep them straight into my mouth. They're delicious. As I'm munching away at my perfect breakfast while gazing at the stunning frozen lake, and listening to Lola launch into a presentation of why raccoons are superior to cats, I can't think of anywhere I would rather be than here, and when I hear Sean's rumbling voice in my head asking me if I'm going to cum for him, I know for certain there is no one I'd rather be with.

14

Sean

It's the night of the grand opening of Talley's. I hate to jinx myself, but everything is pretty perfect right now. Not only is the love of my life back in Lake Mistletoe, but I've got the taste of her on my lips and I can't stop smiling. Add the wine and seafood arriving on time and the gas-fitters finishing two hours ahead of schedule, and I could just be the luckiest man on Earth. I'm not going to let a prick like Jack ruin this for me. If he shows his face in Lake Mistletoe... , if he even looks at Lexie... , it'll be the last mistake he ever makes.

Again, she's been in my head all day, and I've relived that night in my truck over and over. There are two things I'm certain of: That tonight is going to be a success, and that I'm going to taste Lexie again as soon as I get the chance.

I waltz about the restaurant taking care of the finer details, like straightening some chairs and centering the table arrangements. I inspect the silverware to be sure it's so polished I can see my reflection, and I drag my finger along the oak bar top to check for dust. Spotless. Perfect.

Talley's will be the premier dining destination, not just for the people of Lake Mistletoe, but for all the north. I've got a space for live bands to perform and a small dance floor, as well as a VIP area with a personal sommelier. My chef is Michelin starred and local produce and producers will always be the focal point of his menus. I want everyone to know what a special place Lake Mistletoe is, and after building restaurants in other places, it feels right to finally have one at home.

At the entrance I have an art installation, where local artists and designers can display their pieces and put them up for sale. I'm adjusting the satin drapes that conceal our debut exhibit when Blake walks in the door, dressed smartly in a navy suit and black loafers.

He looks me over, decidedly unimpressed, resting his chin on his palm.

I roll my eyes. "What?" He's staring at my jeans, but I paired them with a blazer and tie which counters the casualness, or at least that's my opinion.

"You can't wear jeans to this opening. I gave you a pass when you wore that heinous striped polo in South Hills, but not tonight. Tonight is special."

I frown. "We open in two hours. I don't have time to go home and..."

Blake holds out his hand to silence me, then reaches into his satchel, pulls out a pair of black trousers and chucks them at me. "Here."

I cock an eyebrow. "Did you bring these knowing I would need them, or do you always have an extra pair of trousers in your man purse?"

"Fuck you, it's a satchel and you can never be too prepared," Blake replies. "I discovered that the day I went into business with you."

"I owe you one," I say, taking the trousers.

"I'm glad you said that. I'll need a tab tonight for a sexy redhead called Tamara, and maybe we can get her and her equally attractive friends a table near the garden?"

"Well, well. A garden table. This Tamara must be pretty special."

"Not really," Blake says nonchalantly. "Oh, and I thought maybe we could seat Char right next to the kitchen. Even move the table closer to the doors, so she keeps getting bumped every time they open. It'll be hilarious."

"Is that really the way to treat your soon-to-be sister-in-law?" I sigh.

Blake nods confidently. "There are so few true joys in the world. When you find something that makes you happy, you grab it with both hands and don't let go. For me, it's the face Char makes when I've ruined her day."

"Do you know why little boys pull little girls' ponytails in the playground, Blake?"

He shrugs, only half listening. "Because it's fun? I don't know. Go put the pants on."

I feel the allusion is lost on him, so I turn and head for the bathroom while he orders a glass of very expensive scotch from the bartenders, who aren't on the clock yet.

While I'm in the bathroom, I'm thinking about two things. These trousers are buttery smooth, and I get to see Lexie in one hour and thirty-seven minutes. I've got a surprise for her tonight, something I hope she'll love. I miss her so much and it's been less than a day. I can't get enough of my girl. The way she smells, the way she tastes, the sounds she makes when I please her. I grip the basin and pull myself together as I feel my member harden. The last thing I need is my dick tearing a hole in Blake's fancy pants.

Now that I look professional enough, I sit at the bar, order myself a beer, and wait for the opening. The servers arrive, their red aprons designed to match the tablecloths. Next is the string quartet I booked, and the musicians file through carrying their black instrument cases. A couple of local teens I hired as valets turn up close to opening time, and Blake gives them shit for not wearing ties. Glad to know I'm not the only one. When the clock chimes 7pm, the staff break into applause and Blake and I stand to thank them.

"Talley's is officially open," I announce.

The hostess opens the door, and I'm pleased to see the line outside, despite the snow. The hostess seats the first guests and I recognize the food critic that Blake sacrificed his finger for. When the server walks by me on her way to the table, I touch her arm to get her attention.

"Critic," I whisper, and she acknowledges me with a discreet nod.

Within thirty minutes, Talley's is full. The kitchen roars into action as the servers pin the orders, and I always get a rush when I hear the commotion of a busy restaurant. The thrum of polite conversation, the clink of glasses, the chef barking at his staff and the sizzle of premium wagyu when it hits a hot pan. Blake catches my gaze across the room and gives an approving nod just as the string quartet breaks into Jingle Bell Rock. Now there's only one thing that will make this night even better.

The door opens, and when Lexie walks in I can't remember how to breathe. She's wearing a red dress that hugs each full curve of her stunning body, and I fight to drag my eyes away from her thick thighs wrapped in black stockings, like a Christmas present just for me. She's pinned up her hair, but a few blonde tendrils fall over her jade eyes, framing her face. A shade of deep, decadent red stains her lips and, when she parts them and laughs, I imagine that gorgeous mouth wrapped around my cock.

She sees me and smiles, and I don't think she has a clue how long I've waited for her to look at me that way. Stan and Beth stand on either side, looking stunned and a little worried by how full the restaurant is. But they don't need to be. I've saved them a special table in the back. The hostess checks the list and nods her head, gesturing to the VIP area by the garden. She leads the Moores through the dining room, and when Lexie reaches me, she stops.

"I'll catch up with you," she says to her parents.

They look us over with enthusiastic grins as they carry on to their table, and as I'm gazing at Lexie and inhaling her sweet, candied scent, I wonder how long it will be before I've got her propped up on the bathroom sink with her amazing pussy in my face and a black stockinged leg over each shoulder.

"You look beautiful," I breathe.

She shuffles nervously, her cheeks reddening. "What. This old thing?"

Lexie's so shy, she can barely keep eye contact, but there's no way I'm looking away. I don't want to miss a moment of her. I gesture around the room. "So, what do you think?"

She seems grateful to have permission to look somewhere else. "It's fantastic, Sean. I can't believe this used to be Deena's."

"It took an industrial steamer to get the grease off the wall behind the old fryer, and I had to gut the bathrooms, but the bones were good." Miraculously, I've worked the bathrooms into the conversation. Now do I offer her a tour? I go to speak, but Lexie beats me to it as she checks the contents of her purse.

"Sorry, where are the bathrooms? I just want to freshen up before dinner."

Now I'm rock hard. I just hope I don't poke anyone's eye out when I'm weaving my way through these tables. I cough to clear my throat. "Let me show you."

My hand finds hers, and I lace our fingers. Again she smiles, and there's some uncertainty there, as if no one has wanted her the way I do, savored the little things like holding her hand and making her laugh just to hear the sound. The feel of her skin alone is enough to make me blow my load and ruin Blake's loaner pants. Speaking of Blake, he immediately clocks me guiding Lexie through the restaurant. He chuckles, and I know he's going to grill me about it when we have our debrief over a beer tonight.

We get to the bathrooms and I've gone with this deep, forest green damask wallpaper, gold fittings and marble sinks. The lowlight of the sculpted sconces creates a moody, brooding atmosphere, which is equal parts classy and sexy. I lean into the wall and gesture to the door. "Here you go."

"Thanks," Lexie replies, but she doesn't go straight in, and I can tell by the way she's fidgeting with the clasp on her purse she wants to ask me something.

"Was there something else?" I move away from the wall and stand over her, and she trembles when she looks up at me. Lexie takes a step back, but only finds the closed door, and I stretch my arms above her, gripping the edge of the frame. "Lexie. Do you need...," my eyes devour her, "... help?"

"I...," she mutters.

She's trembling, her breasts heaving with anxious breaths. I take one hand away from the door frame and trail a finger along her upper arm. Her eyes close as she leans against the door, and I dip my head to lay a whisper-thin kiss in the smooth curve where her neck meets her shoulder. She shivers beneath my lips. My hand slides away from her arm, my fingers gently dragging along her collarbone and finding the sumptuous seam of her cleavage. I follow the inviting groove all the way down to the fullness of her perfect breasts, and it doesn't take long for my searching thumb to find her nipple. It hardens instantly under my touch and Lexie moans softly.

"Sean," she murmurs.

I trail kisses up her neck, some soft and barely there, while others are hard as I breathe into her skin. I reach her ear. "Baby, if I don't get you in this bathroom quick, I'm going to have to take you right here against this door."

She gulps, leaning into my kisses. "But people will hear."

I clench my teeth and pull her hips against me. I growl, drawing out each word. "I don't. Fucking. Care."

Lexie puts her hand against the door, her fingers desperately seeking the handle, and when she finds it and gives it a turn, we tumble into the bathroom. She stumbles until she backs into the basin, her hands gripping the marble edges. I gaze at Lexie, framed by the dark wallpaper bathed in the amber sconce light. She's got one knee slightly bent, her black heel pressed against the cabinet, her dress riding up those thick thighs. I reach behind me and close the door, then flip the lock without taking my eyes off her. I feel as if I'm a man starving, as if I'm staring down my prey, toying with it, making seconds feel like hours while I decide where I want to start with her.

I yank my tie loose and take my time walking over. She's breathing so heavily already. I pin her hands to the edge of the basin. My nose brushes against hers, and a guttural growl groans its way out of my throat as our eyes meet. "Open your legs for me, baby," I whisper.

Lexie gulps, but does not deny me. I feel her legs part, and she grinds against me, my cock pressing at her stomach. I dip my head to her lips and kiss her deep and passionately, my tongue exploring the warmth of her mouth, my appetite for her insatiable as I kiss her, our heaving breaths uniting in a sensual chorus that makes me harder than I thought was possible. When I've had my fill of her mouth, I drop to my haunches, ready to taste the rest of her. My girl opens up for me, and her scent sends something feral through me. I don't want to pull her stockings down. They'll bind her legs. I want her wide. I want to sink inside her. I want those thighs over my shoulders, just like I imagined. I lift Lexie's thigh and lean into the welcoming warmth between her legs. Her stockings stretch taut over her groin, and through the sheer fabric I make out her glistening juices gliding along her open folds.

"No panties today?" I ask.

She blushes and giggles. "I was hoping this might happen. Maybe I shouldn't have worn stockings either."

I gaze at her thigh over my shoulder, gripping the tender flesh, the silkiness of her stockings fueling my need to taste her. With my free hand I grip the fabric, twisting it in my fingers and with a sharp grunt I tear a hole, exposing her beautiful center.

"Sean," she gasps.

I inhale her exquisite scent. "I'll buy you a new pair," I mutter before pressing my mouth against her glistening crevice.

Lexie's fingers grip the basin tighter as a rush of breathless groans escapes her. God, she tastes amazing. I want to go slow and tease her, but my tongue laps hard and fast, my head bobs back and forth, and my nose swipes against her swollen clit as I claw at her thigh over my shoulder. Lexie grinds against my mouth and I wish there was more room in this bathroom to lie down so she could straddle my face.

I can feel her getting close to her release, her muscles tightening, the pace of her swirling hips escalating. I need to finish her off. I move my tongue to her pretty pink bud. I lick her and suck her, and she covers her mouth as she tries to stifle her moans. But, like I said, I don't fucking care. I want Lexie to scream out. I want everyone to know that she's mine, and this is how I make her cum. My two fingers enter her with ease. I pump in and out while I lap hungrily at her clit, and it doesn't take long for her to explode all over me.

She restrains the sound of her orgasm, and it leaves her as a long, agonizing whimper. I'm proud of her, but I like it more when she's loud.

I stand up and straighten her dress. Her eyes are closed and she's still struggling to catch her breath, sweat beading at her temples. I cup her face in my hands and run my thumbs along her cheekbones.

"How long can you keep this up?" she laughs lightly.

"I can do this every day, Lexie. I'll eat your pussy for the rest of your life, if that's what you need."

A blissful smile blooms on her face, and I feel her fingers trail down my abdomen and over my belt until they find my bulging cock.

I shake my head. "I told you, you don't have to do that."

Her eyes open glazed and exhausted and fucking gorgeous. She bites her lip and squeezes the head. My member stirs and I don't know how much longer I'm going to be able to deny him his own taste.

"I know I don't have to. I want to," Lexie says softly, and my eyes lock on her glistening red lips.

My hands leave her face, coming to rest on either side of her and gripping the basin so I have her caged. She's running her hand up and down my shaft, and I gulp when I feel a drip of precum. Lexie drops to her knees and pulls down the zip of my trousers, then reaches inside and frees my swollen cock.

"I thought you were a good girl," I groan as she licks my head.

"Oh baby," she says, sliding her tongue around my engorged tip, "you don't know how good I can be."

15

Lexie

I've been wanting this cock in my mouth for so long and I'm not disappointed. Sean is so big that I can barely get my lips around his head and only halfway down his smooth shaft before he hits the back of my throat. Because I can't treat his entire length to the warmth of my mouth, I work him with my hands as well, wrapping both of them around his thick base and jerking up and down.

He's groaning, and the noises he makes are so sexy that I'm getting wet all over again. I draw my mouth back and tighten my lips around the tip, and he reacts with a subtle thrust. His hands are still on either side of my head, gripping the basin while I kneel in front of him, and when I slurp again, he responds with another thrust, then another, and soon I'm not moving my head at all. Sean pumps into my mouth and the back of my head presses against the wood cabinet below the sink.

"Fuck, that's good, baby. That's so fucking good," he growls.

He plants his feet and ups his pace, and when he hits the back of my throat, I gag.

"Can you take this whole cock like a good girl?" he asks me.

I look up to meet his eyes, my mouth stretched wide over his shaft and all I can do to reply is nod.

Sean leans his hips into me and inch by inch, his cock disappears past my lips.

"Open your throat, baby," he instructs. "Remember. You wanted this."

I relax my throat muscles as he eases in his length into my mouth. Sean thrusts, slowly at first, but when he sees how well I am taking it, he moves faster and harder. He grips the sink, his teeth grit.

"Good girl, Lexie. Good girl," he groans.

He grows even thicker, and my eyes roll back in my head.

"Fuck, I'm cumming," he grunts.

His member throbs, and Sean explodes, flooding my mouth with his seed. I do my best to take every drop and he groans, holding my mouth over his head until he's completely emptied. Then he slips his spent cock from between my lips and tucks it back in his pants. Sean reaches down and picks me up, his arms encircling my waist and pulling me hard against him, his head resting on my chest.

"Holy fuck," he breathes into my skin. He looks up at me with a dreamy gaze, and I'm stunned when he leans into my lips and kisses me, our tastes mingling with each other. When he pulls back, he's staring at me deeply, so intense I feel he sees the real me, the Lexie below the surface, and I've never felt more wanted.

"Stay," he says breathlessly. "Now that I've had you, I can't let you go." He cups my face. "Stay with me, Lexie."

A bang at the door startles me before I can respond.

"Sorry to interrupt, but we're trying to run a respectable restaurant here?"

I recognize Blake's voice and stifle my giggle.

Sean laughs. "I think we're past that, don't you?" He tips his chin to the door. "I'll be right out." He pulls up his zip and checks himself in the mirror, pushing his hair back from his brow. "No harm done."

"Lucky for you," I frown. "I've got a pretty decent draft going on down there."

Sean shoots a downward glance and rolls his bottom lip between his teeth. "That's going to drive me crazy all night."

He takes me by the hips and, for a second, I think we're going to get into it all over again. But Blake persists.

"It's time for this art thing. Move your ass," he grumbles.

We laugh before Sean kisses me one more time. "Think about it. Okay?" He laces his fingers with mine, then unlocks the bathroom door and opens it. We walk out together and find Blake leaning into the wall looking far from pleased.

"About time. Let's get on with it," he grumbles.

Blake walks into the main dining area. "Good evening, everyone," he announces, and I barely recognize him as the grump outside the bathroom from five seconds ago. With his bright, bold smile and rumbling voice that oozes charisma, Blake is a charmer, just like he was in high school.

"Sean and I can't thank you enough for making Talley's opening night such a massive success. It's an honor to bring a restaurant of this caliber to a place that means so much to us both, and the way you have supported us is just a reminder that Lake Mistletoe is the greatest town in the entire world." He steeples his fingers and tips his head to the guests hanging on his every word. "Thank you again."

There's a roar of applause and even the odd whistle and Blake bows, not hesitating to soak up all the adoration. He turns toward Sean and extends his arm.

"Now let's hear from the mad genius behind Talley's. The hometown boy made good, Mr. Sean Talley."

The cheers increase, and one by one the guests slide out their chairs and rise to their feet to applaud. Sean bows his head and he's almost tucked behind me, the opposite of Blake's response to the attention.

"Go on," I giggle behind my hand. "They love you."

His chin lifts and our eyes meet. I feel his fingers tighten around mine as I place my hand on his chest.

"You can do this," I whisper.

He gulps, and it blows my mind that this man who takes me so boldly and passionately in a restaurant bathroom is nervous about public speaking. There's so much more to Sean than I realized.

Sean nods and I see his shoulders heave as he takes a step forward, only releasing my fingers when he absolutely has to. The applause continues, and when his cheeks redden I can't help but swoon.

"Thank you, thank you," he says, waving his hand to quieten the guests. He's mostly looking at his feet, but now and then he glances upward and gazes straight at me, as if he's making sure I'm still there. "This was a bit of a passion project," he starts. "I remember coming to Deena's when I was in high school. I'd sit right over there, near the window," he points. "Alone, of course. I wasn't one of the cool kids back then, but I'd like to think I'm pretty cool now." The guests laugh and he has them eating out of his hand. "It was hard changing this place, and I know a lot of you were hesitant at first. But more than anything I wanted somewhere friends and families could come together and eat and drink and laugh and enjoy cuisine from all over the world right here in Lake Mistletoe, and I'm proud to say I think Blake and I have accomplished that."

He scratches at his neck and his shoulders stiffen, and I look at him curiously. He's doing so well. Why the sudden change? He was looking at me for reassurance before, and now he can't meet my eyes at all. I can't figure out why.

The guests look just as confused as they wait for him to speak, and I can see their whispers are making him even more anxious. Shit. I've been so preoccupied with how good Sean has been making me feel the last couple of days that I've completely forgotten that underneath the success and the muscles, and the way he makes me orgasm so hard that I actually see God, he's still Sean from next door. Nervous, awkward, and alone. And he needs me right now.

I cross the room, an urgency in my step, and I grab his hand as soon as I can reach it. He looks up, and I can see the sweat pooling on his brow.

"You've got this," I say softly, enclosing his hand in mine.

It takes a second for his shoulders to loosen. He exhales and nods and, finally, a smile blooms onto his face. "You all know Lexie Moore," he says.

The guests applaud, and the tension in the room seems to ease, but now I'm the one blushing. I tuck my hair behind my ear and give a timid wave.

"Lexie is an example of how talented and creative folks are in Lake Mistletoe, and as well as good food, I want to make sure when you come to Talley's, you're surrounded by great local art. So, even though Blake didn't think it suited the layout, I installed a space to show off our artists, with new displays each week." Sean extends his arm toward the satin-curtained wall near the entrance. "Maybe Lexie can help me unveil our first exhibit?"

I frown at him and he gives me a cheeky grin. I didn't mean to suddenly become part of the speech, but if it makes him feel more comfortable, then sure I'll be his assistant. Sean leads me over to the wall and gestures to a green rope alongside the curtain. I take hold of it and prepare for the grand reveal. How exciting for an artist to have their work on display for everyone to enjoy. I don't dwell on how envious I am; I want to make sure I'm ready when Sean needs me.

"Our debut artist at Talley's has a real eye for color and movement, and I must admit her work is so vibrant, so emotive, that viewing her paintings can be quite an emotional experience." Sean looks straight at me as he speaks, and I feel as if I'm the only person in the room. "This artist is beautiful and kind. She makes me laugh… and not always with her, and in moments like this, she makes me feel like someone has my back, no matter what."

I knit my eyebrows. This all seems very specific and somewhere along the way I think it stopped being about brush strokes and got really personal. He nods at me, and I take that as my cue to pull the rope. The green satin curtain comes billowing down revealing the paintings and when I see them my eyes well with tears. I recognize all twelve of them, because I painted them. Painted and sold them to a mysterious online buyer.

"It was you?" I murmur as I gaze upon my art on display. "You bought them all!"

Sean nods and I tuck my head into my shoulder when I feel a tear run down my cheek. He's at my side in an instant, stroking my arm with one hand while the other cups my face and wipes away the tear. "I'm sorry. I didn't mean to upset you."

I laugh softly at how ridiculous that notion is. "I'm not upset, Sean. I'm happy. Thank you."

"That's not all," he says, as he turns back to the guests. "As some of you may know, our arts center is struggling to keep its doors open, and places like this are vital to our community. Beauty and passion and creativity are traits that need to be given space to grow, and it's something so incredibly close to Lexie's heart. So Talley's will be putting all her stunning work up for auction, and all the proceeds will go to the arts center."

The restaurant erupts with applause.

I shake my head, dumbfounded. "But Sean. These are yours."

"No. They're yours," he replies. "And it seems right that it's your art that keeps the center open."

"This is incredible," I say, breathless.

He cups my face with both hands and gazes into my eyes. "I'll spend my whole life making you happy if you'll let me, Lexie."

The butterflies in my stomach take flight and I lean into him, the warm comfort of his lips making me feel as if I'm floating on air. He holds me tight, and even though we're in a room full of gawking people, it's only me and Sean and nothing else matters, and I wonder if it could always feel this way if I was to give Sean what he wanted. Me. Forever.

16

Sean

Lexie and I spend the rest of the evening drinking wine while sharing a bowl of fettuccine. We laugh and flirt, and her foot nuzzles me under the table but, more than anything, we talk for hours and never run out of things to say. She's always been enchanting, but when that curtain dropped and she saw her paintings, something came alive in her. This light that had been dwindling has suddenly sparked, and the glow on my girl is intoxicating.

As the evening grows late, Tom and Sophie wander past and, while I shake hands with Tom, Sophie takes a seat beside Lexie.

"The auctions are going well," Sophie says.

Lexie nods her head, her lips tightly drawn together, too excited to speak.

"This is huge, Lex," Sophie gushes, gripping Lexie's hands on the table. "The center can stay open."

Lexie finds her voice, though her cheeks are still flushed with color. "I want to do more. Let me take over the volunteering. You need to focus on getting married."

A weight seems to lift from Sophie, and she lets out a long, deep breath. "That would be great, Lexie. Thank you." She shoots me a quick glance. "Does that mean you're staying?"

Lexie smiles and I'm hanging on her answer. "It's beginning to feel that way," Lexie says.

"Don't tell Daisy," Sophie warns as she stands from the table. "She's got this crazy idea for a softball team."

Tom and Sophie say goodnight, and Lexie glows even brighter before me. Gradually the guests disperse. They tap my shoulder to thank me or tell me how amazing their meal was, and I try my best to be polite and grateful, but all I want to do is listen to everything Lexie has to say. Before I know it, the staff are clearing the tables and the string quartet have packed up their black cases and are heading out to their cars in the snow. Then it's just me and Lexie laughing together, and I can't think of anywhere else in the world I would rather to be.

"Do you want me to drive you home?" I ask.

"I have my parents' car," she replies. "They left with friends for a late night game of Yahtzee. So I guess it'll just be me at home."

"That's such a shame," I say, grazing her arm with my finger. "Maybe I should come over and keep you company?"

Her eyelashes flutter around her jade eyes and I feel my heart melt. "Maybe you should," she says.

"Well, consider me there."

Lexie blushes and I like I make her feel that way. She deserves to feel desired. I'm so obsessed with how she shimmers under these dimmed lights, I don't notice when Blake ambles up beside me.

"Sorry to interrupt, but I need to grab you in the kitchen for a debrief before everyone heads home."

God, all I want to do is get Lexie into her house and naked as soon as possible, but the debrief is important, especially after opening night. I can make it quick, though. Before I can ask her if that's alright, she's already nodding at me.

"It's fine. I'll meet you back at my place."

I lift her hand to my lips and kiss her knuckles. "I won't be long. I promise."

Lexie shuffles out of her chair and when I'm at eye level with her thighs, all I can think about is that tear in her stockings. She crosses the room and heads for the exit. The hostess opens the door for her, and the entire time she's glancing over her shoulder at me, giggling and blushing, and I'm not doing much better. I feel like I'm in high school with my first love, except this time maybe she could love me too one day.

I stand up and walk to the big misty window, leaning on the glass and watching to be sure she makes it to her car safe. She sees me and waves before she ducks inside, and the headlights of her parents' sedan flick on, streaking the snow with harsh yellow beams. Lexie drives away and from that instant I'm counting the seconds until I get to hold her again.

"Come on, lover boy," Blake sighs. "This will be quick."

He's not wrong. We go over the menu, what worked and didn't, and concerns the servers had with the POS system, as well as a saffron shortage and guests mentioning strange noises coming from one of the bathrooms. Apart from that, Talley's opening night is a success with a tidy profit to boot.

Blake takes a seat at the bar, helping himself to a bottle of scotch. "Drink to celebrate?"

I've already got one arm in my coat and I'm fishing my car keys out from behind the hostess stand. "Not tonight. I've got somewhere to be."

Blake pours himself a scotch. "First Tom, now you. Another good soldier lost to the trenches. Us bachelors are becoming an endangered species around here."

I work my other arm into my heavy navy coat and straighten the collar. "Maybe you need to settle down, man. Stop fucking around and find yourself a keeper."

Blake sips his scotch, then stares at the amber liquid as he swishes it in his glass. "Easier said than done. Guess I'm not as brave as you."

I laugh and dig my hands into my pockets. "Brave? Did you see me shit myself when I had to talk to people?"

Blake grins. "You're letting someone in, man. Allowing yourself some genuine fucking happiness. That's as brave as taking a grenade in my books."

I open the door and the bracing breeze ruffles my hair. "It'll happen, Blake. Just gotta let it."

He shakes his glass at me. "Yeah, yeah. Have a good night."

I dip my head at him before I leave, closing the door behind me. He would have spent the entire night drinking and shooting the shit if I didn't get out of there. He's a good guy, and one of my closest friends, but dude's got some serious emotional hang-ups, and when it comes to relationships he's fucking dead in the water.

I head to my truck at a decent pace, but before I know it I've broken into a jog and I'm flicking the unlock button on my car remote. I climb in, buckle up and crank the stereo, and when I glance to the empty passenger seat, the image of Lexie with her legs spread is enough to get my foot on the gas.

I need to get to her house quick, but I also don't want to die on these roads. It feels like forever before I pull into the street and I don't bother with my driveway, instead pulling straight into hers. But when I turn off the engine, I realize there's another car parked behind Stan and Beth's sedan. A black BMW. The sedan's driver side door is wide open, and when I get out of my truck I can see the keys are still in the ignition. I immediately train my eyes on the house and, just like the car, the door is open, white light spilling onto the porch. I can see figures moving inside. Then I hear a man yell. Then I run.

17

Lexie

My heart is beating a hundred miles an hour, and I wonder if this is how a rabbit feels when it's cornered by a wolf. I couldn't get into the house quick enough. I got out of the car and ran when I saw him pull up in the rearview, but by the time I got to the front door, he was already right behind me. I told him to get out, that I didn't want to talk to him. I fought my way inside, but when I tried to close the door, he jammed his foot to keep it open. When I backed away, he let himself in, and now we're standing here staring at each other, and I'm so terrified I can barely breathe. He's never laid a hand on me, but he's also never shoved a door open when I've told him to leave, and that look in his eye... so full of anger, and I can smell the booze on his breath. This isn't the same Jack I left in the city.

He takes a seat and throws his arm on the table, knocking over my mom's center piece. "Fuck," he snaps, clumsily standing it back up. He looks around the room through glazed, half-shut eyes. "Talk about being stuck in a time loop. This place hasn't changed, has it?" He flicks his eyes up the stairs. "You still got that squeaky twin bed up there?"

I feel nauseous. "Please leave, Jack. We have nothing to discuss."

"Oh, I beg to differ, babe. Let's start with the fact that you just disappeared on me. Who does that? We've been together since we were kids, Lexie. I deserve better."

I almost choke on my tongue. "Are you serious? The last time I saw you, you were balls deep in Jewel. What was I supposed to do? Stick around? Check if either of you needed an Evian?"

He shakes his head. "You know I've been under a lot of stress. I wasn't thinking straight, okay?"

"Get out, Jack," I yell.

He bolts to his feet, and the chair skids away behind him before falling to the floor. I gasp and take a step back, and he rolls his eyes.

"Why are you acting like that? What, do you think I'm going to hurt you?" He takes a step forward, so I take another step back until I'm against the wall. He smirks. "You think I'm going to hit you, Lexie?" His eyes darken beneath his brow. "That's not me. But if you don't get your ass in the car and come home, who knows what could happen?"

I can feel the tears building behind my eyes, but I won't give him the satisfaction of knowing he's getting to me.

"You're shaking..." he mutters. He looks behind him to the open door and slaps the side of his head so hard it startles me. "Of course. You're cold. Let me close this for you, babe."

He walks toward the door and I panic. I can't let him close it. Then I'm locked in here with him, and the way he's acting, god knows what he's capable of. Before I know what I'm doing, my feet are running and I'm rushing for the door, desperate to get there before he does. But it takes almost no effort for him to grab my wrist, pinching it in his hand so tightly I wince and cry out.

"Where do you think you're going? We're staying right here, babe, until we sort this mess out." He pulls me to him, and when I try to get free, he squeezes my wrist tighter until I settle. With his other hand, he pinches my chin between his thumb and finger, forcing me to look at him. "Why are you making this so fucking difficult?"

As he presses against me, I realize he's leaning closer, his eyes trained on my lips. "I miss you so much, Lexie."

He kisses me, and I want to vomit, and not only because of the sickly beer that soaks his breath. I'm done with him. Finished. I've moved so far past Jack that he's barely visible in my rearview, and as he gropes at me my fist tightens. No one is allowed to touch me but Sean. I swing and connect just above his eye and Jack groans, turning his head away from me. It takes him a minute to register what just happened, and the stunned look in his eyes slowly morphs into rage.

"Oh, you want to get physical?" He digs his hand into my hair and grips the back of my head. "I'll show you physical."

"Let her go," a voice demands from the doorway, and my heart thumps hard in my chest.

Jack turns. "This is a private discussion. Now get out of here."

From behind his back, Sean pulls out his hockey stick and taps it methodically on his shoulder. "Not going to happen. Now let her go."

Jack laughs smugly. He still grips my wrist like a vise and he yanks me behind him. "Listen buddy, I'm having a conversation with my girlfriend and things got a little heated, but everything's fine now, okay?"

"She's not your girlfriend," Sean snarls.

Jack cocks an eyebrow. "Oh really? How would you know?"

"Because she's mine," Sean breathes, his eyes narrowing on Jack like an arrow aimed at a bullseye. "And if you touch her again, I'll fucking kill you."

Jack's throat quivers when he gulps, and I'm ecstatic to see him nervous, but the deep intent in Sean's tone makes me worry that if Jack doesn't back down, Sean will follow through on his threat, and the last thing I want is to lose him.

"He's not worth it, Sean," I say.

Jack's head jerks sharply and he looks at me. "Sean?" His eyes dart back to the doorway. "Sean Talley? Is that you?" He looks him up and down and rolls his shoulders. "Bulked up a bit, huh? Good for you, man, good for you. Now get the fuck out."

I struggle in Jack's grip, and he shakes me. "Enough, Lexie!" he booms.

Suddenly Sean charges across the room, holding the hockey stick lengthwise. Jack scrambles when he sees him coming and releases me, and I move away just as Sean puts the hockey stick to Jack's throat and pushes him against the wall.

"Get off me," Jack gurgles. He grabs hold of the hockey stick and tries to push Sean away, but Sean doesn't move an inch, instead he presses harder.

"Who do you think you are that you get to touch her? You're nothing. You're worthless. You don't even deserve to breathe the same air she does."

Jack coughs as Sean applies more pressure, and I notice a sickly blue tinge to his skin.

"That's enough, Sean," I yell.

Sean doesn't stop. A fury has overwhelmed him, and I know he will kill Jack if I let him. But I won't. I put my hand on Sean's shoulder and press my forehead to his back.

"Sean. That's enough."

Sean heaves with breath, his frame shuddering under the pressure of his rage. But slowly his arms slacken as he takes the hockey stick away from Jack's throat, and Jack erupts into sputters and coughs as he tries to breathe.

"Him," Jack croaks. "You're with him now?"

Sean looks over his shoulder at me and the answer sings in my heart. "Yes. I'm with him now."

Jack stumbles toward the door, then pauses, bracing himself on the frame. He looks at the ground, unable to meet Sean's eyes. "Your truck. It's blocking me in," he stutters.

"Then fucking walk," Sean snarls.

Jack nods, staggering out the door and into the snow without another word.

I take the hockey stick from Sean's hands and lean it against the wall, then I caress his face as his anger leaves him, and soon he's my Sean again. His arms encircle my waist and he closes his eyes and kisses my thumb as I drag it across his lips.

"Are you alright?" he asks.

"I am now," I reply.

"I don't know what I would do if anything happened to you, Lexie." His eyes are wide and he's breathless.

My heart swells. I rise on tiptoes to reach his lips and kiss him, and he hungrily breathes me in like I'm oxygen.

18

Sean

I held Lexie in the kitchen until her parents came home. She wanted me to stay, but it was best that Beth and Stan take over. Family is what she needs more than anything. I didn't go far, though. Headed straight home, pulled up a chair on my front porch, and sat there with my hockey stick to be sure Jack didn't come sneaking back around. Even after the chill settled into my bones, I stayed put, watching the silhouettes move around in the Moore house, making out the lush curves of Lexie's figure. I'll stay here until morning if I have to.

Not long after midnight, I hear the front door of the Moore house creak open and I'm on my feet with a start. It takes me a second to make out Lexie's blonde hair through the snowfall and I loosen the grip on my hockey stick. She walks gingerly across the slippery porch and down the stairs, then jogs through the snow to join me at my house. I lean my stick against the siding and sweep back my damp mop of hair.

"Is everything okay?" I ask.

She nods. "What are you doing out here? It's freezing."

I gesture to Jack's black BMW. "Seeing if he comes back for it, or for any other reason. I want to be here if he does."

"I don't think we'll be seeing Jack for a while," Lexie says.

She shivers and I whip off my jacket without a second thought, bundling her up and encircling her in my arms. "Any way, what are you doing out here? There's no point in both of us freezing."

She looks up at me, her long lashes blinking over round, glassy jade eyes. "Then maybe we should go inside."

My heart races at the thought of having her to myself. But I can't be selfish, even if all I'm imagining is sliding my cock in and out of Lexie's sweet pussy. I shake my head.

"No. After what you've been through, you need to be with Beth and Stan."

"I'd rather be with you," she argues, and there's a snap in Lexie's tone, as if she's not interested in my reasoning.

"I just want you taken care of," I protest, sliding my hand along her jaw to cup her face. My girl is cold. She can't be standing out here. She'll catch a chill.

Lexie rolls her bottom lip between her teeth. "Will you take care of me, Sean?"

My breath hitches in my throat, my eyes fixed on her glossy lips as she speaks.

"Please," she mewls, and her tone is so close to the way she sounds when she cums that I'm rock hard in seconds.

She glances down and smiles. I'm so fucking stiff that she can feel it through my pants, pressing against her stomach. I'm embarrassed at first, recalling the loner nerd in high school who kept busting out random erections whenever Lexie walked by. But that memory fades when she grasps hold of me with both hands and strokes me slow from base to tip.

A deep groan escapes my lips, and my hand slides to the back of her neck where I grip her tight at the nape. "Do you have any idea what I'm going to do to you if you walk through that door?"

Lexie smiles and licks her lips. She's a tease, and she knows it, but the way she's working my cock, we won't be messing around with the foreplay for long.

"Show me," she says.

I need no further encouragement. She had her opportunity to go home, but she pushed me too far. Now I'm not stopping until I'm so deep in her she can feel it in her belly. I slide my hands under her ass and lift her up by those gorgeous, thick thighs. She hooks her legs around my waist and squeezes, and already I can feel the heat from her core through my shirt. I walk backward to the door and give it a hard kick with my heel to get it open. Once we're inside, Lexie reaches behind to close it and then her mouth is on mine.

Our tongues collide like we're starving for the taste of each other. She's breathing hard and when the mound of her breasts escapes her dress, I tear myself away from her lips to bury my face in her cleavage. She smells so good. I clench the bust line of her dress between my teeth and pull down until her full, beautiful breasts pop out. Her pretty pink nipple falls into my eager mouth and I suck while groping her ass, pulling her warmth harder against my stomach.

Lexie groans, gripping my hair and pushing my mouth deep over her nipple. "Fuck, yes, just like that," she murmurs.

My cock is throbbing and I can barely think straight, but I need to decide where I'm going to make love to Lexie for the first time. Against the wall, on the stairs, on the couch. Maybe bent over the kitchen counter. Then it comes to me and a pearl of precum beads on the tip of my cock. I carry Lexie up the stairs.

She grips me by the shoulders, and when the old stairs creak, she jolts. "What are you doing?"

"Shhhh, baby," I whisper. "I'm just taking you to bed."

She wraps tighter around me. "You're going to drop me!" she squeals.

"No, I'm not," I chuckle, giving her full ass a squeeze. "You fit perfect in my arms."

A contented smile melts onto her face, and she wraps her arms around my neck and rests her head on my shoulder. I make it to the top of the stairs, then it's a quick four steps to my old bedroom.

She laughs when she realizes which room I'm going to have her in. "Sean! Really?"

"Seems perfect to me. I finally get Lexie Moore right in the place I dreamed about her every night."

She kisses me, and it's such a long, deep kiss that everything else fades away. It's just her and me, and I'm completely under her spell. I'm hers to use, however she wants, in whatever way that pleases her. I don't care. As long as she doesn't stop kissing me. Ever.

I lie her on the bed, and it's a little creakier than I remember. I look down at her and I never thought in a million years I'd be gazing at Lexie on my blue tartan bedspread, her dress riding up her thighs, the crotch of her stockings ripped open, and her pussy waiting to be fucked. She giggles as I stand over her, lifting a leg one at a time and flicking off her shoes. I lean down, taking a thigh in each hand and clawing my way up toward where her dress sits just below her hips. I hook the band of her beautifully defiled stockings, peeling them away and tossing them over my shoulder.

Lexie giggles, bringing her knees together, but I'm not going to allow that. I cup a knee in each hand and roughly spread my girl until she's wide open. Lexie gasps as I drop to my knees in front of the bed, sling her legs over my shoulders, sweep my hands under her hips, and pull her pussy onto my face. I find her hard bud and flick my tongue with relentless speed, parting her folds so I can work deeper on her clit.

Lexie grinds her hips and her arms shoot out, clawing at the bedspread. I feel her muscles tightening, and her hot, sweet juices stream down my chin. She's close, so it seems like a good time to loosen her up so she can take my cock easier when I decide it's time. I ease a finger inside her, and Lexie arches her back and cries out, propping herself on her elbows. I look up from her mound as I lick, and the sight of her gaping mouth and glassy eyes is enough for me to bust this nut before I even get my pants off.

She grinds against my hand, choking my fingers within her warm folds and with one final pump, Lexie throws her head back and cries out. "Oh my god," she breathes, falling flat on her back, her eyes closing. "That was amazing."

I wipe her delicious juice on my forearm, then climb to my feet. "Don't quit on me now, baby. We're not done yet."

I undo the notch on my belt and unbutton my trousers, allowing them to fall open and my smooth, hard cock to spring out. Lexie's eyes widen and she gulps, and I'm pleased with that response.

I grin, licking her taste that lingers on my lips. "Don't worry. I'll make it fit."

I stay on my feet and take Lexie by the thighs, dragging her toward me until her hips are just off the bed. I lift her, then bend my knees slightly, lining up my purple head with her entrance. God, I've wanted this for so long. I ease every inch inside her, her hot walls closing around me. Each second I'm sinking into her is bliss. I close my eyes and throw back my head, groaning at how tight she is, and I'm not even all the way in yet.

She winces and whimpers, and bites down on her fist.

"It's okay, baby," I groan. "You're doing so good."

At last my balls tap against her ass, and I'm so proud of my girl. But now that it's in, and I know she can take it, I'm going to give it to her hard. I slide my cock out, but before Lexie has time to relax, I plunge straight back into her.

"Oh my god!" she cries.

I grip the back of her thighs, sliding her up and down my cock. She gasps every time I enter her, leaving my shaft slick when I pull out. I fuck her faster and harder, my hips thrusting roughly against her, sweat shimmering across my chest as I take Lexie the way I've always wanted to. I feel the familiar sensation of her muscles tightening, but when it's around my cock instead of my fingers, it's exquisite. I feel my seed building, but I'm not going to cum yet. Lexie gets to cum first. She props herself up on her elbows and lifts her hips higher so I can bury my length deeper inside her.

"Fuck, yes, Sean!" she screams as she explodes on my cock.

I fight to hold back my own orgasm. I want to make love to Lexie all night, but her pussy's so tight I'm not going to last another five seconds.

I shuffle her back so I've got enough room to kneel on the bed, then I lift her legs straight up, resting them on my shoulders. My cock is soaked in her juices, and I growl when I slide inside her. I thrust while pressing down on her soft belly, her gorgeous tits bouncing, her beautiful face contorted somewhere between pleasure and agony.

"Fuck, Lexie. You feel so good," I groan, my shaft lengthening. "Can I cum in you?"

Lexie looks at me and bites her lip, then nods. "Yes."

My back stiffens on my last thrust, my body quivering as I empty every last drop. Then I collapse beside her, lying on my side and hooking her leg over me.

She's panting, breathless, her body shimmering with a layer of sweat, and I don't think I've ever seen her more beautiful. "I'm sorry," I murmur. "I wanted to go longer."

"Well, if you did, I would have died, so this is absolutely fine," she says.

We laugh and I lean over to kiss her. I gaze into her glassy eyes. "I still can't believe you're here with me," I mutter.

"Well, get used to it," she yawns, leaning into my chest. "Because I'm going to be here for a long time."

We fall quiet, and I hear the wind whistling through the fir trees outside. Lexie's naked and sweaty in my arms, and I've never felt so complete. If I could, I would keep us here in this room, in this moment forever.

"Hey, Lexie," I say, tucking her damp hair behind her ear.

"Mmmm," she mumbles, half asleep.

"Do you want to be my date for Tom and Sophie's wedding?"

She looks up at me and a smile blossoms on her face. "I'd love to."

Epilogue
Sean - Three Years Later

I'm sitting in the lobby of the Marlow Hotel in a leather chair a week out from Christmas, bouncing my knee as I check my watch for the tenth time. Lexie always wants to look her best and I'm not complaining, but a little time management in these situations might be helpful. We're already fifteen minutes late.

A beanpole-thin guy in a nice, grey suit walks through the revolving door, passing a Christmas tree draped in silver and gold, and makes a line for the front desk. I don't want him to see me, so I lean my face into my cupped hand, peering at him through the gaps between my fingers. It takes Lexie two hours to get ready, but it takes this guy four hours before he shuts up. I must have been thinking too hard because his neck cranes and he looks straight at me.

"Shit," I mutter, but I paint on my friendliest smile when he waves and heads over.

"Sean Talley. What are you doing in town?" he asks.

We shake hands, and he winces in my grip.

"Just some family business. How are you, Mike?"

"Good, good," he replies. He puts his briefcase on the ground and I silently grumble. "Are you opening a restaurant out here?"

"No, not here for me," I reply.

"I was going to say," Mike starts, "if you were looking for property out here, I should have been the first person you called." He puts a hand on his hip and pouts. "I'm still broken-hearted that you and Blake cut me out of that Karmela deal."

I sigh. The fucking Karmela deal. He brings this up every time. "We didn't cut you out, Mike. We just didn't need the extra finance, that's all."

He snorts a laugh and slaps my shoulder and I glare at the sleeve of my suit that he disheveled.

"I'm just pulling your chain, Sean. But you know, you could make some fantastic money out here. The city is full of opportunities and a great place to live."

"I prefer Lake Mistletoe," I say. I glance at my watch. "I'm late for an appointment, Mike. You'll have to excuse me."

Mike whines, "That's a shame. I would have loved to catch up. You know, I can get you some great interest rates if you're looking at refinancing."

I wave my hand. "No, I'm good, but I'll be sure to call you."

I see Mike's eyes train on the gold band around my finger and he gasps. "Holy shit, did you get married, Talley?"

Whenever I glance at my wedding ring, I can't help but smile like a lovesick kid. "Yeah, I did," I reply.

"Well, hell, who's the lucky lady?"

The elevator dings and the door slides open, and Lexie strolls into the lobby, looking effortlessly stunning. She's wearing a red pencil dress that molds itself to every curve of her gorgeous body, her waist cinched with a wide black belt, accentuating her full, round hips. The fabric hugs those thick thighs that I think about at least fifty times a day, and all that sexiness teeters on a pair of shiny black stilettos She has this confidence about her now, like she's completely comfortable in her own skin, and she's never been sexier. My dick twitches and after three years I still can't believe how lucky I am.

"Sorry," Lexie chirps. She reaches for me and I grab her hand, pulling her into a kiss. I dart my tongue between her lips and she squeaks, but soon her tongue joins with mine and we tangle as if no one is watching.

"Get a room, you two," Mike laughs uncomfortably.

Lexie looks at him while I keep my arm around her waist. "I'm Lexie," she greets.

"Mike. I guess congratulations are in order."

"Thanks," Lexie says. "But it's not new. I've been Mrs. Talley for almost three years now."

I love it when she calls herself that. After the first night we made love, I knew I was going to marry Lexie. I waited a couple of months. I didn't want to take the shine off Tom and Sophie's special day. But as soon as the coast was clear, I bought the biggest pink-diamond ring I could find, flew her to Hawaii for the weekend and proposed. Boy, the noise complaints we got that night. Let's just say Lexie gets better at taking my cock every time we fuck, and we fuck a lot. But then Mike's sour face ruins my daydream and I guess it's because I didn't invite him to the wedding. I'm not sure why I would, though. I barely know the guy, but he seems pretty emotional.

"Sorry, Mike," I say politely as Lexie and I exchange looks. "I didn't have your number."

"No, no, it's fine," he says, but the high pitch in his voice hints that it clearly isn't fine.

The three of us stand there suffocating under the weight of an awkward silence, and eventually I just can't stand it anymore. "Anyway," I puff, rubbing my hands together. "We better get going."

Mike slaps his forehead, which feels unnecessary. "Right. Your appointment. Well, don't let me keep you."

He's barely finished his sentence and I'm halfway to the door, towing Lexie behind me, her heels clacking frantically as she tries to keep up.

"Lovely meeting you, Mike," she calls over her shoulder.

He gets to watch my wife's fantastic hips swishing as she leaves, the lucky son of a bitch. But I won't beat his ass for staring. That would mean having to interact with him again, which is a hard pass.

"He seemed nice," Lexie says as we leave the hotel and join the bustling rows of people on the sidewalk.

"He is literally the most painfully annoying man I have ever met. He took me and Blake to a business dinner once, but when we got there they had no record of his reservation and they were all booked out. Blake and I didn't care, but Mike loses his damn mind. Starts screaming that his cousin is a DJ in Florida or some shit. I mean, what does that have to do with anything?"

Lexie laughs and pinches my arm. "You're mean. He's just being friendly."

I sigh. She always sees the good in people. "So, what took you so long?" I ask.

"I was just on the phone organizing the last few details for the exhibition night at the arts center." She can't shift the smile on her face whenever she talks about the event she's been planning for months. "The kids are so excited, and I think some charities could be interested in coming on board."

"I'm so proud of you," I say, cupping her hands in mine. "Lake Mistletoe's Christmas miracle."

She frowns. "Stop. It was you. You auctioned the paintings."

"You keep saying that as if you weren't the one who painted them," I chuckle. "And you've kept that program running ever since."

A smile tugs at the corner of her mouth. "I suppose. Now can we get going? You're going to make me late." She laughs as she trots by me, and I can't resist giving her ass a cheeky slap.

The sidewalks in the city are way too crowded, and it makes me immediately miss the quiet streets of Lake Mistletoe. Not only do I have to watch where I'm going, but I'm mindful of someone knocking into Lexie. They're all going so fast. I place her on the inside of me, closest to the shop fronts, and keep her safely tucked away under my arm. She suddenly hits the brakes and I'm on the defensive.

"What. What is it?" I ask, putting her behind me as I look for trouble.

She stares at a building across the street with her mouth gaping open. I follow her eyes to the For Lease signs hung in the blacked-out windows. The place is well rundown and looks like it hasn't housed a business for some time.

"You know that place?"

She grabs me by the collar and pulls me down to her eye level, then points at the faded sign. It's hard to make out what it says. The yellow block letters have cracked and faded and some are missing all together.

"Get Ed With Ja," I say slowly, squinting my eyes. It takes less than a second to feel like a complete idiot.

Lexie bursts into laughter. "Get Jacked With Jack," she corrects. "Guess it didn't work out." She takes a deep breath and loops her arm with mine. "It all feels so small now. Like it was this tiny part of my life I had to live while I waited for you."

My heart thumps hard against my ribcage, and I lean down to kiss her brow. "Now we get to live our big life together."

She nods, nuzzling into my chest and we carry on down the street, once again leaving Jack far behind us. We round the corner and the buzzing of a large crowd and clicking of cameras interrupts our conversation. A young girl with a slick black bun dressed in a bright red pantsuit spies Lexie and runs toward her, pinning her wire thin glasses to the bridge of her nose so they don't fall off.

"Lexie," she chirps. "Oh, Lexie."

"Hey Rachel," Lexie says with a smile. "How are you?"

"How am I?" Rachel fakes a laugh. "Well, Lexie, I'm a little stressed because the guest of honor is almost an hour late and there are hundreds of people inside waiting and they're getting very impatient. Plus, we are apparently out of smoked salmon bites."

"Well shit," I grumble. "Might as well go home then."

Rachel oversells a sarcastic smile. "Lexie, can we just go inside? Please. Now."

"Sure," Lexie replies, indulging her incredibly anxious but amazingly organized personal assistant.

Giant white pillars and spherical topiaries frame the ivory double-doors of the building, while a long red carpet stretches across the sidewalk to the curb where valets open car doors for guests. Banners billow above, stretching over three stories, and when the wind settles and a banner deflates, I make out The Lexie Talley Exhibit in bold letters.

We walk inside, and the waiting crowd erupts with applause. Lexie reddens and squeezes my hand. I squeeze back to let her know I'm right here and everything's going to be fine. She takes in the sight of walls dressed with her artwork and hundreds of strangers here to see it. I don't know why she's so surprised. I've always believed she could do it, that this is what her life should have been. I believed it when I was just the boy next door in high school, and I believe it even more now as a proud, loving husband.

"You did good, baby," I whisper in her ear. "Your first gallery exhibit and you've not even graduated yet."

"Stop," she grumbles, pinching my arm. "You'll make me cry."

"Never," I whisper, kissing her cheek. "Go get em."

She smiles. "I love you, Sean."

It's the words I never dreamed I'd hear. Now she says them to me every day.

"I love you too, Lexie."

Rachel takes Lexie by the elbow, and reluctantly, I loan my wife to the adoring crowd.

"Ladies and gentleman," Rachel announces. "I present the artist, Lexie Talley."

The patrons come alive with applause, and all I can do is stand there and not get blinded by how bright my girl is shining. She's found herself and she finally sees what I always have. That she deserves respect, devotion, and the kind of love that leaves you breathless. She's powerful. She's perfect. And she's mine.

The Reindeer Games

BOOK TWO
BLAKE AND CHARLOTTE

1

Charlotte

"I wouldn't recommend that," I say, peeling off my heels and tossing them into my gym bag. "The jute rug suits your color scheme better." Next it's my clip-on earrings and I swap my phone from ear to ear as I tug them loose. "I realize it's rustic. That's the whole point, isn't it?" I stand up from the worn bench and shimmy out of my camel silk dress pants. They fall to the floor, crumpling at my feet. "Yes, it's expensive." I roll my eyes. "Yes, it's worth every penny." I grin. "Yes, all your friends will be jealous." I give a sigh of relief. "That's a brilliant decision, Vera. No, it's not a problem. That's why you hired me. I'll get you an invoice for that. Okay then. Bye, bye now."

I end the call and pinch the bridge of my nose. This one's going to be trouble. I can feel it. I glance at my gym bag, and the blades of my skates glint at me. Immediately, the stress melts off my shoulders. This will make everything better. When I'm on the ice, I don't need to worry about color schemes or bench tops or hijacked clocks. It's just me and my stick, gliding.

I drop my phone into my bag and fish out my black tights and long socks, yanking them over my legs. I can't wait to get my silk blouse off. The high collar feels more like a noose than a chic fashion statement. Once I've wrestled with the sleeves and rolled it into a ball, I expertly toss it behind my back. I'm not surprised when it lands perfectly inside my gym bag. These hands never miss. Finally, I get to put on the most comfortable shirt in the entire world. It's so well worn that it's practically threadbare, with a few faded stains I'm certain have seeped into the molecules of the fabric at this point. It's baggy around my arms and belly, which is not only great for skating but also for cheering at Mayhem games and gorging on hot wings afterwards. But the biggest reason it's the best shirt ever is because it belonged to the best man ever. Dad's been gone almost four years now, and I wear his old team shirt almost every day.

I pull it over my head and it fits me like a hug. I glance at myself in the mirror and rub my fingers over the crackedstaunch red print. Mistletoe

Mayhem 03. Defend The Lake! Damn, I miss him. Hockey's not the same without him around. I don't just love the game; I love how special the game was because of him. He always told me I could go pro if I wanted to, and I got some interest when I played in high school. But once he was gone, the drive kind of went with him. What's the point of being a pro hockey player if he's not watching me from the stands? So, instead, I argue with bored housewives over what rug looks better in their sunroom.

I grab my skates and throw my gym bag over my shoulder. I'll put these on in the rink. I leave the changing room and open the swinging doors to the rink, butt first. It's so quiet right now, with only a couple of kids passing a puck and a cute little girl in a blue tutu practicing a pirouette.

I take a seat beside the gate and pull on my skates, lacing up extra tight, just like Dad taught me. I know they're perfect when I lose all feeling in my toes. When I open the gate and launch myself onto the ice, nothing else matters. The brisk whip of cold on my face, the weightlessness, how my feet feel barely there, although that could be the numbness from my ridiculously tight laces.

I do a couple of laps with my hockey stick stretched across the back of my shoulders, hoping that these kids go home for dinner soon so I can get the rink to myself. My ears prick up when I hear a couple of moms call out from the door, and try not to smile too excitedly when the children leave, but Jesus, I wish they'd do it a little faster. I'm this close to booting the pipsqueaks off the ice myself when the last one stumbles out the gate. Finally. I roll my shoulders and crack my neck, then dig a puck out of my pocket, tossing it onto the ice. I eye up the net. Is today the day I smack this thing 120 miles per hour? I pull back my stick and let it fly, shooting the puck across the ice and straight into the goal.

"You still don't bend your knees enough," a voice calls from the wall. "And your follow through is for shit."

I clench my jaw, and don't even bother to look. I know exactly who it is.

"How about you go fuck yourself, Blake?" I snap, cringing when I hear the gate open and his skates cut across the ice.

"Do you kiss your pillow with that mouth, Char?" he says, skidding to a stop beside me.

I reluctantly look up at him with a scowl. "I'm really not in the mood for your bullshit today. I just want to skate, smash this puck and go home."

Blake howls. "Damn. Talk about a hot Friday night. You must have the boys lining up."

"Well, it's better than the Friday nights you spend at the free clinic," I snap back. "I hear after your ninth genital warts visit, the tenth one's free."

Blake frowns at me and I try not to grin at his lack of a comeback. Blake zero. Charlotte one.

"Your follow through is shit though. You need to angle your hips more and you're swinging way too high. Here, let me show you." He drops his stick on the ground and reaches for my hips.

"You wish," I snap, pushing off the ice and getting some distance.

He rolls his eyes and picks up his stick. "Char, get over yourself. I've seen better hips on a mop."

"Is that right?" I say, taking another puck from my pocket. I drop it on the ice and take a slow skate around it, staring narrowly down my nose at him. "A mop you say?" I scrape to a halt and line up the puck.

He furrows his brow. "What are you doing?"

I clench my tongue between my teeth and squint at him. "This is for my clock." I shift my weight to my front foot, swing my stick and fire the puck at him.

"Hey!" he shouts, curving his body like he's in the Matrix.

The puck just misses its target, and I pout. "Damn. I was aiming for the balls."

"Well, that's why you're still a virgin, Char. You weren't anywhere near the balls, sweetheart," he says with a rakish grin.

"I am not a virgin. I have loads of sex," I blurt. It only takes a second after my word vomit for me to realize that was not a great flex.

Blake chuckles and swipes a hand over his blond waves of hair. "Good for you, Char. Good for you." He skates over to me and, if I didn't know him, I'd think he looked hot doing that, with his muscled physique and coiffed waves of golden-blond hair. But I do know him. Well. He's a smug, clock stealing man whore, and this time next week he's going to be my brother-in-law. Of all the girls in Lake Mistletoe my brother could have fallen in love with, why did it have to be Blake's sister? He comes to a stop in front of me, and I dread what he's about to say next.

"I'll make you a deal. Let's have a shootout. Best of five, and the winner gets that heinous clock you keep going on about."

I sigh. "No thanks."

"I won that clock fair and square, by the way. It's not my fault you have shitty time management and missed the auction," Blake declares.

My blood boils. "You wouldn't even have known about that clock if I hadn't talked about it at Sophie's party. You bought it just to piss me off. You don't even use it."

"Now that's where you're wrong, Char. I use it constantly. I hang my coat on it when I get home from work. I rest my coffee on it, and one time when I got wasted and couldn't make it to the head, I popped open that cute little door and barfed all over it."

I screw up my face and stare daggers. "Best of five," I snarl.

"Nice," Blake says, speed-skating to his bag on the wall before returning with a handful of pucks. He drops one in front of me. "Ladies first."

I give a quick bow and gesture to the net. "Then, by all means, you start us off."

Blake rolls his eyes again, but this time I try not to laugh. "Good one, Char. Where'd you learn that? Kindergarten?"

"Yeah, I stole it from one of your girlfriends," I tease.

He looks at me, but his only reply is his grin. We're hassling each other like always, but it's actually an enjoyable conversation. I wonder if he feels the same.

"Fine. I'll go first," he says. He lines up the puck and smacks it, and it shoots across the ice into the net.

I drop my puck and shoot it, and just like his, straight into the net, it goes.

"One all," he comments, before smacking his second puck into the net as well.

"Two all, I add," after adding my next puck to the challenge.

On our next turns, our third and fourth pucks find the net just as easily and my competitive nature gets the better of me. I've seen Blake play. He's good, but I'd never admit that to his face. He could fire in fifty pucks with his eyes closed if he wanted to. But that's when he's playing for the Mayhem, and in those situations, I want him to be scoring too. I've got season tickets for Mistletoe Mayhem home games, and he better not waste my money by playing like shit.

But this is different. This is me, and him, and the stolen grandfather clock, and I'll be serving him a big fat L tonight.

Blake eyes up the puck, then locks his steel gaze on the net. I watch him bend his knees and shift his weight onto his front foot, then draw back his stick, but just as he's about to swing, I poke him right in the backside with my stick. He gasps, his knee jerks to the side and when he connects with the puck, he sends it well off its target and into the boards.

"Oh no," I pout. "That's so sad." A smile swipes onto my face. "My turn."

I line up the puck and lean in, practically giddy with excitement.

"You know, Sophie told me she's having second thoughts about the wedding," Blake blurts out of nowhere.

I gasp and swing around. "What!"

My leg shoots out like a goof and my skate catches the puck. Before I know it, both my feet slip from under me and I'm looking at a nice bump on the back of the head once I hit the ice. The last thing I expect is for Blake to catch me. He's got one arm under my shoulders and the other curled around my waist, and when I look into his brown eyes swirled with gold, I struggle to remember exactly why I can't stand him.

Blake gazes down at me and chuckles. "Shit. I'm sorry. I didn't realize you lose control of your body when you get surprised."

Why am I looking at his mouth when he's talking? I drag my eyes to meet his. I inhale deeply, trying to find anything remotely close to calm, but all I smell is vanilla. Is that him? Lucky he's holding me because I think my knees just gave out. He stands me up, but keeps his hands on my waist and holds me steady once I'm back on both feet.

"Are you okay?" he asks, and I could be in shock but it sounds like he actually might care. With his fingertip, he slides away a lock of brown hair that's escaped my ponytail. "Sophie would never forgive me if her third favorite bridesmaid got concussed on my watch."

Christ. He's such an asshole, but he also has the sharpest jaw line I've ever seen.

"I'm not interrupting anything, am I?"

The squeaky voice snaps me from my daydream. I bat Blake's hand away and take a step back.

Blake scratches the back of his neck. "Oh. Tamara. Did I ask you to meet me here?"

The redhead giggles and leans on the rail, her boobs half out of her low cut top. "It's a surprise, silly. I thought we could grab some dinner."

Suddenly Blake can't look at me, even though seconds ago I felt like I was the only person who existed.

"Umm... sure," he finally spits out. He gives me a timid wave, but still doesn't meet my eyes. "See you later, Char."

I look away too. "Yeah. Whatever."

Blake skates to the gate and, against my better judgment, I glance up just in time to see Tamara wrap herself around him like a boa constrictor with a fresh blowout. I hear the arena doors clap shut when they leave. Good. I wanted the ice to myself, anyway.

2

Blake

I'm sitting in Talley's and sipping scotch while the day's events roll around in my head. Spoke to Sean this morning. We're planning another restaurant out west in the new year and I'm excited to get started. But I have a feeling he'll be hard to lock down for a while. Talley's has been open less than a week and he's already taking the night off. Fair enough, I guess. Jack showing up like an asshole and scaring Lexie wasn't right. I'm surprised the prick is still breathing. It makes sense that Sean takes some time off to look after her. He's only been waiting for this his whole life.

Then, this afternoon was the gym, and some meetings after lunch, and then... oh yeah... the rink. I don't normally go there around that time, but when I saw Char's car in the parking lot, I had to drop in and yank her chain for a bit. I always have my gear in the trunk, so why not? She actually had some pretty good chirps going on today, but she looked terrified when she thought she was going to fall. Like I would allow that. She was never hitting the ground while I was there.

I take another sip of scotch, and grin. It was strange how she fit perfectly in my arms, like someone designed them specifically to hold her, and the smell of her... Jesus Christ. It was earthy and clean, like rain or grass or something like that. Definitely a welcome change from the fruits and flowers these other girls drench themselves in. They make my eyes water something wicked. Not Char's scent. I could happily breathe that in all day.

"Blake, are you listening?"

I snap out of my thoughts, and just in time, too. Why do I care what Char smells like?

"Blake," Tamara groans again.

"Yes, I'm listening." I cough and take another sip of scotch.

She's sitting across the table from me, pushing some broccoli around her plate with a fork. "Oh really? What did I say then?"

I slouch in my chair, my legs wide, and I undo my jacket button before I suffocate from this conversation. "You were saying the new girl at work is the worst and that you don't know why you're the one who has to train her, and you're not being mean or rude, but she gives off serious bitch vibes and you're almost certain she's had her boobs done. Just saying."

Tamara's jaw practically hits the table. "Yeah," she laughs. "Wow. You were listening."

I raise my glass at her. "Cheers," I say, taking another sip.

Tamara puts her fork down and crosses her arms on top of the table. Her eyelashes flutter, and even though I'm not a hundred percent into her right now, those massive tits spilling out of her shirt are helping.

"I missed you today," she says, her bottom lip clenched between her teeth.

"Me too," I reply. Seems like the right thing to say.

She nods her head toward the door. "Did you want to get out of here? Maybe go back to your place?"

Do I? I ask myself. I take another look at her tits. They're fantastic, but I'm still not convinced. I'm just not feeling it tonight. Something's off. Maybe I need to see a doctor. Any sickness that keeps my dick soft has got to be bad and must be treated immediately. But I'm not telling Tamara about my soft dick.

"I wish I could, babe, but I've got work early in the morning," is my reply.

"That's okay. I'm used to leaving before sunrise. I know you're super busy."

"Jesus," I mutter under my breath.

"What?" she asks.

"Nothing," I reply. "That's sweet, but it's just not a good time. How about a rain check?"

She looks stunned, fidgeting with her red hair, her eyes darting back and forth as if she's trying to figure out where she went wrong. I almost feel bad for her.

"How about I give you a ride home?" I say, offering her a warm smile.

She nods, but doesn't speak. I'm pretty sure if she tries to, she'll burst into tears. I go to stand up, but a hand grabs my shoulder and pushes me back down.

"Don't stand up on my account," Finn chuckles, adjusting the cuffs of his black Armani jacket.

I give it an inquisitive glance. It's nice. Finn has great taste, that's probably why we get along so well. He's also a workaholic and emotionally stunted like me, so obviously he's the first person I call when I need a bowling partner. Tom's with him, and he still does this thing where he punches my shoulder and says, "Hey, sport," like he's going to be my stepdad rather than my brother-in-law. He's actually only two years older than me.

Tom sidles up beside Finn, smiles awkwardly at me, then punches my shoulder. "Hey, sport."

I sigh. "Hey, Tom." I gesture to Tamara, who's doing all she can to keep herself together. "You guys remember Tamara, right?"

"Of course," Finn says. "Your mother had her book club meeting in the Northwellian's tea room last week."

I roll my eyes. Finn remembers most people by the events he organizes for them. There's sweet-sixteen-girl, and bar-mitzvah-boy. Apparently Tamara is book-club-mom's-daughter.

"So, what are you two doing here?" I ask. Hopefully, this stalling will give Tamara time to calm down before I have to sit in a car with her for half-an-hour.

Tom glances out the big window and across the street to the ice cream parlor. "Sophie and the girls are over there getting desserts. Finn and I popped in to see Sean, but apparently he's off for the night?"

I nod. "Lexie." Both of them frown and we exchange knowing looks.

"Who's Lexie?" Tamara asks, perking up.

"You know," I prompt. "Lexie. From high school."

Tamara giggles. "I wasn't in your year, silly. I was three years behind you."

My heart stops in my chest and I can feel Tom and Finn's eyes burning a hole in the side of my head. I'm too manic to do the math.

"Tamara, how old are you again?" I ask anxiously.

She laughs. "I'm twenty."

"Yikes," Tom shrieks, holding out his hands as if she was the plague.

Finn stifles his laugh. "That's a great age, Tamara. A great, legal age."

I resist grabbing the napkin off the table and dabbing the sweat from my brow. I detour the conversation after the relief that I've narrowly avoided a felony.

"Why are they there?" I ask. "We've got dessert here."

Tom shrugged. "Sometimes you just want good old vanilla ice cream, not crème brûlée."

That actually makes sense to me.

"You're going to be at the rehearsal dinner, right?" Tom asks.

Any points he won with the ice cream–crème brûlée analogy he fucked away after mentioning the rehearsal dinner within ear shot of Legal Tamara, which would now be her new nickname. I didn't have to look at her across the table to know she was staring straight at me with her big doe eyes.

"Do you have a date?" she asks.

I glare at Tom, but the big doofus just shrugs his shoulders at me in utter confusion.

"I don't think I'm going," I mutter, scratching the back of my head.

"Why not?" Tom groans with disappointment, and I notice Finn kick my dear, stupid brother-in-law-to-be's ankle. That's another reason I like Finn. He knows when to keep his mouth shut and when to shut other peoples'.

"Work," I sigh, throwing my hands in the air in faux-frustration.

Tamara pouts. "Wow, you work so much." A wide grin swipes across her face. "You must be so rich."

"Not really. I donate it all to charity," I say.

"Which charity?" she asks.

"Sex Addicts Anonymous," Finn answers.

Now I'm the one kicking his foot. And here I was thinking he was my wingman.

"What did he say?" Tamara laughs uncomfortably.

"Nothing, babe. How about we head out?" I don't give her time to decide, already on my feet before the last word has passed my lips. She stands too, grabs her purse, and smiles charmingly at Tom and Finn.

"It was nice to see you," she says. "Hopefully I'll see you again soon."

I notice the eyes Tom and Finn give each other, and I know what they're thinking. They won't be seeing Tamara again. It's not her fault. She's doing everything right, and I can tell she's really into me. I'm just an emotional dumpster-fire and apart from this face, this body, and the best fuck of her life, I've got very little else to offer, and for the love of god, don't throw around the R word. I'm not looking at becoming anyone's boyfriend. I can't stand still long enough for that sort of commitment.

I glare at Tom and Finn as we leave, and they chuckle at each other, knowing exactly the trouble they've caused. I hold the restaurant door open for Tamara and she shivers when the chilled evening wind whips around her. I instinctively take off my coat and drape it over her shoulders, pulling it snug around her neck.

"Is that better?"

Her cheeks fill with a warm blush and she can't look me in the eye without smiling. "Yes, thanks," she says sweetly. "Blake, I really like you."

Fuck. Here we go again. Problem with dating hometown girls is unless you're going to marry them, it makes things really damn awkward when you're trying to end things. Especially when, in Tamara's case, she makes me my double-shot espresso latte every morning. She does a good job, too. Where am I going to get my coffee now? Because, by the looks of things, I can never go to Chilly Bean Bistro again.

But she looks so cute standing there, a foot shorter than me, shivering in the cold with gigantic eyes staring up at me, and I'm not a total fucking monster, and it is a really good cup of coffee.

"I like you too, Tamara," I say. Who knew I could be such a sap?

I walk her to my car, parked out front. Perks of being a partner at Talley's. Like a gentleman, because that's exactly what I am, I open the door for her.

Tamara pauses before climbing in. "Are you sure I can't come to your place tonight?" She curls her fingers around my shirt collar. "It'll be fun. I promise."

If my dick could talk, this is where he'd be reminding me what a total smoke show this girl is, and that tonight's mission is to bed her immediately. And most of my life, I've trusted him at his word. But tonight is different. In fact, the last few weeks have been different. It just all feels so... empty. There's no depth, no connection, no laughs and banter. Not like there is when I'm shooting pucks with Char at the rink.

I catch myself in my thoughts and realize Char's been in my head a lot lately. What's up with that? I heave my shoulders as I exhale, and my dick will probably tell me I told you so in a few hours.

"Sorry, Tamara. Not tonight."

She gives a disappointed but understanding nod, then curls herself into the leather seat and tucks in her legs, giving me one last sweet smile before I close the door.

I don't know what's causing this change in me, but to be honest, I kind of like it.

3

Charlotte

"What do they put in ice cream to make it so good?" I ask with a long, guttural groan, and I'm not sure if the noises I'm making are appropriate for such a family establishment.

Sophie sits across the booth from me and eyes up the melted goo on her spoon. "I think the key ingredients are ice and cream."

Daisy inspects her bowl. "It's really nice. They make it in store here, which is cute." She takes a spoonful and holds it in her mouth for a while, like this is a wine tasting. "Could use a little more vanilla bean, if you ask me. I make a Christmas one with maraschino cherries and brandy. It's delicious, and boozy and all the good things."

"Then why didn't we go to your house?" Sophie sighs.

Daisy shrugs. "I'm testing my new cake recipe too, so there's cut-offs and mixing spoons everywhere."

My eyes widen. "Will you have your cake at the rehearsal dinner?"

"A sample cake, but not the real deal, of course." She nudges Sophie. "No one sees that until the big day."

Sophie's giddy, kicking her feet under the table like a little kid. "I can't wait."

"You're not nervous?" I ask.

"Oh no, I'm terrified," she says matter-of-factly. "I can't wait until it's over and I don't have to think about seating arrangements and bouquets and, I love you Daisy but if you ask me one more time if I want the beef tenderloin or fillet mignon, I may have to straight up murder you. Beef is beef."

Daisy turns up her nose and exhales, whipping her blonde mane over her shoulder. "They're actually totally different cuts of meat, but I get it, you're stressed."

"I am," Sophie confesses, scraping a dollop of ice cream onto her tongue. "Tom's been taking me to the cabin almost every day. It's the only place that calms me. We're practically living there."

"Be careful," I say, my voice winding up a notch. "The snow's getting heavy in those hills. Last thing I need is my brother getting stuck up there, and then I'm the one who has to take Aunt Sheila grocery shopping on a Saturday afternoon."

"Ack. He hates that," Sophie says. "Surely it's your turn soon?"

I shake my head firmly. "A Powell contract is good for a minimum of three years. I've got at least another seven months on this one."

Sophie laughs, and I'm glad I can give her a little peace, if only for a minute. "And what did he do to be on the losing end of this contract?"

"Let's just say, if there's a zombie apocalypse, I hope you guys score a car or something, because he is the slowest runner in the history of slow runners. Lucky you get skates in hockey."

As we're laughing, Daisy's phone buzzes. She swipes it from the table and screws her face up before putting it straight back down.

"I don't take after-hours calls," she grumbles, scooping a glob of ice cream into her mouth.

"That's not Finn, is it?" Sophie says. "Daze, he talked to me today, says you're not taking his calls."

"Well, he can call me at a decent hour," Daisy says curtly.

Sophie frowns and rests her hand on Daisy's shoulder. "He's the venue manager."

"So?" Daisy replies defiantly.

I roll my eyes. "Her wedding's at the venue, Daisy. Now stop being so fucking difficult and answer Finn's calls. Is that so hard?"

Daisy keeps eating ice cream while pretending that she can't hear what Sophie and I are saying.

"Daze!" I snap, and her face turns sour.

"Fine. I'll call him in the morning."

Sophie pouts and bats her eyelashes, and if it was anyone else Daisy would likely be immune to such simpering. But the bonds formed at kindergarten last a lifetime.

"Fine," Daisy groans as she stands from the booth. "I'll call him back now." She snatches her phone off the table and storms to the other side of the parlor near the jukebox.

I shake my head. "I get that if you wanted the Northwellian, you had no choice but to sign on Finn. But then why in the world would you hire Daisy as your caterer?"

Sophie shrugs innocently, as if she didn't know Finn and Daisy have hated each other since the dawn of time. "She's the best."

"Well yeah, duh. But they're adding more stress to an already super-stressful situation, don't you think?"

Sophie looks over at Daisy as she's on the phone, pacing the checkered floor like a tiger in a cage. "I'm sure they'll sort out their differences. It's all about me and Tom at the end of the day. Right?"

"I told you I don't care that it won't fit through the door. That sounds like a you problem, so fix it," Daisy yells.

The other parlor patrons turn from their booths to eavesdrop on the disturbance, and I cringe when a toddler bursts into tears at hearing Daisy's shriek.

"Sleeping at the cabin again, then?" I ask.

"Yep," Sophie replies in the same breath, spooning ice cream into her mouth like they were going out of business.

I laugh, scooping out the last of my chunky monkey. "Oh, and I don't need a plus one, if one less beef product saves you a headache."

"Really?" Sophie asks, raising an eyebrow. "You're not seeing anyone at the moment?"

"I'm not seeing anyone, period. The last time I got screwed was when I bet on the Sabres to win."

Sophie's eyes light up and she puts her spoon down for the first time since we got here. "Let me set you up."

"Nooooooooooooooooooo," I drawl, pushing my bowl aside. "That is not going to happen."

She scoops up my hands. "Come on, Charlotte, please. I know just the guy. He's cute, and he's sweet..."

I roll my eyes and put my finger down my throat for effect.

"He plays hockey..." Sophie continues.

I tilt my head to the side. "What position?"

"Defenseman."

I'm still not convinced, but I'm not all together disgusted by the idea anymore. Somehow, men are sixty percent more attractive when they're hockey players. Take Blake, for example. The biggest skanky shit bag you'll ever meet. But put a hockey stick in his hand and throw him on the ice and you get yourself a pretty decent dude. Okay, maybe that's a little extreme. He's kind of cute as a civilian too... well, maybe a little more than kind of. His hair waves in the most adorable way, and it's cut so close and clean at the back of his head. I pay attention to this because there is something about Blake's neck that fascinates me, and I hate to admit that I think about sliding my hand around his nape more than a normal person would. And damn, what was that smell today? Was it vanilla, or caramel, or some other sexy creamy scent? I'm not sure what happened between us at the ice rink, but what I do know is that when that man caught me and had his arm around my waist, I felt a sweet tingle in a place that's been a barren wasteland for quite a few months now.

"Charlotte," Sophie says, shaking my hands.

I awaken like a disturbed drunk. "Huh?"

"What are you doing? Did you hear me?" she laughs.

I furrow my brow. "Yeah, I heard, but I don't know, Sophie. I'm not sure if I want to date someone right now." That wasn't completely true. I could date someone, if that someone was the right someone.

We table the conversation when Daisy returns, somehow looking grumpier than when she left. "All sorted," she says with a clenched jaw.

Sophie smiles appreciatively. "Thank you."

Daisy sits down and glances out the window toward Talley's across the street. "I didn't realize he was having dinner over there with Tom. He could have come and talked to me, but I suppose he's far too important to care about little things like professional courtesy."

I can practically feel the stress oozing through Sophie's skin, and thankfully Daisy senses it too. She grips Sophie's shoulder.

"But it's all sorted. I promise. You won't have to worry about another thing when it comes to me and Finn. You're going to have the perfect wedding, Sophie."

"Really?" Sophie asks with pleading eyes.

Daisy isn't great with social cues sometimes, so I'm hoping she says the right thing.

"I promise," she replies.

A smile cracks the thin line of my mouth. Yep. That'll do it. Sophie's shoulders loosen and she relaxes, sinking into the booth like a marshmallow melting into cocoa.

Daisy sits back down, but just before she turns her attention to the bowl of soup that was once her ice cream, a little scoff escapes her. "God. Who's Blake with now?"

My head snaps back so hard I might have whiplash. I look out the window and across the street, just in time to see Blake put his coat on the redhead who showed up at the rink.

Sophie takes a nosy peek. "I think that's Tamara. He's been on a couple of dates with her."

Daisy's eyes widen. "A couple? That might as well be a marriage proposal." They laugh and I join in with a half-hearted chuckle.

"I wonder if he'll bring her to the rehearsal dinner," Daisy muses.

"Maybe," Sophie says. "He hasn't told me he's not bringing anyone."

Really? Her? That's who he's going to bring to the rehearsal? That's the first girl he's going to introduce to the friend group? Tamara? What's so special about her? That's she's beautiful, has a great body and probably smells like candy or fruit or some shit? Typical men. Typical Blake. Who cares who he brings to the rehearsal! It doesn't take long to realize the answer to that question is... me... apparently, I care.

I gulp and hope my friends don't see it. "Hey, Sophie. Maybe I'll take you up on that offer."

"What offer?" Daisy asks, leaning in to get brought up to speed.

I roll the words over in my head and still can't believe I'm about to say them out loud. "Sophie's going to set me up on a date."

"Bullshit," Daisy spits.

Sophie squeezes my hands. "Yay, this is going to be so much fun!"

I force a smile and try not to make it too obvious when I watch Blake put Tamara in his car then drive away.

"Yeah. Totally. So much fun," I reply.

4

Blake

The moment I hit the ice, I'm at peace. It's the one constant in my life. The thing I know will always be there, no matter what. Hockey hasn't been a lifelong passion for me. I only got into it in middle school. It was Tom and Char's dad, Joel, who gave me my first pair of second-hand skates and a taped up hockey stick. I mean I could have asked my dad I guess, but he was always so busy on the hunt for the next Mrs. Ward that he didn't pay much attention to me and Soph. We had more dinners at the Powell's than anywhere else.

Mom passed when we were barely out of kindergarten. Hit by a drunk driver. So, when Joel died, I knew what Tom and Char were going through. I was kind of going through it again myself. He was a good guy, and probably more of a father to me than my own. I still remember so clearly how broken Char was. I would have given anything to take that pain away from her, take it on myself if I had to. Just as long as she didn't have to be sad for another second. It fucking killed me.

Henry's already on the ice, pulling his gloves on, and he flicks up his eyes when he sees me skating over. That's high praise from someone like Big Henry. He doesn't talk much, smiles even less, but you can bet your ass if you ever need someone to show up, no questions asked, with a shovel and some rope in the middle of the night, Henry would be there in a heartbeat. And, as rough and gruff as the town veterinarian and Mayhem goalie likes to act, he's like a ball of warm butter if you're within a hundred yards of a puppy.

I dip my chin at him. "Henry."

He's a massive guy, height and width. There's few people in Lake Mistletoe I have to look up to talk to.

"Blake," he replies with his gravel voice. "Fucking freezing in the clinic today."

"Your heater out?" I ask.

"Waste of money," Henry replies.

I frown. "We live in the far north. It's winter, and it's snowing, Henry. I don't think it's ridiculous to put the heat on this time of year."

"You sound like Lola," he grumbles.

I roll my eyes. "You don't leave poor Lola to freeze her ass off, do you?"

"Of course not," Henry snaps, sounding offended at the insinuation. "I keep the heat on in reception. I know she gets cold easily."

"Big softie," I tease, pinching his bristled cheek.

Henry bats my hand away like he was slapping a puck. "Don't fucking touch me, Ward."

"Roger that," I reply with haste, adding an awkward salute at the end.

A group huddles together at the edge of the rink near the arena entrance, and I look past Henry's wide shoulders to see what's going on. I recognize Tom straight away as he strokes his dark beard with his hockey gloves tucked under his arm. He's in what looks like a deep conversation with Hayden, one of our defensemen.

"What's that about?" I ask.

Henry slams his helmet onto his head. "Like I give a fuck. I'm here to play hockey."

He skates off, leaning hard into every stride. I wonder if society forced him to become a vet because someone with his lack of a bedside manner could never cut it as a doctor. I keep my eyes on the chat unfolding between Tom and Hayden. We're all on the same team, but this doesn't feel Mayhem related. Tom looks uncomfortable, and that's confirmed when I see him clench his fist and playfully punch Hayden on the shoulder, then mouth the word sport. What the fuck is going on here?

The arena doors open and Sophie walks over to them. She's got a big smile on her face while she talks to Hayden, and when she whips her phone out he reaches into his back pocket and grabs his as well. They're swapping numbers or something. Why does my sister want Hayden's number? Before I can skate over, Sophie waves goodbye and turns her back, leaving the arena with as much mystery as she arrived.

Hayden puts his phone back in his pocket and pulls on his gloves. Tom gives him another arm punch, and I'm a little hurt. I always thought that was our thing. Then they both skate over to where the rest of us are waiting. Well, most of us; we're just waiting on Sean, and as if he knew, Sean stumbles through the gate.

His hair is a bushy mess and he hasn't shaved. In a nutshell, the kid looks like shit. It doesn't take a rocket scientist to figure out that Lexie is the reason behind his haggard appearance. Between the Jack drama and about ten years of pent up sexual frustration, they're probably on their hundredth headboard by now. But there's something else about him, too. Something in his eyes. Sean looks happy. Good for him. It's not a luxury we can all enjoy.

I'm still curious what all the commotion on the other side of the rink was about and, as luck would have it, Tom skates up right beside me. I immediately notice no arm punch. I even extend my arm like a common shoulder whore. Nothing.

"What was that about?" I ask him, deciding the best way to get an answer is to ask a question.

Tom leans closer. "Just your sister playing matchmaker."

Typical Sophie. Always trying to find someone willing to be introduced to their future ex.

"For Hayden? Who's the lucky girl?" I'm being sarcastic. If I'm a dumpster fire because I lack commitment, then Hayden's one because he wants it too much. He's sent his last two girlfriends running for the hills because he'd already bought a ring and picked out baby names before the third date.

Tom says her name out of the corner of his mouth. "Charlotte."

I get the weirdest feeling between my ribs, and I can't figure out why I'm having trouble getting my next breath out. On top of that, I think I'm going deaf. "Who?"

Tom chuckles as if we're sharing some sort of inside joke. "You know. My sister. Charlotte."

I definitely heard it that time, and the pang in my chest worsens. "You mean, Char?" Tom nods.

"Char's going on a date with Hayden?"

Tom nods again. I point my glove in his direction. "That Hayden?" Once more, Tom nods.

And my Char? I catch myself before I say that part out loud. "And your sister, Char?" I correct.

"Yes," Tom exclaims, clearly over all the head bobbing.

"Bullshit," I laugh.

We're interrupted when Hayden skates over, and suddenly I can't stand the sight of his smug rat face.

"Hey, Blake. How are you?" he says.

"Never been better, Hayden. Why do you ask?"

Hayden's back stiffens. "Umm, no reason." He pivots his attention to Tom. "Hey, I was just wondering what kind of flowers Charlotte likes?"

Tom scratches his head. "Geez, I don't really know."

I roll my eyes. Fucking gardenias, dipshit. Her prom corsage was gardenias. But like I'm going to share that information with Hayden.

He shrugs and smiles. "No problem. I'm sure I'll figure something out."

"I'm sure you will," I say with a sneer.

Now Hayden's scratching his head. He and Tom will get on like a house on fire. "Okay... well... see you out there," he says before skating off.

I keep my eyes trained on him as he moves around the rink, and for some reason all I want to do is punch him square in the face. Something about how straight his nose is.

Coach leans over the wall and spins his cap around. "Alright. Puck protection. Pair up."

My eyes widen and I stand tall. "Hayden, I'm with you," I yell out to him. He looks just as surprised as everyone else. I don't think I've ever partnered up with Hayden.

"Sure. Sounds good," he replies.

Look at him. Being so fucking friendly and accommodating. What an asshole. I grab a handful of puck's from the gear bag and race over to him, startling the guy when I hit the brakes and spray him with ice.

"So, did you want to..."

"You protect first," I say, dropping the pucks at his feet. "Get the net."

Hayden gulps. "Okay."

He taps his stick on the ice and moves the puck left and right, but when he lunges forward, I give him a strong push back. It's nothing out of the ordinary. We use our arms and sticks to defend, but he looks nervous. Hayden moves again, this time trying to get around my right side, but I lean into my knee and take away his space, this time adding some elbow when I push him back.

He laughs uneasily. "You know, maybe I'll just go with Tom."

I laugh as well to ease the tension, but when he's looking a little too comfortable, my mouth falls into a straight line. "Get to the net, Hayden." And it can't be taken any other way than a threat.

He gulps and taps his stick on the ice. With a sudden burst he drives forward, only for me to bump him back. He tries again, flanking my left, but I shift my feet quick to cut him off, forcing him to the wall side and I couldn't be happier. Hayden puts his head down and tries for the narrow space and I don't hold back when I throw my full weight into him, bumping him off my chest and hard into the boards. He collides shoulder first and grimaces on impact, and the resounding thud is enough to draw the attention of the rest of the team. Even Coach hauls his ass off the bench to skate over to us.

"What's your problem?" Hayden snaps, holding his arm at the elbow.

"What?" I chuckle while everyone watches on. "It's practice. Sometimes things get physical at practice."

The guys are stunned, and no one's saying anything. Not even Coach. But I can tell what they're thinking. I'm acting like a prick and I know it. But I can't control this anger stirring in my gut. No, not anger. Annoyance? Irritation? What is this fire that's burning me up from the inside, and why does it blaze like an inferno whenever I imagine Hayden putting his hands on Char?

"I think you should hit the showers, Ward," Coach says finally.

Yeah. Maybe I should. I shove my hand under my arm and tug off my gloves one at a time, and my chin drops as I skate toward the gate.

"I'll text you," Sean says as I pass him.

I can barely hear him with my heart beating in my ears. When I'm off the ice, I charge straight for the shed, and the second the door closes behind me, I pound my fist into my locker. I don't know what's come over me, but I know one thing for sure. Hayden's not getting anywhere near my Char.

5

Charlotte

Why am I so nervous? I've been on a date before. Okay, maybe it's been a few weeks. Fine. Honest? A few months. Oh my god, when was the last time I even had a conversation with someone I found attractive? My mind drifts to Blake and I chide myself. Blake doesn't count. Blake's annoying. I would never date Blake. Now if I could just stop thinking about him for five seconds, maybe I could figure out what shoes go with this dress.

After I spend far too long deliberating, I decide to go with a nude pump. I don't wear this dress often, but it's one of my favorites. It's off the shoulder and cinches me at the waist, then flairs out at my hips and sits just above my knees. I had to wax my legs, which was a pain and probably qualifies as my workout for the day, but as I take a top-to-toe look at myself in the mirror, I have to admit I don't scrub up too bad. My hair was another conundrum, so I face timed Sophie for her opinion. It's brown, and boring with about as much bounce as a deflated beach ball. Personally, I think it looks best tucked under a baseball cap. But the cap doesn't go with this dress. Sophie says it would look nice up, to accentuate my bare shoulders, with a few loose strands to frame my face. By that point I'm already running late, so screw it. Up it is.

The door bell rings just as I clip on my earrings. Great. I'm late and he's early. I check myself in the mirror one last time before wrestling my coat off the rack and dashing for the front door. I take a second to compose myself. Woman up, Powell. He's just a guy.

A fanned bouquet of red roses greets me when I open the door, and somewhere behind the mass of stems and petals I can see Hayden's blue eyes peeking out at me.

"Good evening, Charlotte," he says, and there's this nervous squeak to his voice, which is mildly cute. He thrusts the flowers at me.

"Wow. These are beautiful," I say, giving them a polite whiff. They're not my favorite, but how would Hayden know? I doubt anyone would. But it's very sweet all the same. I look for a place to put them, then notice the Thank You carnations a client sent a week ago have conveniently wilted and died in the vase on my hall table. I snatch the dry stems in my fist and toss them aside, then pop Hayden's roses in their place.

"Perfect," I say, giving a thumbs up.

He laughs awkwardly and matches my thumbs up with one of his own. "Shall we?" he asks.

I nod. I'm still not convinced this is a good idea, but I'm way past the point of no return. I step outside and close the door and Hayden is quick to offer me his arm.

"Oh, alrighty," I say, linking my arm with his.

My apartment is on the third floor of the complex. This has its perks, like having the best view of the lake right in my front living room. But then again, I almost needed a defibrillator when I had to haul my couch up six flights of stairs last spring. The elevator is always out of order. Luckily tonight I don't have a velvet arm chair strapped to my back, so the walk downstairs is relatively painless.

Hayden walks me out of the complex and down the front path, and his car's waiting at the curb. It's a terribly sensible camel-colored sedan and, with the way this date started, I'm willing to bet a million to one that he's going to open the door for me. When we near the curb, he gently un-loops from my arm, then scurries to the car and opens the door. The cynic in me wants to roll my eyes and remark how cliché this all feels, but there's a part of me that appreciates the effort Hayden is making. He obviously wants to take me out, and what's wrong with trying to make something special?

I slide into the cream leather seats and decide not to give Hayden such a hard time tonight. "Thanks," I say to him.

Hayden scratches the back of his neck, unable to meet my eyes. "Of course." He closes the door when I'm tucked away, then jogs around the car and hops in the driver's side.

"So," I say, putting on my seatbelt, "where are we going?" Please, not Talley's. Please, not Talley's.

"I've got us reservations at The Lake Bar and Grill," he replies.

I give a sigh of relief. "That sounds perfect."

He seems relieved as well. "Originally, I was thinking Talley's, but Blake was acting really strange today, and I didn't want to bump into him there tonight."

My eyebrows knit together. "Blake was being strange?"

Hayden starts the car and nods. "Yeah, it was weird. He was more of an asshole than usual. He even bumped me into the boards at practice."

"That is weird," I reply, curious what might have set him off.

"But Tom and Sophie mentioned you really like the steak at The Lake."

I smile. "I do." Geez, he's being really nice.

We drive away, and The Lake Bar and Grill isn't far from my place, just on the other side of the lake. Hayden parks and, as expected, helps me out of the passenger side. When I stand beside him, I notice how tall he is, lean with wide shoulders. I look up at him, and still his blue eyes shy away from me. I suppose Hayden is pretty hot. He offers his arm again, and this time I take it without cringing. We walk up the stairs and I glimpse the giant frozen lake bustling with activity. Night skating has just started and the surrounding snow dusted pines are glowing with twinkle lights. I can smell the hot chocolate and pie vendors from here, and if I wasn't about to have the best steak in Lake Mistletoe, I'd be first in line for cocoa and peach cobbler.

The interior of the restaurant resembles a log cabin, featuring an enormous stone fireplace as its centerpiece and a rack of antlers proudly displayed over the mantle. Every piece of furniture is made of thick, carved wood, and above us hangs a gorgeous candle chandelier made from worn wagon wheels. We're seated at a table near the roaring fire, and it's warm enough for me to get my heavy coat off. I slip the cashmere from my shoulders but Hayden is quick to help, sliding the coat down my arms, his knuckles grazing my skin.

"Thank you," I say.

A server comes along and takes the coat from him, and I have to admit, I'm looking forward to tonight much more than I was an hour ago.

"So," he starts, "you're an interior decorator?"

"Designer," I reply, trying not to sound too pretentious. "And, yes. It wasn't my first choice, but I kind of fell into it after high school. Who would have known my super power was layered lighting?"

The server returns and places two glasses, then pours the red wine.

"I'm pretty sure you'd be amazing at anything you put your hand to. So, what was your first choice?" Hayden asks.

I don't want to answer at first. It's too ridiculous.

"Come on," he coaxes with a smile.

"A professional hockey player," I say from the corner of my mouth, with one eye scrunched up. The silence that follows makes me wish I'd said nothing. "Stupid, right?"

Hayden shakes his head. "Not at all. I think a woman can be whatever she wants to be, as long as she's happy."

A smile blooms on my face, and I pick up my glass of wine. He's getting more attractive by the second.

"Well, until she gets married anyway," Hayden adds.

My head jerks, and my wine sloshes. I lean forward, ear first. "What was that?"

Hayden picks up his own glass and takes a sip. "You know. It's important for women to get an education and find themselves when they're younger, but once they become a wife, taking care of their husband, home and family is their job."

I raise an eyebrow. "Sure, if they want that. But if they prefer to keep working, that's fine too. Right?"

Hayden chuckles, and the tension in my shoulder eases. "No," he says bluntly, and my back stiffens. "My father always told me that making a woman a wife is the most fulfilling gift a man can give, and from that day on it's her duty to serve her husband, and she's forever grateful. Just ask my mom."

Jesus Christ, his fuckwittery is hereditary. I scull back my wine in one gulp then slap the glass on the table.

"Whoa. Go easy there," Hayden says. "A lady doesn't drink like a sailor. Especially in public."

My jaw clenches and I'm doing my best not to smash the glass and stab him in the eye with the pointy stem. "Listen, Hayden..."

I'm interrupted by the ear-wrenching sound of a chair being dragged along the floor before being dropped in front of our table, then rocking until it stands still. I turn just in time to see Blake drop his weight onto the seat. He sits with his legs splayed and one elbow resting on the table, while his hand sweeps back his golden-blond hair.

"Evening, Char," he says. His eyes linger on my bare shoulders. "You look... nice."

Hayden almost spits out his wine. "Blake, what are you doing here?"

He shrugs. "Just passing by."

I'm skeptical. "Just passing by The Lake? Shouldn't you be at Talley's?"

"I'm an owner, not the chef, Char. I don't have to be there all the time." He takes my empty glass and refills it, then knocks it back in a single gulp. His face sours.

"Fuck me. I thought I was interrupting an actual date, but there's no way she's going to put out for a three-dollar bottle of wine, Hayden."

While Hayden gets flustered, I simply grin. "So you knew you were interrupting a date, then?"

Blake stares at me from beneath his heavy brow, his tongue sliding between his lips. "You look really nice."

Out of nowhere, my core tightens as his eyes devour me, and I worry he can tell. I turn away as a blushing smile swipes over my face.

Hayden stamps to his feet. "I think you should leave, Blake."

Blake looks at him unbothered, but I notice his fist clench and the toned sinews of his forearm tighten. "Oh, you do?" he replies. "Things going that well?" He turns to me and heat swells between my legs when I feel his gaze again. "What do you think, Char? Is Hayden going to get lucky tonight?"

Hayden grips the edge of the table. "That's enough, Blake." Soon annoyance fuels the heat building inside me, rather than arousal. I don't dignify him with an answer.

He chuckles, but there's a raw, angry edge to the sound. "Well, Char? Is he?" When I still don't answer, he leans onto his knees. "I didn't think you were that kind of girl. If I knew you gave it up on the first date, I'd have taken you for a spin long ago."

My hand shoots out and grabs Hayden's glass, and I throw the wine at Blake's face. "Fuck you, Ward," I snap.

The red liquid runs in crimson veins down Blake's cheeks and along his sharp jawline before trailing down his throat. I'm furious, but still my eyes can't look away from the line of red, trickling across his collarbone and staining his white shirt.

Blake swipes his hand over his jaw and flicks the wine off his fingers. "Guess I hit a nerve," he mutters.

Suddenly Hayden grabs him by the collar of his shirt and yanks him to his feet, and I'm surprised when Blake doesn't fight back. The arrogance he wielded a second ago has vanished. He looks almost defeated now.

"We can deal with this outside if you like," Hayden snarls. "No net this time, Blake."

Blake laughs and shoves Hayden away. "No need for that, friend. I'm leaving." It stings when his eyes find me again. "I've seen all I need to see."

The manager arrives, but Blake waves him away as he heads for the door, and the thrum of whispering diners follows Blake all the way out. A server arrives at our table with a cloth and begins wiping up the spilled wine from the floor, while another tries to change the tablecloth without disturbing the place settings.

I drop my head into my hands. "I'm so sorry for the mess. That was really rude of me."

The brunette server shakes her head. "Please. This is my pleasure. It's about time someone made an asshat of Blake Ward. I'm just jealous I didn't get to do it." She winks at me when she finishes. "I'll send you over another glass of wine. On me."

I smile politely as she wanders off, and between the train wreck that just happened and the room full of people staring at me, I feel like I'm going to be sick all over this freshly changed tablecloth.

"Can we go?" I ask Hayden, standing from my chair and using the table to keep steady.

He hurries to my side and even though I don't want anyone to touch me right now, I also don't want to fall flat on my face and add to this awful date night. "Of course," he says softly, taking me by the waist. "I'll get you home."

6

Blake

I'm such a fucking asshole.

I tap my fingers on the steering wheel and keep my eyes trained on her apartment. What was I thinking, saying something like that to her? To my Char? I deserve to be dragged naked through the snow by my balls. When I got Tom to tell me where Hayden was taking her, I didn't actually think I was going to turn up. But before I knew it, I was in my car and breaking every speed limit to get to The Lake Bar and Grill before Char somehow fell in love with Hayden. Did I feel like a creep when I got to the parking lot? Yes. Was I entering stalker territory when I asked the hostess what table they were at? Yes. And should someone have had the good sense to call the cops on me when I sat my ass at that table? Fuck yes.

But the idea of Char laughing, smiling at... touching... anyone but me, well, it feels like my chest is being ripped apart just thinking about it. I shouldn't have said what I said, though. If she never talks to me again after that, I'd totally get it. So I guess I'm going to have to beg for forgiveness until she does. Starting the moment she gets back from this date.

It feels like I've been waiting forever and I'm pretty sure my dick has frozen to the inside of my thigh. Finally, Hayden's beige-mobile turns the corner, and I duck so I don't get caught in his headlights. He pulls up to the curb and the next few seconds feel like hours. I can see them talking, and slowly a milky fog clouds the glass until I can only make out their silhouettes. I grip the steering wheel and my jaw clenches.

It's okay... they're just talking.

I tell myself this over and over, yet my fingers curl harder around the wheel until my knuckles are aching. Then the driver door opens and I release the breath I've been holding when Hayden steps out and I glimpse Char in the passenger seat. She looks upset. Hayden walks around the back of the car, then opens Char's door and helps her out. He pulls her coat around her shoulders and snuggles the collar against her neck. God, I wish that was me. They're talking, but Char's head is down. I watch as Hayden lifts her chin with his curved finger. Their eyes meet and as Hayden leans forward, I grit my teeth and grip the door handle. But Char pulls back and turns away from him, then shakes her head.

My eyes set on Hayden as I anticipate what his reaction will be. But luckily for him, he takes her response like a gentleman, and the two of them shake hands before Char makes her way into the apartment complex. I watch Hayden drive away, once again dipping behind the steering wheel to avoid getting caught in his high beams.

When his taillights disappear into the distance, I get out of my car and trudge through the snowy parking lot to the building. With each flight of stairs, I'm still trying to figure out exactly why I'm here. I could have called her to apologize, or at least waited until the morning. Why did I have to see her right away? Was that really going to make that much of a difference or just get her angrier?

By the time I reach her door, it's too late to change my mind. Whatever the reason, it's brought me here, and it's willing me to knock.

I hear footsteps inside and a shadow moves across the peephole, but there's silence. "Hey, Char. Are you there?" I cough, clearing my throat.

"Go away, Blake," she replies tersely.

I bite my lip and press my fist against the door. "Char, listen, I'm sorry. Okay?"

She says nothing, but her shadow lingers over the peephole.

"What more do you want me to say?" I carry on, leaning my forehead into the wood. "Things got out of hand. I shouldn't have said what I said. But come on, of all the guys in town you pick Hayden? You had to know I was going to give you a hard time."

I hear her shriek and the door flies open. She's still wearing that green dress that sits perfectly on every soft curve of her body. Curves I didn't even realize she had until tonight. I can't drag my eyes away from the smooth skin of her bare shoulders, and all I'm imagining is pulling her into my arms and smothering her neck with starved kisses. I don't understand the way I'm feeling. I've known Char since we were kids, and not once have I looked at her as anything more than a friend. She's one of the guys. The way I can shoot the shit with her and give her a hard time like I do with Sean or

Henry, and she gives it right back, sometimes worse! That's why I like her. She challenges me, and humbles me, and never tells me what I want to hear just to make me happy. And, as of recently, she's the most beautiful girl I've ever seen.

I'm swiftly brought back to earth when she pounds both her fists against my chest.

"For your information, I didn't pick Hayden. Sophie set me up with him," she snaps. "And that still doesn't give you permission to sit yourself down at the table and tell an entire restaurant full of people that I give it up on the first date."

I roll my eyes. "I didn't say that."

"Yes, you did!" she yells.

Her foot shoots out and kicks my shin. I wince. "Surely those weren't my exact words."

"I can't repeat your exact words because if I do, I'll have to murder you."

She's all flustered, and her skin is flushing pink. She's so mad, and my dick is so hard.

"You were cruel, Blake," she mutters as her chin drops against her chest. "I can put up with you being a lot of things to me, but you've never been cruel."

My heart breaks and I can't stop from reaching for her and curving my hand around her cheek. She closes her eyes and leans into my palm. "Char... ," I breathe.

Her eyes snap open, and suddenly she's staring daggers at me. She shoves away my hand and takes a step back. "Don't. Don't you dare pull the same shit with me that you pull on those other girls. You think you can just look at me and spew your bullshit and I'm going to forgive you for humiliating me in front of half the town?"

"I didn't mean to... I just..."

"Just what? Had nothing better to do than crash my date? Were you that bored, Blake, because it felt like you really put some effort into ruining my night?"

I can't get the words past my teeth and it's driving me crazy. "I just..."

"Just what!" Char yells.

Still, the words don't come and now I can't even look her in the eye. She shakes her head and goes to close the door on me, but I need to say my piece. I straighten my arm to keep the door open and she groans.

"What!"

"I just couldn't stand knowing that you were there with him," I mutter at last.

She gulps, and it's so quiet right now that the sound booms in my ears.

"What?" she says again, but this time it's soft.

I find the strength to meet her eyes. "The thought of you being with another man is fucking agony."

She clenches her bottom lip between her teeth. "Why, Blake?"

The answer comes to me with such ease I know it can't be anything but true. "Because the only man I want you to be with is me."

She trembles and her eyes glaze over. She parts her lips to speak, but all I want to do is kiss her hard and long. We can talk later. If I don't have her on my mouth soon I feel like I might die. I grab her by the waist and pull her against me, then scoop her face into my hand and wrench her desperately to my lips. At first she fights me, her palms pressing against my chest, her lips sealed shut. But slowly I feel her body relax in my arms. Where she was once pushing me away, now her hand slides onto my shoulder, while her other finds my waist.

I kiss her softly, my lips parting to taste hers even though she resists me. But I keep kissing, soft and long. I grip the nape of her neck, holding her to me until at last she surrenders, and when she does, my tongue finds hers and I gasp for breath. My heart races, my blood boils like lava in my veins, and my cock throbs with an exquisite ache. Now Char's kissing me back, her sweet tongue darting in and out, her teeth hungrily tugging on my lip. Now it's her breathing hard, clawing at me as if she's finally allowed herself to give in to something forbidden and she's ravenous.

There's always been an emptiness inside me. A void that I've never been able to fill, no matter how hard I've tried. I pull Char tighter against me, my hand reaching behind and cupping the sweeping curve of her plump ass. This feeling, this blissful feeling. I finally understand what it is. Char makes me whole.

I walk her backwards until she's against the wall, never taking my lips away from hers for a second. I fold my hand around her neck, dragging my fingers down past her shoulders and across her collarbone before spreading my fingers to take her full, heavy breast in my hand. My thumb skims over her nipple through the sheer fabric of her dress and she gasps, her hips writhing against me.

The mound of her pussy brushes my rock-hard cock and a deep groan escapes me. All I can think about is burying my fingers inside her while she cums all over them. I lean over her with my hand against the wall and give her nipple one last pinch before dragging my fingers down her soft belly. I press my knee between her legs, nudging them apart.

"Pull your dress up for me," I whisper in her ear.

Char gulps as her hands slide down her hips. She balls the fabric up in her fists and lifts. I watch as the dress inches up, revealing her gorgeous thick thighs, but I want even more.

"Higher," I whisper.

Char keeps going until at last I glimpse her white lace panties. I give her a rakish grin. "Fuck, that's so pretty, Char," I breathe.

I lean down and kiss her. When I pull away, I take two fingers and put them in my mouth, making sure to get them nice and slick before reaching down and rubbing my palm over her panties. Char closes her eyes, her back stiffening against the wall as I trace her crevice through the thin lace. I trail my fingers all the way down until I feel the hot wetness dripping from her entrance, and when I catch her sweet scent, my girth lengthens in my trousers.

"Open your legs wider for me," I whisper.

Char does as I ask and now, with her open to me, I hook her panties to the side, allowing myself full access to her pretty pink pussy. My thumb finds her swollen pearl. Char whimpers as I draw circles around her clit while my fingers tease her soaking wet folds. I watch her face intently. She bites down on her lip when I slowly slip a finger into her eager entrance. She swallows me up, her juices streaming down my hand, and she's so wet that my second finger slides in with ease. Char flings her arm over my shoulder, then grips a handful of my hair while her other hand braces against the wall. Her hips are grinding, swirling, and I pump my fingers against her movements so that my slick digits plunge deep inside her. She needs to be careful. With the way she's riding my fingers, I'm tempted to see how well she does on my cock.

But that can wait. Her muscles tighten around me and she grips my hair tighter, her pussy thrashing against my fingers while her juices trickle down my arm. Suddenly she cries out. Her body trembles before she falls limp against the wall. I ease my fingers free from her swollen folds and dip them into my mouth, releasing a low moan as I savor her taste. But there's not nearly enough to satisfy me.

I drop to my haunches, spreading her legs even further apart. "Keep your dress up," I instruct her.

She's uncertain at first, shuffling away from me, but I pin her to the wall and swiftly take her into my mouth before she can move another inch. Just as I hoped, Char is still soaking wet and I lap at her juices while darting my tongue in and out of her folds, and rolling the tip over her tender bud.

Char shivers as she stands over my face, handfuls of my hair twisted through her fingers. I feel her muscles tightening again, this time around my tongue, and it doesn't take long for her to explode, spilling more of her sweet taste into my waiting mouth.

When the bliss of her orgasm fades, I climb to my feet, take her face in my hands and kiss her deeply, and even with my nuts weighted and aching, I've never felt more satisfied. I pull back and gaze at her, waiting for her to say something, and at last, she does.

"Get out," Char tells me coldly.

7

Charlotte

I didn't go to work today. There's no way I can get any adulting done with the state I'm in. The early afternoon sun sneaks through a crack between my curtains and cuts my face with a stripe of pale light. I snuggle into my quilt, wrapping myself tight like a human burrito of confusion. What the hell was that last night? Of all the scenarios I could have possibly imagined, ending up with Blake kneeling between my legs at my front door was not one of them. The memory flashes before my eyes and my core tightens, like it has a million times since I woke up. I can still feel his hands on me, his lips, his tongue, and even though I can't make sense of it, I know for certain I've never cum that hard in my life.

There's a knock at my front door, but I've got no intention of moving from this spot. I've molded a Charlotte-shaped cavity into the mattress and it's perfect. The knock comes again, and again, and eventually it's followed by a voice.

"Charlotte, I know you're home. I called your office. They said you didn't come in," Daisy yells. She follows up with another loud bang on the door. "You better not be dead in there. I can't deal with that trauma. This wedding is stressing me out enough. Charlotte!!"

"Alright!" I yell, unfurling myself from the safety of my quilt. I rock myself to my feet, and though I've been avoiding it all day, I glimpse my phone sitting on the nightstand. My curiosity gets the better of me. I pick it up and check my messages, and I'm not surprised to find nothing from Blake. While I'm in bed sweetly suffering through orgasm kickbacks, he's probably lining up the next girl stupid enough to think she means something to him. That or he's spiraling with regret. Neither option is great for my self esteem.

I drag myself out of my room and down the hall, and Daisy is still pounding on the door when I get there. I yank it open and she recoils at the sight of me.

"Jesus. You look like shit."

I glance at myself in the mirror above the hall table. I mean, yeah, she's had better days, but 'shit' is extreme. "Nice to see you too, Daisy."

Daisy invites herself in and heads straight for the kitchen. By the time I've closed the door and meandered to the breakfast bar, she's already got the coffee machine going and is scouring for something sweet.

"Top left," I yawn.

She opens the cupboard and her face lights up when she finds a tub of brownies. Daisy then goes on the hunt for a cute little plate to put them on and a couple of mugs for our coffees. I'm not complaining. My kitchen is strictly for show. I think I still have the plastic wrap on the oven, so I love when Daisy comes over and makes use of it. Mostly because it means she's making me coffee and serving me treats.

"Are you sick?" she asks as she putters about, opening drawers and closing cupboards.

"Not entirely," I reply, leaning on my hand.

"Well, it's not like you to not go to work. So if you're not sick, what's wrong with you?"

I'm just exhausted and confused from being finger banged by our friend's brother last night. That's what I want to say. But there's just no delicate way to put it. I can barely admit it to myself. How am I supposed to tell someone else?

Instead, I go for old reliable. "Cramps," I say, clutching my stomach.

Daisy grimaces. "You poor thing. You should have told me, I would have brought over my hot water bottle. Works wonders." She fills two mugs with coffee then heads to the fridge. "I came by your work to maybe grab some lunch and see how the date went."

"Right," I say. "The date." I'd almost forgotten that part of the evening had happened. For some reason the face sitting bit at the end has been taking up more space in my head. "It was fine."

Daisy returns from the fridge with creamer. "Just fine? The way Sophie was talking up Hayden, I thought you'd be engaged and knocked up by now."

"I get the feeling that's how Hayden would have liked things to happen," I sigh, reminded of our dinner conversation. "He's very... traditional."

Daisy pours the creamer into our coffees. "So, no dice then?" She nudges the cup toward me, and I grab the handle.

"No dice." I'm startled when Daisy claps her hands excitedly.

"Good, it's my turn then."

"Your turn for what?" I ask.

Daisy smiles. "Anthony."

I sip my coffee, and I have no idea how she makes it so delicious. It never tastes like this when I make it. "What's an Anthony?"

"About six-three, gorgeous brown eyes, smooth tanned skin. Absolute rehearsal date material."

"And why have I never heard of this bronzed god before?" I ask.

"He's new in town. You know how I was advertising for a pastry chef? Well, I hired him over the phone and he arrived yesterday." Daisy leans on the counter. "He's gorgeous, Charlotte."

I frown. "Then why are you in my kitchen making me delicious coffee when you could take this gorgeous pastry chef for a test drive yourself?"

Daisy scowls and shakes her head. "I don't have time for that nonsense, Charlotte. I've got a wedding to plan and memories to make."

I laugh. "Will you ever have the time?"

Daisy glances at her apple watch. "I have some space available in 2066."

"By then we'll be living on Mars with robot husbands," I say.

Daisy's shoulders slouch. In fact, her whole body seems to relax, which is rare. "God, that sounds perfect. A programmable hottie who requires zero maintenance. Except maybe servicing or something, like a car, I guess? But that's still more appealing than remembering anniversaries and going to the in-laws for Thanksgiving."

"You need to take a day off, Daisy," I laugh, taking a brownie off the plate and stuffing it into my mouth.

"I will," Daisy smiles. "When every town in the north has a Gingerbread House Bakery and a life-size cutout of me greeting them at the door." Her smile wilts. "But first I need to get this wedding sorted."

"You're going to do amazing," I say reassuringly.

Daisy throws back her coffee and I'm not sure how she didn't burn her throat. "So are you," she says. "On your date tomorrow with Anthony."

I frown. "I don't know if I'm cut out for this dating thing. The Hayden project was a real flop."

"I'm telling you, Anthony is a catch," Daisy persists. "The real deal. You know when you're a kid and you close your eyes and imagine the man you're going to marry? Well, close your eyes right now and I'll bet you a triple layer chocolate cake that you see Anthony."

I wish I could tell her that all I see when I close my eyes is Blake leaning over me, that all I can hear is his deep voice telling me to open my legs for him. But I know exactly what reaction I would get. First there would be the shock, followed by screaming. Then it would take another thirty minutes to convince her I wasn't joking. Then curiosity would get the better of Daisy and she would want every single graphic detail, and when the novelty passed, she would tell me I'm a fucking idiot because Blake Ward is incapable of caring about anyone but himself. I know all this because it's exactly what I would say if Daisy went through the same thing, and I just don't have the stamina to deal with all that right now.

"Triple layer chocolate cake?" I ask. Daisy smiles and nods, and I breathe out slowly. "Fine. But you better make it extra fudgy."

Daisy bites into a brownie. "How dare you? Fudge is my middle name." She sweeps the crumbs into her palm and pops them in the trash. "Well, I better get back to work."

Her phone rings and she fumbles through her purse, and I can tell by her sour expression who it is, but I point my finger at her before she can ignore the call. "Remember. For Sophie," I remind her. "Finn's not that bad. Some people might even say the guy's hot."

Daisy frowns. "Some people also say that CrossFit is fun, Charlotte. The world is full of idiots." She gives her phone a second look and holds it to her ear. "For Sophie," she mutters, before answering Finn's call.

I hear her ranting on her way to the door, but pay little attention to the words. All I'm thinking about is how once upon a time, Blake and I used to have slurpee sculling competitions to see who could take a mega brain-freeze without crying like a bitch, but last night he was knuckles-deep inside me.

My core tightens again, and I squirm on the stool. I consider going back to bed, but it's probably best to take a cold shower instead.

8

Blake

The score is deadlocked. I take a deep breath, feeling the cold air fill my lungs as I step onto the ice. The puck drops and the clash of sticks echoes through the arena. The Devil's goalie eyes me from the other end of the rink and I grip my stick tighter.

Skating hard, I catch a pass just past the blue line, weaving through defenders like they're pylons. Dangling the puck on my stick, I deke left then right, out-stepping the flat-footed Devil's defensemen, who are dreaming if they think they can get anywhere near me. The crowd's cheers become a distant hum as I focus on one thing—the back of the net.

I wind up for a slapshot, aiming for the top corner. The goalie moves, quick as a cat, snatching the puck from the air with his glove. The collective "oohs" and "aahs" from the crowd tell me it was a close call. But no time to wonder what could have been. Now I'm battling along the boards for possession. A well-timed hip check sends my opponent tumbling, and I gain control of the puck. The opposing defenders converge, but I slip through like a shadow.

The crowd roars, sensing something big is about to happen. My eyes lock onto the net, liquid magma burning in my veins. A quick deke to the left, a feint to the right, and I'm in the clear. It's just me, the puck, and the goalie. I grit my teeth, my muscles tightening as I unleash a snapshot, aiming again for that coveted top corner. The puck sails through the air and time seems to slow. The Devil's goalie stretches, but he's just a fraction too late.

The arena erupts in a deafening roar as the puck finds the back of the net. I throw my arms up in triumph, and Sean, Finn, Henry and Tom rush in to celebrate. I notice Hayden heads for the bench instead. The crowd is on its feet, showering the ice with cheers. But there's only one face I'm searching for amongst them.

I can see Sophie and Lexie on their feet, and naturally Lola and Daisy missed the whole thing, arriving back at their seats with sodas and hotdogs and confused at what all the fuss is about. But there's no sign of Char. She didn't come. The guys are grabbing at me, slapping the back of my helmet and shoving at my chest as they howl in victory. But it all feels numb. She never misses a game. Is it because of me? Fuck. I knew I should have called. What the fuck is wrong with me?

"Dude, you okay?" Sean asks, patting my back.

I clear my throat. "Fuck yeah!" I yell, like I'm supposed to. "Let's get some shots."

The guys cheer and head for the bench but I stay a second longer just to be sure she's not there, but as the crowd thins it's depressingly clear she isn't. I pull off my helmet and let out a deep breath. What's the point of winning if Char isn't here to see?

I follow the guys to the bench, and they're still on cloud nine while the Devil's wander glumly to the sheds.

"Drinks at Talley's," Sean announces.

Finn nods agreeably. "I knew there were perks to having you as a friend."

"I'll catch up with you," I say as I yank my gloves off.

The way they all turn to look at me you'd think I've never said no to free drinks after a win. Come to think of it, that's true. But tonight I've got something else, or someone else, taking up way too much space in my head.

"All good," Tom says. "We'll drink your share until you get there."

The guys head to the locker room, but my head is so messed up, even taking the time to change feels like time wasted. I need to see Char now and explain to her why I didn't call. I throw off my gloves and fight my skates off my feet, discarding all my gear on the bench before heading out of the arena. Sophie sights me immediately and cuts me off before I get to the door.

"Where are you going?" she laughs, and there's a nervous pitch in her voice.

There's this strange flutter in my stomach. I feel like I'm burning up from the inside and my jersey's trying to strangle me to death.

"I just have to be somewhere," I reply. I don't want to be rude to my sister, and I'm not ready to tell her the truth, but I'll say anything she wants to hear if it gets me to Char's apartment quicker.

She looks me over with a raised eyebrow. She can always tell when I'm keeping something from her. Maybe it's a big sister super power. If it's something she can do on all men, then Tom is fucked.

"You're not wearing any shoes," she says, crossing her arms.

"My car is right outside," I reply.

She eyes me suspiciously. "Where are your keys?"

I gulp and pat my pants, but I know they're not there. "I'll call an Uber."

"Where's your phone?" she continues, eyeing me suspiciously, and it feels like she's interrogating one of her three-year-olds after finding drawings in permanent marker on the kindergarten wall.

"I'll catch a bus!" I snap.

She glares at me. "What's going on, Blake?"

I grumble and drag my hands through my hair before cupping them behind my head. "Soph, I don't have time to explain, okay? There's somewhere I have to be and I have to be there now."

She frowns at me, then reaches into her purse. I hear the dangle of car keys before she tosses them to me. "Take the truck. Tom has a change of clothes in the back seat. Including shoes."

I clutch the keys tight and smile. "You're the best, Soph."

She waves me away with a swish of her hand. "I know."

I head for the exit, but she calls out to me just before I vanish out the doors. "You'll tell me everything when you're ready, though, right?"

I clutch the keys in my fist and press it to my heart. "I promise."

She smiles and waves me away again, just as the girls arrive and ambush her with questions.

Christmas lights dangle from the arena, illuminating the parking lot with flashes of red and green. I spy Tom's blue truck and dash over, wincing every time I sink into the freezing snow. By the time I get to the driver's door and climb in, my socks are completely soaked and I can barely feel my toes.

I lean into the back seat and find Tom's bag. After rummaging through shirts and pants, I find a fresh pair of socks and trainers and waste no time getting them on. Now that I'm a step closer to not dying of hypothermia, I push the keys into the ignition and start the truck. It's cumbersome driving with all my gear on, but I've already wasted enough time as it is. I get the wipers going and hit the gas.

Char doesn't live too far from the arena. Even so, I seem to hit a hundred red lights and get stuck behind every grandma out for an evening drive, so it's taking forever to get there. Her apartment complex peeks over the treetops as I round the corner, teasing me with how close yet how far she is.

I pass the lake. Everyone not at the Mayhem vs Devils' game tonight is skating. There's a towering 80 foot artificial tree right in the center of the frozen lake. It beams with thousands of golden, twinkling lights, and a big crystal star crowns its peak. I notice couples skating hand in hand, and I realize I've never taken a girl to the lake at Christmas time. It's never occurred to me. But the thought of me and Char holding hands and talking shit like we always do while gliding over the ice urges my foot to push harder on the gas pedal.

Finally, I drive into the parking lot and hit the brakes so suddenly I jolt forward. I'm out of the truck in a flash, my untied shoe laces flapping about as I trudge through the snow to the entrance of the complex.

By the time I reach the glass double doors, I'm out of breath. This gear is really heavy. I drag myself through the foyer, then brace myself on my knees when I reach the six flights of stairs. I glance at the elevator, and I let out a winding groan when I read the OUT OF ORDER sign. I suck in a heap of breath before embarking on my climb.

By the time I hit the fourth flight, my feet are aching. Tom's got such small feet that his shoes scrunch my toes at the top. I can feel the sweat seeping through my pads and soaking my jersey. I'm pretty sure I didn't sweat this much in the game I played thirty minutes ago.

When I reach the third floor, I feel like I've climbed Everest and barely survived. I stagger to her door and collapse against the wood, mustering what strength I have left to knock. It opens immediately and I catch myself before I fall in.

Char is standing there in a tiny little pair of shorts and her dad's old Mayhem shirt. I can't help but notice her breasts sit a fraction lower, and the thin fabric clings to her hard nipples. The realization she's not wearing a bra gets my cock thick in seconds. Thank god I'm wearing all my hockey gear so she's not greeted by my erection like a fucking savage. I notice a smear of jelly around the collar as well, but I know how often Char wears this shirt. That stain could be from two minutes ago or two years ago. What's for sure is that I've never seen her look sexier.

"What do you want?" she asks curtly, and that's not the response I was hoping for.

"Hello to you too, Char," I pant, still catching my breath.

She looks me over curiously. "What are you wearing? Did you come straight from the game?"

"So, you knew there was a game," I say.

She frowns. "Of course I knew there was a game. Hockey is life."

"But you weren't there."

She pauses, her eyes softening for a second. "You were looking for me?"

"No," I blurt. My first instinct to tease and banter with her is so trained it takes over, but I don't want to hide behind that bullshit right now. Her eyes turn down and I can see I've upset her. "Wait. I mean, yes. Yes, I was looking for you."

She seems to slightly warm to me again. "Why?"

I gulp as sweat streams down the back of my neck. I thought the stairs were the hard part. "Because I needed to see you."

She shakes her head. "You didn't call, Blake."

Fuck. I knew that wouldn't be an easy one to get out of, and she's got every right to be pissed at me. "I know. I'm sorry."

"Sorry is fine, but why? Why didn't you call?"

The words are there on the tip of my tongue, but I'm not used to spilling such sentimental truths. Char's staring daggers at me though, and if I want her to trust me I've got to be honest with her.

"I was scared," I mutter, gripping the back of my neck.

I don't expect Char to laugh when I'm trying to be vulnerable. It catches me off guard.

"Scared of talking to me on the phone? Of reassuring me I wasn't just another notch?"

I get that she's mad, but the way she's being so dismissive is getting me upset, too. "I'm trying, Char. This isn't easy..."

"A phone call is easy, Blake," she sighs.

"Hey, are you forgetting that you told me to leave last night?" I snap defensively. "I would have stayed." I gaze up at her from under my heavy brow. "I would have stayed forever if you let me. But you didn't want that."

Now Char is the one on the back foot. When she speaks, there's a tremble in her voice. "I was scared too. I didn't know you felt that way about me." She gulps. "I didn't know I felt that way about you."

I need to touch her. My hands reach out before I have a chance to stop them, cupping her face and pulling her to my lips with urgency. We breathe hard in unison as we taste each other, and my tongue flicks hungrily inside her mouth. I reach around and scoop her beautiful, round ass cheek into my hand, pulling her against me while my other hand finds one of her perfect tits. She inhales sharply when my thumb grazes her nipple, before I close my hand around the soft flesh and squeeze. Her shirt is so threadbare I can feel every inch of her, and it's got me hard as a rock.

Char grinds against me, her fingers tangling in my sweat-soaked hair. I'm a hot, stinking mess, an animal rubbing up against a sweet angel I don't deserve. But she tastes so fucking good, and her body responds to my touch so naturally you'd think we were created for each other. I promise I'll make it up to her. The teasing, the bullying, being a complete and utter asshole. I'll fix it all. But god give me the strength to not pin this beautiful woman against the wall and fuck the shit out of her. Not yet anyway.

Then I feel her hands against my chest, pushing me away as she turns her face from me.

"What?" I say breathlessly, desperate to feel her lips again. "What's wrong?"

"What is this?" she asks. "What are we? Is this just screwing around at my door again or is it something else?"

Her lips have me mesmerized, and all I want to do is kiss her. "It's anything you want it to be."

"No, Blake," she says sternly, pushing me back again. "Tell me what I am to you."

My shoulders heave as I try to catch my breath. I can barely think straight, and I can hear my heart beating loud in my ears. "You're... Char."

Her head drops, and the disappointment in her eyes strikes my chest like an arrow. "Thanks for stopping by."

I stand there dumbfounded for a second, with my heart in my throat and my cock aching in my pants. "Just tell me what you want to hear, Char," I say.

"That's just it," she replies, folding her arms over those perfect tits. "I shouldn't have to tell you. At the very least, you should know what you want from me. What the end game is."

I exhale. "This is all pretty new to me, Char. Can we just keep whatever this is going and figure out the details later?" I move toward her, but her arm straightens to hold me back.

"Not tonight," she says coldly. "Maybe I'll call you tomorrow."

With that, the door closes in my face. How do I keep fucking this up?

I drag myself back down the stairs, and it feels even longer going out than it did coming in. When I'm back in Tom's truck I want a few minutes, maybe twenty, on the off chance Char changes her mind and wants me to take her against that wall like I imagined. But she doesn't, so I start the truck and head home. Horny and miserable. The worst possible combination.

I pull up at my place and park in the driveway, kicking snow as I walk to the front door. It's dark inside, with only the soft twinkle of my tree lights guiding the way to my living room. I roughly strip off as I wander to the couch, grabbing the back of my jersey and pulling it over my head then tossing it onto the hardwood floors, followed by my shoulder pads. I hike my legs onto the couch one at a time, tugging off my shin guards, then unfasten my hockey pants and shimmy them off while I head to a laundry pile on an armchair in just my long sleeve, shorts and jock.

I fish around in the pile, using the sniff test to confirm if this is clean or dirty, and take the risk with a pair of grey sweatpants. I slip off my jock and shorts and decide to free-ball for the rest of the evening, pulling on the sweatpants and heading to the kitchen for a late-night snack.

I've barely been in the fridge for a minute when the doorbell rings. It's probably the guys coming to see what's taking me so long. Normally, a drink would be exactly what I needed after such a shitty night. But all I want to do is mope around and figure out a way to prove to Char that the way I feel is real.

I head for the door, pulling off my long sleeve while I'm at it. It's soaked in sweat and smells rank. I ball it up and fire it into a corner to deal with later, then answer the door shirtless. But it's not my friends at the door. It's Char standing on the porch, still in her dad's Mayhem shirt and those tiny little shorts.

If I'm going to figure this out, I better be quick.

9

Charlotte

I don't know why I'm here. I'm struggling to remember the drive at all. But when I closed the door on Blake, I instantly regretted it. By the time I found the courage to ask him to stay, he was pulling out of the parking lot. I could have gone back inside and taken another cold shower. It's surprising that my skin isn't permanently like a prune at this point. But instead I ran upstairs, grabbed my keys, and broke every speed limit to get here. Now I'm standing at Blake's door, freezing my ass off, gazing wide-eyed at the sexiest man I have ever seen.

He looks stunned, his mouth wide open. It's not often I catch Blake speechless. I'd love to enjoy it, but I'm starting to lose feeling below my knees.

"What are you doing here?" he finally asks, and I feel a bit of reverse déjà vu coming on.

I try not to make it blatantly obvious that I'm staring at his chest, but it's almost impossible. With every breath, every subtle movement, his muscles flex and ripple beneath his smooth skin. I just hope I'm not drooling.

"I shouldn't have sent you away," I say through chattering teeth.

He grips the door frame and stares down at me. "Really?"

I nod, the cold spreading up my thighs. His eyes take in every inch of me, but I notice when he pays special attention to my pebbled nipples, sharp enough to cut glass through my thin shirt.

His teeth graze his bottom lip. "Did you want to come inside to talk?"

I shake my head.

"Did you want to come inside... for something else?"

I nod as the cold continues to creep. "I want you to make me feel the way you did last night."

A rakish grin takes hold of his mouth. His fingers skitter down his chest, coming to rest in the waistband of his sweatpants. If his chest wasn't distracting enough, his grey pants are leaving about as much to the imagination as my shirt. His bulge is clear through the fabric, and I'm not left wondering whether Blake is hung. The proof is hanging halfway down his thigh.

"But I want all of you," I say, and even I'm surprised by my demand.

Blake's hand drifts further down and my core tightens when he grasps himself through his sweatpants. "If that's what you want, Char. But we're at my house now. Once I start kissing you I'm not going to stop, and if you want all of me it's not over until I'm finished. Do you understand?"

Every word that drips from his mouth has me getting wetter and wetter before he's even laid a hand on me, and I desperately need him to touch me.

"I understand," I mutter.

Blake steps aside of the doorway. "Then, please come in."

I'm shaking, but I'm not convinced it's just the chilly night air. I step over the threshold, and as I pass Blake I feel him lean over me, his hot breath on my ear.

"Stop," he says, and I freeze in place.

I hear the door close and his steps on the hardwood floor as he comes up behind me. His hands fold around my neck, his thumbs drawing circles on my nape. I melt into the warmth of his touch, my every nerve electrified as his hands slide along my shoulders. Soon I feel his lips smothering the curve of my neck with tender kisses. He grips my upper arms and pulls me back so I'm hard against him, and when his hips move I feel the length of his cock rub against my back. His hands continue to trace along my arms as he kisses my neck, his gentle caress sending shivers down my spine. When his fingers reach mine he spends a moment delicately circling each digit, each tiny tickle filling my veins with fuzzy warmth. He laces his fingers with mine, then draws my hands behind my back and pins them against my tail bone.

I gasp when I feel one of his hands close around my wrists, holding them in place, while the other hand finds its way under my shirt and caresses my stomach, inching higher and higher until his fingers brush the bottom of my breasts. Blake's lips stay at my neck, and he switches between deep kisses and swirls of his tongue against my skin. His hand continues to explore me as he cups my breast in his hand and squeezes softly. His thumb glides along my goose-pimpled skin and I moan when he rolls his thumb over my nipple. His hips grind against my ass and he tightens his grip on my wrists as his kisses grow hungrier at my neck.

Suddenly, I feel him walking me slowly across the room and toward the wall. I move with him, savoring the shivers he's sending through my core every time he pinches my nipple between his fingers. He presses me against the wall, my face turned to the side so he can see my eyes. The hand that was taking care of my nipple disappears into his mouth and emerges slick with his saliva, and he keeps his dark eyes locked with mine as he slides his hand under the waistband of my shorts and between my folds, to find my clit.

I groan, and he kisses my lips softly as he circles my clit with his fingertips. His touch is tender at first, but as his spit moistens my swollen bud, his rhythm quickens. His hand vibrates, faster and faster, and the pressure building between my legs feels like a bomb ready to explode. The friction he's creating sends jolts of blissful agony through my entire being, and the more I groan the more he kisses me, until I cry out into his mouth.

"Good girl," he whispers. His pace on my clit slows and I whimper, feeling a gush of wetness escape from between my folds and soak my panties. He gives a guttural, grunting laugh at my ear. "Are you ready for my cock already, Char? I was going to rub your clit some more, but if you want me inside you now..."

He releases my wrists and frees his hand from my shorts, before hooking a finger under each side of my waistband and easing them over my hips and ass and down my thighs until they're crumpled at my feet. I hear him groan with pleasure, happy with what he sees. He grips me by the waist and his thumbs press down, arching my back.

"That's nice," he growls.

One of his hands leaves my waist, fidgeting with something behind me. That's when I feel a weight slap against my ass and I may only be an interior designer, but I'm pretty sure I know what it is. He uses his foot to spread my legs wide, and my slick folds part as well as I wait eagerly for what will come next. Suddenly I feel his swollen tip nuzzle my clit before he drags the head of his cock along my crevice, all the way to my ass and back up again. I bite my lip and lean into the wall, my pussy getting wetter and wetter each time he strokes.

The anticipation builds when he passes my entrance, and my muscles clench as if trying to draw him inside me. I've never wanted something so bad, and waiting desperately for the moment he fills me is absolute agony. Just the thought of Blake easing into me makes me wet, and I feel my hot, sticky juices running down my thighs.

"I think you're ready now," Blake says, sliding his bulbous head along my folds one last time.

The tip hovers over my entrance, and I'm so horny I'm tempted to buck back into him, but before I get the chance, he eases into me inch by inch, his groan getting throatier as he buries himself deeper inside me. My lips part and I whimper, and when I feel the last ridge of his cock pass through my folds, he slams into me hard and I cry out. Blake grips my hips, his fingers hungrily kneading at my skin as he pulls his cock from my slick pussy, only to drive it straight back in. I barely have time to recover and brace myself from his last thrust before he's balls-deep inside me, releasing a guttural grunt every time he plunges.

I try to put my hands on the wall but he grabs them, pinning them behind my back by the wrists again. The side of my face presses hard against the wall and my legs splay even wider as he dips his hips to get deeper inside me, now thrusting up, bouncing me on the edge of his cock like I weigh nothing.

"You're so fucking tight," he groans as he slams into me again. "You're going to make me cum."

He grips my wrists tighter, pushing them hard against my back as he hungrily pounds my pussy for all it's worth.

"Don't come in me," I stammer as my eyes roll back in my head, my ass growing numb from the punishment it's taking.

"Better tell me quick where you want this cum, baby," he says, " 'cause your pussy feels too fucking good."

He releases my wrists and I turn around to face him. I sweep my shirt over my head, then drop to my knees, grasping my breasts in my hands and opening my mouth wide for him. The sight of me kneeling before him sends Blake over the edge. He grabs his cock by the base and jerks his shaft for only a few seconds before ropes of cum explode from his swollen, purple head. He throws his head back, growling through grit teeth as his seed spurts into my mouth and splashes my tits. It's hot when it hits the back of my throat, and I keep my mouth open until he's shot every last drop.

Blake shivers when he's done, his hand sliding along his cock, his eyes fixed on the sticky strings that he's painted across my chest. His vein-ridden member is still hard when he releases it, and it slaps hard against his thigh. He holds his hand out and pulls me to my feet. One hand folds around my neck and pulls me to his lips, while the other smears his cum all over my breasts. He kisses me hard and long, his tongue exploring my mouth with such intensity that I don't think he's had his fill yet. He leaves one last kiss on my lips before pulling back, then grips my hand, leading me toward the hallway.

"Where are we going?" I ask.

He looks over his shoulder at me, his blond hair hanging over one eye. "To bed. I need to fuck you at least ten more times before morning."

My eyes bulge. "You're not serious? I'm already swollen."

He turns, pulls me to him, then scoops his hands under my ass cheeks, pulling me onto his hips.

"Good," he whispers, kissing my chin. "Then you'll be even tighter for me."

Heat reignites between my legs, and I can already feel myself getting wet again. Our lips melt together as Blake walks me to the closed door, kicks it open, and carries me inside.

10

Blake

I've never been so happy to wake up, because I know when my eyes open, Char will be lying next to me. Except she's not. I blink a few times, and it takes a second for everything to come into focus, but her side of the bed is still empty, with only a crumpled pillow and her forest morning scent on my sheets as evidence she was even here.

I feel a sting under my rib cage. Is this what it's like being abandoned before the sun comes up? Here I am thinking I've found the one. It makes sense she would end up being my ghost of dating past. I'm not mad at her, though. I like that she's challenging me, playing hard to get, treating me mean to keep me keen. It's all a part of the game, and I love to play. But it's a little different now. The rules have changed, and I don't want revolving partners. I just want Char. Now and forever. I just need to find the courage to tell her that.

I hear the doorbell and I smile. She's back. Part of me is relieved, only believing half the hopeful story I told myself. The truth is, I want to put an end to the games. It took the idea of Char being with another man to make me realize I've fallen for her. I've wasted so much time with this schoolyard bullshit. Suddenly, I remember what Sean said to me that night in the restaurant. Why do you think little boys pull little girls' ponytails? What an idiot I've been.

I leap out of bed, buck naked. I'm tempted to answer the door like this. I'm taking Char straight back to bed, anyway. But I decide to knot the bed sheet around my waist instead. Last thing I need at Christmas time is Mrs. Bearenstein from across the street, keeling over from a heart attack after she catches a glimpse of the yuletide log that hangs halfway down my thigh.

The bell rings again and I jog from my bedroom, clutching the sheet in my fist. I throw open the door, feeling like a kid on Christmas morning and it's Char on my wish list. But it's Legal Tamara standing on my porch with a big smile on her face and two coffees in her hand. I try not to look disappointed, but I feel my expression drop.

"Good morning!" she exclaims.

Her eyes scan my chest and abs and I pull the sheet higher over my belly button. "Tamara. Hi." I scratch the back of my head. "What are you doing here?"

She shrugs, her eyes eventually meeting mine. "You've normally popped by the coffee shop by now. So I thought I'd make a special delivery in case you were busy or sick. But I guess you're just sleeping in?"

I nod. "Yeah. I had a late night."

"I know," she says, her voice bursting with the same awe as her smile. "I saw the game. You were amazing. I tried to find you at the bar after."

"I decided to celebrate at home," I reply.

Her cheeks blush. "You should have called me. I would have loved to celebrate with you."

I give half a smile. I can see the girl is besotted with me, and it's my own stupid fault. I don't want to hurt her, but I'm not going to pretend there's something here when there isn't. Tamara is lovely, but the only girl I want for the rest of my life is Char.

"Look, Tamara, I've got to tell you something."

Her nose twitches as she shivers on my porch, her hair dotted with snowflakes and her blue lips trembling. "Can you tell me inside?" she asks. "It's freezing out here."

I can't figure out which is better. Telling her I don't want to see her anymore in my entry way or inside my front door. But she's cold, and if she gets upset the last thing I want is her crying on my porch while I'm standing here in nothing but a bed sheet.

"Sure. Come on in."

I hold the door open for her and she scurries inside under my arm. I close the door behind her and when I turn she beams that big smile at me again.

"It's much warmer in here," Tamara says. She holds up one of the Chilly Bean Bistro coffee cups in her hand. "Double shot espresso latte for Blake?"

"That's really nice," I say, "but I need to talk to you."

"Okay, but let me go first," she interrupts. "I've been working up the nerve the whole drive here, and if I don't ask you now, I know I'll chicken out."

I exhale, and I'm still politely smiling and nodding like a dork. The new Blake is a pain in the ass. Old Blake would have closed the door in Legal Tamara's face and sent her into the cold without a second thought. Scrooge style. Old Blake would have even tried to get a for-old-time's-sake blow job if we're being honest. But new Blake wants to make sure Tamara is comfortable, content, and apparently warm before ruining her morning.

"Okay, sure. You go first," I say.

Tamara takes a deep breath, tapping her shoes nervously on the floor. "I know we've not been seeing each other for long, but... I really like you," she gushes. "And I haven't been able to stop thinking about the rehearsal dinner your friends mentioned the other night."

I almost swallow my tongue. Please don't let her ask what I think she's going to ask.

"Your friends all seem to know who I am, and I think that's a good thing, and it's weird that I'm the one suggesting this, but the book I'm reading says I should trust my inner goddess and not be afraid to take what I want."

Fuck my life. Here it comes.

Tamara takes another deep breath. "So, Blake, I think you and me should be exclusive and you should take me as your date to the rehearsal dinner to show everyone that I'm your girlfriend," she spits out.

I'm rarely tongue tied. But here we are. I stare at her blankly as I search for the kindest way possible to say no, but my silence is making it worse. I can see her eyes welling, and the tremble in her lips isn't just from the cold.

"Blake," she says, her voice softer, "what do you think?" When I still don't respond, her head drops. "Oh, my god. I'm such an idiot."

"No, you're not," I say at last. I reach out and put my hand on her shoulder, keeping the other firmly latched onto the bedsheet. "It's me. I'm a fucking asshole. You deserve so much better."

"No, I don't," she whines. "You're the hottest guy in town. There's no one better."

I try not to allow my ego to take that compliment and run with it. "Yes, there is, Tamara," I say, though she's partially right. I'm getting better, but I'm not a fucking saint. "Someone who will give a brilliant girl like you all the love and attention in the world."

"Did I do something wrong?" she asks through her tears. "Is it the inner goddess thing? Because I can throw that book in the trash."

I shake my head. "Tamara. Stop. It's me. I'm not the guy I used to be. There's something else I need in here," I say, pointing to my chest. "And I don't think it's something you can give, no matter how hard you try. I'm sorry, but I want to be honest. You and I just won't work."

Her chin lifts and the tears recede. Maybe she understands. "Oh," she sniffs. "Why didn't you just say so?"

I cock an eyebrow. "Really? So you're okay with everything?"

She tilts her head to the side. "Of course. I'm happy for you."

My chest heaves with relief. "Thank you."

"It's really brave for someone with your reputation to come out as gay. I mean, it actually makes sense now."

"Wait, what?" I choke. "That's not what I meant."

"So, are you taking a guy to the rehearsal dinner, then?" Tamara continues.

"I'm not gay," I state firmly. "I can't be with you because I've fallen for another woman."

Suddenly the floodgates open, the tears worse than before. "What!" she cries. Tamara squeezes both coffee cups and the milky brown liquid squirts into the air like a geyser, soaking through her white blouse. A few drops splash my chest. Luckily we've been talking so long the coffee's cold.

"Let me get you a towel," I stammer, cautiously relieving her of the squished, empty cups and rushing to the kitchen. I come back with a cloth and, after awkwardly dabbing at her chest, I decide just to give it to her instead.

Tamara does her best to wipe up the coffee, but her shirt is toast. "How long has this been going on?"

I screw up my face. "It's all pretty recent, if that makes it better?"

She glares at me. "Not really."

"I am truly sorry," I declare. "I never meant to hurt you. Let me get you a clean shirt."

"It's fine," Tamara mutters tersely.

"No, it's the least I can do," I say, rushing over to the laundry basket on my couch. There are clothes everywhere because my housekeeping is atrocious, so I grab hold of the first t-shirt I see and hand it to her. "You can clean up in my bathroom. Hey how about I make you another coffee?"

Tamara says nothing, but it's plain to see by her death stare that if I died of syphilis right now, she'd be the first one dancing on my grave.

I point down the hallway. "Bathroom's that way. Help yourself to the lotions and I'll get you that coffee."

She sneers at me, then turns on her heels and marches to the bathroom, slamming the door behind her. I scurry to the kitchen, still clutching the sheet, and get the kettle going.

"Do you take sugar?" I call, tapping my fingers impatiently on the counter as the water boils. "You know, I really hope we can still be friends after this, Tamara."

Suddenly, I hear another door slam, but this one is closer. I peek around the corner. "Tamara? Everything okay?"

I see the bathroom door open, and notice that my front door is also ajar, the frosty breeze swishing through my front room. I jog to the door, tripping over the flappy edge of the sheet on the way, but catching myself before I fall flat on my face. I pull the front door open just in time to see Tamara's car sputter off down the street.

I exhale. "Well, that went well."

As Tamara's car disappears into the drizzle of snow, I look up and glimpse Mrs. Bearenstein across the street, standing at her own front door with a newspaper in her hand. I grip the sheet tighter and wave to her with my free hand.

"Morning, Mrs. Bearenstein," I call.

She looks down her nose at me and shakes her head disapprovingly before slamming her door shut. I sigh as I hear the kettle click. Suppose I had better learn how to make a double espresso latte.

11

Charlotte

Have I fallen for Blake Ward? When I woke up this morning and saw him asleep next to me, it felt like a dream. I've known him for so long, and I always thought what we had was rivalry. The teasing, the taunting. I truly believed Blake lived to make my life a living hell. It might have started like that, but somewhere along the way, things changed. I started noticing the gold flecks in his brown eyes, the way he tries not to laugh at his own jokes before getting to the punchline, how he can be kind and sweet when he thinks no one is looking, and how when he touches me, my body feels like it's on fire.

I panicked this morning. I didn't even have time to find my shirt, just grabbed whatever was closest and headed out the door before he woke up. We can't ignore last night. I don't think I could if I wanted to. But what scares me, and is probably the reason I ran this morning, is I'm not sure how Blake feels. He's a player. That's not a secret, and he's a master of the games he plays. But I will not allow him to move me around his board with the other pieces. I truly want to believe I mean something more to him, that he's falling for me in a way that makes fools out of grown men. That strips their hearts bare for the world to see.

It's a question I never thought I'd be asking myself. Is Blake falling for me like I'm falling for him?

I take a long shower and I need it. He wasn't lying when he said he was going to have me another ten times before morning. I'm so sore I can barely walk. But it's a pain I'd be willing to suffer through any day. Thank god I don't have to be anywhere today. That's when my doorbell dings and my stomach drops. Is it Blake?

I pull on a pair of jeans and a powder-blue sweat shirt before rushing to the door, my skin prickling nervously with each clumsy step. My heart thumps hard in my chest as I peer through the peephole, and I can't shift this goofy smile. But I'm confronted with a shock of black hair and dark eyes under a heavy brow. I take a step back.

"Who is it?" I ask.

"Hi. My name's Anthony. I'm here for our date."

Fuck. My. Life. I totally forgot. I open the door and look up at the tall, tanned, handsome man that Daisy promised. His eyes widen when he sees me.

"Wow. Daisy said you were beautiful, but I still wasn't prepared."

I give an involuntary snort. "That's sweet, thanks, but..."

"But something's come up and you can't go out with me anymore?"

My head jerks. "Something like that..."

Anthony nods. "Daisy said this might happen, so she wanted me to let you know––no date, no cake."

I laugh. "Oh, my god. She's holding my cake to ransom?"

"She also told me that if I'm not man enough to get you out of this house, I can pipe my butter cream at someone else's bakery." I laugh again, and Anthony smiles. "I can't be sure, but it sounded kind of sexual."

"That does sound like something Daisy would say," I reply.

"Your have a beautiful laugh too," Anthony says, dipping his chin.

Geez, this guy is a charmer, and he's firing at me with both barrels. But Blake is still at the forefront of my thoughts.

"Look," Anthony continues. "I know this is awkward, and there are some real pity-date vibes going on here. But I'm new to Lake Mistletoe, and I'd love to get to know the place a little better. So how about I take you out for skating and hot chocolate and you give me the tour?"

I furrow my brow. "So, not a date, then?"

He holds up his hands placatingly. "Date? What date? Gross. I would never. You're not even my type." He grins. "I'm not into perfect, beautiful girls with amazing laughs, so you're out of luck."

The guy's really going in for the kill here, and I want that cake. "Okay. A skating and hot chocolate non-date is acceptable. I'll get my coat."

When I'm all bundled up, Anthony shows me to his emerald-green truck in the parking lot and opens the door for me to climb in.

I take a deep breath and my eyes widen. "It smells like cinnamon in here."

"Well, of course. I have fresh cinnamon rolls in the back, just in case."

"In case of what?" I ask curiously.

"In case my non-date gets peckish on the way to our non-date activities."

Anthony takes me ice skating at the lake. The air is brisk, but the afternoon sun is bright and glistens upon the snow-topped pines that line the lake's edge.

"Do you get winters like this where you're from?" I ask as I lace my skates.

Anthony's sitting next to me, lacing his own. "Just scorching summers where I'm from," he replies.

With a response like that, I expect him to topple over immediately, but when his skates are laced, he jumps to his feet and zips out onto the ice, skating a full loop of the Christmas tree before returning to me. He offers me his hand and smiles.

"Non-date," he says.

I laugh and take his hand and he pulls me up. "Non-date," I reply.

"So tell me," he starts as we skate alongside each other, "did you really have something else to do today?"

I sigh. "No, not really."

He grabs at his heart like he's been shot. "So why the rejection? If you don't mind me asking?"

"I'm seeing someone," I say. "Sort of."

Anthony cocks an eyebrow. "Sort of?"

"I'm not sure what we are right now. It's complicated."

Maybe it's just because Anthony knows nothing about me or Blake or Lake Mistletoe, but it feels good to talk to someone.

"Excuse me if I'm speaking out of turn here," Anthony says, "but if I had the chance of having you as my girl, there'd be nothing complicated about it. That's for damn sure."

I wish I had an answer. Some sort of reason Blake hasn't told me how he feels. But I don't. Anthony skids to a stop and gestures to the cafe above the lake.

"Hot chocolate?"

I nod. "Sounds good."

We head up, and after we find our seats, the server comes around to us with the menus, her hair adorned with a cute reindeer headband. Anthony barely glances at the drink list.

"Two hot chocolates. Extra foam. Double extra marshmallows. With a chocolate fish on the side, please."

The server nods, the antlers on her headband flopping back and forth, and I nod my approval while leaning back in my chair.

"So, I hear you like hockey?" Anthony asks. "Did you catch the Mayhem-Devil's game last night?"

I exhale. "No, I missed it. I heard it was great, though."

Anthony nods excitedly. "It was tight the entire way. Then the right wing scores this amazing snapshot on the buzzer. The arena went crazy. I can't remember his name."

I cough. "Blake Ward."

"Yeah, that's him," Anthony says. "He's good. You know him?" I pause, and apparently Anthony is a pretty perceptive guy. "Oh, he's Mr. Complicated?"

I nod. "Yeah. He is."

Anthony exhales and leans into his fist. "Well, no wonder I don't stand a chance. It was a hell of a snapshot."

The server arrives with our hot chocolates. Anthony smiles and thanks her, then pinches his chocolate fish's tail between his fingers and holds it out to me.

"To uncomplicated friendships," he says.

I smile and pick up my own fish, knocking it against his. "To uncomplicated friendships."

I dip my fish's head in my milky hot chocolate, just long enough to melt his candy noggin before popping him into my mouth. My eyes roll back in my head and I give Anthony a thumbs up while I maneuver a mouth full of marshmallow.

The bell on the cafe door jingles and I hear a group of girls chatting and giggling long before I see them. They walk past in single file, and my eyes drift up when I glimpse faded red text on the back of one of the girl's shirts. To most, it wouldn't mean anything. But to me, I immediately recognize it as the roster of the 2003 Lake Mistletoe Mayhem Hockey Team. I strain my eyes to make out the face of the red-haired girl wearing what looks like my dad's shirt, but it can't be. My dad's shirt is at Blake's house.

The friend behind her says something amusing, and she spins around laughing. That's when I see the red jelly stain around the collar and I'm positive that, just for a second, my heart stops beating. Anthony notices my interest and looks at the group.

"Something wrong?"

"I'll be right back," I say, rising to my feet and heading straight for the redhead. She notices me coming and our eyes meet. She looks nervous, which isn't surprising. I'm practically storming her way, staring daggers at her. "Hi," I say tersely. "Where did you get that shirt?"

The girl raises her eyebrows at me and folds her arms across her chest. "Excuse me?"

"The shirt," I snap, losing patience. "It belongs to a friend of mine. Where did you get it?"

"Not that it's any of your business, but this is my boyfriend's shirt," she says, swirling her head on her neck. "So unless your friend is Blake Ward, I think you've got the wrong shirt."

I gulp, anger pooling in my stomach. "Blake gave you that shirt?"

The girl looks down at it and shrugs. "Yeah. I needed something to wear after he got the shirt I was wearing all dirty this morning."

My rage is in my veins now, pumping through my limbs. My fist clenches. "Really?" I say snidely.

The girl glares at me. "Who are you?"

I take a deep breath, slowly unfurling my fingers. "Apparently, nobody," I say, turning on my heels and returning to the table. I slam into my seat.

I can't believe this. One out the door, another straight in? I guess this answers the question I've been tossing and turning over. Blake doesn't care about me. Not at all.

"Is everything alright?" Anthony asks. "Do you know her?"

I fight to drain the anger from my veins, like venom from a snake bite. I won't let Blake get to me. He doesn't deserve my anger. He doesn't deserve any part of me. I look straight at Anthony.

"Do you want to come to a rehearsal dinner with me?"

Blake

I open my front door and Sophie shoves me hard in the chest.

"What the hell is wrong with you?" she yells.

She pushes past me, and I close the door behind her.

"Good to see you too, sis," I say. I follow her to the kitchen where I find her helping herself to my sugar cookies. "Is something wrong?"

"What's going on with you and Charlotte?" she mumbles as she chews.

I turn my head, pretending to find something interesting about the corner of the room. "I don't know what you're talking about."

She frowns. "Oh really?"

I scratch the back of my neck. "Why? Has she said something about me?"

Sophie rolls her eyes and grabs another cookie. "I thought you were supposed to be some suave Romeo, but you're just a little boy playing games, aren't you, Blake?"

I hear the fire in her voice and meet her eyes. "Sophie, what's going on?"

"Joel's Mayhem shirt. The thing Charlotte loves most in the world. Do you have any idea why that redhead you've been messing around with is wearing it all over town?"

My brow furrows. "No. I literally have no idea what you're talking about."

"Well, you should," Sophie scoffs. "She's telling everyone her boyfriend Blake gave it to her the other morning."

The puzzle pieces slip into place as I think hard on what Sophie's saying. Shit. The shirt I thought was from my laundry basket, it was Char's shirt, and I gave it to Tamara. My stomach drops. "Does Char know?"

Sophie laughs tersely. "Oh yeah. Charlotte knows. She was on a date when the girl walked into the cafe wearing it."

I've barely had time to process stupidly giving away Char's favorite shirt when I get blindsided by the revelation that she was on a date the same day.

"Date? What date? With Hayden again?"

Sophie shakes her head. "That was a disaster, apparently. No, this was someone that Daisy set her up with. A pastry chef from her bakery."

My head is spinning. Here I am, feeling like a piece of shit after sending Tamara away. Meanwhile, Char is out on a second date with a different guy!

I clench my jaw. "What's his name?" I mutter through grit teeth.

Sophie ponders for a bit. "Anthony, I think. You'll get to meet him at the rehearsal dinner. He's her date."

My chest feels like it's caved in, crushing my heart into dust. I can't speak. Fuck, I can barely breathe. I walk to the couch and grip the back to keep myself steady, my fingers digging deep into the fabric.

"Blake," Sophie says, her voice soft for the first time since she's arrived, "are you okay?"

I hear her footsteps across the hardwood floor and my body jerks when she grips my shoulder.

"Blake," she says again, "why did you have Charlotte's shirt in the first place?"

"Because she was here," I breathe. "She spent the night."

God, it feels good to say it out loud. I turn to Sophie, but she doesn't look surprised. She smiles and nods.

"And how did the shirt end up on the redhead?"

"Tamara," I say. "When I woke up the next morning, Char was gone. Tamara showed up at my door, and I told her there was someone else and I couldn't see her anymore. She got upset and spilled some coffee on herself. I gave her a shirt to wear, but I swear to god, I didn't know I had given her Char's shirt, and nothing happened. I don't know why she's telling people I'm her boyfriend."

Sophie ruffles my hair and for a split second I can see Mom's kindness in her eyes. "I think that's pretty obvious. You're Lake Mistletoe's most eligible bachelor, little brother."

I shake my head vehemently. "Not anymore. I only want Char."

"Does she know that?" Sophie asks.

I gulp. "I mean, I've shown her..."

Sophie screws up her face. "I'm fine without the details, thanks. But have you told her, Blake? Said the words out loud?"

I shake my head. "I think I've said more to you than I ever have to Char."

Sophie sighs and leans on the back of the couch. "You need to tell her, Blake. You need to prove to her she's not just another notch on your belt. I'm talking screaming from the rooftops so that every hopeful girl in Lake Mistletoe who ever dreamed of having a shot with Blake Ward hears loud and clear that he is off the market. That his heart belongs to someone else."

I nod. "You're right. She needs to know she's not some little secret. I want the entire world to know. Do you think that will be enough?"

Sophie shrugs. "Might have been, before she RSVP'd her plus one to the rehearsal dinner."

I clench my fists, and the muscles in my forearms tighten. "I have to talk to her."

Sophie shakes her head. "She doesn't want to talk to you. That's the other reason I'm here. She wants her shirt back, and she wants you to leave her alone."

"But it's just a misunderstanding," I protest. "If I could just explain..."

Sophie looks at me sternly, and I feel the big sister coming out in her. "Blake, I love you, and it makes me ridiculously happy that you've finally sorted your shit out and found someone you want to devote yourself to, and bonus points for it being Charlotte. But she's a mess, and misunderstanding or not, she's going to the rehearsal dinner with Anthony, and I can't have you ruin this night for me. Please."

I release a heavy breath, and my shoulders heave. "So what am I supposed to do? Just sit there and watch her be with someone else?"

"I guess so," Sophie says. She heads back to the counter and grabs another cookie. "Because if you punch that poor man, or make Charlotte cry on my practice special day, I just might kill you." She walks past me on her way to the door and dabs a crumbly peck on my cheek. "And for fuck's sake, get the shirt back."

Sophie leaves and I suddenly have a to-do list for the rest of the day. The first thing is to grab my phone and type out a message to Char, which is pretty much the opposite of Sophie's instructions. But as I'm halfway through my speech, my sister's words haunt me. What if I just fuck things up again, like I always seem to do? I can't risk ruining Sophie's dinner, but the thought of Char with someone else has my blood boiling.

I pause and erase the message. I have to handle this delicately. I write out another text, then hit send. After a quick shower, I throw on a pair of jeans and a green Henley, and drive to Talley's. When I arrive, I maneuver my car around a boom lift set up outside. I park and climb out, walking over to the boom lift and peering up at the roof to see what's going on. Through the snowfall I can see a workman in a neon-orange jacket messing around with the letters on the sign. Sean walks out of the restaurant, pulling his coat tight around his neck to chase off the chill.

"Something wrong with the sign?" I ask.

"The Y came loose in the wind," Sean replies. "No big deal." He nods toward the door. "Someone's in there waiting for you."

"Thanks," I say. "How's Lexie?"

Sean glows whenever I mention her name. For a while I thought it was sentimental nonsense, that you could be so wrapped up in a girl that it literally made you shine from the inside out. But that's exactly how I feel whenever I think about Char and the noise she makes when I lift her thigh over my hip so I can bury myself deeper inside her.

"She's great, man," Sean sighs contently. "We're great. Everything's great."

I pat his back before heading inside, and when the door closes behind me, I look up to see Tamara sitting at the bar. The hostess greets me as I walk by, and I take the stool next to Tamara.

"Can I get you a drink?" I ask.

She can't make eye contact with me, but she shakes her head. Tamara pushes something across the bar to me. "This is what you wanted, right?"

I lay my hand on the worn, white cotton and give a sigh of relief. "Yeah. I'm sorry about the mix-up."

"It's the girl who came up to me in the cafe, isn't it? The one you're seeing."

I nod. "I know I've hurt you, Tamara. But you can't keep telling people I'm your boyfriend."

Tamara's cheeks redden, and she laughs lightly as if to hide her embarrassment. "Yeah, I guess it was a little desperate."

"No, I get it. The problem is the girl who owns this shirt thinks you and I are still seeing each other. It's created a bit of a situation for me."

Tamara exhales. "I see. I'm sorry."

I shake my head. "This wouldn't have happened if I'd just been honest with her from the beginning." I offer Tamara an apologetic half smile. "And honest with you, too."

Tamara's expression warms, and slowly a smile appears on her lips. "It's never too late. When two people care about each other enough, there's always time," she says, standing from the stool and pulling her purse over her shoulder. "She seems nice." Tamara frowns. "Feisty, and a little scary, but nice."

"She's all the above," I chuckle.

Tamara holds out her hand to me. "Well, good luck, Blake."

I stand and shake her hand. "You too, Tamara."

Her eyes drop to the floor as she walks past me and I watch her leave Talley's, a mixture of guilt and relief stirring in my belly. Tamara deserves someone who lives and breathes her, the way I do with Char, and I sincerely hope she finds him one day. Making peace with Tamara is ticked off my to-do list, and getting back Char's shirt is another job taken care of. I head back outside and find Sean standing in the same spot I left him.

"She wasn't screaming or crying. Must have gone well," Sean says, watching the worker at the top of the boom lift straighten the Y. "Got your sights set on someone else, I suppose?"

"Yep," I reply, the icy wind nibbling at my lips. "Char."

Sean chuckles, but once again and just like Sophie, doesn't seem surprised. Did everyone know but me?

"That's great, man," Sean says, slapping my back. "Don't fuck it up."

I roll my eyes. "Am I getting relationship advice from a guy who choked out his girlfriend's ex with a hockey stick?"

"Didn't have a choice," Sean replies. "He was trying to get between me and the woman I love, and that's just never going to happen. Not while I'm breathing."

His words stir something in me. "I feel that way when I think about this guy Char's going to the rehearsal dinner with. But Sophie begged me not to make a scene."

"It's just one night," Sean says. "What's one night when you're going to be with her for the rest of your life?"

I chuckle. "You think?"

"You tell me," Sean says. "When you close your eyes, do you see you two getting married, having kids, growing old together?"

My skin goose pimples. "Kids... me... a dad?" I've never thought about it until now. I don't know if I'm up for the job, but I'm positive I'd do a better job than my father did, that's for damn sure. It's about as hard imagining Char with a baby in her arms as it is me, but then when I imagine the two of us together, suddenly she's right there. A little girl, with my blond hair and Char's hazel eyes, and she's perfect, and we're so happy.

"Do your sister a favor, don't wreck her dinner. But as soon as it's over, make sure Charlotte knows exactly how you feel. Trust me. Shoot your shot, Blake. You won't regret it."

To think of all the time I wasted in high school not getting to know Sean. Now, I don't know what I'd do without him. But it seems like wasting time, instead of spending it with people I care about, is more common than I thought. My heart races in my chest, and I can't wait to start spending my life with Char. I look over the boom lift once more and furrow my brow.

"How long have you got this thing rented for?"

13
Charlotte

The Northwellian stands out regally against the winter evening as the cars pull up and the guests are greeted. As I look over at Anthony in the driver's seat, I'm sure I've done the right thing. Even after all that's happened, he's not the one I wanted to be here with. Blake. It's always been Blake, and the truth of that hurts more than anything else.

We pull up to the curb outside the hotel and the valets are immediately there to open our doors. I struggle to get out of the truck in my long, slinky dress that gives zero room for movement but looks fantastic. Anthony notices and is quick to my aid, lifting me down. My heels clack on the concrete when I touch the ground.

He gazes at me for a second and I blush under his dark eyes. "Did I mention you look stunning tonight?"

"Only a few hundred times," I reply.

"As long as I'm being clear about that," he says.

I nod. "I'm definitely picking up what you're putting down. Don't worry about that."

He's sweet, and so nice, and anyone else would think I'm a fucking idiot to not be jumping all over this tall, dark opportunity of a man. But my blood doesn't race when I look at him the way it does with Blake. My skin doesn't feel like it's on fire when he brushes by me. And when I picture a man with my legs wrapped around his hips, kissing me passionately as he buries himself deep inside me, it's Blake's face. Not Anthony's.

But for tonight at least, I'm here with Anthony, my friend, and I'm going to make the most of it.

Anthony offers his arm, and I loop mine through as we stroll toward the hotel entrance. A sign in the lobby for 'The Rehearsal Dinner of Tom Powell and Sophie Ward' directs us to the ballroom.

I remember talking to Tom today, and trying not to laugh at how nervous he was. He loves Sophie so much, and has been waiting for this day forever. I'd be jealous if I wasn't so happy for him.

Two giant wooden doors open and I gaze in awe as the warm draping of twinkling lights welcomes Anthony and me into the ballroom. Fresh snow powders the glass-domed ceiling overhead, and a tiered chandelier dangles above us, its prisms catching the golden sparkles of light.

Then we're seated, our tables dressed in crisp white linens and crowned with a gorgeous centerpiece of mixed winter blooms––white roses, red amaryllis, and wild sprigs of evergreen––the scent of pine and flowers mingling and creating an intoxicating fragrance.

The place settings are like pieces of art, with polished silverware, crystal-clear glasses, and delicate chinaware plates that look almost too lovely to use. Tall candles stand proudly in the center, their flames flickering romantically.

"Wow," Anthony says, pulling my chair out and pushing it in once I'm seated. "This is amazing."

I nod. "Finn does a great job. He's the venue manager." I lose my train of thought when the grand doors open and a three-tiered cake is wheeled down the aisle between the tables. I see Daisy hovering by the door, her heart in her throat as she watches.

Anthony sits himself next to me and nudges my shoulder when he sees me eying the cake. "I piped the butter cream on that, you know."

"It looks fantastic," I say.

"And that's just the rehearsal cake. Wait until you see the one Daisy's got for the big day."

"Will you be butter-creaming that one as well?" I ask.

His eyes lower, and he grins. "I'm not sure how much longer we can keep talking about butter cream without me getting the wrong idea."

I put my hand on his. "Then maybe we should stop talking about it."

I can read the disappointment in his eyes as he exhales. "Of course. If that's what you want."

I'm thinking of what to say next when the doors open again, but this time it's not a gigantic cake that distracts me. Blake stands in the doorway in a navy suit with a white shirt, his blond hair coiffed to the side, and his hands resting casually in his pockets. He tilts his head up to admire the chandelier, and my core tightens when my eyes settle on his jawline. He's the kind of handsome that takes your breath away, and I still can't believe I've had him between my legs.

Suddenly Blake turns to me, and I look away before he catches me staring. Instead, I keep watch from the corner of my eye as he crosses the room, taking a seat at the Ward family table on the other side of the aisle. I can't stop looking at him, but when I turn away I can feel his eyes on me. It's like we're playing another one of our games. Who can catch the other staring?

Luckily, there are enough distractions that I'm able to catch my breath between rounds. Lola and Lexie wave at me from a few tables away while Sean and Henry are grabbing drinks at the bar. Daisy potters around in the background, checking each tray of starters before it goes out to the tables, and Finn asks me for the tenth time how the temperature in the room is.

Finally, the doors open one last time and Tom and Sophie enter hand in hand. The guests rise to their feet as they welcome the happy couple with a round of applause. I've never seen my brother look so handsome in his black suit, while Sophie's white-lace pencil dress drapes elegantly over her curvy frame, sitting just below her knees. They wave as they walk down the aisle before stopping at the bride and groom's table at the front of the room.

"Sophie and I want to thank you all for coming," Tom says, looping his arm around Sophie's waist and pulling her close. "This is a very special evening, and we wouldn't want to spend it with anyone else but our family and friends."

"We would also like to thank our good friend, Finn Ross, for hosting the event here at The Northwellian, as well as the actual wedding next week. And the wonderfully talented Daisy James and her team for creating the amazing meal that we'll be sharing tonight. Thank you both so much."

"Finn and Daisy mentioned in the same sentence," I mumble with a laugh. "Be careful. Something might burst into flame."

Anthony smiles politely. "Why, what's their deal?"

I realize Anthony isn't in on the intricacies of Finn and Daisy's relationship, and when I notice Blake chuckling, I wonder if he's thinking the same thing. You take for granted how simple a conversation is with someone who knows you back to front. After the starters, dinner is served, and Daisy's roast beef with seasonal vegetables are exactly what I need right now.

The table guests chat, between mouthfuls, about everything, from how beautiful the flowers are to how the big day is just around the corner. But all of that drowns out whenever I sneak a glimpse of Blake across the room. I'm still so mad at him, I know that in my bones, and I can't decide whether I want to rip him to pieces or just rip off his clothes. But either way, the power he has over me is agonizing, and I want more.

He's here alone. Maybe he feels the same. No sign of the redhead who stole my shirt. Perhaps bringing Anthony was over-dramatic. Or maybe it's just what Blake needs to show him he's not the only man in Lake Mistletoe who wants me.

When dinner is over, Tom and Sophie address their guests once more. "And to finish our evening, we would love you to join Sophie and me for a dance." Tom scratches the back of his neck. "God knows, I need the practice," he says, and the room laughs with him.

A soft, slow ballad fills the air and the lights dim above us. Tom and Sophie take a prime position in the center of the dance floor, and the guests applaud as they hold each other, their bodies melting into one, Sophie's head resting on Tom's shoulder as he kisses her brow. It's so romantic, and everything I didn't know I wanted.

Sean and Lexie are next, and slowly, couple by couple, the dance floor fills up. I'm so focused on catching glances of Blake between the shuffling bodies I don't notice Anthony standing beside me, holding out his hand.

"May I have this dance?"

I wince. "I'm not a great dancer. I believe the phrase 'god, my eyes' has been used to describe the way I dance."

"Perfect, because everyone says I look like I'm being electrocuted when I dance, so hopefully you being horrible will take the emphasis off me."

I laugh, and against my better judgment I take the hand he offers. Anthony draws me to my feet and leads me onto the dance floor. I stifle my laughter when he opens with a shimmy, followed by a rumba, before pulling me close to him. His hand finds my waist, while the other cups my fingers.

"There. That's not so bad," he says, his eyes meeting mine.

I gulp as my arm drapes over his shoulder. "No, not bad at all." Our bodies press closer until I can feel his heart racing in his chest.

"Mind stepping away from her?" a voice growls.

I know that voice, and I look up to see Blake standing there.

Anthony cocks an eyebrow. "Excuse me?"

"I said take a step back," Blake says. "She's not your girl."

Anthony doesn't shrink and keeps me in his grasp. "Are you saying she's your girl?" He turns to me. "Do you know this guy, Charlotte?"

I gulp, struggling to find my voice. "Anthony, this is Blake."

Anthony glares back at him. "Oh. You're Mr. Complicated. Well, sorry to disappoint you, Mr. Complicated, but Charlotte is here with me tonight."

Blake grumbles before reaching out and folding his hand around my wrist. "Char. Can we talk?"

"Hey. Don't touch her," Anthony snarls. "Charlotte, do you want me to kick this guy's ass?"

Blake grins and leans into Anthony, their heavy brows meeting. "Try it, asshole. You'll be out cold before you hit the ground."

I wrestle my wrist away from Blake's grasp. "Okay, that's enough testosterone for one night. Just calm down, the both of you."

"Wait, Char," Blake pleads, grabbing for my wrist again. "I need to explain."

"What the fuck is wrong with you?" Anthony snaps, standing between us. "She doesn't want to talk to you. Get that through your thick head."

Blake grits his teeth and lunges, grabbing Anthony by the collar of his jacket and clenching his fists. I've never seen such unhinged rage in his eyes as his chest heaves with breath. "Say one more word and I will fucking end you, you hear me?"

The room quietens to a hush as the quarrel catches everyone's attention. I see Sean and Henry moving toward us, weaving their way through the crowded dance floor.

"Blake, that's enough," I say, putting my hand on his forearm. "Not here."

Blake's breathing calms as my words stir him from his anger, and his eyes immediately seek out Sophie. I watch him crumble when he sees the disappointment welling in his sister's eyes.

Sean and Henry arrive and hook Blake's arms. "Come on," Sean says. "Let's get some air."

Blake shrugs them away. "No, wait."

Henry glares and grumbles, gripping Blake tight by the shoulder. "He said, let's get some air, Ward." Henry's voice is low and booms like thunder, and it's enough to stop Blake from fighting back.

"Let me just say something, Char," Blake continues to plead.

I wave him away. "You've said enough."

"Charlotte!" he exclaims.

The word catches me out. I'm not expecting it. It's just my name, something I hear dozens of times a day. But never from Blake. I've always been Char. Never Charlotte. And that sound from his lips sends a million butterflies dancing in my stomach.

"What?" I say, giving him the chance to fix this whole mess once and for all. "What do you want to tell me?"

Blake's mouth falls open. "I..."

"You what?" I ask. "Tell me."

All I want to hear is that he sees me. That he wants me. That I'm not just another notch, but something more. Not a proposal or a declaration of love. Just an acknowledgment that this is as real to him as it is to me.

He gulps. "Please, Charlotte. Can we go somewhere private?"

The butterflies fade and I shake my head. "Never mind." I nod at Sean and Henry, and they walk Blake toward the door without a fight, his head dropped against his chest.

My heart feels like it's in a million pieces as Blake leaves the hotel, and all I want to do is go home. I feel a hand grip my shoulder and, when I turn, Sophie is the last person I expect to see.

I go to apologize for ruining her night, but she cuts me off. "Give him a chance, Charlotte. He really cares about you."

I gulp and my eyes water. "I just wish he would tell me. I care about him, too."

14
Blake

As I'm up three stories in the frosty morning air with my teeth chattering and my balls frozen solid, I question whether or not this was a good idea. But hey, it's too late now. I blew it for the last time last night, and I'm done with letting Char slip through my fingers again and again.

The boom lift shudders and I grab the railing to brace myself as it steadies. I lean as far forward as I can, just enough for my knuckles to graze Char's sliding door. I tap against the glass, then rub my hands together to chase away the cold. What if she's not home? Shit, did I check? What if she's in the shower, or has headphones on or something? How long am I going to be standing here for?

Before I have time to spiral, the curtain draws back and Char curiously peers out her sliding door to the balcony, and when she sees me, suspended in midair, she screams. Char throws open the door.

"What are you doing out here!" She looks down and sees the boom lift, then looks back up at me. "What is going on, Blake?"

I steady myself enough to gesture to the bulky item beside me, wrapped in white cloth. "Since your elevator is always broken and your stairs are a nightmare, I thought I'd deliver a Christmas present to your balcony instead."

Her cheeks fill with warmth, and a twinkle of curiosity sparkles behind her brown eyes. I pull away the cloth and she lets out the most beautiful, excited laugh I've ever heard.

"My clock," she says.

I pop open the glass case, drawing attention to Joel's Mayhem shirt, swaying with the pendulum.

She frowns. "And my shirt."

"I didn't give it to Tamara," I blurt. "I told her it was over and she picked it up by mistake. You have to believe me. I would never have done that on purpose. Not when I know what this shirt means to you."

"You've cleaned out the jelly stain," Char says. "I liked that stain."

"No problem, I can make a brand new one for you."

She laughs. "Oh, yeah?"

"Yeah."

I lift my leg and step onto the railing, crouching while I heave my second leg up. Char gasps and puts her hands out.

"Are you crazy!" she shrieks.

"Can you not scream, Char? I'm trying to concentrate," I mumble as I slowly stand up straight, my legs wobbling as I balance three stories in the air. I hold my breath, and with one giant leap, I lunge for the balcony. Char screams when I hit the concrete, shoulder and hip first. "That looked much cooler in my imagination," I grimace.

"You dumbass," she snaps, but I can hear the laugh she's trying to stifle.

She kneels beside me, but I climb to my feet with a long, pained groan before I take her by the waist and pull her close to me.

"Charlotte. I want you. I've always wanted you. It took almost losing you to realize that, and I'll never make that mistake again. If you'll have me, I'll make sure you never doubt that my heart beats just for you, for the rest of your life."

Her arms slide around my neck, and I press my forehead against hers. "Do you hear me down there, Mistletoe?" I yell. "You're my witnesses. I have fallen for Charlotte Powell."

"Yeah, we hear you. Can we go home now?" a voice calls from the ground.

Char's eyes widen as she leans over the railing and looks down at the parking lot to find our friends looking back up at her.

"What are you all doing down there?" She laughs.

"Freezing our fucking asses off," Henry booms.

Lola slaps his arm. "Emotional support!"

Finn and Sean cheer, while Daisy and Lexie clap and shiver. I glance down just as Sophie snuggles against Tom and blows me a kiss.

"I want everyone to know that you're mine. No more hiding."

Char looks up at me. "You drag our friends out in the freezing snow so they can stand in a parking lot and watch us make out?"

I give a rakish grin. "We're going to make out?"

Char bites her bottom lip. "Oh yeah."

I look over the railing. "Thanks for coming out, everyone. Catch you later. Drive safe."

Char laughs, but the sweet sound fades when I press my lips against hers. I've been waiting to taste her for so long, and just the feel of her soft body in my arms has me hard as a rock in seconds. I walk her into her apartment, our lips sealed as we hungrily taste each other, our tongues darting back and forth. I feel Char's hand slide down my abdomen and encircle my shaft through my jeans.

"We don't have to," I whisper to her. "We've got the rest of our lives for that."

Suddenly Char shoves me roughly backwards, and I tumble onto the couch. She's silent as she spreads my legs and kneels before me, her eyes fixed on my belt. She undoes the notches and pulls the leather loose from the buckle, then slowly pops my buttons. When she peels back the denim, she finds my girth strangled by my black boxers, the outline of my member clearly defined. Char hooks the waistband and pulls, releasing my hard-on, and it startles even her when it flops against my abs.

Char licks her lips before taking my cock with both hands, and a drop of precum pearls at my tip just as her mouth envelops me. I groan and lean back on the couch, splaying my arms on the back of the cushions, but my gaze doesn't leave Char. I don't want to miss a thing.

Her head bobs up and down, her hands working in unison with her mouth so that every inch of me is taken care of all at once. As her pouting, perfect lips glide along my shaft, she pays special attention to my swollen head when she reaches the top, lapping and licking at every curve, and slurping at the drops of precum. Her saliva coats my dick, keeping it slick, and her hands work me faster. One hand slips away and cradles my balls as she takes me deep into her mouth, gagging when my bulbous head hits the back of her throat.

I reach down and grasp the base of her ponytail, holding her mouth just there for a while longer. I moan when her throat opens for me, and I slide myself deeper inside.

"Good girl, Charlotte," I mutter.

When it's time for her to take a breath, I pull back on her ponytail and she gasps, but I'm not done yet. I pull up and down, sliding her mouth back and forth over my cock. I'm so hard I can feel her lips catch every ridge. She's sucking me so good... I don't know how much longer I'm going to last.

"Do you want me to cum in your mouth again, Charlotte?" I ask her, my fingers still folded around her ponytail.

She looks up at me and drags the back of her hand across her mouth. "No," she murmurs, moving my hand away from her hair.

She stands up and I watch blissfully as she eases her pajama pants over her round hips and they drop in a pile at her ankles. Char kicks them away, then comes closer to me, her fingers trailing along her soft stomach and grazing the waistband of her pink panties.

"Can you help me take these off?" she asks.

Fuck yes I can. I nod and reach for her, gripping the sides in my fists and dragging them down her smooth skin. The tuft of hair above her crevice nearly has me cumming there and then. I lean forward to get her panties past her knees, nuzzling the hair with my nose on the way down. She lifts her feet one at a time for me, stepping out of her panties and I toss them aside, grabbing her by the ass and pulling that beautiful little pussy to my face.

My tongue dips between her sweet folds, and she gasps, burying her fingers in my hair. I grip the back of her thighs as I probe deeper with my tongue, flicking the tip against her swollen little bud. I could do this all day, but Char has something else in mind.

She pushes my head back and pins my shoulders to the couch before straddling me. She hovers over the head of my cock, her pussy sliding back and forth, her entrance tempting me to buck into her. Char leans forward and kisses me, and we breathe each other in. I slide my hands along her jaw, cupping her face and kissing her deep, and if I died right now, I'd die a happy man.

The anticipation builds inside me until at last, Char lowers herself onto my stiff cock, swallowing every inch of me, whimpering until she's taken me whole.

"You're so big," she moans into my ear.

"That's right, baby. Are you going to treat this big cock good?"

"Yes," she whimpers.

"Are you going to ride me, baby?" I ask.

She nods and lifts her hips, her soaking wet pussy gliding up my shaft before I sink back inside of her.

"Good girl, Charlotte. You're so fucking good," I growl. I grip her hips, guiding her motions as she grinds against me. She bucks faster, her tits bouncing underneath her pajama top, the two top buttons popping loose and a pretty pink nipple peeking out. I pull her closer, close enough to lap at her stiff nipple while she rides me. She's so fucking wet. I can feel her dripping onto my thighs as her ass slaps against my balls.

Char arches her back, leaning back on my knees as she rides me hard and fast. God, she looks so fucking beautiful, and she's all mine. I'm not giving her the option to pull out this time. I'm cumming inside her, hot and thick. My cock lengthens and I dig my fingers into her soft skin as I spurt inside her. After the first stream, I thrust, burying myself deeper in her pussy and grinding her against me as more of my seed fills her.

"Fuck," I growl after the last drop.

I fall back on the couch and Char falls with me, laying her head on my shoulder while her swollen pussy hugs my spent dick. I wrap my arms around her, holding her tight against me.

"Hey Charlotte," I whisper as I kiss her cheek.

"Mmmmm," she replies.

"Do you want to be my date to Tom and Sophie's wedding?"

I feel her warm lips against my neck. "Yes," she says.

Epilogue
Charlotte - Three Years Later

Standing in the dimly lit corridor, I feel a buzz of excitement and a surge of adrenaline rushing through me. The familiar and comforting scent of cold air and freshly polished ice fills my senses, just like any other night in the arena. But tonight is special. This isn't just any game. It's my debut for the Puffins. My first semi-pro hockey match. After years of hard work and training, I finally made it.

The weight of my hockey gear presses against my shoulders. As I adjust the grip on my stick and take a deep breath, I hear the echoes of the crowd grow louder, matching the rhythm of my heartbeat as I stride toward the ice. The anticipation is palpable, each passing second intensifying the energy thrumming within me.

I step onto the ice and straight away I know I'm home. Now it's time to show all these spectators how I earned this spot. As I glide, I position myself in front of the net, eyes locked on the puck. The seconds tick away, each one bringing me closer to a moment I've dreamt of my entire life.

A teammate maneuvers the puck toward me, and instinct takes over. With a quick, precise movement, I receive the puck on the blade of my stick. Time seems to slow as I assess the situation—the goalie poised for action, defenders closing in. In that moment, the training and countless hours of practice converge into a singular focus.

With a burst of speed, I make my move, weaving through the opposition. The ice feels alive beneath my skates, and the crowd's roar becomes a distant hum. As I approach the net, I wind up for the shot, the puck leaving my stick with a satisfying thud.

The arena holds its breath as the puck sails through the air, finding its mark with perfect accuracy. The goalie stretches, but the puck whizzes past, crashing into the back of the net. The crowd erupts in a deafening cheer, the sound reverberating through the arena, but it all fades in my ears. I close my eyes and see my dad's face beaming with pride, and that's all the praise I need.

I glance up at the scoreboard, and there it is--Charlotte Ward--my name illuminated beside the first goal of the game. I hate to be cocky, but it's an absolute stomping on the ice tonight. I'm carving up this ice like it's a canvas and I'm creating a masterpiece. I score another of the five goals that night, and the Puffins keep the Rovers scoreless in their own barn.

"Good game, Ward," Coach Cate says as I skate onto the bench.

I yank off my helmet and slap gloves with the other girls as they come off the ice. "Thanks, Coach," I pant, my sweat-soaked hair clinging to my neck.

The Puffin's goalie Libby hits the bench last, waddling past me with her leg pads.

"Not bad, Ward," she reiterates. "You coming out to dinner with the team after this?"

I nod. "Yeah. Totally. I just have to check in with my family before I go. They're in town for the game."

Libby smiles. "That's great. I'm looking forward to meeting them." She holds out her glove and I knock it with my own. "Good to have you on the team."

As I hit the changing rooms with the rest of the team, I still can't believe this is my life. It didn't come easy, and there were plenty of times I wanted to throw the whole idea in the trash. But there was one person who wouldn't allow that, who pushed me at training and the gym. Someone who would never give up on me, no matter how often I wanted to give up on myself.

I yank off my skates and turn to the bleachers, my eyes scouring the thinning crowd for the love of my life. He's easy to spot, being the most handsome man in the entire arena. He's already giving me that look with his brown eyes when I find him, and I feel my knees weaken when he smiles.

I heave myself up the stairs in my gear, and I can't wait to feel his arms around me and his lips on mine. He's on his feet by the time I reach him, but before I can get anywhere near his mouth, two chubby little arms reach for me, with ten sausage fingers grabbing for my hair.

"Say, congratulations, Mommy," Blake says in a squeaky voice, as our daughter Eliza wriggles in his hands.

Eliza giggles and gurgles when I scoop her into my arms and smother her neck-rolls with kisses. I hold her high in the air, gazing in awe at how her brown eyes sparkle and how her sandy-blonde hair falls in soft waves that frame her perfect, round face. If there's one thing Blake and I know how to do, it's make adorable babies.

Blake pulls the nappy bag over his shoulder before snaking his free arm around my waist and pulling me to his lips. He kisses me and I lose my breath. The way this man kisses gets me every time. Like ten thousand volts of bliss.

"Congratulations from Daddy too, Mommy," he says. "Maybe after Eliza goes down tonight, we can celebrate."

I shiver as his lips drag across my jaw and kiss me behind my ear. "Oh, so you liked what you saw then?"

"That slapshot was nice," he says. "You're welcome, by the way. You're distributing your body weight a lot better on your follow through."

I jiggle Eliza in the crook of my arm as she gets fussy. I need her to settle for just a minute so I can taste Blake's lips one more time. I grab him by the collar of his shirt and pull him down to me, and it feels like gliding on ice when we kiss.

"I wouldn't be here without you," I say.

He shakes his head. "You got here on your own, Char. You just let me come along for the adventure."

"How did I get so lucky?" I sigh.

Blake furrows his brow as he thinks. "I think it all began with an auction for a grandfather clock."

I laugh, and I'm quite content to just spend the evening with the two people I love most. Then Libby's voice echoes across the arena. "Hey, Ward. You coming?"

I let out a deep breath and look at Blake. "I can come back to the hotel. It's fine. I'm actually exhausted."

Blake rolls his eyes. "No you don't. This is your first victory as a pro hockey player. You're going out with your teammates and getting drunk and that's the last I want to hear about it." He holds his arms out to Eliza and she can't wait to get back to him. "Besides, Eliza and I have a hot date with pumpkin puree and Elmo, don't we?" He nuzzles into our baby's neck and she laughs as she holds his bristled face in her little hands.

I smile and wave at Libby. "Coming!" I kiss Blake's cheek one more time. "Thank you. I love you."

He looks at me, and it's as if he's gazing into my soul. "I love you, Charlotte."

In the end, I have to tear myself away from them, forcing my legs down the stairs toward the changing rooms where Libby and the other Puffins wait for me. Who would have thought that in three short years I'd have found my partner, given birth to a beautiful baby with his hair and my eyes, and signed a contract to play the sport I love? It wasn't easy, but nothing worth having ever is, and even though it all worked out in the end, I would recommend you keep an eye on that boy who makes a special effort to tease and taunt you. There's a damn good chance he's the love of your life.

The Gingerbread House

BOOK THREE
FINN AND DAISY

1

Daisy

You might think my job was perfect. I have the cutest little bakery called The Gingerbread House, right on the corner of Partridge Lane, just off the main street in Lake Mistletoe. I always stock the big display case in the front window with sugary treats, from cookies to cream puffs to chocolate éclairs. The peppermint striped awnings and red brickwork give my store a small town vintage charm, and I chose pink and red rose wallpaper for the inside that just makes it feel so sweet and cozy.

The building used to be the old post office, but after selling my soul to the bank for the next thirty years, it's all mine... kind of. I give the bank every cent I earn and they let me stay here with my baking equipment until it's paid off, and with the way my books are looking, I'll be piping cannoli until I'm ninety... if I'm lucky. Still. I'm my own woman, with my own business, and I absolutely love making delicious food and feeding people. But the paperwork part I could do without.

My office is at the back of the kitchen, and I can smell gingerbread cookies freshly baked out of the oven. It's a welcome distraction from the tower of invoices, receipts and bills stacked on my desk. I stare at my phone, willing it to ring as I tap my foot and chew on the end of a ballpoint pen.

Suddenly Cherry Bomb blares, and my phone violently vibrates, shimmying its way to the edge of my desk. I clamp my hand on top of it before mashing the buttons and putting it to my ear.

"Daisy James speaking," I say, hoping my big smile translates over the call.

"Yes. Daisy. It's Grace Ford from Ford and Drummer. How are you?"

My heart races. "Miss Ford. I'm great. How are you?"

"Now, now Daisy. We've known each other for quite some time now. I think we can forgo the formalities. Call me, Grace."

My anxiety eases. I went to high school with Grace, but with her holding my financial future in the palm of her hand, I didn't want to assume our history would benefit my loan application. I'll call her anything she wants to get a big 'APPROVED' stamp on my file.

"Grace. Of course. I've been looking forward to your call."

"I've looked over your business proposal, Daisy, and the idea of franchising The Gingerbread House is very exciting. Your outline for expanding the catering side of your business is attractive as well. All in all, it's a great proposal, and it looks like you've put a lot of effort into putting this together."

I can't shift the smile from my face. She's saying everything I want to hear and I grip the edge of my desk to stop from squealing excitedly. "Thanks, Grace."

There's a brief silence, and I hear her exhale over the phone.

"But I'm sorry to say that Ford and Drummer won't be able to facilitate your loan," she says at last.

My heart goes from racing to stopping flat and my stomach drops. "Oh," is all I can manage at first.

"Yes, unfortunately, we have some concerns around your numbers. We're not convinced you'll be able to repay the loan, based on your forecasts. To be honest, Daisy, they were a bit of a mess."

I give a soft, awkward laugh. "Numbers aren't my strong point."

"It shows," Grace replies bluntly. "Which is a shame, because apart from that, it was a good proposal and the samples you sent were delicious. The office devoured them. You're a wonderful cook. When you have your budgets and estimates a little tidier, I'll be happy to take another look at your application."

All I want to do is throw my phone in an oven and set it to explode. I wouldn't mind bitterly doing the same to Grace.

"Thanks. I'll do that," I say blankly, a numbness swallowing me up.

"Good luck, Daisy," Grace says before ending the call.

I still have the phone to my ear after she's gone as I stare vacantly ahead. Only when Anthony knocks on my door, do I snap out of my daze.

"Hey boss, did you want milk or dark chocolate ganache on these brownies?" he asks, but he jerks his head when he takes another look at me, and I hope he doesn't notice the welling behind my eyes. "You okay, boss?"

I put my phone on the desk. "I'm fantastic!" I exclaim, painting on my smile. "And let's go with milk chocolate today."

He salutes me and turns to leave, but swings back around almost immediately. "Heads up. That Finn guy just walked through the door."

I lean my elbows on the desk and pinch the bridge of my nose. "This morning is just getting better and better."

"Do you want me to kick him out?" Anthony asks.

I laugh, and as tempting as that might be, my promise to Sophie is always at the forefront of my mind. I'm going to make her wedding the most special day of her life, and that means getting along with the venue manager, Finn, regardless of what an asshat he is.

"I appreciate the offer, but it's fine," I say. "Can you hold down the fort while I deal with him, though?"

Anthony nods and heads back to the kitchen, and I notice him glare at Finn as they pass each other. Anthony's great, and I'm glad I hired him. He would have been perfect for Charlotte, too. I still can't believe she's with Blake. Charlotte is so sweet and Blake is so.... Blake. But as long as she's happy, I'm happy. Although, at the rate people are coupling up in this town, it could line me up with wedding gigs for years. Maybe I should put that on my next loan application.

Finn stops at the door and taps on the glass, poking his head in. "Is this a bad time?"

I force a smile. I want to say that anytime is a bad time with him, but I hold my tongue. Sophie. Sophie. Sophie. I repeat in my head. "Of course not, Finn. Do come in."

He almost fills the doorway when he enters the room, his broad, towering frame poured into an Armani suit. His thick, light brown hair is tousled just enough to be effortlessly charming, and even though I can't stand him, I can't deny the magnetic effect of his warm brown eyes. When he sits opposite me, he unbuttons his jacket and swipes it to the side, before widening his legs and leaning back in the chair, a stern expression plastered across his rugged, angled face.

"To what do I owe the pleasure?" I ask as I cross my legs, my red pencil skirt riding up my thigh. I tap my pen in my hands. "Is something wrong?"

Finn takes a breath and retrieves a tablet from his satchel. "I've been going over the numbers you sent me yesterday, and I don't know how we're going to make them work."

I swear, if someone mentions numbers to me one more time, I will beat them to death with my wooden spoon. Sophie. Sophie. Sophie.

"Which part?" I say, my jaw clenching.

Finn flips open the tablet and swipes at the screen. "Well, going by the amount of food being served and the number of guests attending, we don't have enough wait staff for starters."

I shrug. "Okay. I'll hire more."

Finn frowns. "There's no budget for more. You've already overspent on the main course as it is."

"Surely the Northwellian has servers that can help," I say.

"Help?" Finn says, almost choking. "You expect them to work for free?"

"Of course not. Can't you take care of that?"

"I just told you, Daisy. The budget won't allow for hiring any more servers. As it is, Sean and Blake are supplying the alcohol at cost because you didn't budget for that either."

"Well, at least they're helping," I say, and Finn's brown eyes grow more irate.

"This is a business arrangement, Daisy, not Habitat for Humanity. Vendors expect to be paid, and right now, you are in the red." He flips his tablet closed and grumbles. "You need to tell Tom and Sophie."

I gulp. "Tell them what?"

He folds his thick arms over his chest, straining the dark fabric. "Frankly, that you're completely mismanaging this."

"But you're the venue manager," I argue. "Isn't that your job?"

Finn shakes his head and his smug laugh makes me want to slap him across the face with a baking tray.

"I handle the hotel, Daisy. I make sure the facilities suit the client's needs, but you're the caterer. Staff, menu, food and alcohol budget and delivery, that's your responsibility. How do you not understand that?"

I can feel sweat building at my nape as he glares relentlessly. I suddenly feel very foolish thinking I could go from running a small town bakery to catering a two-hundred person wedding without batting an eyelash. God. I don't want to let Sophie down, and I sure as hell don't want to tell her I the mess I've made, especially after promising everything would be perfect.

I look at Finn with venom. I can guarantee he's loving this. Seeing me fail. I'm surprised he hasn't told Tom and Sophie already. Swooping in to save the day while making me look like an incompetent amateur. Damn it! I hate him so much! But he's got me over a barrel.

"Just give me a day to sort this out," I say, and I can't believe I have to compromise with him. "Sophie is really stressed right now, and I don't want to add to that."

Finn nods. "Tom says he's having to take her to his family's cabin almost every weekend. She's wound tight. It's the only place that relaxes her."

"Exactly," I say. My eyes plead with him. "Let me try to fix this. If I can't, then I'll tell Sophie myself."

Finn stares at me, and the seconds feel like hours. He returns his tablet to his satchel and stands up, fastening his button with one hand. "Fine. I'll give you a day. But if you can't fix this, you're telling Sophie straight away, or I will."

I glare. "Yes, Finn. I understand."

He exhales and drops his chin. "You brought this on yourself, Daisy. Maybe you're just not cut out for running a business. I'll call you tomorrow." He turns and heads out the door.

"Can't wait," I yell after him, the bell on the door jingling as he exits the shop.

When he's gone, I shriek, hurling my pen at the wall and kicking at my desk with the heel of my black pump. I don't know what's worse. Disappointing Sophie or having to beg Finn to keep his mouth shut. We've known each other since we were kids. You'd think that would earn me some brownie points. The way this day is shaping up, I'd even take pity. But as Call Me Grace painfully reminded me, history doesn't account for shit in business.

There's one thing that keeps me from giving up, and that's Me. Finn is wrong. I can cut it. It might not be pretty, and I'll definitely make mistakes along the way, but I'll get there, because this is my dream, and nothing will stop me from chasing it down. Not even Finn with his tablet and his spreadsheet.

Suddenly, I have a flashback to Phillip Meyer's fifteenth birthday party. About thirty hormone-riddled-full-sugar-soda-hyped-tweens in a basement blasting Uptown Funk and stuffing themselves with pizza rolls. It doesn't take long for a game of spin-the-bottle to break out and before I know it, the chubby girl with the frizzy blond hair and braces, that would be me, and the tall, gangly boy in the Bruins shirt are sitting at either end of a coke bottle. Our friends swiftly herd us into a closet, where we sit awkwardly in the pitch dark while they chat and giggle right outside the door.

God, I remember it so clearly.

"Hey. I'm Finn," he says, his voice trembling.

I'm just as nervous when I reply with, "I'm Daisy."

He gulps. "So, do we kiss now?"

I cringe just thinking about it. If only I could go back in time. I would never have gone to Phillip's party, and maybe then I would never have met Finn.

2

Finn

I tighten my scarf when I leave the bakery, a pocket of snow shaking loose from the awning and dusting my hair as I close the door. Of one thing, I'm certain. Daisy James is the worst businessperson I have ever met. She doesn't pay attention to simple things like estimates, cost, staff, resources, or time-lines. Yes, her food is amazing, and whenever I could sneak away from hosting Tom and Sophie's rehearsal, I stuffed myself rotten with her cream puffs. You can taste the care she puts into everything she makes. But there's not going to be anyone to enjoy it if she can't figure out the staffing issues or fix the budget. And I meant what I said. If she doesn't tell Tom and Sophie. I will.

I glance at my watch. I've got another meeting in a couple of hours, but the way I'm feeling right now has me wound up. Do I have time to smack a couple of pucks at the rink? I glance at my watch again. My gear is always in my truck. If I head straight there, I can let off some steam and still make my meetings. It's decided then. I quicken my pace to my red truck in the bakery parking lot and climb inside, rubbing my hands together for warmth as I fumble the keys in the ignition. I look up and see Daisy's office window straight ahead of me, and between the blinds I just make out her curvy frame, pacing back and forth.

I exhale. She's probably pissed and hates me more than she already did. But our relationship has never been sugar and spice and all things nice. Not since. Shit. When was it? I shudder as I start the engine. Philip Meyer's fifteenth birthday party. Who would have thought that seven minutes in heaven would end up being eight years of hell?

I feel a sharp jab in my chest when I see her slump into her chair and bury her face in her hands. I straighten my shoulders and clear the lump in my throat. She should have thought about this before taking on Tom and Sophie's wedding. This is strictly business and I'm here to do a job. Not concern myself with Daisy's feelings. I throw my truck in gear and roar out of the parking lot before I can see any more of her sulking.

I head to the arena, sitting through some Christmas shopping traffic when I pass the Mistletoe strip mall. I arrive at the rink and recognize the midnight blue Range Rover parked close to the entrance. Looks like Henry is playing a little hookie as well. Good. It'll help burn off some of this frustration if he can add some physical defense.

I grab my bag from the back seat and jump out of my truck, trudging through the snow until I reach the doors of the arena. The Mayhem mascot, a white snow leopard wearing a red helmet, emblazons the overhead signage. I love this place, and I love this team. I was a Magpie in high school, and I may not end up in the National League, but my Friday night games with the Mayhem are more than enough for me. I've been on the team for four years, and captain for the last two.

There's always this hollow echo when the arena is empty. When I close the doors behind me, it's like thunderclaps, and my footsteps reverberate through the stands. I spot Henry already on the ice, and if I didn't know this big, hulking guy, I might be tempted to turn around and leave rather than share the rink with him. Actually, even if you know Henry, that might be the right thing to do. He's not exactly a ray of sunshine. But he's a good friend, a great veterinarian, and the most terrifying goalie in the league. I'm just glad he's on my team.

I take a seat on the bench and drop my bag at my feet, fishing out my skates. I make a quick switch out of my shoes and take off my work blazer, then roll up the sleeves of my white business shirt. When I'm almost done, Henry notices me and skates over.

"Hey, Cap. What are you doing here?" he asks, his voice like gravel.

"Just need to have a skate. Clear my mind. What about you?"

His shoulders drop and he grumbles. "Same. Lost a bunny this morning."

I raise an eyebrow, but know better than to pull his chain. Henry genuinely cares about the animals he treats. "Sorry to hear that, man."

He shrugs. "What about you? What happened?"

I lace up my skates and frown. "Met with Daisy this morning, and it went as well as it always does."

With my skates on, Henry extends his big hand and pulls me up from the bench. I follow him onto the ice.

"What's the deal with you two?" he asks as he skates towards the goal. "You must have some epic back story to explain this hate you have for each other."

I keep forgetting Henry is new in town. He fit in so quickly with me and the team that it feels like he's always been here. But being a newbie means he missed out on all the fun and games of Phillip Meyer's fifteenth birthday party, but more specifically, what happened the week after.

"You don't want to know," I say, resting my stick across the back of my shoulders.

Henry grabs his mask off the net and pulls it over his stubbled face. He picks up his stick, leaning against the boards, then tosses a puck at me before setting himself up in front of the goal.

"No. I don't want to know. But if it pisses you off some more, you'll really hurl these pucks at me and I can get some good stopping practice in."

The puck skids across the ice before it stops against my skate. I nod my head and tap the blade of my stick on the ice. "Fair enough." I line the puck up, narrowing my eyes on Henry as he fills the net like a yeti. "It all started at Phillip Meyer's fifteenth birthday party," I start, before smacking the puck with all my might.

Henry effortlessly snatches it out of the air, and even through his mask, I can see the disappointment. He tosses it back at me, and I line it up again.

"Someone started a game of spin-the-bottle, and it ends up pointing at me and Daisy. I'd seen her around school, but we never talked or anything like that."

"What was she like back then?" Henry asks, widening his stance as he waits for my next attempt.

A smile creeps across my mouth from nowhere when I remember her back then. "She was cute," I say. "She had braces, and this frizzy blond hair, and her eyes... she has the most amazing blue eyes." I check myself and clear my throat. "Had... she had the most amazing blue eyes," I correct. I fire the puck again, harder this time, and though Henry still catches it, it knocks him a little off balance. He tosses it back to me.

"Then what happened?"

I move the puck around with my stick as I recall. "So we're locked in this closet, and they tell us we have to stay in there for seven minutes."

"Seems like a precise amount of time," Henry says.

I line up the puck. "So we're in this closet, and it's super awkward. We say nothing for the first minute, but eventually, we introduce ourselves. Now there's no rule saying we have to kiss, but even in the dark, she is just crazy pretty, and I think that maybe I want to kiss her."

"Sounds a little inappropriate. A girl being locked in a closet with you and forced to kiss."

"No, that's what I'm saying. We didn't have to, but I kind of wanted to, and I think she kind of wanted to as well," I say.

Henry lifts his mask and frowns at me. "We don't need to have a talk about consent, do we, Finn?"

"It wasn't like that!" I grumble, slapping the puck, which goes completely off target and hits the boards.

Finn groans and fishes a spare puck out of the net, tossing it to me. "Good. Then what happened?"

The puck makes its way to the edge of my skate and suddenly I feel lightheaded. I look at Henry. "If I tell you something, can you keep it between you and me?"

"Sure," he nods. "As long as it's not something weird. I'll tell the police immediately if it is."

"You remember when the team went on that submersible last summer when we played down south?"

"Yeah. You were sick or something," Henry says.

I exhale. "Truth is, being in enclosed spaces terrifies me. It feels like everything gets smaller, crushing me like I'm in a trash compactor and I can't breathe."

"You're claustrophobic." Henry says.

"Apparently, and I discover this during minute four. At first I think I'm just nervous about kissing Daisy, but then I start sweating and my throat tightens up. Now I'm thinking about my buddies outside, and how embarrassed I'll be running out of this closet having a panic attack."

"What does Daisy do?" Henry asks.

I smile. "That's the thing. She puts her hand on my back and tells me to breathe. She tells me to close my eyes and imagine I'm in the arena, on the ice, with everyone cheering for me." My chest heaves with warmth as I remember the softness of her voice at my ear. "And it passed."

I smack the puck, but rather than slicing through the air, it ambles its way across the ice, sliding to a stop just in front of the net.

Henry frowns. "I thought you were going to get angry when you told this story. This sounds like a show on the Disney channel." He kicks the puck at me with a disgruntled groan.

"Oh, we're getting there," I promise when the puck returns to me. "We decide not to kiss..."

"I'm actually relieved to hear that," Henry interrupts.

"So we just talk and it's awesome. We talk so much that when the closet door opens and thirty kids stick their heads in to catch us kissing, we're disappointed because now we have to go back to what was a mediocre birthday party if we're being honest." I line up the puck again. "Anyway, we plan to meet up at school and, you know, maybe go on an actual date that's not in a closet." I exhale. "Then shit falls apart."

I smack the puck and it speeds at Henry and when it hits his glove, he stumbles backwards in the net.

"That's more like it," he laughs, throwing it back to me.

"Some guys at school hassle me, asking if I need a night light at bedtime, or if mommy and daddy check under my bed for monsters." I line up the puck. "Then my friends say Daisy's telling the entire school I'm scared of the dark and that I nearly pissed myself in the closet."

I slap the puck again, and this time when it drives for the corner, Henry needs to fully extend himself to grab it before it hits the net. He groans as he stretches his arm, pulling it in just in time. He nods approvingly before throwing it back to me, but the lifts his mask again, his eyebrows knitted together.

"Why would she say that if she was trying to clam you down?" he asks.

I feel a lump lodge in my throat as I move the puck left and right with my stick. If I'm telling the story, it should probably be the whole truth.

"I might have said something to my friends after the party that got back to her," I mumble.

Henry frowns. "What did you do?"

I smirk. "Really? Not too Disney channel for you?"

He shrugs. "Well, I'm fucking invested now, aren't I? What did you say about Daisy?"

I line up the puck, but the will to smack the shit out of it is fading. "My friends asked if we made out..."

Henry's stare is pointed. "Yeah."

"And they just kept asking, saying how cool I'd be if we had."

Henry groans. "Yeah."

I lift my stick off the ice and rest it along the back of my shoulders again. "So I said we did."

Henry shakes his head. "You dick."

"I was a kid!" I say in my defense. "Just a stupid dumb kid trying to look cool in front of his friends. It was Daisy who kicked it up a notch when she told everyone I was afraid of the dark."

"I don't think that'll hold up in court," Henry grumbles. "And you're full-grown adults now, at least biologically."

My shoulders slump. "It was years ago. We could have fixed it, but we're both just too proud, I guess. Feels like it's too late now."

I see Henry taking off his mask and gloves, and I get the feeling that practice is finished. He skates towards me and skids to a stop.

"Well, that was depressing, but I guess I asked, so that's my fault. I'm going back to work. I've got a chinchilla with a cold coming in at 2pm." He heads back to the bench, but pauses and looks at me over his shoulder. "If you need a night light, I keep one in the recovery room for the animals that need to stay over. It's a rotating moon with stars and planets. All yours if you need, big guy."

"Sure, why not? I mean, that recovery room will be empty tonight anyway, won't it, bunny killer?" I chirp with a grin.

Big Henry's brow drops and his eyes darken as he swings around to face me. "What the fuck did you say, Ross?"

For a second, I forgot who I was dealing with. Apparently, Henry's the only one allowed to chirp, and that's fine by me.

"Nothing!" I blurt. "Have a great day at work."

Henry turns his back on me and continues to the bench. He's right. Telling him the details of mine and Daisy's past didn't make me feel any better. In fact. Now I'm thinking about her even more. I try to shirk the thoughts away. That's it. I'm going to tell Tom and Sophie about the budget. Then this woman will finally be out of my hair. Tom mentioned last night they were heading to their cabin for a couple of days, so I guess I'm heading there, too.

3

Daisy

Time seems to crawl by. Every time I look at my watch after what feels like hours, only minutes have passed, and I know it's because of this guilt swirling around in my belly like bad seafood chowder. Should I tell Sophie that things aren't going as well as I've been leading on? The last thing I want to do is ruin her special day. I'd rather slide buck naked and tummy down across Lake Mistletoe than upset her. But if there's even the slightest chance something could go wrong, she deserves to know. Even if she ends up hating me because of it.

I slam my fist on the workbench and startle Anthony, who jumps a foot in the air and squirts his piping bag of vanilla frosting all over a batch of cupcakes.

"What!" he shrieks.

"I'm going out," I state, untying my apron. "You're the boss."

He tips his chin at the radio blaring in the background. "In this weather? The snow's going to pour down soon."

I roll my eyes. "They say that all the time. Don't worry."

I hurry into my office and lean over my desk to grab my phone. Sophie's taken time off work at the kindergarten leading up to the wedding, which means she could be anywhere. I search her name and dial her number, and each ring feels like a death knell. I'm slightly relieved when she doesn't answer. I call Charlotte next. She might know where Sophie is.

Charlotte answers. "Hey Daze, what's up?"

"Nothing much. How are you?"

"She's got her hands full right now, Daisy," a man calls in the background.

Charlotte laughs and I cringe, recognizing Blake's voice immediately.

"Sorry about that," Charlotte says, stifling her giggles. "What do you need?"

"I'm looking for Sophie," I say, hoping the loved up couple can't hear my eye rolls. "Have you seen her?"

"Pretty sure she's at the cabin," Charlotte replies.

I hear kissing in the background and gag. "The cabin?"

"Yep," Charlotte confirms, giggling again. "That's where they were when I spoke to Tom this morning, but his phone cut out. The reception is terrible."

"Okay, thanks. I'll head up there now."

"Is everything okay?" Charlotte asks.

"Oh, sure," I say, my tone arching. "Everything's great."

"Good," Charlotte sighs. "The wedding's so close. Sophie would probably have a meltdown if something went wrong now."

If it were possible for me to feel any more like a piece of shit, Charlotte just flushed me.

"Okay, thanks for that, Charlotte. Bye now."

I end the call and pinch the bridge of my nose when I feel a migraine swelling behind my eyes. Off to the cabin, I guess. I grab my bag and keys, and when I come back into the kitchen, Anthony still appears unconvinced.

"Okay, so maybe I'm new around here. It seems to snow a lot anyway, but boss, have you forgotten that your car is on its deathbed? I practically had to Fred Flintstone that trash-heap when it broke down on the way back from the grocery store."

I frown. "You didn't put in your resume that you were a drama queen, and if this is a hint to buy a new work van, then forget about it. I've got enough to deal with." I march past him, but pause to snatch a cupcake from his tray. I take a huge bite, my eyes rolling back in my head. "Jesus, this is delicious, Anthony, you're very talented," I mumble with my mouth disgustingly full, before carrying on through the pink and red rose wallpapered shop front and out the door.

My car is in the parking lot out back and every time I lay eyes on my lady Sharona, I'm reminded of how desperately I need a new car. She was a birthday present when I turned seventeen and if she was a fixer-upper back then, she's ready for the scrap heap now. But every penny I've ever had, I've invested into The Gingerbread House. A new car is way at the bottom of the list, right below a decent bra with underwire that's not trying to amputate my boobs.

I jog to Sharona, which is such a rare sight that this must be important, and climb inside. I kick open the glove box and a dozen disposable hand warmers tumble onto the passenger seat. As I start up Sharona and wait for the engine to defrost, I tear open the hand warmer's packaging and strategically place them inside my clothes. One between my thighs, one under each arm, and another held tightly between my hands. A puff of thick, black smoke from the exhaust pipe lets me know she's ready to hit the road, whether she likes it or not, so I crunch the gearstick into drive, hit the squeaky gas pedal and with a sputter off we go.

The main street is gorgeous as always, with red velvet ribbons and bows wrapped around the streetlamps and a wreath hanging from every shop door. Folks weighed down with either shopping bags or children, litter the snowy sidewalk, and I can make out Rockin' Around The Christmas Tree crackling out of the old tinny township speakers. It might be clearer if I wind down my window, but the handle fell off years ago. I have to open the door to place my drive-through orders.

Still. Sharona will get me there. She always does. She might break down for Anthony, but she knows when I'm behind the wheel. I smell smoke, that means it's time to dig the hand warmer out from between my thighs, which is the most heat I've had down there for a while, and as the main street traffic clears and I set eyes on the rural road past town, I question whether or not this is a good idea. But there's no turning back now. Literally. It's best to keep Sharona moving in a straight line, otherwise she gets bitchy.

I pass the arena. God, I could really demolish a rink hot dog right now. But there's time enough for that later. Soon the township is in my rearview, and the wide open road framed with snow dusted pines stretches out before me. The cabin has been in the Powell family since the town was settled, or at least that's the story Tom likes to tell. For a place that's existed so long, he seriously needs to take to it with a hammer and a paintbrush. Rustic is an understatement. Last time I was up there, I fell through one of the porch steps, which was a great curvy girl nightmare I manifested for myself. But Sophie insists it's perfect the way it is, and at the end of the day, it's Tom's job to make sure she's happy. To hell with anyone else. Plus, who am I to judge? I'm literally driving a dumpster on wheels. At least the cabin has hot water.

I'm about halfway there and the road gets steep and Sharona is not having it. The engine groans and grinds and even though my foot is pushed all the way to the floor, she's barely moving.

"Come on, girl!" I plead, putting all my weight behind the gas pedal. "We're almost there! You can do it!"

Sharona replies with a big Fuck You as she sputters to an abrupt stop and I'm almost certain I hear the engine drop right onto the road.

I slump back in the driver's seat. "Great."

I fumble around in my bag and dig out my phone, navigating straight to Charlotte's number. But when I hit call, nothing. I check the signal. No bars. Shit. I spin around in my seat, looking up and down the long road, but there's not a soul in sight, let alone another car. Quickly, panic sets in. Am I going to have to walk? I'm reminded of Anthony's weather warning, which I'm taking seriously all of a sudden. Oh god, I don't want to die out here. I'm wearing a massive pair of underwear. It's laundry day.

While I'm debating whether to brave the cold in my pencil skirt and black pumps, I hear an engine revving in the distance. Sounds like a truck coming up the mountain. Yes!

I push against the door and it opens with a long creak, and by the time I clamber out I catch sight of a red truck under a veil of falling snow. I strain my eyes. Lake Mistletoe is a small town, but I'm sure there's more than one red truck. It comes closer and I pretend I don't recognize the head of thick chestnut hair behind the steering wheel, and wide shoulders like a cliff's edge.

The truck rolls to a stop behind Sharona, and I take a deep breath when Finn steps out into the snow.

"Car trouble?" he asks.

I fold my arms to keep warm. If only the anger steaming in the pit of my stomach was hot enough to heat my whole body.

"Yes. Obviously," I sneer.

Finn swipes the snow from his brow and looks up the mountain. "You headed to the cabin?"

I realize that apart from the cabin, there's little else this way. So what's Finn doing here?

"Yeah. What about you?" I ask suspiciously.

He pulls back his shoulders and puts his hands on his hips. "Actually, I was going to talk to Tom and Sophie about the situation."

I glare. "You were going to give me more time."

He shrugs and looks away from me. "I just think they should know."

I stare daggers at him. If he thinks I'm going to let him tell Tom and Sophie his version of events, he's got another thing coming.

"Well, you can't talk to them, because I'm going to talk to them first," I snap.

"Oh, really?" he laughs smugly. "How are you planning on getting there before I do?"

"I'm not," I say, swaying my head side to side and giving him the eyes. "We'll get there together because you are giving me a ride."

"I am, am I?" he says.

I take a step forward. "Yes. You are, and when we get there, we will sit down like adults and have a real conversation to sort this whole mess out."

"Will we?" he scoffs.

I take another step and now I'm right in front of him. "Yes. We will. Because Tom and Sophie are our friends, and making sure this is the best day of their lives is what matters more than anything. More than you, or me, or even my giant fuck up, and because for some reason, you would rather drive all the way up here to see me fail, then actually try to help me fix this." I poke his chest and try not to get distracted by how firm he is under his shirt. "So open your passenger door like a gentleman and drive us to the cabin now!"

Finn gulps and I can see the cogs moving as he tries to find something to say. But in the end he just coughs and nods, and opens the passenger door for me. To be honest, I'm surprised that worked. I grab my bag from Sharona and don't bother to lock her up before climbing into Finn's truck. If someone steals her, they'd be doing me a favor.

As soon as my butt hits the heated seats in Finn's truck, I relax, melting into the leather. But when he jumps in beside me, I sit up straight and look out the window. I don't want him to know for a second that this is the nicest car I've ever been in.

He closes his door and starts the engine, pulling his truck back onto the road as we continue up the mountain. He turns the heat on, and I can't help but feel that it's for my benefit.

I feel something sticking to my thighs and reach under, retrieving a flyer from the seat. I hold it out in front of me. Pucks for Presents. Holiday Charity Hockey Game Friday Night. Your Mistletoe Mayhem vs Southills Sabres.

"This is a good cause," I remark. "So couldn't have been your idea."

Finn frowns. "Actually, it was the team's idea. All ticket sales go towards buying Christmas parents for kids having a tough time."

I wish I could say something extra bitchy, but it's genuinely a decent thing they're doing, so I stay silent. For now.

"That was a real mouthful out there," he says. "Been holding onto that long?"

There's the asshole. Now I get to talk..

"About eight years," I reply tersely, although I'm relishing the relief of the heat crawling up my stiff legs. "Not much has changed with you, Finn. You're still so desperate to maintain your reputation and impress people you don't care who gets hurt in the crossfire."

I hear him grumble. "That's not what this is."

"What is it then?" I ask. "Because I've been having flashbacks to Phillip Meyer's closet since I saw you this morning."

His hands tighten on the steering wheel. "Me too."

He looks me in the eye and a strange tingle sweeps between my legs. I assume the flashback is as triggering for him as it is for me, but I can't shake the feeling we're not remembering it the same way. When I can't keep eye contact with him for another second, I turn and look blankly out the window, but I can still feel his eyes flitting back and forth between me and the road.

I gulp as sweat beads at my temples. What is going on? We're silent for the rest of the drive.

4

Finn

Why is Daisy always so pushy? She drives me crazy the way she orders people around like she runs the place, when in reality she's the most incompetent, infuriating person I've ever met. The fact The Gingerbread House hasn't fallen under is a miracle. She shuffles in the passenger seat and her skirt inches up around her thick thighs. That's another thing driving me crazy. Those black stockings hugging the sweeping curves of her legs and the way she looks walking around in those heels. I jerk my head roughly and clear my throat, fixing my eyes to the road in front of us. Focus, Finn. It was seven minutes in a closet eight years ago. Grow the fuck up.

The silence is deafening, which is just fine by me. She was out of line mouthing off about my need to impress. That couldn't be further from the truth. I've worked damn hard to get where I am today, and I will not risk my reputation on Daisy's ineptitude. Once Tom and Sophie know the truth, I'll never have to speak to her again.

She coughs and I look over just in time to see her breasts heave when she clears her throat. I glimpse her black lace bra beneath her blouse and the tantalizing sight is enough to send a surge of electricity through my shaft. I look away before she catches me gawking like a creep. What is happening? Once again, I train my eyes on the road ahead. The cabin should only be a few minutes away. Please God, let it only be a few minutes away.

As if an answer to my prayers, Tom's cabin appears over the rise, tucked away amongst a dense crop of pines. The sort of place you'd only be able to find if you knew were to look. I hit the gas, keen to get there as soon as possible. The sharp jolt startles Daisy and she's flung forward. I grimace. Of course she hasn't put her seat belt on. Instinctively, my arm flies out to catch her before she hits the dash, and though I manage to stop her from getting hurt, I've ended up with a handful of Daisy's breast in the process.

In any other situation, having this gorgeous, soft mound in my hand would be a dream come true. But not when it's attached to the woman whose level of hate for me is something normally reserved for terrorists. And for whatever reason, I'm not letting go. I'm staring right at her and not letting go.

Daisy furrows her brow. "Do you mind?"

Her glare is enough to snap me into reality, and I swiftly release her. "Fuck. Sorry."

She adjusts herself and does up the two top buttons of her blouse, tucking away that sexy black bra. Good. It was a distraction.

"Are we there yet?" she nags.

I point up ahead. "Yeah. It's right there."

The first thing I notice is that Tom's truck isn't parked out front. That's enough of a red flag to get me worrying I've driven all the way out here for nothing. As if she's in my head, which she has been far too much lately, Daisy pipes up.

"Tom's truck isn't here. Does that mean they're not here?"

I shrug. "Only one way to find out."

Daisy groans. "I swear to God, if I've come all this way for nothing, I'm going to be pissed."

I'm not going to agree with her out loud, but I feel exactly the same.

My truck roars over the snowbank, and I'm sure it's deeper than usual. I can't even see the tracks from Tom's truck with the latest dusting. I turn off the engine and peer towards the dormant cabin, noticing no smoke wafting from the chimney. Another red flag.

"Wait here," I tell Daisy. But that goes as well as you'd expect.

"And let you run your mouth to Tom and Sophie without me there? No way," she snaps.

I sigh. "I don't think they're here. Let me go check so you don't freeze out there."

She shakes her head vehemently and throws the door open. "And what if they are there, huh? I'm not risking it. Not today, pal."

She throws her legs over the seat and leaps into the snow. I'm not surprised by the tirade that follows.

"Stupid damn snow. Stupid damn shoes. Shit. I'm stuck," she yells.

I roll my eyes and unclip my seat belt, then take my time getting out the driver's door and making my way around to her side. That's where I find her flailing her arms around, knee deep in the snow. I dip my chin and try to conceal my laugh behind my hand, but that just seems to make her more mad.

"Are you just going to stand there, or are you going to help?" She catches herself and frowns at me. "Oh wait. Isn't that what you're good at? Not helping?"

I turn my back on her and take a step towards the cabin, but she calls out immediately.

"Wait!"

I look over my shoulder at her shivering in her snow hole. "Yes?"

Finally, she spits it out. "Can you help me? Please."

I turn around and trudge through the snow to her, then hold out my hands. "Of course. I'm not a monster."

Daisy grips my wrists, and I pull until she pops free, falling into my arms. Her body presses against me and I'm suddenly much warmer than I was a second ago, the sweet floral scent of her hair strong despite the frigid cold. It's happening again. I should let her go, or at least set her upright and walk away. But I'm not. I'm holding her, and she feels so perfect in my arms. It's Daisy who pushes away first.

"Thanks," she mutters, forcing the words past her clenched teeth.

"My pleasure," I reply, but that's not what I wanted to say. I wanted to say, whatever, or even better, nothing at all. Even Daisy doesn't know how to take my response. Now she's looking at me like I've got two heads. "I mean. Whatever."

Oh, God. I can't believe I'm still talking. All I want to do is dive headfirst into that snow hole she made and have her fill it in. But instead of something snide, she laughs, and the sound is like soft wind chimes in my ears.

"Are you okay, Finn? You're acting kind of... weird."

I frown at her grumpily. "I'm just cold from standing out here, pulling your butt out of snowbanks. Can we get inside?"

She stifles another laugh and nods. "Okay. Fine. Let's go then."

There's a snowflake on her red nose and it's taking all the restraint I possess to not brush it away. I quickly turn and head for the cabin before my resolve crumbles. I hear her trudging along behind me and soon we're up the stairs and on the porch, just as the snow comes down heavier.

I blow into my cupped hands, trying to warm them up before knocking on the door. The glass rattles in the wood, and the door shakes more than it probably should. This place could really use some repairs.

"Tom. Sophie," I call, knocking again. "Are you two there?"

"No one's home," Daisy adds, standing on tiptoes to peek over my shoulder.

"Hold on," I groan. I knock once more. "Tom. It's me, Finn."

"And Daisy," she yells right in my ear.

I grimace. "Can you give me some room here?"

"They're not here," Daisy moans. "Open the door. I'm freezing!"

"I don't have a key," I reply.

She pushes me aside and grabs hold of the handle. "This place is in worse shape than Sharona." She gives the door a shove, and it clicks, then falls open with a creak. "See." Daisy hurries inside, breathing warm breath into her hands. "Come inside and close the door!"

I reluctantly enter and don't so much close the door behind me as jam it back in the frame. A mustiness hangs in the cold air, and the peeled wallpaper and faded paint adds to how well-worn this place feels. Old, tattered curtains sway gently in a breeze that's creeping through the loose boards, I imagine, offering glimpses of the snow-covered surrounds.

The furniture, though aged and a bit rickety, has a kind of unique charm. A wooden table in the center of the room, and mismatched chairs around it. A faded quilt, folded haphazardly over the back of a tired old orange couch. Then there's the little kitchen, its solid wood counters marked by years and years of scratches and nicks, and most of the cupboards dangling loose on their hinges.

The rustic fireplace stands proudly as the cabin's centerpiece with a worn rug in front of the hearth. There's some Christmas lights strung along the stone, and stockings hanging from the mantle. Daisy huddles over it, and I join her with an unenthusiastic amble.

"Look," she says, pointing at the grill. "Those ashes are still smoking. They couldn't have left long ago."

I roll my eyes. "Great work, Detective Daisy. What does that mean?"

"It means that we probably only just missed them," she replies.

"But if we just missed them, wouldn't we have seen them driving down the mountain?" I ask.

Daisy's lips fold over and her eyes scrunch up. "Okay. Fine. They've been gone for hours. How the hell am I supposed to know?"

"You're the one who came over here and went full C.S.I. on the fireplace. I don't know what the fuck you're doing!"

"Don't yell at me!" she yells.

"I'm not yelling, you're yelling!" I admittedly yell.

Daisy sweeps her blond hair away from her soft, round face, which is growing ruddier by the second. "We're both yelling! So what happens now?"

"We go back to town," I snap.

"Sounds good!" she snaps back. "Just let me go to the bathroom super quick. I drank half a gallon of peach Snapple before I left and my bladder's about to implode."

"Okay!" I shout.

Daisy waddles past me towards the bathroom, and I'm doing my best not to chuckle at how silly she looks. She disappears inside, and again my mind goes back to Phillip Meyer's birthday and how being stuck with a girl in a closet for seven minutes ended up being one of the best experiences of my young life, regardless of the shit storm that followed.

I can't help but wonder what if the same thing happened now? Not in a closet, obviously, but if we were stuck here in this cabin, all alone with only each other for company. Could we put everything behind us? Resolve this stupid feud that's lasted eight years, and maybe find some common ground? Could we just talk like we did then?

I can't believe I'm even thinking about it. I can't stand Daisy. She's an unorganized mess. I'm efficient and precise. Everything about her makes me want to run as far away as I can. But yet, here I am, and some force I can't explain is desperate to stay.

5

Daisy

This could be really bad. Please don't let me pee myself all over my friend's cabin. In retrospect, I probably should have gone to the bathroom before I left town, but that would require the sort of forward thinking I'm not well known for.

My legs are crossed so tight you couldn't fit a pin between my thighs as I shuffle into the bathroom. I'm grateful that the door is in its frame, but when I go to close it behind me, I can't help but notice the lack of a knob. Instead, the locking mechanism juts out, and the brass knob is on the wooden floor. A broom sits oddly at the side, and I realize it's holding the door open. It's lucky I didn't accidentally kick it out of the way when I came in.

Great. A broken, non-closing door, an engorged bladder, and annoyingly handsome Finn Ross all at the same time. I clench my legs together and add a little mince to my hips for good measure. I glimpse the toilet, then glance through the gap in the door to see how good an eyeful Finn will get. My face scrunches as I weigh up my options, but the decision comes to me pretty easy. I am not peeing my pants. Not today.

I shimmy my way to the toilet, then check the open door again for any sign of Finn. Gah. I can just make out his shoulder. I can't risk him walking in. We have enough shared trauma.

"Hey. The door is broken, so don't come in here, okay?" I call out.

"What?" he calls back.

I grumble. "I said, don't come in here!"

Suddenly I hear his heavy footsteps and before I know it, he's at the door.

"What?" he asks again.

I watch as he steps inside, and his big stupid foot kicks the support broom. I reach out, trying to stop him from taking another step.

"No!" I shriek.

But it's too late. The broom topples to the floor and the door slams behind Finn, sealing us both inside the bathroom.

I shake my head. "Oh, my God! I told you not to come in here!"

"I couldn't hear you," he moans. "What's the big deal?" He turns and reaches for a knob that ordinarily might be there. "Oh," he mutters.

Finn spies the knob on the floor and drops to his haunches, picks it up, then starts fiddling with the mechanism. I look over his shoulder, hopeful that's whatever he's doing will actually fix the door, but I'm also mindful of my ticking bladder.

"Well?" I ask impatiently, bouncing up and down.

"Well, what?" he replies, trying to fit the knob into the lock.

I tighten my legs, twisting them like a barber's pole as I bite down on my bottom lip. "I've just got a bit of a situation here."

He looks over his shoulder at me and frowns. "Just go. I don't care."

His words slap me across the face and I laugh uncomfortably. "Can't you just fix it?"

"Oh sure. Few people know I moonlight as a locksmith-slash-handyman-slash-door-fixer-guy."

I furrow my brow. "Okay, smartass, but I really, really need to pee."

He jabs the knob at the lock, his patience quickly waning until he eventually growls at it and tosses the lock aside like a caveman. "Then you're going to just have to go. This is broken."

"Yeah. I know," I drawl. "That's why the broom was there."

Finn climbs back to his feet, unbuttoning his cuffs and rolling his sleeves up to his elbows. "Well, how was I supposed to know that?"

"I called out to you!" I argue.

"And I didn't hear you!" He turns his attention back to the door. Now he's trying to jam his fingers between the door and the frame.

I've never needed to pee so badly in my entire life. I look around the compact room. Apart from the door, the only other exit is a small window that I could barely squeeze my butt through. I puff my cheeks and close my eyes. Why is this happening to me? When I open my eyes, I'm looking at the bath with its navy shower curtain. I can't believe I'm about to do this.

"Get in the shower," I say firmly.

Finn steps away from the door and eyes me curiously. "What now?"

I point. "Get in the shower and close the curtain."

He sighs. "What are you talking..."

"Get in the fucking shower now, Finn or I swear to god you will not survive this!" I scream.

He raises his hands in surrender, and I can sense a hint of a smirk on his full lips. He climbs into the tub and gives me one last glance before pulling the curtain across.

"Now face the wall," I order.

I hear him grumble. "Okay. I'm facing the wall."

I keep my eyes trained on the shower curtain, ready for even the slightest sign of movement. Slowly, I hike up my skirt and inch my stockings down my thighs before lowering myself onto the seat. I sit there with my knees drawn together, watching the tub like a hawk. But there's one more thing that needs taking care of.

"Run the tap," I say.

"Are you serious?" Finn snaps. "I'll get wet."

"Just do it!" I shriek. At this point I've lost all self control.

His grumble is becoming a familiar sound. I hear the squeak of a turning tap and water pouring into the tub. "Fuck! It's cold!" he calls out. "Hurry up!"

With the proper noise cover, I unclench every muscle I have, literally opening the floodgates and unleashing a tide of peach Snapple.

"Oh, thank God," I exhale, bracing my hands against the wall as relief sweeps over me. This must be what having a baby feels like.

"Are you done?" Finn calls over the loud, running water.

"Shut up," I yell, closing my eyes. "Don't talk."

After what feels like forever, the raging rapids slow to a trickle, until at last my Snapple tank is empty. I tidy up, practically exhausted, my knees wobbling when I clamber to my feet, pulling up my stockings and adjusting my skirt. I flush, quickly wash my hands at the basin, then close the toilet seat before perching myself on the lid.

I let out a deep, satisfied breath. "Okay. You can come out now."

The tap turns off and the curtain whips back, and Finn glares at me as he steps out of the tub. His soaked shoes and ankles of his dress pants slosh when they hit the floor as he pulls a towel from the cabinet and dabs at the water splashes on his shirt.

"Congratulations on not pissing yourself," he grumbles. "Now what?"

I look at the door again. "No luck with the pulling?"

He sighs. "No. Unfortunately, I couldn't bear strength the door open, Daisy, and that there's no way that knob is working."

When he's soaked up as much water as he can, he discards the towel and I can't help but notice how his shirt clings to his toned stomach where the water has seeped through.

His attention turns to the window and he points. "That's the only way out, then."

"And that would be a great plan if we were small children," I say snidely.

His eyes narrow, and I don't like the way he's looking me up and down.

"You could fit through that," he declares.

I laugh loudly. "Are you having a stroke? There's no way I can fit through that window."

"You've got a better chance than me," he explains. "My shoulders are too broad."

I roll my eyes. "Okay. Calm down."

He frowns. "I'm just saying. If it's going to be either of us, it's you."

I shake my head vehemently. "I don't think so. We'll just sit here and wait. Tom and Sophie will come back eventually, and now that we've figured out a peeing system, I can stay here for as long as that takes."

Finn leans on the bathroom sink and folds his arms. "Fine. We'll stay right here then." His eyes dart around the room. "In this small bathroom." He gulps. "With no way out."

My eyebrows knit when he squirms uncomfortably. "Are you okay?" I watch him tug at the collar of his shirt and it hits me. "Are you still claustrophobic? This is bigger than a closet."

"Yeah, and I was fine until the whole no way out thing. Now this is a giant coffin with his and hers sinks."

I laugh, and the sound seems to give him some relief, inching a smile onto his face.

"I'll be fine," he says, but I'm not sure which of us he's trying to convince. "I just need to take deep breaths." He looks at me. "Someone told me that once."

"She sounds like she's pretty smart," I say. "Can't stick to a budget to save her life, but definitely a cool chick."

"She is when she wants to be," Finn says. He runs a hand through his chestnut hair. "Is it getting hot in here?"

I shake my head. "Not at all. It's a frigging ice box."

"That's not good," he mumbles. "Now that we've got the peeing scenario mapped out, what do we do in case of panic attacks?"

I turn to the small window and start doing the math, terribly, in my head. I'm mostly boobs, belly and butt, which could be malleable enough to squeeze through. Sort of like how an octopus can squish into a tiny bottle. It's definitely going to leave some marks, though. I look back at Finn.

"Do you really think I can fit?"

He squints and puffs his cheeks. "I mean. Yeah. Maybe."

I groan. "You're not a great salesman."

"No. Sorry," he laughs. "Yes. You will fit."

I'm not sure I believe him, but we don't have many other options. Part of me doesn't know why I'm bothering to help. I'm not the one with claustrophobia. I'm quite happy to sit here on this toilet seat and wait it out. But I can see the sweat building at the back of his neck and he isn't normally this pale. Besides, you know the old saying. When someone stands in a running bathtub so they can't hear you pee, you owe them one.

I stomp to my feet and slap my hands together. Okay, Daisy. Think thin.

6

Finn

Never in a million years did I think I'd be in a bathroom in the middle of nowhere with my hands overflowing with Daisy's perfect, ample backside. I'm trying to stay focused on the task at hand, which is getting her through this window and now that I see it, maybe we were a little optimistic. Every time she shimmies forward, her red skirt rides up, and the sight of her thick thighs wrapped in black stockings is getting me hard as a rock. I look at the wall instead. That's what a gentleman does. But then I've still got handfuls of Daisy's ass to contend with as I push her through the window.

"Harder," she yells. "I'm so close."

My eyes widen as my dick pulses. "Pardon?"

She reaches back and tugs her skirt down. "I'm almost out," she says. "Keep pushing."

I gulp. "Right. Okay."

I keep my palms flat and push.

She groans. "Harder. Really lean into it."

I nod. "Okay." My fingers curl, my hand folding over the soft curves of her backside. I push again and she shunts forward.

"That's it!" she says. "Almost there! Harder!"

I can feel sweat dripping down the back of my neck and I don't think it's just the claustrophobia. Is she doing this on purpose? Not even a monk could avoid impure thoughts with this view and her sexy voice groaning some pretty blatant double entendres.

"Come on, Finn. Do it!" she yells.

I grit my teeth and dig both hands into her ass, my thumbs finding that gorgeous, gentle dip at the top of her thighs. She squeaks when I squeeze, then squawks like a goose when, with one final push, she topples out the window. I rush to the ledge when I hear her land with a heavy thud on the deck.

I expect to find her rolling in agony. But instead she's flat on her back, clutching her belly and laughing loudly, even throwing in the odd uncontrollable snort when the mood takes her. It doesn't take long before I'm laughing as well, until we're laughing together, and God, she looks so beautiful.

"Are you okay?" I manage to get out between chuckles.

She nods and sits up as her laughter fades to a breathless rasp. "I'm fine. You really went to town on my butt, though."

"You told me to," I say defensively.

She smiles. "I'm joking, Finn." She climbs to her feet and looks at me through the window. "We make a good team."

Her words sink into me. "Yeah. I guess we do."

She glances around the outside of the cabin, but there's not much to see through the dense pines and the constant sheet of snow falling from the sky.

"Does that snow look heavier to you?" I ask.

"I was thinking the same thing," she replies as she shivers. She leaves the window, walking around to the front of the cabin where I can't see her. "Uh, Oh," she calls.

I stick my head out the window as much as I can before my shoulders jam against the sill. I crane my neck, trying to catch sight of Daisy. "What is it?"

Daisy returns, her tongue rolling in her cheek. "I don't think we're getting out of here anytime soon."

"Why? What's happened?"

"Well, your truck is over there doing its best impersonation of Mount Everest," Daisy replies.

I furrow my brow.

"It's completely covered in snow," Daisy clarifies. "The whole road is. I can't even see how we got here." She wraps her arms around her shoulders and I notice her full lips turning blue. "And it's fucking freezing."

"See if you can open this door so I can take a look," I say.

She nods and disappears around the deck again. I hear the front door of the cabin open and close and the pitter patter of her shoeless feet outside the bathroom. The knob on the other side jiggles, the mechanism rattling in the frame.

"You got it?" I ask. Nervous needles prickle at my skin as my throat tightens, and a sudden anxious surge races through every muscle in my body. The bathroom walls close in around me and the weight of the air pushes down on my shoulders with the force of a cave in. I can't breathe.

"Almost," she says, though her voice is hollow in my ears, my heart beating far too loud to hear her clearly.

I stagger to the door and lean into the wood. "Can you hurry?"

"I'm trying," she says. "It's loose. I think I can screw it back in."

I press my forehead to the door. My heart feels as if it's going to burst right out of my chest as the room spins around me. "I just really need to get out of here, Daisy. Please."

She falls silent for a minute. When she speaks again, her voice is urgent. "Finn. Just breathe. I'll be there in a second. I promise." The door knob rattles as she shakes frantically. "I've almost got it."

I close my eyes. Maybe that way the room will stay still. I feel a darkness wrapping itself tightly around my body, its hands at my throat, choking the life out of me.

"Daisy..." I mutter.

Suddenly there's a click, and her weight pushes against the door.

"Take a step back, Finn. I've got it," she says.

I do as she asks, stumbling backwards, grasping the sink to stay on my feet. The door flies open and Daisy's right there, her face stricken with worry. She rushes to me, one hand stroking my hair while the other rests gently on my chest.

"You're okay," she says softly. "Just breathe. Deep breaths, Finn."

I fight her words at first. It seems almost easier to let the fear take over.

"Breathe," she says again, her voice drifting over the air and filling my head. "You're at the rink, on the ice. You've got your stick in your hands and your eye on the net. You're okay."

I take a breath and slowly the weight lifts from my shoulders.

"That's it," Daisy says. "I'm right here. You're going to be fine."

I breathe again and the darkness fades away. I open my eyes at last and see her before me. Her liquid blue eyes glazed with concern, her full, pink lips pursed together as she breathes in and out, mirroring my own breaths. I glimpse her hand resting on my chest, mesmerized by her warmth with every rise and fall. I feel the burden leave me, but I almost wish it didn't. I don't want Daisy to stop touching me.

"There you go," she says, a smile drawing upon that hypnotizing mouth. "You did it."

She withdraws her hand, and it's as aching as I imagined it would be.

"Thank you," I stammer, finding my voice again.

She pinches my arm, and her sweet laugh takes the last of the pressure off my shoulders.

"Don't get soft on me. I'm a mess. Remember? Terrible with budgets, unorganized, not cut out for business?"

I nod slowly and give half a smile. "Right. All of that."

"See," Daisy says. "Can't have you taking a liking to me. I think the world would literally explode if that ever happened. Plus, we have bigger problems." She pats her stomach. "I am starving."

She waltzes out of the bathroom with such a lightness to her you wouldn't think she had just saved me from a full-blown anxiety meltdown. This was a bad one too, and when they usually strike, it can take hours for me to calm and pull myself free. How does Daisy James do it in minutes?

I can't stop thinking about the way her hand felt on my chest and how her voice filled my head, and as the cloud lifts from my mind, I'm reminded of her ass and her stocking clad thighs. I wish my thoughts didn't regress to such a carnal place, but I'd be lying to myself if I didn't admit that Daisy's body drives me crazy. Even when we're fighting over budgets and menu plans, the way she fills a blouse and skirt is breathtaking, and I'm grateful to have such a good poker face. The way I pull off not constantly staring at the soft curves of her body is impressive if I say so myself.

Daisy has no clue that I'm utterly attracted to her, and I have been for eight years now. Since the night she saved me in that closet, right up to today, when she did it again in a bathroom. I've tried to fight it, tried to stay professional while carrying around this bitterness that's as silly as Henry thinks it is. But my claustrophobia isn't the only burden I feel freed from right now. Admitting to myself I have feelings for Daisy lifts just as much weight.

7

Daisy

I rummage through the kitchen cupboards in a desperate search for anything packed with carbs. But when all I find is tinned sardines, salt and a bag of rice, I struggle to figure out what Tom and Sophie eat up here. Then it occurs to me they probably don't come to the cabin to eat. Well. Not food, at least.

Finn emerges from the bathroom, rolling his broad shoulders as he strides towards me. His face is so chiseled, his jaw line so sharp. He's gorgeous, and that always catches me out before I remember how much he despises me.

"Any luck?" he asks, joining me in the kitchen. He leans on the counter, his arms folded over his barreled chest. I take a second to remember how to make words.

"Nope. Apparently, our friends love a good sardine risotto, heavy on the salt."

Finn's face sours. "I hate sardines."

"Well then, we'll be starving to death together, because I'm also not a fan," I reply. I lift onto my toes to get a look at the back of the cabinet, and I can't help but notice Finn's eyes wander over my legs. "Maybe you can help me with this, since you're a giant?"

His head jerks as if he's woken from a spell, and he clears his throat. "Yeah. Sure."

Finn comes up behind me, and I don't expect him to lean over me, his chest pressing against my back, his pelvis hard against my butt as he reaches into the cabinet. He's so close I fold slightly over the counter, my hands gripping the wood, and a tingle sweeps between my legs.

"Jackpot," he says excitedly, and at first I'm not sure what he's referring to, but whatever it is forces him closer and harder onto my back and I'm not complaining.

I hear a rustle in the cupboard before his hand emerges, holding a bright red box decorated with green bows and a picture of a gingerbread house on the front.

"It's one of those build a cookie house things," he declares.

"Gingerbread house," I correct. "How old is it?"

He flips the box around and checks the small print, then his face droops. "Yikes. Best before 2020."

My stomach rumbles so loudly that even Finn hears it, and he takes a step back. When I turn around, he looks terrified.

"Is there a monster living inside of you?"

I snatch the box out of his hand, looking at the details myself. "There'll be a monster right here in front of you if I don't get some food quick." I squint to read the little letters. "I mean. Best before dates are more of a guideline than a rule."

Finn smirks. "Is that your professional opinion?"

I peel open the top of the box and peek inside, getting a brief whiff of gingerbread. It's like blood in the water and I'm a ravenous shark with dubious credit.

"I'll take possibly funky gingerbread over tinned sardines any day. How about you?"

Finn nods eagerly and reaches for the box, but I swipe it out of his grasp and tuck it behind my back. "You think you're going to get cookies off me that easily? In your dreams, pal."

I spin around, putting the box on the counter and huddling around it so Finn can't even get a look in.

"You're going to share, right?" he pleads, as I shove a hand in the box to retrieve the contents.

"What's that saying?" I ask with my brow furrowed. "Women and children first?"

"Well, we're not on the Titanic and if I let you go first, they'll be nothing left," Finn grumbles.

I glance at him over my shoulder. "Rude," I puff.

He chuckles and I feel him on my back again, his arms snaking around my shoulders as he tries to steal the box away from me. Again, I'm not complaining. One of his hands sneaks to my waist and pinches my side, and

I laugh loudly, trying to push him away with my elbows as I fight to secure the gingerbread house. When he sees how I react, both of Finn's hands find my waist and he playfully squeezes again and again. I can't stop laughing, and soon I'm breathless from squealing. He moves closer behind me, his nose brushing against my ear, and I'm sure I hear him inhaling my hair.

My core tightens and I bite my lip as my skin goose pimples. Finn's hands rest on my hips and it's not long before I feel him thicken against me. Suddenly Finn jumps back and when I turn, he's facing the other way, his head bowed as he adjusts his pants.

I grin. "Everything okay?"

He straightens and his head jerks back. "Fine," he snaps as he kicks out his leg. "Absolutely fine."

I laugh lightly. It doesn't take a rocket scientist to figure out what I've stirred inside him. The real mystery is why? Is it just a normal guy thing that he has no control over? Or did he feel the same wonderful sensation when our bodies melded together so perfectly? I decide to take pity on him.

"Good news," I announce, and he looks over his shoulder at me. "I'm going to share this with you."

When he's figured out his situation downstairs, he turns around to face me, and I must admit I'm disappointed that I don't get a look at what was developing in his trousers. It felt amazing.

"How generous of you," he says with a cough, giving his pants one last tug. He holds his hand out. "I'll take the door and the gumdrop roof tiles."

My jaw drops. "You, animal. We have to build it before we eat it."

He stares at me, stunned. "Really? I thought you were starving?"

I roll my eyes as I turn back to the counter and start sorting the items out of the box. "Luckily, we're not building an actual house, Finn. It should only take five minutes."

He sidles up beside me and there's something about the way he breathes that sends shivers down my spine.

"So, where do we start?" he asks.

I arrange the pieces in front of us. "Okay, we've got two sides. A back and a front. Two roof panels, and then a bunch of gumdrops, chocolate buttons, jelly beans and some icing to hold it all together. Step one. Foundation. Let's get the sides together."

The white icing is pre-made, so I rummage around the kitchen drawers and find a pair of scissors to snip the end of the plastic bag. Finn has already started putting the front and left side of the house together, but I shake my head at him.

"Let's put it on a plate, and put some icing down first so it sticks."

He raises an eyebrow. "Seems like a lot of effort for something we're going to eat in a minute."

"Nothing wrong with putting in a little effort. It's all about the journey, Finn, not the destination."

He smiles, and the way his brown eyes fix on me makes my knees wobble. They're dark, warm and flecked with gold, and apparently they sparkle when he's happy.

"I'll have to remember that," he says. He looks away and dips his head to focus on the pieces, but I keep staring, quietly fixated on how gorgeous the back of his neck is.

After a minute, he looks up at me. "Are you getting a plate?"

I catch my breath. "Right. Plate. Foundations." I rummage through the cupboard again, and thankfully, they're easy enough to find. I sit it on the counter and draw a rough square on the surface with the icing. "There."

Finn mushes the front and the side of the house into the icing like mortar, holds them for a second, then removes his hands ridiculously slowly, as if he were in slow motion.

"It's holding," he announces, and I can't help but giggle.

"Excellent. Now the back and the other side. I'll put some icing to keep it all together."

I pipe the icing onto the gingerbread edges and Finn delicately slots the pieces into place.

"Steady," he mutters as he takes his hands away. When he's satisfied the building won't collapse, he nods his approval. "What next?"

"The roof," I state. I pipe more icing onto the top of the panels and when I'm finished, Finn is standing ready and alert and holding the roof pieces. "All yours," I say.

His eyes narrow, and the intensity he's putting into building this house is admirable, as well as adorable. Finn holds his breath and carefully slots the roof into place. When he's done, he exhales as if he's just performed heart surgery.

"How's that?" he asks, his eyes yearning for praise.

Never in a thousand years did I think Finn would ask me if he did a good job.

I smile and nod. "Looks great."

He pinches his chin between his fingers and inspects his work thoughtfully. "What now?"

"Chocolate button roof tiles," I say. "Then we put the gumdrops along the edge of the roof and decorate with the jelly beans."

"Fantastic," he replies.

I pipe a layer of icing onto the roof, and Finn gets to work layering the chocolate buttons. Then he takes a handful of gumdrops and meticulously places each one. His attention to details is impressive, but maybe I was wrong when I estimated this wouldn't take as long as building an actual house. My stomach rumbles as he secures the last gumdrop, squishing it into the icing for maximum hold. Once again, he inspects his work.

"What about a little jelly bean garden out front?" he asks.

I want to laugh out loud, but I hold it in when I read the seriousness of his gaze. "Would you like a jelly bean garden?" I ask instead.

He exhales. "Maybe it's too much."

"I disagree," I reply. "It's never too much if it makes you happy."

He raises an eyebrow. "That's a dangerous philosophy."

I shrug. "I'm not the one who wants a jelly bean garden."

He lifts his chin, a warm glow filling his cheeks. "You're right. Jelly bean garden it is. Snow, if you wouldn't mind?"

"Right away," I say, squeezing what's left of the icing onto the plate.

I watch as Finn uses the green jelly beans as a retaining wall, then the red and yellow as flowers. He takes the blues and builds a path leading up to the front door, then finishes with a gumdrop door knob.

He looks at me for approval. "Well?"

I roll my lips together to stifle my laugh. "It's breathtaking, Finn."

"It is, isn't it?" he agrees, admiring his work. "Seems a shame to eat it."

We look at each other, and it's clear we're thinking the same thing when we both reach out, snatch a roof panel each, and stuff it in our mouths so fast you'd think there was a gingerbread shortage, and oh my God. It tastes so fucking good.

8

Finn

You know. I don't even like gingerbread, and maybe it's the starvation talking, but this is the most delicious thing I've ever eaten. Before I know it, I've demolished one side of the roof and the back, but I'm not done yet. That jelly bean garden is looking like dessert.

Daisy does this thing when she eats where she nods and inspects the cookie before each bite and you can tell she's savoring the taste, analyzing as she goes. I'm curious to know how her mind works.

"So how does it taste?" I ask, catching a crumb as it falls from my mouth.

Her nose scrunches up and her mouth twists from side to side while she ponders.

"I like mine a little sweeter. But it's not bad for something that's been sitting in a cupboard for three years."

I see she's finished her piece, so when I rip off the side panel, I snap it in half, handing one half to her. I raise my part in the air. "Cheers."

She smiles, and I love the way it lifts her rosy cheeks and draws out the dimples in the corners of her mouth.

"Cheers," she replies as we toast our gingerbread.

The house is looking like an earthquake hit it, with only the front door and one side left. The mortar is already melting, and one by one my meticulously placed gumdrops tumble off into a slurry of runny icing.

"All that hard work," I say, just as a pink gumdrop falls to its death.

"Yeah, but it's a nice memory," Daisy sighs, nibbling on her gingerbread. "Those last a lot longer."

Something prickles in my chest. "Bad memories too."

She looks up from her cookie. "Sometimes those are worse."

A silence cuts through our easy banter. There's so much I want to say, but the words won't get past my teeth. When our eyes meet, I can see she's waiting for me to speak first, to rip the bandaid off this thing that turned us against each other, that kept us petty and bitter for eight years. Maybe here and now, in the safety and solitude of this cabin, with the snow packing us in like those nasty tinned sardines, maybe at last we can resolve this.

"You're right," are the words that finally fall from my mouth. "I am terrified of what people think of me."

Daisy tilts her head to the sound, and her reply isn't smug but sympathetic. "Why is that?"

I shrug. "I like being liked. I like succeeding. It makes me feel good about myself."

Daisy lets out a deep breath. "Do you know after you said those things about me, the next boy who asked me on a date got mad when I wouldn't make out with him? He said he only did it because he heard I put out."

My brow sinks, and my face hardens. "What?"

Daisy nods. "And the one after that, and then a couple more in high school. I got this reputation for being easy. Funny thing is, no one had even kissed me yet. All because of seven minutes in a closet when I was fifteen."

I hang my head, ashamed. "Daisy. I'm sorry. I never meant for that to happen."

"Yeah. Well. Boys can be lame, I guess. It doesn't bother me now, but it's hard when you're a teenage girl."

I scratch the back of my neck and wish I could crawl under a rock and disappear. "I had no idea."

"I'm sorry too," she says. "For telling people you were afraid of the dark. I figured the kids at school would find it funnier than claustrophobia. I don't think half of them could spell it claustrophobia, anyway."

I laugh softly. "It sounds so stupid when you say it now. What I did was so much worse."

"It's not a competition," Daisy replies. "Back then, it hurt. That's all that matters, and I'm sorry."

Her words lift a weight from my shoulders that I'd always suffered with, but never truly understood until now. Even though it feels like a lifetime ago, I was so angry with her back then for embarrassing me in front of my friends. But if I had been honest in the first place, told them that nothing happened in that closet. That Daisy was a beautiful, kind person who helped me through my anxiety like no one ever had, or has, since. Then none of this would have happened. It was me who started it. The one who lied first. Why have I been acting like this was her fault? Then I realize what that weight is, what it's always been. Guilt.

I shake my head as the bitter truth slaps me across the face. "I'm an idiot."

Daisy reaches out and puts her hand on top of mine, her warmth sending shivers through my skin.

"You were a teenage boy," she says softly, still trying to comfort me when I was the one who started this.

With my warped memories and all this business nonsense, I forgot about Daisy's kindness. The kindness that had me crushing on her all those years ago when we were two kids in a closet.

"I liked you," I blurt. "I was really looking forward to our date, but then, well... you know."

"I liked you too," Daisy says. "That's why it hurt so much when you said what you said. I thought I meant nothing to you."

I gaze into her eyes and my hand cups the side of her face, her smooth skin warm against my palm. She closes her eyes and leans into my touch.

"Daisy. You meant everything to me." I gulp. "You still do."

She turns away from me, but I won't let her. I bring her face back, my fingers grasping her behind the ear as I pull her lips to mine. It's like a lightning bolt when we connect, and when she gasps, it sends my heart pounding. She tastes like peaches and gingerbread, and her lips are so full and soft that I can't stop kissing them. She breaks free from me and it's agony.

"Finn. Wait," she whispers, her hand presses against my chest.

I want to be kissing her again so badly, but I stop when she asks.

"I appreciate your apology, and I enjoyed building the house with you," she exhales. "And you're really freaking hot. But I'm not looking to get involved with anyone right now. I know I'm not great at running my business, but I will be, and I can't let anyone or anything distract me."

"I'm in the same place, Daisy," I say, trying to steady myself, resisting the urge to take her now right on this counter. "I was hauling bags at the Northwellian long before I was planning events there. But there's still so much I want to do. The few relationships I've had over the years have fallen apart because my work has always taken priority. So you don't need to explain. I get it."

I didn't realize we were so similar when it came to our passions, and I feel like an ass for assuming I knew how Daisy ran her business, or the commitment she had to her success. I should have respected she was a proud small business owner, doing the best she could.

"Few relationships?" she asks, and that's not the part of the discussion I thought she'd latch on to.

I chuckle, and my chin drops against my chest. "That might be generous. More like one, but after enough canceled dinner dates, she didn't stick around for long." I swallow a nervous lump in my throat. "You?"

Daisy shakes her head. Her fingers reach for me, her bright red nails dragging across my abdomen. Her tongue slides between her lips. "I've not been with anyone for a long time."

I fold my hand around her wrist and pull her close to me, then walk her backwards until her backside hits the counter. I hover over her, my lips on her forehead.

"What's happening..." she murmurs as she nuzzles into me.

I gaze down at her and slip my hands beneath the collar of her blouse, rolling my fingers over her smooth shoulders. "Anything you want to happen."

Her arms curl around my neck, and she lifts to her toes to reach my lips. I bend for her as our tongues explore each other's mouths. Her breathless gasps are like a melody I never want to stop hearing, and each raspy moan gets me harder.

My hands leave her neck and run over her shoulders and down her arms before settling on her sexy, wide hips. I snatch her harder to me, our pelvises pressed tightly together, and I grind my length against her stomach before scooping the soft curve of her ass in my hands and lifting her onto the counter.

She squeaks when what remains of our gingerbread house tumbles to the floor, her eyes flashing open as she giggles.

I smooth her blond hair away from her face so I can look at her, our eyes locking, a sudden commonality surging between us I can't believe I overlooked before. Sure, we did things differently, but our hearts beat for the same reasons, our minds shared the same goals, and we dreamed the same dreams. I'd always taken her abrasiveness as attitude, but now I realize it was drive and determination and passion. Fuck. Just thinking about it adds another inch to my cock.

"Daisy," I whisper. "This can be as much or as little as you want. But even if it's just a moment with you, I'll take it."

She closes her eyes and parts her lips. I feel her hand slide down past my waist and she preses her palm firmly against my shaft. Daisy strokes me from my base all the way to my tip and I release a rumbling groan. I kiss her deep, my tongue seeking hers as we taste each other, her skilled hand sliding up and down until I feel a slick drip at my tip.

I reach down and grip her skirt, pushing it up over her hips until I feel the waist of her stockings. I hook my fingers under the silky fabric and drag them down her thighs, past her knees, and slip them off her toes before throwing them over my shoulder. Daisy giggles into my mouth when they catch on the handle of the overhead cabinet.

I take her plump ass in my hands and pull her closer. Her legs part for me, caging me between her milky, thick thighs. I can't wait to feel the warmth inside of her as I drag my fingers anxiously along her skin towards her entrance. I admit I've assumed a lot about Daisy in the past, but when I look down, eager for a glimpse of her pussy, I don't expect to find her wearing the thickest, biggest, baggiest beige underwear I've ever seen.

She senses me pause and her eyes flicker open, and when she sees me staring with a broad smirk across my face, her cheeks turn bright red.

"Fuck. I forgot," she whines, her hands covering her face. "It's laundry day."

I try to pry her hands away from her face. "It's fine," I say, trying not to laugh. "They're sexy."

She uncovers her face just so she can frown, unimpressed at me. "You fucking liar."

"No, wait," I continue. "Look." I swiftly undo my belt, followed by my button and zip, and when I open my trousers for her, I reveal the oldest, holiest, most worn-out pair of pinstriped boxers that I own. "It's my laundry day too."

She bites her bottom lip, and my attempt at soothing her has a fucking outstanding side effect. Her hand dips inside my boxers and she grasps my shaft, her hand expertly sliding over each ridge. I close my eyes and throw my head back as her other hand joins in, encircling my cock and stroking me so well another drop of pre-cum beads at my tip.

"Fuck," I murmur. "That feels so good." I open my eyes to gaze at her. "I want to make you feel good too, Daisy."

I move closer to her, grabbing those gigantic panties by the waistband and wrestling them off. She giggles the whole time and I love how, even though we are both horny as hell, there's an easiness to it. It's fun being with Daisy, even when all I want to do is bury myself inside her. With those industrial cotton monstrosities discarded, I press my palm against her crevice. She's already warm and slick down there, and it doesn't take much more rubbing before my fingers are slippery.

Daisy groans, her hands still working my shaft as I slip a finger between her folds. Our moans are a chorus as our tangled limbs please each other. I push another finger inside and she cries out. When I quicken my pace, so does she, matching me stroke for stroke while our lips hungrily devour each other and gasp for air. She chokes me hard at my base, her fingers catching every ridge as she glides up and down, her thumb rolling over my slick tip when she reaches the top.

I growl, clenching her bottom lip between my teeth, and I bury my fingers deep inside her to the knuckle. She whimpers and rolls her hips, bucking against my hand. Her muscles tighten and her body quivers. She pushes harder against me, using my fingers like an instrument solely for her pleasure.

She chokes my cock, and I lengthen the pressure building at my base. "Fuck, Daisy. I'm cumming."

"Not yet," she commands, her eyes burning with intensity. "Don't stop fingering me,"

I grit my teeth, fighting the desperate urge to spill my seed all over her. I thrust my fingers in and out of her glistening pussy as she holds me strongly in her gaze, her mouth open as she moans.

"Yes... that's it... right there," she whimpers as she bucks against my hand.

Daisy throws her head back and cries out, and when her hands tighten like a vice around my cock, I can't hold it back any longer. My tip erupts, my cum spurting in ropes over Daisy's lap.

"Fuck," I groan, shivering as I spill every drop.

When I've got nothing left, Daisy releases me before falling back onto her hands on the counter.

I steady my breaths, nuzzling myself between her legs and leaning over her.

"Well, I guess it's true what they say," Daisy sighs. "The bigger the ego, the bigger the..." she glances at my spent cock hanging over my boxers.

I give her a rakish, yet exhausted, grin. "Well then, my ego must be huge."

Daisy laughs. "I always thought so."

I lean forward and kiss her softly, taking comfort in the tenderness of her pillowy lips.

She pushes against my chest to hold me back. "I meant what I said, Finn. That was amazing, but I can't make you any promises about what happens when we get back to town."

"I know," I reply. "Just let me enjoy you while I have you here. You're mine. For now."

Her smile is like warm sunshine on my skin as she folds her hand around the back of my neck and pulls me close, our lips melting together.

9

Daisy

After scrubbing out the mess Finn made on my favorite red skirt, I hang the wet fabric over the shower rail. I've borrowed a pair of Sophie's shorts. They're a little tight, and half my ass is hanging out, but as I walk past Finn to the kitchen, his wide grin lets me know he doesn't mind. I grab a washcloth and start wiping down the counter, but no matter where I look, all I can see is me and Finn kissing and writhing all over it. Sophie can never know about this. This is one of those things that goes to the grave.

I glance at him, picking up the gingerbread house debris from the floor and when our eyes meet, I feel my cheeks burn red and I look away. I feel like a kid again, but what we did on this counter was definitely R18.

I ring out the cloth in the sink and hang it to dry over the tap.

"Do you need help?" I ask.

He shakes his head, rising from his haunches with his cupped hands overflowing with cookie bits and gumdrops. "I think I got it all." I open the cupboard under the sink and he dumps the remains in the trash can. "It was a cute little house," he says.

I can't stop staring at his lips as he talks, and he notices immediately. He takes me around the waist and pulls me to him, bending over to reach my mouth so I won't have to tiptoe. The way he kisses takes my breath away. It's as if he can't get enough of me and I've never felt so wanted and desired. He's confident when he touches me, taking my curves into his hands with a passionate urgency that sends shock waves to my center all over again, and the way he looks at me. Jesus Christ. It's as if no one else exists in his world. He makes me feel beautiful.

Finn pulls back from me and stands upright, his hands rubbing up and down my arms. "You feel a little cold. Should I make a fire?"

"Sounds good," I reply.

He sighs. "But that would mean letting you go. I don't know if I can do that."

I frown and slap his arm. "Hugs are nice. Hypothermia, not so much."
Finn chuckles. "You make me laugh."

His voice is deep and rumbling and makes me lightheaded. "Go light
the fire," I say, before we end up with my butt on the counter again.

Finn reluctantly peels away from me, dragging himself to the open
fireplace. Tom's stocked it with logs, kindling and matches, and Finn
quickly gets started. It grows darker outside as the sun sinks behind the
mountains, and the wind whistles through the pines. When I look out the
window, it's impossible to see anything more than a few feet away. The
white veil of snow blankets everything, falling in slanted sheets across the
landscape. I guess the weather report was right for once, but I'm glad I
didn't pay attention as usual. If I had, I wouldn't have ended up in this cabin
with Finn.

The fire crackles and the flames roar, casting dancing silhouettes upon
the walls. Its warmth chases away the harshness of the cold, but a chill
still lingers in my bones. Finn stands behind me and drapes a chunky knit
blanket over my shoulders, then wraps his arms around me. He breathes
tender kisses onto my neck, and his nose brushes by my ear. My body
shivers, but it has nothing to do with the temperature. We stand there,
gazing at the fire, entranced by the flickering waves of red and orange as the
snow continues to tumble past the windows.

I'm so completely at peace that it seems like a lifetime ago I was
stressing over bank loans and budgets. How could those little things have
been so important, so crucial, when here in this moment, nothing matters
but me and Finn? This is all I want. For now, I remind myself. The
Gingerbread House means everything to me. I do not have time for another
priority. How long do I need to keep telling myself that before it sinks in?
But it's not just that. Something else is holding me back from falling for
Finn. A past that still triggers me, as much as I try to convince myself I'm
over it.

But as he whispers in my ear, the warmth of his breath sending tingles
over my skin, that all seems to fade away. For now. He's mine.

"It's getting late," he says. "We should get some sleep."

I flick my eyes at the only bedroom in the cabin and the queen cast iron
bed within. "Do we share?"

"No. You have the bed. I'll take the couch."

I can't hide my disappointment. The thought of falling asleep beside Finn with his enormous arms wrapped around me sounds like a dream come true.

"Are you sure?" My voice arches into a squeak.

He chuckles and kisses me softly behind the ear. "I would love to go to bed with you. There's just one problem."

I exhale when I realize what he's talking about. "That's Tom and Sophie's bed."

Finn nods. "I don't need to be that close to my teammates. But maybe..."

He lets me go and losing his warmth is not something I like at all. I watch him walk around the front of the tattered orange couch and inspect between the lumpy cushions. A pleased grin swipes across his face and he tosses the cushions aside, revealing a pull out wire bed.

He grabs hold of the bar and yanks it out and after he's set up the worn bundle of wires and thin mattress, I'm not confident of its weight bearing capabilities.

"You want to sleep on that?" I ask skeptically.

He nods. "With you, I do."

I blush and tuck my hair behind my ears. "Okay, but if I snap this thing in half, you can buy them a replacement."

Finn tosses the pillows back onto the foldout. "Sounds like a challenge."

I unwrap the blanket from my shoulders and throw it over the bed. "What has gotten into you?" I smile.

Finn comes back to me, resting his hands on my hips and pulling me against him. "You have. The way you laugh. The way you make laugh. The way you smell." He leans to my ear and whispers. "The way you taste." My body shivers when his warm breath glides over my skin. "I've missed out on so much time that I could have spent holding you, Daisy. I'm not missing out on another second." He looks down at the rickety fold out. "Even it means lying with you on this death trap."

How can I argue with that? I frown. "Fine."

I start with a single knee, and when I put my weight down, the wires stretch with a long creak, and I practically touch the floor. I look over my shoulder at Finn for reassurance.

"These old things are very well made," he says. "It's just got a little give in it, that's all."

I'm not as convinced as Finn, but I climb on anyway, holding myself precariously like a tight-rope walker getting their balance. I hear the creak again, but it's louder this time, as if the springs are screaming at each other to hold steady! I move an inch at a time, scrunching my face with every new, unnatural sound this bed is making.

"Now lie down," Finn says, and I can see him trying not to laugh at how overcautious I'm being. I guess I am only a foot and a half off the floor, not teetering on the edge of a cliff.

I close my eyes and hope for the best as I drop my weight to lie on my back. The springs wobble, bouncing me up and down like a mini trampoline. But soon the creaking dwindles to nothing, and the pullout grows still, and I'm not folded in half on the floor.

"See," Finn says. He unbuttons his shirt, and I can't help but think this show is for me with how slowly he's working.

A thin layer of brown hair dusts his pecks, trails down his rippled stomach and past his belly button before disappearing beneath his waistband. The sight of his body tightens my core as I admire how he can be so thick yet so toned at the same time.

He slides off his shirt and tosses it aside before climbing into bed. But unlike me, he throws caution to the wind and leaps, landing on his back with such force that we're both launched into the air. When gravity forces us both back down, he laughs while I brace myself through the bouncing that seems to last forever. This contraption feels more like an amusement ride than a bed.

Eventually the bed groans to a stop, and now with Finn and I both weighing it down, we're barely off the floor at all. But it doesn't seem to bother him, and I'm not used to this version of Finn.

"Come here," he says, hooking his arm around my stomach and dragging me across the mattress. He pulls me onto my side, then curls around me and snuggles deep into my back.

I feel his lips on my neck again and soon our breaths are in unison. The soothing crackle of the fire becomes a lullaby, while the whistling wind and pattering of snow joins the chorus. My eyes grow heavy, and the strain of the day seems to have finally caught up with me. I may be lying in bed with a beautiful man whose body I crave like oxygen, but I'm so tired I can barely keep my eyes open.

I back into him and he curves around my butt, curling his arm tighter around my belly while his other arm scoops under my neck to hold me across my chest. Between his body, the fire and the chunky knit blanket, I'm so ridiculously warm and comfortable, I could fall asleep any second.

My eyes flutter, and I feel myself slipping into dreams.

"Finn," I murmur as my body melts into his. "Do you snore?"

I feel his kisses weaken on my neck. I can tell he's as tired as I am.

"No," he replies, his voice slurred and dazed.

"Good," I reply half-heartedly. "I do."

"Oh, yeah?" he yawns, snuggling into my neck.

"A-ha," I mutter. "Like a chainsaw."

"That's nice, Daisy," he says.

"Finn," I say.

"Yeah," he replies.

"Good night."

"Night," he replies, and that's the last thing I hear before we both fall asleep.

My dreams are an easy haze of feelings and colors. I feel as if I have one foot in and one foot out, my body exhausted beyond compare while my mind is a hive of activity, with most thoughts leading back to Finn.

I don't know what the time is, or how long I've been sleeping, but I stir when Finn's hand slides up my stomach and cups my breast through my blouse, dragging his thumb over the fabric until he finds my nipple. His lips are on my neck, smothering me with soft, lazy kisses, and I moan lightly as a thousand tiny pleasurable prickles find my center. I grind my ass on his pelvis. He pushes back, and I feel his girth growing against me.

His nimble fingers pop open the top few buttons of my blouse and free my breasts, kneading my skin while his thumb draws circles around my nipple. The arm under my neck adjusts so he can touch my face, his finger tracing my lips as I moan again. His other hand leaves my breast, drawing lines along my sternum and across my belly until he reaches the waistband of my shorts. His fingers dip beneath the fabric to find my clit and he rubs me so slowly and gently that I feel like butter melting in the sun.

I'm still half asleep, and not sure if I'm dreaming or if this is actually happening, but either way, every time he touches me, my body trembles.

He pushes against my ass again, and it's impossible to ignore how hard and thick he is. His fingers explore my slick folds before he slides one inside of me and I gasp. The hand near my face closes around my jaw as he puts his thumb in my mouth. I bite down, clamping the knuckle between my teeth as his finger dips in and out of my entrance.

"You're so wet," he whispers, his voice soft, almost foggy in my ear. "I want to know what that pussy feels like wrapped around my cock, Daisy."

He slips his finger out of me, moving his hand to my waistband, easing my shorts and underwear down my thigh. I bend my leg to get them off quicker, the sensual anticipation of what's coming escalating inside me. When I've kicked them to the floor, I hear Finn's zipper and feel his cock slap against my ass once it's released.

Finn hooks me under the thigh and lifts my leg before positioning himself on his side behind me. His tip glides back and forth between my folds, and I get wetter and wetter with each pass. He lifts my leg higher and lines himself up with my entrance before easing inside of me so slowly that I release a long, whimpering moan.

"You feel so fucking good," he whispers as he buries himself deeper, and I bite harder on his knuckle to keep from screaming.

His pace is slow, rhythmic, deliberate, sliding every inch of himself inside me, back and forth, his hips bumping against my ass with each tender thrust. I'm still not sure if I'm dreaming, but if I am please God, never let me wake up. I feel my orgasm building, the blissful agony surging through every nerve until at last it bursts from inside me. My muscles tighten around him and when I cry out, he pushes his thumb deep into my mouth.

As if my orgasm gives him permission, he quickens, raising my leg even higher, allowing him full access to my aching pussy. He plunges deeper and harder, his hand folding around my throat as he throws his head back and releases a deep, rumbling growl. I gaze at him over my shoulder, his eyes closed and teeth grit as he fills me with every sweet drop of his cum.

When he's spent, Finn pulls out and once again he curls around me, hooking me around the belly and pulling me tightly against him. It feels warm and safe, and whatever word which means more than perfect. I yawn and melt into him and he kisses my neck as we fall back to sleep.

10

Finn

As the warm water rains over Daisy's beautiful face, I kiss her open mouth. Her arms snake around my neck while mine loop her waist, and the way her heavy breasts press against my chest has me so hard.

The tub is small, barely wide enough to fit us both, but comfort doesn't concern me. All I know is that this is the happiest I've ever felt, and this stunning woman, naked and perfect, is the reason. When we arrived at the cabin yesterday, there was no possible way I could have imagined things ending up like this. But now I don't want to live any other way. I'd give anything to call Daisy mine, but I can feel her pushing back. If she gives me a chance, I'll spend my whole life making hers easier.

Her hand slides away from my neck, her fingers trailing over my pecks, through my soaking wet chest hair and along my abdomen until they close firmly around my shaft. She strokes me, up and down, her thumb rolling over my tip and I reach around to the back of her head, gripping her hair.

"I've been waiting for you to do that," I growl in her ear.

She giggles as I walk her backwards until she's against the wall, our mouths locked together, each kiss desperate and urgent. I take hold of her thick thigh, lifting it to sit at my hip as my cock lengthens, my tip grazing her entrance.

"Finn! Daisy! Are you guys okay?"

Daisy and I freeze, and our eyes widen. Our heads swing around and look at the door, propped open by the broom.

"Guys! Are you in here? Oh, my god!" Sophie screams as she walks in, copping a full eyeful of me and Daisy, naked in the shower, with her leg hoisted up and my dick on display. She covers her eyes. "Oh, my god. Oh, my god. Oh, my god. I'm sorry. Oh, my god!" she shrieks.

She spins around, trying to make a hasty exit, but I can see exactly what's about to happen. She staggers towards the door and kicks the broom. The door slams shut in her face and when she takes her hand away from her eyes, she's right back where she was, getting a closeup view of Daisy and I still standing like statues in the shower.

"Oh, gross!" she screams again. "What are you doing?"

Daisy slings an arm across her breasts, then crosses her legs tightly and cowers behind me, joining Sophie's chorus of sobbing, Oh, my gods.

I reach out and snatch the shower curtain, ripping it right off the railing. "What does it look like we're doing!" I yell as I wrap the curtain around me and Daisy.

Sophie spins towards the door, searching for the knob. "How do I get out of here?"

"It's broken!" I snap. "Now we're stuck in here. Again!"

Sophie pounds on the door. "Tom! Help me! Tom!"

Daisy peeks her head over my shoulder. "You really need to get that door handle fixed, Soph."

"Tom!" she screams again.

Suddenly the door opens and Sophie tumbles into Tom's arms.

"What? What is it?" he asks. He looks behind Sophie into the bathroom, and his jaw drops when I greet him with a wave.

"Hey, Tom," I cough, scratching the back of my head while my other hand holds the shower curtain in place.

Daisy waves from behind me. "Hi, Tom."

He waves back. "Cap. Daisy. Hey, guys."

"Do you think maybe you could give us a little privacy?" I ask.

He jerks his head and nods vehemently. "Right. Yeah. Of course." With Sophie tucked and traumatized in his arms, he reaches for the door handle.

"Don't close the door!" Daisy and I yell in unison.

He slaps his forehead. "Right. I really have to fix that thing." He jams the broom in the frame while Sophie refuses to let him go. "We'll just wait out here," he says.

He and Sophie disappear from the doorway. Daisy and I look at each other, and it only takes five seconds before we burst into laughter. She wraps her arm around my neck and snorts into my shoulder, the shower curtain almost slipping as we convulse in hysterics.

With the moment officially over, we get dressed before joining Tom and Sophie in the living room. Daisy's got her hair wrapped up in a towel as she walks barefoot beside me while I button up my shirt, and we find Tom and Sophie taking in the scene. Tom moves a jelly bean around on the floor with the tip of his boot, but his eyes are soon drawn to Daisy's stockings hanging from the kitchen cabinet. Oops. Forgot about that. Sophie stands over the foldout couch, her hand now covering her mouth rather than her eyes.

Daisy gulps. "Well thank, god you guys are here. We were worried we'd be stranded forever."

Tom grins as he flicks the stockings with his fingers and they sway back and forth. "Really? You guys didn't look worried."

Daisy power walks to the kitchen and yanks down her stockings, then rolls them into a ball and tucks them behind her back.

Sophie slowly turns around to look at us, the disbelief scarring her face. "But... you hate each other..."

Daisy nods. "That was true. Yes."

"But you had sex... in my cabin?" she mutters.

"Yes, but not in your bed!" I blurt. I take a moment to clear my throat. "Out of respect."

Daisy nods. "Yes. Respect."

"So you just screwed in our shower, on my nana's couch, and God knows what happened in the kitchen," Sophie asks.

Daisy and I look at each other, our lips sealed and in a straight line as we try not to laugh.

"Mhmmm," we mumble in unison.

Tom furrows his brow. "What did you use the jelly beans for?"

Sophie shrieks and shoves her fingers in her ears. "Don't answer that. I don't want to know."

Daisy stifles her laugh and walks over to Sophie. "Don't worry. I'll get in here with some bleach and kerosene. You'll never know we were here."

"What about my eyes, Daisy?" she barks. "They have seen things that cannot be unseen." She moves closer to Daisy, but keeps her eyes trained on me. "You told me once you wouldn't piss on his gums if his teeth were on fire... I don't understand..."

Sophie's like a robot having a malfunction and every so often her head jerks to the side like she's glitching.

Daisy looks at me and smiles. "I don't either, to be honest." She looks back at Sophie and grips her by the shoulders. "But how about we sort it out together?"

Sophie's still trying to process the information. She staggers backwards and goes to sit on the arm of nana's couch, but then promptly bolts up and leaps two feet away from it. To be fair, that's a little overdramatic. I made love to Daisy on the mattress, not the arm.

Tom wanders over to me, trying not to smile, and I know that's for Sophie's benefit. He's a lot less bothered by the whole thing.

"I see you're alright. Couldn't track you down last night. Then Charlotte mentioned Daisy was headed up here, so Sophie and I came to check as soon as the road was clear." He nudges my shoulder. "You hate each other for years and it takes less than twenty-four hours before you're in the sack? Were you two that bored? We have monopoly in the closet, you know?"

I shake my head as I gaze at Daisy, who's still trying to talk Sophie off a ledge.

"It wasn't like that," I say. "We just talked, and she forgave me, and now I can't get her out of my head."

"I mean that's great, Cap," Tom says. "I just need to know one thing."

I fix my eyes on him. "What's that, man?"

His eyebrows knit. "Seriously, what did you use the jelly beans for?"

I chuckle and slap him on the back. "We built a garden, buddy. We built a garden."

Tom shrugs his shoulders. "What the fuck does that mean?"

I watch as Sophie puts her hands on her hips, and her head hasn't stopped shaking in the last five minutes.

"I can't unpack this all right now," she says. "The snow's cleared. The road is open. Let's just go back to town." She points a finger at Daisy. "And you and I are going to do a lot of talking... and a lot of day drinking."

Daisy nods. "Sounds like a plan."

Sophie stomps through the cabin towards the front door, but pauses long enough to shoot me and glare. She speaks to Tom, but keeps her eyes on me. "Burn nana's couch.".

11

Daisy

Once Finn and Tom shovelled the snow off his truck, we were on the road and headed back to town. Sophie's ranting continued right until we left, and I'm not sure what traumatized her more. The idea of Finn and I being together, or having firsthand knowledge of what his penis looks like now. Either way, it won't be long before the girls find out, and I'm dreading it. Not because I regret anything that happened in the cabin. I wanted every second, and I wouldn't change a thing, except maybe having him inside me one more time before Sophie started screaming. I just don't know what to tell them when they inevitably ask, What now?

Finn and I are both focused on our goals. I mean, sure, he's doing a shade better than me right now, but it doesn't make me any less driven to achieve what I set out to do. I want to expand my business. I want The Gingerbread House to be global, like Starbucks or The Kardashians. I want The Kardashians eating at The Gingerbread House! And I'm just not sure how much room there is for someone else in those plans. How much of myself will I have to share with someone when I'm giving it all to my dreams?

Finn's got to be thinking the same thing. He's the venue manager for one of the most booked hotels in the country! The last thing he needs is me getting in his way, making a mess, like I always do. The cabin was fun, but it's better for the both of us if it ends when we get back to town.

I see the main street growing closer ahead, so it feels like the right time to make sure we're on the same page.

"Finn... I..."

"Did you want to get some lunch?" he asks, leaning back in the driver's seat and slinging his arm behind me. "I don't know about you, but I am starving." He chuckles. "I kind of feel like gingerbread. Can you believe it? I hated gingerbread before I got there. Hey, do you make gingerbread? I bet it's amazing."

I can barely believe my ears. Maybe there's still water in them from the shower.

"No," I murmur.

"No, you're not hungry or no, you don't make gingerbread?"

I'm silent as we reach the main street, and when the arena flies past the window and the billboard flashes the time for Friday night's game, Finn lets out a loud groan.

"Fuck. That's right. I play soon." He reaches out, his thumb smoothing over my cheek. "Are you going to come watch me?"

I slink away from his touch. "What's going on?"

He jerks back. "What do you mean?"

"We talked about this, didn't we? About how our careers were our top priorities?"

He shrugs. "Yeah. But that was before."

"Before what," I snap. "Before we screwed in our friend's cabin?"

I watch his face drop. "I mean, I wouldn't have said it like that, but yeah, actually. Are you saying you don't feel any different?"

I don't know if my heart will let me answer that question, so I avoid it. "I have a lot going on right now, Finn. I need to fix the bakery and my loan applications. Jesus, I need to fix Sophie's wedding." I slump in the passenger seat. "I should have told her when we were up there. Got it over and done with."

"We don't need to tell her anymore," Finn says as he takes a corner.

I cock an eyebrow. "What do you mean?"

"I'm just saying things are different now. Maybe we don't need to tell her at all."

"Stop talking like that," I say curtly. "Nothing has changed. Not you. Not me. Not us."

Finn clenches his jaw, pulling his truck over to the side of the road and slamming on the brakes. He turns to me, his eyes piercing with frustration.

"Why are you acting like this?"

"No, why are you acting like this?" I retort. "We're out of that cabin five minutes and you've got lunch plans and a hockey date set up. I thought I made it clear. I can't fit you into my life right now. I thought you felt the same."

"I thought I did too," Finn replies, his voice cracking. "But you blindsided me, Daisy. You made me care about something other than myself for the first time in my life, and now that I've felt that, now that I know how your body feels in my arms, I can't go back to the way things used to be. I won't go back. Please..." He grips my hand. "Let's give this a shot."

I slide my hand free, look out the window, and shake my head. "I'm sorry," I mutter.

"There's more to this," he says through grit teeth. "What is it?"

I'm silent and his voice growls at me.

"Tell me!"

"I'll mess it up, Finn," I say at last, our eyes meeting. "That's what I do. Mess things up."

He shakes his head and laughs lightly. "What are you talking about? You won't..."

"Yes, I will. What we had in that cabin was so perfect. I won't jinx it by letting it go on any longer. I'd rather us enjoy that memory than have me ruin it forever."

"Are you serious?" He reaches out and folds his hand around my fingers. "You can't let that be the reason you won't even try."

I pull my fingers loose from his grip, grab my bag, then throw the door open. "I'll walk from here."

Finn throws his head back and exhales. "Don't to this, Daisy. Get back in the truck."

I climb out and look over at him in the driver's seat. "I'm going to get Tom and Sophie in for a meeting tomorrow. I'll tell them everything. Don't worry. It won't affect you."

"Daisy, wait," Finn calls out, but I slam the door shut before he can finish.

As I walk down main street in crinkled, slept in clothes and black pumps, I fight with myself to not turn around, to not look back, to not run into his arms. I'm not going to do that to myself, not when it's taken this long to get where I am, and though it may not look like a lot to some, it's the whole world to me, and I just can't trust that Finn won't break my heart, or my dreams.

When I get to the bakery, it feels like I'm doing a walk of shame as I strut past the morning customers. I fidget with my hair and smile politely.

"Morning," I chirp brightly. "Try the apple donuts. They're delicious."

I quicken my pace to get to my office as Anthony watches gob smacked from behind the counter. I hear him mutter some instructions to our part-timer before he follows me out the back.

"Weren't you wearing those clothes yesterday?" he asks.

I collapse into my office chair and fling my bag in the general vicinity of the coat rack. "Obviously," I groan.

"I've been fielding calls all morning. The arena wants to know if you can put on some desserts on for the hockey game Friday."

I exhale and scavenge around my desk for a pen and paper beneath the piles of past due bills. "Okay, let me know what they need and I can get an invoice together."

"I think they're looking for donations," Anthony says through his teeth.

"Right. Pucks For Presents," I remember. I toss aside the pen I found and sink back into my chair. "Yes. Of course. Let them know we'll put something together."

"Sure thing," he replies. He purses his lips and glances at the ceiling. "So, are you going to tell me why you're wearing the same clothes from yesterday?"

I sigh. "Sure. Why not? I went to the cabin, like I said, but Sharona broke down, so Finn picked me up. Then we went to the cabin together and got caught in the snowstorm, so we had to stay overnight. We made a gingerbread house together and then Sophie found us naked in the shower this morning," I say in one long breath.

Anthony's jaw is practically on the floor. "You... and Finn Ross?"

His warm smile flashes behind my eyes, and the memory of his touch lingers on my skin.

I exhale. "Yes. Me. And Finn Ross."

"So what now?" Anthony asks. I didn't expect him to be the first one to ask that question.

"Nothing," I reply. "It was just a one off. We're both way too busy for it to be anything more."

"Well, that's bullshit. Busy people have relationships all the time," he scoffs.

I gulp. "I guess."

"So what's your real excuse?" he continues.

I narrow my eyes at him. "Don't you have bread to bake?"

"Daisy, I've not been here for long, but I'll tell you this for free. If you find something that gives you even a moment's joy, grab a hold of it with both hands and don't let it go. Especially this time of year."

"What's Christmas got to do with me and Finn?" I snicker, trying hard to ignore the sense he's making.

"It's not just you and Finn. Everybody. Christmas is a time for new beginnings, right? For forgiveness? Seems like a good opportunity to start fresh, and maybe if you get laid more, you won't make me work so much overtime."

A smile tugs at the corner of my mouth. "And how did that work out for you and Charlotte?"

Anthony moans and stabs a fist against his heart like he's been shot. "She already had Mr. Complicated in her life when I came around. Sometimes even a keeper like me can't compete with history. It was a really nice rehearsal dinner, though, so not a total loss."

I laugh. "I just don't know if I can do it."

"Do you care about him?" Anthony asks.

I only mutter out loud what my heart is screaming. "Yes."

"Then sure you can," Anthony says. "You're a bulldog, boss. So get over yourself and get to work. Now, if you'll excuse me, I have bread to bake."

He turns on his heels.

"Hey, Anthony," I call before he leaves, and he looks over his shoulder. "No overtime tonight," I state.

He puts his hands together like he's praying and casts his eyes to the ceiling. "Thank you Finn's penis."

I growl, pick my pen back up, and hurl it at him as he ducks out the door.

12

Finn

I didn't get a wink of sleep last night. I rolled around in my sheets, soaked in sweat even though it was fucking freezing. I can't stop thinking about Daisy. I was a fool to have agreed with everything she said at the cabin. I should have told her straight away that I didn't just want her for the night. That I wanted more. I keep picking up the phone and dialing her number, but I have no idea what I'd say if she picked up. I'm even tempted to use the wedding as an excuse, anything, just to get her to talk to me. It's been less than a couple of days, but already the distance between us is agony.

I'm sitting in my office at the Northwellian, tapping a pen against my knee while staring at the same bronze paper weight for the last hour. The only time I look away is to glance at my phone on the off chance it might ring, but so far nothing.

I held out hope that maybe she would change her mind, that everything she said was just noise cover, like running the tub in the bathroom. A distraction so she wouldn't feel embarrassed or appear vulnerable. I know enough about Daisy to understand how fiercely she values her independence. But as another hour ticks by, maybe I was wrong. Maybe I was the only one that fell, and fell hard, that night in the cabin.

To be successful in business, you must be disciplined, decisive and sometimes ruthless, no matter who gets hurt. I guess that's another thing I was wrong about. Daisy is cut out for this.

Suddenly my phone rings and after all the silent waiting, it scares the shit out of me. My leg flies out and my knee bangs hard against my desk.

"Fuck!" I yell. I throw away the pen and grab my phone. I put it to my ear, then groan when I realize it's upside down. I flip it around. "Hello?"

"Hey Cap, it's Tom," he says.

"Oh," I reply, my voice heavy with disappointment. "Hey, man. What's up?"

"I was just wondering if you're going to be at this meeting Daisy called at the bakery. It sounds pretty important."

"She mentioned it," I reply. "But I don't think I'm invited."

It's hard talking to Tom when I know exactly what the meeting is about, and even harder knowing how rough it's going to be on Daisy. She's brave, I'll give her that, but I would do anything to make sure she never had to suffer an ounce of sadness.

"She says it's about the budget," Tom continues. "Do you know anything about this? Sophie's getting nervous."

Again, I hate to lie. But I'm not going to fuck up again. Daisy wants to tell them, and she doesn't want me involved. She made that perfectly clear.

"Sorry," I say, my shoe tapping against my desk. "I don't know."

I can hear Tom breathing heavily over the phone. Sounds like Sophie's not the only one who's nervous. "Well, would you mind coming down?" he says finally. "If it's about the wedding, I think we should all be there."

"Tom. I'm really busy, and we've got the game coming up..."

"Finn," he says sternly, and I've never heard that tone in his voice before. "Can you meet us at the bakery in an hour, please?"

"Sure, man," I reply. "Of course. See you then."

Tom ends the call and I'm left not knowing what the fuck I'm supposed to do now. Daisy will be pissed if I show up. This is something she wants to do herself, plus there's the added factor that she wants nothing to do with me. But Tom and Sophie are not only my friends, but my clients. If there's a problem, I need to solve it.

I stand from my desk and button my jacket. Daisy wants to keep it professional. Well, this is me being professional. I leave my office, but my assistant Liz flags me down from her desk near my door.

"Finn, the arena called. They want to know if we're able to provide some donations for the charity game? They're giving away a bunch of free tickets for the kids, so wondered if we had something they could take home with them."

I nod. "Get I touch with Jim at ToyLand. Ask him if he can get some toys delivered to the arena asap. Tell him to invoice me directly."

Liz smiles and picks up the phone on her desk. "Right away."

As I stride through the opulent lobby of the Northwellian, a wave of festive warmth greets me. The air is filled with the scent of freshly cut pine, mingling with cinnamon and cloves. Glittering ornaments dangle from the towering Christmas tree, casting a soft glow over the marble floors.

The walls are dressed with elegant garlands, their golden ribbons intertwined with twinkling lights, while gentle strains of classic Christmas carols echo through the corridor, played by the pianist stationed in a corner.

The front desk staff nod their heads at me as I pass them, and I fish my keys out of my pocket as I stroll to my truck parked in the lot. I pass a trailer towing a stack of tables and chairs towards the marquee set up out back for Tom and Sophie's wedding. The linens arrived yesterday, and I believe the cutlery is being polished as we speak. Everything is going as planned. Let's just hope everyone gets paid.

I jump in my truck and head for the main street, and this anxiety is playing havoc with my stomach. What I wouldn't give for a small enclosed space with no way to escape. That would probably be less stressful than what I'm walking in to.

In a little under thirty minutes, I'm at The Gingerbread House and it's bustling as usual. Yes, I'm early. But I always am. That's the best way to never be late. Once I park and walk around to the entrance, I hold the door open for almost twenty people before I can get in myself. I bend in half to avoid a woman piled high with baguettes as she passes me, then flick my eyebrows at Anthony to get his attention.

I'm sure Daisy's newest employee sees me, but he doesn't react. He keeps serving customers. I frown and raise my hand at him over the crowd, but still nothing. I begrudgingly join the line, tapping my foot and checking my watch every five seconds while I wait my turn. When I finally reach the front, Anthony once again attempts to look past me.

"Hey," I say before he gets the chance. "I need to see Daisy."

He finally acknowledges me and lifts his chin towards the kitchen. "She's in her office. But she's having a meeting soon."

"I know," I reply, scratching the back of my neck. "Is she okay?"

"Why don't you ask her yourself?" Anthony says. "I can already see the problem with you two. Too much screwing around."

I furrow my brow. "Aren't you new in town?"

Anthony laughs. "I've lived a lifetime in Lake Mistletoe the last few days. I'll tell you that much. Next!" he yells past me.

An elderly woman shoves her elbow into my side as she pushes me out of the way. "Move, pretty boy."

"Jesus," I mutter, nursing my rib as I weave through the crowd towards the kitchen. I push open the double doors and Daisy stands from her desk when she sees me.

She points back at the doors. "No. Out!"

I shake my head as I carry on through the kitchen, headed to her office. "Tom asked me to be here."

Her face is already steaming with rage, her nostrils flared and her blue eyes wild like a lightning strike. "Oh he did, did he? How fucking convenient."

"You called a meeting about the wedding and he wanted me to be here. That's all there is to it, Daisy," I say sternly. I don't want to fight with her, but if I have to be short and cold, so be it.

"Do you know how hard this is going to be for me?" she asks, and there's a frailness in her voice. "I'm about to break my best friend's heart and completely humiliate myself. I really don't need you here to watch."

"Again," I say firmly. "This is just business, Daisy. Isn't that what you wanted?"

"Don't turn this around on me," she snaps. "This is what you wanted as well."

"I want you, Daisy!" I yell as my facade slips, and she falls silent. "I wanted you even when I didn't know that's what I wanted, but I sure as fuck know I want you now."

She gulps, her bottom lip clenched between her teeth, and when she looks at me, the rage is gone, and her eyes glaze over. "Finn..." she mutters.

The double doors swing open, the noise from the front flooding through the kitchen. Daisy and I turn to see Tom and Sophie standing there.

"Are we interrupting?" Tom asks, his arm around Sophie's shoulder.

Daisy smooths her hands over her emerald green skirt and shakes her head. "Of course not. Come in. I just didn't realize you had asked Mr. Ross to join us."

Sophie raises an eyebrow. "Mr. Ross? When did we start calling each other by our last names?"

I move out of the doorway and lean against the wall as Tom and Sophie enter. "Miss. James and I are trying to be professional. That's all."

Tom guides Sophie into one of the chairs in front of Daisy's desk, then sits down next to her.

"Sorry, Daisy. I asked Finn to come down. It sounded important on the phone," he says.

Sophie leans forward, resting her hand on the desk. "What's going on, Daisy. You're making me nervous. Is something wrong with the wedding?"

It's as if I can feel Daisy's heart pounding in her chest as I watch her search for the words. Tom and Sophie might not be able to see, but she's trembling, her fingers curled, her red nails digging into her palms. All I want to do is charge across the room and hold her. Of all the things we argued about wanting, this definitely wasn't one of them. This is killing me.

"Sophie," she starts, her voice wavering. "I need to tell you something. It's about the wedding."

Sophie puts one hand to her mouth, while the other grips Tom's arm. "Oh, my god. What's happened?"

Daisy's lip trembles. "Sophie... the budget..."

"...allows enough wiggle room to add the extra outdoor heating we talked about," I interrupt, crossing the room to sit on the edge of Daisy's desk.

Sophie's eyebrows knit. "What?"

"I think we're actually going to come in under budget," I add.

The stress melts away from Sophie's face. "Really?"

"Really," I say.

"Sophie..." Daisy starts, but I swiftly cut her off.

"Miss. James. Doesn't Sophie look so happy?"

Daisy gulps. "Yes. She does."

"And isn't the most important thing that Tom and Sophie have the most beautiful wedding possible?"

"It is," Daisy replies.

Sophie relaxes in her chair while Tom pets her hand.

"See," he says. "I told you everything was fine. Not sure why we had to drive through Christmas traffic to hear it... feels like this could have been a text."

"Miss. James and I just wanted to present you with a united front. We know our relationship has been tense and a stressful for you the last couple of weeks. We just want to assure you we're a team when it comes to your special day."

Sophie frowns. "Finn, I found you both naked in the shower. Why are you talking like this is strictly business?"

"Because it is," I reply. I look over my shoulder. "Right, Miss. James?"

Daisy is still shaking. "Right."

I clap my hands. "Great. So the tables and linen have arrived, and we realized we didn't properly plan for enough servers while going over the budget, but that's not a problem. The Northwellian will happily provide the extra staff to keep things running smoothly at no extra cost."

Sophie stands and wraps her arms around my shoulders, and I hear a heavy sigh of relief.

"Thank you, Finn. Thank you."

Then she walks around the desk and flings her arms around Daisy. "I'm so glad you agreed to cater my wedding, Daze," she gushes. "I'm so proud of you."

Daisy and I lock eyes and there's a palpable mix of rage and regret steaming between us. Tom nudges me and I turn to face him.

"Cap, why didn't you just tell me over the phone?" he says. "Sophie was pulling her hair out all the way here."

"Sorry, man," I say, slapping his back. "I should have said something."

"No harm done, I guess," he replies. "See you at the game?"

I nod. "Can't wait. I need to burn off some steam."

"I hear that."

We shake hands as Sophie finally releases Daisy from her death hold and rejoins Tom. He takes her in his arms and I have no doubt in my mind I did the right thing. I can't wait to see my friends get married.

"See you later," Sophie says as she and Tom leave hand in hand.

I know as soon as they vanish out those doors, Daisy is going to unload on me, and once again, she doesn't disappoint.

"What the fuck, Finn."

I stand up from her desk and head for the door. "I don't want to fight with you, Daisy. I said what I said and now it's done. Let's just get on with it."

"I was going to tell her the truth!" Daisy snaps.

"And what would that have achieved? Sophie leaving in tears? That doesn't sound like a great outcome to me," I state.

Daisy gulps, switching between crossing her arms and having them loose at her side. "So what happens now?" she mutters.

I can't help but chuckle. "Nothing right? Nothing at all."

I leave before she can say another word.

13

Daisy

Lottie, the local Lake Mistletoe mechanic, shakes her head dejectedly as she looks under Sharona's hood, her oversized, dangling Christmas tree earrings swaying side to side.

"I don't know what to tell you, hon," she says out the corner of her mouth. "I've seen crash test cars in better shape than this."

I lean against the garage wall with my arms folded across my chest, tapping my fingers. I'm only half paying attention. My focus is on the flashing neon lights at the arena down the road, and the stream of cars causing havoc as they compete for a parking spot. The Pucks For Presents game starts in ten minutes. I'm also nursing a teeny sore stomach. My own fault for rolling the dice with mystery meat burritos for Boss Buys Lunch day.

"So, what's your advice?" I ask, flitting my eyes between the Lottie and the arena.

"Insurance scam?" she replies.

My ears catch that part, and I give her my focus. "What?"

Lottie scratches the messy bun, that looks more like a bird's nest, on top of her head. "Sorry, Daze. It's time to put the old girl down. I can try to do you a deal. Buy her off you for scrap and give you a decent discount on a runabout. What do you reckon?"

My eyes are back on the arena. "Sure. Sounds good."

Lottie stands beside me, following my gaze. "Why are you here, anyway? Don't you normally go to the games?"

"I was going to skip this one," I reply.

"For Sharona?" Lottie laughs. "I towed it back tonight, but this could have waited until tomorrow."

"Not just Sharona," I say. "Other things."

"Oh lord," Lottie sighs. "What man has got you bothered, then?"

I roll my eyes. "It's not a man, Lottie."

"Fine, what woman, then?"

I laugh lightly. "It's not a man or a woman."

"Well, what is it then?"

"It's me," I say, letting out a long held breath. "I'm the problem."

"Should be easy enough to fix then," she says.

"It's that simple, is it?" I ask skeptically.

"Sure it is," Lottie replies. "Problems are like car repairs. Something's wrong. You pop the hood, figure out what the problem is, then fix it. The hard part is finding out what's wrong, but like you said, it's you. You're the problem. So just fix it."

"But what if I just make it worse?" I mutter.

"That's the great thing about cars. You can just keep fixing them. Flat tire. Busted alternator. Squeaky brakes. It's all repairable."

"Like Sharona?" I ask.

Lottie grits her teeth. "Oh, no. Sharona's a shit show. It's just a metaphor, hon."

My eyes widen as if a light switched on inside my thick skull. "You're right. You and Anthony. You're both right."

Lottie screws up her face. "Who's Anthony?"

"Lottie, do you have a car I can borrow? I need to get to the arena by intermission."

"Sorry, darling. Tad Junior just took the tow truck to a breakdown on the highway and the thing about a garage is most of the cars are here because they don't run."

"Damn it," I mutter. I my gaze falls on my beloved Sharona, but Lottie shakes her head vehemently. "Whatever it is, it's not worth risking your life for, hon."

"Dramatic," I mumble. I walk out of the garage and set my eyes on the arena. It's not that far. I can make it by intermission if I... oh my god, I can't believe I'm thinking this. Run? "Thanks, Lottie," I say as I leave. "I'll call you tomorrow."

I start down the road, the snow squelching under my feet. It's melted a little during the day, so it's not as deep as it can get sometimes. I walk to begin with. I've got to pace myself. I quicken my steps when I get comfortable and before I know it, I've broken into a comfortable jog. My heels clack on the sidewalk, but they're the least of my problems. I can do anything in pumps. The bitch is these boobs banging about once I get some speed going. Now I'm running with my arm across my chest so I don't give myself a black eye. The cold, dry air isn't helping and I'm barely halfway there before I'm completely out of breath.

"Don't you stop running, Daisy," I chide myself. "It's you. You're the problem." I force my feet to keep moving, my tongue hanging out the side of my mouth. "You're a bulldog, Daisy. A cute, messy bulldog."

By the time I reach the arena, I'm really trying to convince myself that Finn is worth it. The parking lot is still filling even though the game's already started. I drag myself past the front gate. There's no more running. There will never be running again. I'm staggering around like a zombie, straight into the path of cars hunting out empty spots.

A horn toots loudly at me, and when I turn, the stark yellow head lights flash me in the eyes.

"Hey. Watch where you're going!" the driver yells as she hangs out the window.

I clench my jaw and slam my fist on the hood. "Don't mess with me, lady! I have a very sore tummy!"

She raises her hands placatingly before receding back through her window.

I make it to the doors of the arena, and not a moment too soon. A second longer and I was going to puke all over the place. If I've learned anything from this journey of self-discovery, it's that I am not built for speed.

I push through the doors, and I'm immediately greeted by the ticket scanners. The lanky teen boy points his little beeping machine at me. That's when I realise I don't have my purse, my bag, nothing.

I look over his shoulder to see the game still going, but the period is in its last minute. I glance at the scoreboard. Mayhem up by two.

"I don't have a ticket," I say. I'm finally able to stand up straight, and it's nice to breathe again. "But I really need to get in there."

The kid laughs. "Yeah. I'm sure everyone would. This game is sold out."

"No. I really, really need to get in there."

The kid raises an eyebrow. "And why is that?"

Think, Daisy, think. Great, now the stress has my tummy ache coming back. I slide my hands around my belly, which inspires possibly the best and worst idea I've ever had.

"Because I'm pregnant," I state, plopping my belly out as far as it will go. I add a loving pat for good measure and nod towards the rink. "And daddy's on the ice."

"Shit," the kid gasps. "Of course. Go on through."

He moves aside and I give a warm smile, rubbing my belly one more time as I pass through. When I'm far enough away from him, I stand up straight and suck my stomach back in, and I frown when it doesn't retract as much as I thought it would. I'm either an amazing actress, or I pass a little too well for a pregnant lady when I'm, well... not.

I hurry through the stands, weaving between Mayhem fans screaming Go Home Sabres! I near the Mayhem bench, and spy Anthony at our Gingerbread House stall wearing the dark orange polo with the gumdrop buttons I designed, teamed with a matching visor. He's dividing his time between watching the game and serving free cookies to all the kids, but I gave him the night off. It's supposed to be one of our part-time staff hauling baked goods.

"What are you doing here?" I ask.

He's surprised to see me. "The new girl felt sick. I think it was those burritos. I couldn't get a hold of you, so here I am."

"I left my phone and all my stuff at Lottie's, sorry."

He grins at me. "And what are you doing here?"

I shrug. "Being a bulldog."

I climb behind the stall and rummage around the back, grabbing a takeaway box, then I scavenge through the cookies.

"Do you have a pen?" I ask, as I'm making a mess.

Anthony hands me one just as the crowd roars.

"Score!" the announcers booms. "That's another one on the board for Ward after a great steal from Ross! Ten-thousand dollars donated to the children's wing at Lake Mistletoe Hospital!"

I look up just in time to see Finn skate along the boards in his red jersey before he and his teammates gather around Blake to celebrate. The hooter blows, signaling the end of the period. I need to get to Finn before they head to the locker rooms.

I grab the box and plow my way down the aisle, fighting against the flow as spectators make their way up for hot dogs and beer.

"Excuse me. Pardon me," I yell as I weave through them.

I jump up to see over the crowd. Finn's on the bench, but they're heading towards the locker room.

"Finn!" I call. "Finn!" My patience has dried up and I'm straight arming people now. "Finn. Wait!"

I see him pull off his helmet and look up at the stands. His eyes find me in the crowd and he waves away his teammates, instead making his way towards me.

I finally reach him at the bottom of the stairs and I'm puffed again. I really need to get in shape, but who are we kidding? Finn stands over me, his hair soaked with sweat and clinging to his flushed face. He's sucking in air as heavily as I am, but I'm sure he looks much hotter doing it.

"What are you doing here?" he breathes, tucking his helmet under his arm.

"I came to see you," I gulp, my heart racing, my stomach in knots.

He looks towards the locker room, where the last of his teammates disappears. "I can't really talk now, Daisy."

"I know, I know. It's actually really stupid me just yelling at you in the middle of a game. I should have waited for you to be done. Maybe I shouldn't have come at all," I say in one long breath.

He laughs. "Okay, okay. Calm down. Why are you so red?"

"I ran," I say.

"You ran? Here?"

I nod. "From Lottie's."

"Gees," he says. "That's at least an eight-minute run. This must be important."

I frown. "I don't appreciate the sarcasm, but I came all this way so... here."

I shove the small white box at him. He puts his helmet on the ground, shoves his gloves under his arms, and pulls them off one at a time.

"Are you proposing?" he asks with a smirk.

I smile. "You wish."

He takes the box from me and opens the lid. Inside sits a gingerbread man and the note I scribbled about two minutes ago. Let's give this a shot.

A grin tugs at the corner of his mouth, and he narrows his eyes on me. "How do you know I still want to?"

"Fine," I say, turning on my heels.

He laughs and grabs my elbow to spin me back around. "Wait. Wait." He pulls me towards him and holds me in his arms. "I want you, Daisy. I really want you."

My cheeks flush red as my arms circle around his waist. "I want you too, Finn."

He leans down and kisses me, and the roar of applause from the crowd startles us both.

We laugh together and give the fans a wave.

"I better get to the locker room," Finn says. "I'm kind of the captain."

"Right," I say. "See you later?"

He picks up his gloves and helmet and nods as he walks backwards towards the shed. "Absolutely."

My heart swoons as I watch him go, our eyes locked in a teasing gaze that sends tingles through every nerve. But the spell's broken by a loud, slow clap and I recognize the ticket scanner kid standing beside me.

"Woo! Yeah, go Ross!" he howls. "Congratulations, bro! Way to put a bun in that oven!"

Finn's eyebrows leap up his forehead and he pauses before the locker room door with his mouth agape.

I laugh awkwardly, shake my head and give a dismissive wave. "It's nothing," I yell. "See you after the game."

I frown at the ticker scanner kid and his hand shoots over his mouth.

"Oh shit," he laughs. "Did I ruin the surprise? My bad."

For the rest of the game, I help Anthony at the stall and we clear out our inventory halfway through the third period. When the final hooter sounds, Mayhem wins 6 - 3.

"Thanks for coming along tonight folks," the announcer calls over the speaker. "And a special thanks to the local businesses who made this special charity game possible. ToyLand; Ford and Drummer; The Northwellian;

Talley's; Purr-fect Health Veterinary Clinic, and The Gingerbread House. I know I've eaten enough snickerdoodles to sink an aircraft carrier. Thanks again for supporting Pucks For Presents. Drive home safe, folks." The fans stand and slowly meander towards the exits. "Oh. One last thing, folks," the announcer says, and the crowd pauses. "This is a message from our very own Mayhem captain, Finn Ross. He wants to know if Daisy would like to go to Tom and Sophie's wedding with him."

The crowd erupts into applause and swooning woos as I feel my face burn an unnatural shade of red.

"What do you say, Daisy?" the announcer asks.

I look down to the bench and see Finn on his feet, a cheeky broad smile plastered across his face.

I let out a deep breath and nod at him. "Yes," I mouth.

Epilogue
Finn - Three Years Later

I lift Daisy's thigh higher on my hip and ease myself deeper inside her. Her nails dig into my shoulder as she whimpers softly into my chest. She's keeping quiet like she promised, but when I thrust harder, she can't help but cry out. I put my hand over her mouth and bury us further in the coat rack amongst the cashmere and fur jackets.

"You said you'd be quiet!" I whisper roughly, her muscles still clenched around me.

She giggles, the sound muffled inside my hand. I widen my fingers so she can speak.

"I'm sorry! I wasn't expecting that. I thought you were going slow."

I give a rakish grin. "That wasn't going to last long. Not with the way you're wearing that dress tonight."

She bites her lip and grabs me by my tie, dragging me to her lips. "Speaking of this dress, don't you dare make a mess of it."

I lift her thigh higher and her eyes roll back in her head. "Don't worry yourself with what I'm doing. Just keep quiet for once."

"Ummm... Mr. Ross... Miss. James. Are you in there?"

Daisy and I freeze, our eyes wide, and locked in a silent stare. This feels just like the time Sophie caught us in the shower at her cabin.

"Ah, yeah. We're here. Everything okay?" I ask.

"Ummm... we're out of cheesecake bites and the bartender says they're low on eggnog."

"Thanks. We'll get onto that straight away." I reply.

"Okay..."

Her footsteps trail away and Daisy and I burst into laughter. I pull out of her and quickly refasten my pants and belt. "I knew that would happen," I grumble. "I hate when we can't finish."

Daisy shimmies down her black sequin dress, the gorgeous smile on her bold, red lips immovable. "Yeah, but it's so much fun seeing if we can get away with it."

I poke the notch on my belt, then take her in. Her blond hair in loose curls over her bare shoulders, her skin buttery smooth, and it's hard to look her in those blue eyes too long without feeling unworthy.

"You look beautiful, Daisy," I say. Not sure if my words can hope to convey how much I mean them.

She drags her thumb over my lips, and I imagine she's wiping away traces of her lipstick. "Now Mr. Ross. That's not terribly professional."

I take her by the hips and pull her against me. "Fuck professional."

She giggles again and slaps my chest. "Enough. I need to get more cheesecake bites from the van and you need to sort out the eggnog. What's a Christmas Party without eggnog?"

I shrug. "Better?" I hate the stuff, but it was the client's request. Daisy frowns at me, so I relent. "I'll sort that immediately, Miss. James."

I hold my hand out, palm down, and she puts her hand on top.

"Break on three," she says.

"One, two, three, break," we say in unison before throwing our hands in the air.

She gives her dress a final adjustment before opening the closet door. Instantly, the thrum of Christmas music and banter and clinking glasses fills the air.

I stay behind for a second. It looks less suspicious that way, and Daisy and I have done this enough times to have it down to a fine art. We started as a way to work through my claustrophobia. She would sit with me in the closet and I would do visualizations and breathing exercises to manage the stress as best I could. But then something happened, and by something I mean one day in the closet, she climbed on top of me and fucked my brains out, and you know what? The small confined space was the last thing on my mind.

Now I'm not saying I'm cured by any means. But over the last three years, it's been a lot of fun trying.

Once Daisy is in the clear, I duck out of the coat closet as well, shutting the door behind me. I make a beeline for the bar, buttoning up my black blazer as I go. The bartender is mixing up a martini when I arrive.

"Did you hear about the eggnog?" he asks.

I nod. "I've got another keg in the van. I'll be back."

Waltzing through the glass-walled mansion feels like prancing through a winter wonderland on steroids. Daisy and I have planned a few celebrity parties, but never like this, and never on Christmas Eve. But with the amount of money the client was throwing around, we weren't going to say no. When it comes to work, Daisy and I are all in. The cherry on top? That we get to live our dream together.

This place is decked out like Santa's workshop on a designer budget; fairy lights, wreaths, even nine life sized fiber-glass reindeer pulling a sleigh, with an actual Santa sitting inside, greeting the famous guests who add their own sparkle to the festive chaos.

As I make my way outside, I pass a towering Christmas tree that could give Rockefeller Center a run for its money. The van is parked out front amongst Lamborghinis and Range Rovers, with the words The Gingerbread House Catering Company written across the side. Daisy and I have been in business for just over a year now and it's going great. I handle the finances; she takes care of the food, and everything in between, we do together. With Daisy still running the bakery, and me maintaining my role at The Northwellian, it makes for a pretty hectic schedule. But we make a great team, and there's no one I'd rather be utterly exhausted with.

I notice the sliding door is already open, and I'd recognize Daisy's backside even if I was a blindfolded blind man in a cave at night. I resist the urge to give it a pinch as guests stroll by.

The van's refrigerated and when she turns with a tray of cheesecake bites, her teeth are chattering. I give her arms a rub, then lean into the back myself to wrestle out the extra keg of eggnog.

"They're going to clean us out," Daisy says as warmth slowly returns to her.

"Good," I reply, heaving the keg onto my shoulder while sliding the van door closed with my free hand. "We can charge them a surplus product requirement fee."

She furrows her brow. "Do we have that?"

"We do now," I sigh.

Daisy smiles. "Fuck, I love you."

She lifts onto her tiptoes and purses her lips, so I bend to kiss her. "I love you, too," I whisper.

"Holy shit," a rugged voice with a southern twang calls out loud.

Daisy and I part and turn in unison to find a tall, ginger-haired man wearing a suit and Jordans walking excitedly towards us. He has a glass of champagne in one hand, while his other hand hangs loosely in his pocket, and it's hard not to notice he's wearing a silver, shimmering visor across his eyes when it's 11pm at night.

"Do you know who that is?" I ask.

Daisy shakes her head. "Never seen him before in my life. Maybe he's confused us with someone else?"

"Daisy? Finn? Is that you?" he chuckles.

"Guess not," I mutter. I stand up straight and clear my throat. "Hi there," I greet with a smile. "How are you?"

He gestures to himself, but I'm not sure how that is a sign of success.

"I'm doing amazing," he replies. "I thought I recognized you two." He nods at the van. "Are you catering this thing?"

Daisy nods. "Sure are. This is our business." She narrows her eyes. "And how's your work going?"

I try not to snort as Daisy begins the inquisition. Neither of us knows who this guy is, but we don't want him to know that. It's going to come down to a series of open-ended questions until we can get a hint.

"Work's great," he says. "Producing a new album this month. Another hit, no doubt."

Daisy shoots me a sideways glance, but I still don't know who he is.

"And how's the wife?" I ask. "And kids?"

He laughs. "Come on now, Finn! You know no one can tie down this mustang!"

Daisy and I exchange looks again. We're nowhere closer to knowing this man's identity.

"I couldn't help but notice you two smooching," he teases, giving my arm a playful punch. I remind myself he's a guest and force a smile. "Guess I had a little to do with that, eh?"

I furrow my brow. "You did?"

"Well, it was my closet, wasn't it!" he laughs, slapping his knee.

Daisy and I look at each other and the answer blooms on our faces.

"Phillip Meyers," we almost sing in unison.

He swipes off his visor and gives us an overly vigorous shimmy. "Fuck Yes! You didn't recognize me?"

"Of course we did," Daisy replies. "It's just been such a long day. You look great!"

Phillip bows. "Thank you, thank you. Not too shabby yourselves. So what's the dealio here, you two married?" he asks, waggling his finger at us.

I grit my teeth and cringe as Daisy holds up her hand, displaying a very bare ring finger.

"Great question, Phillip," she says snidely.

"It'll happen soon," I stutter. "But enough about us. You're a producer?"

He nods. "Indeed, I am. Business is good... in fact... here comes the star right now..." He puts his fingers in his mouth and lets rip a high-pitched whistle, attracting the attention of an ethereal, elf like girl hovering around the empty dessert tray near the door.

Her face beams when she sees him, and she swiftly prances over in her bejeweled shoes, dabbing a peck onto each of Phillip's cheeks.

"Hollie!" he gushes. "I want you to meet my friends from Lake Mistletoe."

I recognize the young woman, that's for certain. But I'm struggling to remember just what it is she does. Actress; singer; model? I look at Daisy to swap theories, but I find her standing bug eyed with her jaw on the ground, gazing in awe at this smiley, blond girl.

"This is Finn and Daisy," Phillip says. "Guys. This is Hollie Arrow."

"Nice to meet you," I reply.

"Oh, my god!" Daisy screams suddenly, and I realize her eyes are welling with tears. "I love you so much. Your last album changed my life." She sniffs. "You're so beautiful."

"Oh, my goodness. Thank you, you're so sweet," Hollie says with a bright smile, wandering over and touching Daisy's arm.

Daisy's eyes lock on the patch of skin, and I'm certain it'll never know the touch of soap again.

While Daisy obsesses over her celebrity encounter, the cheesecake bites on her tray have Hollie fixated.

"Where did you find these!" she gasps, reaching out and snatching one, then immediately stuffing it in her mouth. "I've been looking everywhere. I can't get enough of them."

"I made them," Daisy says.

"Get out of here!" Hollie squeals. She taps Daisy's other arm and now I'm worried about the future of bathing all together.

"No. Really," Daisy says, practically sobbing. "It's my own recipe."

"Well then, this is fate," Hollie starts. "You have to cater my engagement party."

She holds up her hand, and wriggles her ring finger dressed with the biggest yellow diamond I've ever seen, and even though Daisy is pretty star struck right now, I can still feel her death stare boring through my head.

"Please say you will!" Hollie pleads.

Daisy's lost for words, so instead is communicating with only nods and babbling. I step in front of her and smile.

"We would love to cater your engagement party, Miss. Arrow." I reach into my jacket pocket and retrieve a business card, handing it to her. "Please email us at your earliest convenience and let us know how The Gingerbread Catering Company can make your special day unforgettable."

She giggles and jumps and takes the card. "This is perfect!" She pecks Phillip on the cheek again. "See you in the studio, Philly." She glances back at Daisy and I. "And so lovely to meet you both!" She grabs two more cheesecake bites off the tray. "Thank you!"

Hollie skips off and Phillip slaps his hands together.

"Well, would you look at that? Congratulations you two. Hope you're ready for your business to take off overnight."

"Yes. Gees. Thanks for the introduction, Phillip," I say, shaking his hand.

"My pleasure," he replies. "Just call me your guardian angel, I suppose." He swipes on his silver visor, and now that I look at it, I guess it is kind of cool. "Have a great night, you two."

Phillip returns to the party, and a short time later, Daisy returns to the real world.

"Did that just happen?" she murmurs.

"Yes. It did," I reply.

"Are we catering Hollie Arrow's engagement party?"

I smile. "Yes. We are."

There's a slight wobble in my knees and she looks up, realizing I've been holding a keg of eggnog on my shoulder the entire time.

"Do you want to put that down?"

"Yes. I do," I groan, placing the keg on the ground.

I lean over her tray, and our lips connect in a way that still takes my breath away. I never knew what true love was before Daisy. I always thought I had to pick and choose which successes life would allow me. Surely I couldn't have it all. But as I gaze upon this beautiful woman who agreed to give it a shot, think back on the life we've built, and the life together still to come, all I can say, is thank god for Phillip Meyers and his fifteenth birthday party.

The MistletoeGrinch

BOOK FOUR
HENRY AND LOLA

1

Lola

I've always been a cup half full kinda girl. I can't think of any situation that's ever made better by hoping for the worst, so why waste your energy on worry and unhappiness? Waking up every morning, excited for a day of surprises, and unexpected pockets of joy, is all I ask for. Well, that and Lucas' car not stinking of crusty old socks and decomposing hamburgers. I mean, I'm optimistic about life and all its possibilities, but I still have a sense of smell.

I kick at the half-empty cans and drink bottles littering the floor of the passenger side, and grumble when a dribble of red Powerade stains my perfectly white sneakers.

"You must have been switched at birth," I groan. "There is no way a brother of mine could be this disgusting."

Lucas looks over at me, one hand lazily on the steering wheel while the other taps his knee in rhythm with the indie grunge music blasting from the speakers. He has my same big brown eyes with swirls of caramel, and warm brown hair that we both keep long. He's obviously taller than me, with dimples in the corner of his mouth and an immovable cheeky grin. My friends tell me all the time how cute he is, but all I see is my lifetime tormentor and destroyer of teddy bear tea parties.

"We came out at the same time, Lola," He groans. "Well, technically, I was five minutes before you."

"See! More than enough time for a quick switcheroo. I wonder what my actual brother is doing right now? Probably driving around in a lovely clean car, picking up the diamond bracelet he's giving his imposter twin sister on Christmas morning."

Lucas clenches his jaw. "Were we supposed to get each other something?"

I frown. Sounds about right. Buying presents would mean thinking ahead, and Lucas is too spontaneous for that. For example, he's just let the family know he's moving to Macaroy Beach. Already has a bartending job lined up. So, because I am the superior twin, I got him some new luggage. That way, he won't show up with everything he owns in two black garbage bags.

It will be the first time Lucas and I have ever been apart, and although I'm happy for him, it's going to feel as if half of me is missing. I'm jealous in a way, but not because he's leaving. I love Lake Mistletoe. I plan on spending my whole life in this town. I envy how brave he is to take the leap. I crave what's familiar and safe, and I'd much rather celebrate someone else's accomplishments. You'll never see me being the first to jump in the lake when the ice melts, but I'll be the one bounding up and down on the bank, cheering when someone else does.

Lucas, on the other hand, would bellyflop buck naked off a two-twenty-foot rickety platform blindfolded, whether the lake was thawed or not. Sometimes I wish I could be that sure of myself. People assume that because I'm the human equivalent of Tigger, I must be ridiculously confident. I'm actually the opposite. If I was, I'd probably be in the city, lead singer of The Thornes, with Dylan on bass.

God... why does he keep popping into my head when I least expect him to? Every time I think of him, I promise myself it'll be the last time. But that was about a million last times ago. Don't forget, Lola, I keep telling myself. He left you. For her. The cool, sexy blonde singer with the chic dark roots and gorgeous green eyes. No more thinking about Dylan. Starting from... now.

Okay. Let's see how long it lasts this time.

Lucas pulls up to my work and brakes hard, as usual. I jerk forward and kick a can of Dr. Pepper, spilling more sticky, sugary liquid onto my sneakers.

"Lucas!" I shriek.

"What! You asked for a ride. I don't guarantee a five star experience."

"I'll have my car back in a couple of days," I grumble, pulling a wet wipe from my bag and doing my best to tidy up my shoes. "So you'll have to do your best impression of a decent brother for a little longer."

He exhales. "Fine. I'll pick you up after work."

"No," I say. "Sophie is getting me. We're going out for drinks tonight. But I might need a ride home after."

Lucas rolls his eyes. "Oh, great. Because wasted Lola is so much fun. Can you promise I won't have to listen to My Heart Will Go On at full blast before you burst into tears again?"

I open the door, and the frosty morning wind whips against my face and sends a shiver down my spine. "All I'm saying is there was enough room for Jack on that door as well."

"Yeah, yeah," Lucas sighs. "We all know Rose was a royal bitch. Now, can you shut the door? I'm freezing my balls off."

I screw up my face. "Gross, Lucas," I grumble as I slam the door shut.

He takes off, spinning up snow behind him, and I hurry across the sidewalk to the doors of the clinic. There's a big sign across the building that reads Purr-Fect Pet Health, with a picture of a fluffy white cartoon cat wearing a stethoscope. I've been working here as a veterinary assistant to Henry Gallagher for almost two years, and even though I never envisioned a future where I'd have such a vast knowledge of pet suppositories, I love my job.

I fumble my keys out of my pocket and a bell jingles over the door when I open up. It's almost as cold in here as outside! I shiver my way to the thermostat and roll my eyes when I find the handwritten note taped to the control. Keep it respectable. We're not in the fucking Bahamas.

"That's a dollar for the swear jar," I say, snatching up the note and screwing it into a ball.

If you don't tread carefully, Henry has a temper on him. Usually all I have to do to soothe the bear is feed him meat and Red Bulls, but sometimes the Grinch in him gets out, and it only took one case of jamming his finger in a door during an exam and screaming motherfucker at a nine-year-old, for me to implement the No Swearing rule. One f-bomb equals one dollar. It's been working so well at the clinic that I've implemented it outside as well. It'll be good for him, plus I find it hilarious poking the bear.

I can't help but feel like a menace when I crank the thermostat to eighty-five. I know it drives Henry nuts, and when he arrives in the morning he heads straight for the control to turn it down. But it's just a little game we like to play, and his brow furrows in the most adorable way.

With the heat on, I slide out of my oversized baby-blue puffer jacket and hang it on the rack near the door, then head over to my desk and switch on the computer. Henry's not too fussed on Christmas decorations, but like that would stop me. You can barely see my desk beneath the layers of tinsel and Santa ornaments. I'm especially proud of my most recent addition. An animatronic dog in a Santa hat that barks We Wish You A Merry Christmas when you press his foot.

I do my rounds. Turning on lights, restocking supplies in the examination room, making sure the fridge in the lunchroom is full of Red Bulls for Henry. I pop into the overnight room, where we keep animals who need to stay after surgery. We don't have any right now, but there are five little guests who have been the highlight of my morning for the last few weeks.

I can hear them crying when I open the door and I scurry over with a bowl of kitten food in hand. They're all awake, tumbling and tangling with each other on a soft, fur bed in the corner of the room.

"Good morning, beautiful babies!" I gush as I drop to my knees, placing the dish in front of them.

Nick and Kevin are immediately face down and gorging, as always. AJ totters along a few seconds later, followed by Howie, who cautiously nibbles. It's always Brian who needs coaxing.

"Come on you," I say softly to the ginger, who is the smallest of the litter. "Time for breakfast."

I give him a scratch under his fuzzy chin and slowly Brian unfurls himself and wanders to the dish, finding a spot to eat amongst his siblings. While they're distracted, I give each one a gentle tickle around the ear, and try not to lose my mind over how cute they are. We found these babies at the front door of the clinic. Left in a box, along with an anonymous text on Henry's work phone to let him know they were there. He came in early to get them out of the cold, and they've been our guests ever since. They're almost ready to find their forever homes, just in time for Christmas. I'd love to keep one for myself, but Dad is allergic. Oh, the joys of still living at home.

I hear the bell jingle over the door and head out into the reception area. There's a young, sad-looking girl holding the hand of a man I'm guessing is her father, and the lead of a Golden Retriever. The door closes behind them and they approach my desk. I tuck my hair behind my ears and swipe on my brightest smile.

"Good morning and merry Christmas! Welcome to Purr-fect Pet Health," I say.

"Morning," the man says, and I immediately notice the somberness in his voice. "We're here to drop off Comet for his surgery."

I keep my smile warm and tap on my keyboard. "Yes. Good morning Comet." I scroll through the notes that Henry has left on his file. "This will be a quick fix," I say. "You'll have Comet back in no time."

The man nods, but the girl is unconvinced, and I see her eyes welling with tears. I lean over my desk, taking in the vibrant red of her coat.

"That's a lovely coat," I say. "I love the color."

She looks up at me with those sad eyes. "My grandma bought it for me."

"Well, it's the loveliest coat I've ever seen." I tap the name tag on my emerald-green shirt. "My name is Lola. What's yours?"

"Alice," she sniffs.

I smile. "Alice, I promise that Comet will be home soon. You have nothing to worry about."

She gulps. "Really?"

"Really, really," I reply.

Alice gingerly extends her hand, offering me the lead, and her dad gives half a smile as I lead Comet around the desk toward the overnight room.

"Thank you," he says.

"Not a problem. Have a great day, and I'll call you as soon as Comet is ready to be picked up."

The tears recede behind Alice's eyes and there's the tiniest curve to the corners of her mouth. "See you soon, Comet," she calls.

I wave goodbye as they head out the door and take Comet to a large crate with a big, fluffy bed inside. He twirls twice before dropping himself onto the bed, but as soon as I close the crate door he whimpers, and the sound is enough to break my heart.

I kneel. "It's okay, Comet. You'll be back with Alice soon."

Comet continues to whimper, and it's clear to me just how much this dog and his little girl mean to each other. I reach into the crate and scratch Comet behind his floppy ears.

"Well, I can't have you sad all day," I say. "Do you like music? I love music."

I stand up and grab my phone out of my pocket, then head over to a speaker sitting on a bench. It beeps when I turn it on, and I scroll through my phone, smiling when I find just the right track. I hit play, then return my phone to my pocket.

"Now this isn't everyone's favorite," I say as I walk back to Comet, "but it's impossible to be sad when it's playing." I turn my back to him, tousle my hair, then look at Comet over my shoulder when the song starts.

I threw a wish in the well

Don't ask me, I'll never tell

I looked to you as it fell

And now you're in my way

Comet looks at me, cocking his head to the side.

I trade my soul for a wish

Pennies and dimes for a kiss

I wasn't looking for this

But now you're in my way

Now I have the kittens' attention, with the five of them standing in a row, a twitch to their pointy ears.

Your stare was holdin'

Ripped jeans, skin was showin'

Hot night, wind was blowin'

Where you think you're going, baby?

With that I spin around, hands above my head, and it's at this point I'm not sure if I'm performing for Comet and the Backstreet Boys or just myself.

Hey, I just met you, and this is crazy

But here's my number, so call me, maybe

It's hard to look right at you, baby

But here's my number, so call me, maybe

Comet is up on his paws, his tail wagging ferociously, his tongue hanging clumsily out the side of his mouth as he pants, and I can tell by the shimmer in his eyes that he's also a huge Carly Rae fan.

God, I love my job.

2

Henry

I can hear Janie's voice on speaker phone, but the words don't make sense anymore. I was out the door and on my way to the clinic when she called, and now, twenty minutes later, she's still talking and I'm tuning out. It's not as if I don't know the topic, it's the same shit as always. Are you coming home this Christmas? Momma needs you to deal with Dad again. You're the oldest. It's your responsibility, and all I know is, I'm fucking sick of hearing it.

"Janie. Enough. I've told you. I'm too busy with work this year. I've got appointments scheduled right through to New Years."

"Just because you moved towns doesn't mean we don't exist down here anymore, Henry," she snaps. "You were a Gallagher before you were a veterinarian in Lake Mistletoe, and the ranch needs you."

"So this isn't really about me coming back for Christmas, then?" I say tersely.

Janie exhales. I can tell she's frustrated. With me gone, she's next in line and all the bullshit that our parents dumped on my shoulders has shifted onto hers. The ranch, the cattle, Mom and Dad at each other's throats most of the time, and our younger siblings are as useful as tits on a bull. I can't help but wonder if Janie really wants me to come back just so she can run away herself.

"Don't be like that. Of course, we all want to see you," she says.

"I told you last Christmas I wouldn't be back next year, and I'm sticking to that," I grumble.

"Okay. But what about next Christmas? The way you're talking, it's like you'll never be back."

I clench my jaw. "I'm taking it a Christmas at a time."

"Look, Henry," Janie starts. "I know you and Dad are going through some shit, but we're family."

My eyes widen when I spot the fluffy white cat with a stethoscope and it's not a moment too soon.

"Janie, I'm just pulling up at work. I'll have to talk to you later."

"Okay, Henry," she says, the disappointment clear in her trailing voice. "Bye."

I end the call and sink into my chair, then bang my hand angrily on the steering wheel as I park. The whole reason I came to Lake Mistletoe was to get away from the drama that my family carries around like backpacks. No one knows me here, no one has expectations, no one tells me what my responsibilities are. It's a freedom I've been craving my whole life. Somewhere far away from the ranch, and far away from my father. I hate that this is a burden Janie has inherited, but if I didn't get out of Rockford Valley, I was going to explode. She'll probably do a better job than me, anyway. Janie is strong.

I climb out of my car and head into the clinic, and it's not long before I notice the waiting room packed tight with dogs on leads, cats in carriers, all wrangled by their grumpy-looking owners. I push open the door and the bell jingles, drawing the attention of the waiting masses. Suddenly, all eyes are on me and staring daggers. I look over their heads toward Lola's desk. She's not there, which explains the commotion. I quickly shrug off my coat when a blast of heat washes over me. Her and that fucking thermostat. I can't imagine the Caribbean climate is adding to these people's moods.

"Morning, folks," I grumble as I weave my way toward the thermostat. I'm a big guy, so my broad frame shoving people around isn't helping. "I'm sure Lola is around here somewhere. Has anyone pushed the buzzer?"

A thin, wiry woman with gray hair slicked back into a bun and gold-rimmed glasses balanced on the edge of her swordfish nose steps forward and, when I spot her, I wish I hadn't asked.

"Of course we have, Dr. Gallagher. Numerous times, but to no avail. Exactly what kind of medical office are you running here?"

It's a struggle to not roll my eyes, but my low grumble is unavoidable. "Good morning, Mrs Bearenstein."

She reaches down to her feet and returns with a pastel-mint cat carrier, the narrow head and giant ears of her Cornish Rex bobbing around inside.

"Anastasia and I have been waiting for hours," she states. "I don't know about you, Dr. Gallagher, but I am a very busy woman and this simply won't do."

I finally reach the thermostat and see that Lola has paid no attention to my note, cranking it up to eight-five. I turn it down to a respectable sixty-seven.

"We've only been open a half hour, Mrs Bearenstein, but I understand your frustration." I peer around the room for Lola again. "Now let me just find my assistant."

Mrs. Bearenstein scoffs. "I'm not surprised it is chaos around here with that girl running things. Always with her head in the clouds. Why you keep her on is beyond me."

A woman behind her raises her hand to catch my eye, while her other hand grasps the lead of the French Bulldog snorting at her feet. She points down the hall, toward the overnight room, and that's when I notice the music.

"I think she's down there," the woman says.

"Thanks," I reply. "Just a second, folks. I'll be right back."

I have a long stride, so make it down the hall in no time, although not quick enough as far as Mrs. Bearenstein is concerned. The music grows louder with each step and I frown when I recognize that pop shit Lola plays nonstop. I reach the overnight room and glance down the hall to reception to find not only Mrs. Bearenstein standing there watching me like a ghost haunting an old mansion, but the beady yellow eyes of Anastasia tracking me as well.

I force something that resembles a polite smile before pushing the door open to find Lola spinning in circles while a Golden Retriever lumbers playfully in his crate and a cluster of kittens watch on.

Before you came into my life, I missed you so bad

I missed you so bad, I missed you so, so bad

Lola croons at the top of her lungs while the backing track blares from the speaker. She turns on her heels, her arms stretched wide as she spins like a hurricane, and all I can do is brace myself when she heads in my direction, colliding with my chest and coming to an abrupt stop.

I hold her by the shoulders before she can fall, and although I was angry a few seconds ago, when she looks up at me with those big brown eyes, I can't remember what had me upset.

"Henry!" she says, snapping to attention. She still has to crane her neck to meet my eyes. Even standing straight, Lola barely comes up to my chest. "Good morning. Red Bull?"

I exhale a long breath. "Lola, do you know there are people in the waiting room?"

She bites her lip and nervously tucks her brown hair behind her ears. She wears it half up, half down most days, with pretty colored clips to hold it back from her face. Today they're green with bright pink flowers. Her cheeks are flushed, probably because she's been spinning around the room all morning, and it makes her skin glow, as if she's bathed in sunshine when it's snowing outside.

"Right. I'm sorry! I got distracted."

She hurries over to the speaker and switches it off, and the animals actually look disappointed when the room falls silent.

I look at the Golden Retriever in the crate. "And who is this?"

She smiles. "This is Comet. His owner, Alice, just dropped him off. He has a minor surgery this afternoon, and she was worried. So was Comet. I was just trying to cheer him up."

My gaze switches to Lola. "With Carly Rae Jepsen?"

Lola opens her arms toward Comet. "Well, he looks much happier, if you ask me. Music releases endorphins, you know, which is great for reducing stress."

This time I can't contain my eye roll. "Now that Comet is relaxed, can you maybe go out front and calm down all the people sweating themselves silly in the waiting room? Without singing, if possible."

Lola frowns. "It's not that warm out there."

"It's the fucking surface of the sun, Lola," I grumble.

She raises a stern finger. "That's a dollar in the jar, mister." She holds out her hand with a massive smirk on her face while I pull out my wallet and dig a note out. Lola snatches it eagerly. "With how well the swear jar is doing, we'll be able to get one of those massage chairs you see at the mall for the lunchroom."

"Oh, joy," I groan. "Now, waiting room, please?"

She gives me a salute. "Yes, sir!"

I follow her out of the overnight room and can't help but notice the swish in her hips as she jaunts along. I drag my eyes away from her backside and the hypnotic way it bounces behind her, and when I glance over my shoulder, I'm sure that Comet is judging me. He's recently become a member of a popular club here at Purr-fect Pet Health. The We Love Lola club.

Mrs. Bearenstein wonders why I keep Lola on, even though an abandoned front desk and dancing with the animals are regular occurrences. Because, in all my years, I've met no one as kind and sincere and genuine as Lola Nixon. Whether it's helping or supporting pet owners when they're at their lowest, or belting out a pop song to a nervous dog, Lola makes it her job to put a smile on everyone's face, and when you find someone with that special gift, you allow them to express themselves from time to time, and fuck with the thermostat now and then.

Lola is what's great about this clinic, and not just for the pets and owners who walk through those doors. Knowing I'll see Lola every morning definitely makes it easier to get out of bed when it's freezing outside.

Lola carries on to her desk while I take a left and go into the examination room, awaiting my first patient of the day. I take my white coat from the rack behind the door and pop a blue pen and a red pen into the chest pocket. I wander to the desk and collect my glasses from the drawer, blinking my dark brown eyes twice before they adjust. I catch sight of myself in the glass storage cabinet and do my best to tame my shaggy, dark hair. I keep forgetting to get a trim, and it's getting pretty unruly now.

The door opens and my lips fall in a straight line with a hint of an upward turn in the corners, which is about as close to a smile as I get. But that tiny lift falls flat when I see Mrs. Bearenstein stamp in with her pastel-mint cat carrier. She heads straight for the examination table and places the carrier on top.

Lola pokes her head in, her teeth clenched. "Mrs. Bearenstein and Anastasia to see you."

"Yes. Thank you, Lola," I reply as she closes the door. "Hello again, Mrs. Bearenstein." I peer into the carrier. "And what is troubling Anastasia this week?"

Mrs. Bearenstein raises her nose in the air. "I'm not sure I approve of your tone, Dr. Gallagher."

I exhale. "My apologies. It just feels like I'm seeing you both so much, which is a real treat, but I'm just not sure there's anything wrong with Anastasia."

"I think I know my darling better than you do," Mrs. Bearenstein snaps curtly. "Now, I have changed her diet, and I moderate exactly what goes in and out, and nothing is coming out." She leans toward the carrier and her eyes soften, something I'm not used to seeing. "She is so unhappy and I can't stand it. You must help her."

For the first time I feel a tinge of sympathy for Mrs. Bearenstein, who has been a pain in the ass since I moved to Lake Mistletoe two years ago. I see her and this damned cat more than anyone else in town, and no matter how many times I tell her Anastasia is perfectly healthy, she still shows up every week with some new ailment. I wouldn't mind if she was at least pleasant, but Mrs. Bearenstein is the grumpiest witch I've ever met, and that says a lot coming from me. I'm compared to the Grinch on a daily basis.

But I'll give her one thing. She loves her cat like it was her own child and, from what I've gathered, Mrs. Bearenstein doesn't have any actual children, or even family. Not that I've seen, anyway, but her chilly demeanor means I'm in no hurry to ask.

"Okay, let me see here," I say, popping open the carrier and gently retrieving Anastasia. I look her over and run a hand over her belly. "She does feel a little tight."

Suddenly the door flies open and Lola's back, and Mrs. Bearenstein clutches her chest as if she's about to have a heart attack.

"Hi, sorry to interrupt!" Lola says. "Henry, just a reminder that I have to leave a little early today, but I'll make sure everything's spic and span before I go." She goes to leave, then turns back again. "I'm getting sushi for lunch. Did you want some?"

I shake my head, keeping my eyes focused on Anastasia. "You know I don't like sushi."

"What about a salad? Or anything that's not a whole cow between two loaves of bread?"

"Not now, Lola," I sigh.

"Right," Lola says. "Just looking out for you, Henry." She smiles brightly at Mrs Bearenstein, whose expression resembles someone who just ate a lemon. "By the way, love your cardigan, Mrs. B! The little flowers are the cutest!"

Lola finally leaves and Mrs. Bearenstein glances down at her olive knit cardigan with pink embroidered flowers. "Seems very unprofessional, calling you by your first name. Is that allowed?"

I look up from examining Anastasia, and can't believe my ears. Even after doing her best to be friendly, Lola has somehow offended this woman.

"We're pretty casual around here," I respond. I don't want to get into an argument. I just want to make sure Anastasia is fine before sending the pair of them on their way.

"Honestly, Dr. Gallagher. I'm sure you can find someone who takes their job a little more seriously to assist you, and that makeup ... is it appropriate for the workplace?"

"Again, pretty casual," I reply, and I can feel my patience wearing thin.

"And do I understand correctly that the reason we were left waiting for hours in that steaming hot room was because she was singing to the animals?"

I release the breath I've been holding, and it rumbles in my throat. "It was thirty minutes, Mrs. Bearenstein, and for your information, music releases endorphins which help to reduce stress."

"What nonsense," she scoffs. "You're beginning to sound just like that silly girl."

I gently place Anastasia back in her carrier and click the door shut as Mrs. Bearenstein watches curiously.

"All done here," I state, a sharpness in my tone. "I'll prescribe Anastasia some pills to help with the constipation. Can I prescribe some for you while I'm at it?"

Her eyes widen, and her glasses almost fall right off her nose. "Pardon me?"

I lift the cat carrier and hold it toward her. "Lola will have your prescription for you at the front desk. Have a great day, Mrs. Bearenstein."

She reaches out and takes the carrier, her jaw practically on the floor as she slowly makes her way out of the exam room. She gives me one last stunned look before she leaves, and I reply with a wave and a real actual smile, and I can tell by the tightness in my cheeks that my mouth isn't used to it.

Lola walks in, craning her head over her shoulder to watch Mrs. Bearenstein leave. "She's grouchier than usual. Is she okay? Maybe I should follow her out to her car and check."

Lola never fails to surprise me. Even when she has to deal with someone as difficult as Mrs. Bearenstein, who's never had a nice thing to say about her, she continues to look for the best in people, even if they don't always deserve it, and for that I'm grateful. That's another thing Mrs. Bearenstein doesn't realize. I don't put up with Lola. It's the other way around.

"She'll be fine. Back next week, no doubt."

Lola smiles. "Okie dokie. Well, Terry and her French bulldog, Betsy, are next. Are you ready for them?"

I nod. "Yes, but first ..."

Lola holds up a finger. "Red Bull?"

I work my mouth into a smile again. It's always easier when I'm looking at Lola. "Yes please."

3

Lola

I sit at my desk, finishing up the last bits of paperwork so I can get out early today. I'm having drinks with the girls, and I'm so excited for a catch up. Since they've started pairing off, I barely get to see them. It's like Sean and Lexie were a ripple that started a tsunami! Next thing I know, Blake and Charlotte are all over each other. It wasn't a complete surprise. I always got the feeling it was just a mess of sexual tension behind the teasing. But Finn and Daisy! I still don't know if I've recovered from that revelation. But, oh my god, when he asked her to the wedding over the loudspeaker at the hockey game, that was possibly the most romantic thing I'd ever heard. Daisy was so happy. They all are. I wouldn't mind a little piece of my own happiness if it's going around.

I look over at Henry's office. His door is open, and he's washing his hands in the sink. He swipes his glasses off his eyes and rubs the bridge of his nose, then twists himself out of his white coat. His shoulders are broad and his arms thick and muscled. He always struggles to get the sleeves off. I should probably mention it, suggest that he get himself a size up. But then I wouldn't get treated to watching him try to get it off every day, and catch sight of his toned stomach and sharp V-lines when his shirt rides up.

I rest my elbow on my desk and lean into my hand, my jaw slightly open as I gaze in awe at the beauty of this man. I catch sight of the trail of dark hair that starts at his belly button and disappears beneath his belt, and my mind drifts to where that glorious path leads.

"Excuse me," a voice says.

I snap from my trance. "Snail trail," I blurt.

The woman blinks at me. "Pardon?"

"Nothing," I say, dabbing the drool from the corner of my mouth. "I'm Lola, and welcome to Purr-fect Pet Health. Merry Christmas, and how can I help you?"

The woman eyes me oddly, but I just keep smiling.

"I have an appointment," she says, gesturing to a fluffy gray bunny in a cage under her arm. "Buttons, at 5 o'clock?"

I check the computer and nod. "Fantastic. You're Dr. Gallagher's last patient of the day. Follow me."

I walk around my desk and lead Buttons and his owner into Henry's office just as he's hanging up his coat.

"This is Buttons," I announce, patting the examination table.

The woman pops the cage onto the smooth white surface, then leans over to check on her bunny.

"Last one," I say to Henry as I join him by the sink. "I'm all up to date with invoices and I've sent appointment reminders to tomorrow's patients, so I'm going to head out now."

Henry nods. "Right. Drinks with the girls. Well, have fun."

"Always," I reply. I go to leave, then spin on my heels. "Don't forget to give the Backstreet Boys fresh water before you go."

He frowns and nods. "You really shouldn't have named them. It's only going to make it harder when we have to give them away."

I shove my fingers in my ears. "Sorry. I can't hear you. Bye."

I hurry out of the office, and I don't have to look back to know he's shaking his head at me. I heard him perfectly fine, but I'm happy living in my delusional world where the kittens live with me at the clinic forever. Also, in this world, my best friend is Katy Perry and I have a closet packed with Jimmy Choo shoes.

I grab my bag from behind my desk and my coat from the rack before heading out into the windy, cold evening. We decided to have drinks at Big Red's, a great little bar on the main street that's standing room only on Friday nights after the game. Lexie and Charlotte tried to talk us into Talley's, but the rest of us saw through that straight away. No boyfriends tonight. Plus, I'm still traumatized after Lexie told me the bathroom story. Jesus.

Big Red's isn't far from the clinic, so I pull on my coat, pin my ears back and power through the short walk to the bar. I pass the streetlamps wrapped in festive ribbons and bows, their golden glow warming the incoming evening. The loops of twinkle lights hanging from the eaves remind me of fireflies, and when I hear Last Christmas belted out by a throng of croaky, slurred voices I can't imagine anywhere else in the world I'd rather be. The lights from Big Red's spill onto the snowy sidewalk, tinted amber by the foggy stained-glass windows, and the moment I step inside I'm completely at ease.

The doorman, Chaz, nods at me stoically as I pass by, and I'm greeted with hugs and smiles from the people I've grown up with. I spy my friends at a table near the stage, dancing in place and singing along with the couple crooning another verse from Last Christmas. As well as the familiarity of it all, another great thing about Big Red's is their open mic nights, when anyone can jump on the karaoke machine and sing their hearts out. That used to be me, but I'm just an avid spectator now.

At the table, Daisy's the loudest, and going by the amount of empty glasses in front of her, the furthest in. Lexie and Charlotte are showing each other something on their phones, and again, after not being able to erase Lexie's detailed descriptions of her bathroom escapade, I don't want to even imagine what they're looking at. Sophie notices me first and throws her arms around my shoulders, pulling me into a hug. She's warm and giggly and happy, just as she should be a week out from her wedding day.

"You made it! He let you finish early then?"

I nod and pull off my jacket, hanging it on the back of the stool. "Oh, yeah. Henry's a sweetheart like that."

Sophie's cheeks are flushed, which probably has something to do with the prosecco in her hand. "Well, you're the only who sees it, babe," she says, her voice a little slurred. "Tom came home an absolute mess because he asked Henry if he needed his water bottle refilled at hockey training the other day and Henry called him a bitch boy."

I try to stifle my laugh, but a snort squeaks past my defenses. "That's terrible," I quickly deflect.

Sophie frowns. "I'm just saying. If you mentioned to anyone in Lake Mistletoe that Henry Gallagher is a sweetheart, they'd tell you to get a concussion check."

"Lola!" Lexie cries, mincing over to me with a glass of prosecco in each hand. "You have to catch up!"

She hands me a glass, then clinks hers with mine before knocking it back in one gulp. It's an impressive skill. Lexie's been a pro-sculler since high school. Me, on the other hand, slow and steady wins the race. One glass goes straight to my head and turns me crazy stupid. I take a sip and smile for her. "Mmmmm. Yummy."

She laughs and hooks her arm around my neck before joining in with the chorus.

"Thanks for coming out," Sophie says, snuggling up alongside of me. "I've been so stressed out. It's nice to take a break for a night. Who knew it would be so hard to find a night we were all available?"

"Right!" Charlotte adds to the conversation, her voice a little louder than the singing. "Blake wanted to play laser tag tonight. He thinks he's close to beating my high score, but he's dreaming." She nods her chin at Lexie. "And as for her, she barely comes up for oxygen long enough to associate with her friends."

Lexie frowns. "I'm also doing a lot of work at the arts center, thanks very much. If you want to talk about schedules, what about Daisy? Every time I call the bakery, Anthony tells me you're at another long, business lunch with Finn."

Daisy sips her wine and grins at us over the rim of her glass. "Well, it's definitely long and we're absolutely eating."

"Gross, Daze," Sophie says, poking her tongue out. "Do I need to remind you all that I'm the one who caught them in the shower? I wake up screaming in the night when I remember I've seen Finn's dick."

Daisy tilts her glass at Sophie. "You're welcome."

"Well, once I locked down everyone else, I knew you'd be available any time, Lola," Sophie says, raising her glass to her lips, but she pauses once she realizes what she's said.

I give half a smile. "No social life. That's me."

"That came out wrong," Sophie says, slapping her hand against her forehead. "I know you're super busy too."

I laugh and rub Sophie's back. "No. It's fine. I totally get what you're saying. I don't have a boyfriend I need to plan around. In my opinion, that makes me the lucky one."

Daisy raises her glass. "That's the spirit, Lola."

"Besides, after what happened with Dylan... ," Charlotte says. "What a fucking asshole."

Sophie rolls her eyes. "Let's not get started on Dylan, okay?"

My stomach drops every time I hear his name, and even though I promised myself this morning was the last time I'd think about him, what can I do when my friends are bringing him up?

"What's he even doing now?" Charlotte asks.

I shrug. "I don't know."

In reality, I do know. He's living in the city, trying to get a record deal with his new band, living in a cozy apartment with his new girlfriend, the cool, sexy blonde with the chic dark roots, who also happens to be the new lead singer.

"Geez. I wonder if he's still with that girl," Sophie says.

I roll my shoulders and take another big sip. "I don't know," I say, when I come up for air.

I do know. They're very much still together. Her name is Savannah.

"What a jerk," Daisy says. "He was a shitty bass player too."

Actually, Dylan is pretty good. But I appreciate Daisy's effort. It's the thought that counts.

"Such a shit," Lexie adds. "You were always too good for him in high school."

Daisy furrows her brow. "Do you really want to get started on the quality of high school boyfriends?"

The girls burst into laughter, and I'm more than happy for someone else to be the center of attention. How am I suddenly the sad little single girl of the group, and when did it become casual conversation to talk about Dylan like he's the reason I'm alone? I mean, sure, technically yes, he's the one who ended things. But I could start dating again if I wanted to. It's just this pesky lack of self-esteem after a massive act of betrayal that's holding me back. But that's got nothing to do with Dylan. Maybe if I keep telling myself that, it'll sink in.

After the last notes of Last Christmas screech over the speakers, the couple bow to the crowd and receive a round of applause. As I lean on the table, I feel an elbow in my back as someone tries to squeeze between me and the people at the table next door.

"So sorry," the woman says, and I recognize her voice before I turn to see her face.

"Oh hi, Krista," I greet her.

Her skin is pale, her dark hair sitting in waves on her shoulders. She pauses and narrows her bright blue eyes on me, taking in every inch of my face as if she didn't see me almost every day not too long ago.

"Lola," I say, immediately wishing I hadn't bothered in the first place. "From the clinic."

"Oh, right!" she says. "Henry's receptionist."

"Veterinary assistant," I correct.

A grin tugs at the corner of her mouth, and it's then I know for sure she knew exactly who I was. "How is Henry?"

"He's great," I reply.

"Really?" she asks.

"Really, really," I respond.

"Well, good for him. Maybe our break up has given him some focus. Henry has so much potential, but lacks drive and ambition, you know?" She puts her bony hand on my shoulder and I notice she's still wearing the diamond engagement ring, which is pretty ballsy for someone talking trash about their ex-fiancé in a bar. "Lucky he has you around to fetch him sandwiches and Red Bulls."

"I thought you broke up because he didn't want to go to your lame karaoke birthday party with your lame doctor friends?" I blurt.

The girls gasp and whisper to each other behind their hands. My toes are tingling as the prosecco gets to work on me. I know what I said, I even replay it in my head, and I don't regret it. Maybe it's the wine, or maybe it's because Krista is a bona fide bitch.

Her jaw clenches, and she folds her arms over her chest. "There were many reasons things didn't work out between Henry and me. He and his receptionist making moon eyes at each other constantly being one of them."

I take another sip of wine and glare at her. "Veterinary assistant."

Krista's face turns sour and she spins on her heels, turning her back on me as she storms to join a group on the other side of the bar.

"Holy shit, Lola!" Charlotte snorts. "What was that all about?"

Lexie nudges my shoulder. "Look at you. What a badass."

I finish my wine and slap the glass on the table. "Another round?"

The girls raise their glasses and Daisy signals to the server who weaves her way through the crowd.

That's right. I'm Lola the badass. I'm single, happy, great at drinking alcohol, totally over my ex, and one hundred percent not viciously attracted to my boss. Just a few fresh additions to the list of things I need to keep telling myself.

4

Henry

There's nothing I like better than getting home from work, throwing on some sweatpants and spending the evening in front of the TV with Bombay and Goldberg, Bomb and Goldie for short. My German Shepherd, Bomb, likes to curl up right beside the fireplace, while Goldie, a very un-golden Labrador cross, is my dedicated footstool, always nudging his way underneath my feet until they rest on his back. Both dogs are getting on, with flecks of gray through their coats. The animal rescue center said no one wanted to adopt them because they were old, grumpy and slept all day, which made them undeniably perfect for me. Just three grumpy bastards watching Fraser re-runs and snoozing during the commercials.

As blissful as that is, lately I've been wondering what having someone else in my life might be like. Someone on the couch beside me, to fall asleep in my big arms, to kiss goodnight. Not that Bomb doesn't love a good smooch, I'd just prefer less drool. But I can't shake the fear that, even if I go into a relationship with the best intentions, it'll all turn to shit in the end. I watched my parents fall out of love, and I saw firsthand how a loveless marriage turned them cold and bitter over the years.

The worst part was they didn't even have the decency to shield me and Janie, Rob and Stella from any of it. Nope. We got front row seats to the screaming and the blaming and the slamming doors. Now all four of us are terrified of ending up the same. Whether it's being the instigator, like our asshole of a father, or the sufferer like Mom. Seems like the best way to avoid a broken heart is to not let someone get anywhere near it.

My phone rings, the screen lighting up my darkened living room with flashes of neon-blue light. When I read Janie's name, I look away and try to focus on what Marty's getting up to on Fraser, but Janie's persistent. When I don't answer the first time, she calls back. What if this time it's not about going to the ranch for Christmas? What if something happened to Mom or Rob or Stella? I release a rumbling groan from the back of my throat and pick up the call.

"Avoiding me?" Janie asks.

I lay back and sprawl my arm across the back of the coach. "Never. Is everything alright?"

"It's Stella ..."

I bolt upright and I'm immediately alert, figuring out in my head how fast I can get to Rockford.

"She says she's not coming to Christmas if you're not going to be here. You've got to talk to her."

My shoulders slump and I slouch back into the couch. "Really, Janie? It's almost midnight, and this is what you're calling me about? I've got work in the morning."

"If I have to deal with Mom and Dad and the three-ring circus you're conveniently turning your back on, then you can deal with baby sister. You're the only one she listens to anyway."

I exhale. "Fine. I'll call her in the morning." There's silence, and I hope that maybe that's all there is to this phone call. "Is that all?"

"No, actually, got an hour?"

I roll my eyes, then feel my feet drop and hit the carpet. I look down to see Goldie meandering out of the living room. Even he doesn't want to hang around for an hour of phone time with Janie. Lucky bastard. As Janie launches into her tirade, my phone vibrates. I pull it back from my ear with relief to check the notification.

LOLA: Heyyyyyy. Can u pik me up? Big Reddds. Thnx.

My head jerks and I squint my eyes to read the message a second time. I only use my glasses for work, but I wish I had them right now. Nope. Definitely says what I think it says. Weird. She's never asked for a ride before. But her car is at Lottie's, I guess. I furrow my brow and read the text twice more.

"Henry, are you listening?" Janie snaps.

Whoops. I put the phone back to my ear. Even if I have misread Lola's message, I'll take any excuse to escape from this call.

"Yeah. Sorry, Janie. I've got a work emergency. I have to go."

"Another awesome fucking convenience," Janie says, her voice trailing off as I hold the phone at arm's length and press end.

I return to Lola's message. Do I reply? I open the chat box, and you'd think I was re-sitting my vets exam again with the amount of thought I'm putting into this. Then another text pings through.

LOLA: Hurry itz cold!!!!!!!!!!!!!!!$%!!!!#$

I shrug and rock to my feet. Well, fuck. I can't have her sitting out in the cold. I calmly head to the front door, but before I know it, I'm jogging. I pull on my boots and grab my coat from the rack. I can't seem to get the buttons done fast enough. I grab my keys from the hall table and I'm out the door and in my car less than ten minutes after I got Lola's text. All I can think about is her tiny little frame shivering to death on main street, not to mention the men staggering out of Big Red's at this hour. If anything happened to her... suddenly my foot presses harder on the gas.

Luckily in a town as small as Lake Mistletoe, everywhere is practically fifteen minutes from where you live. I drive down main street, my eyes wide open and scanning the sidewalk for any sign of Lola. Then I spot her, standing under a street lamp, its golden glow crowning her snow-dusted hair like a halo. I can see her shivering, even with her big blue coat bundled around her. At the same time, I spy a trio of guys laughing loudly, stumbling out the doors of Big Red's. The hairs on the back of my neck stand on end and I pull up to the curb in front of Lola, with a screech.

She squeals and laughs, taking a jump backwards, and I can tell by the way she lands she's had a bit to drink. She stumbles and struggles to find her balance like a newborn giraffe. I get out of my car just as the scruffy-haired blond from the trio takes Lola by the hips. Suddenly my blood is boiling.

"Steady there, sweetheart," he laughs as his buddies close in around her. "You need a ride?"

I don't recognize these guys, and even though I'm new in town, I don't think they're from around here. There's a game tomorrow night. Maybe they're here to support the away team. As far as I'm concerned, they've already worn out their welcome.

"I've got her," I growl, my eyes narrowing on the man with his hands on Lola.

"We're fine here, man," he chuckles. He tightens his grip on her waist, and I feel my fists clench.

I step onto the curb, my heavy steps crushing the snow on the sidewalk. In a second I'm standing over him, and with the lamplight at my back, he falls under the long, dark stretch of my shadow.

"I said I've got her." My words are not just a statement. They're a threat, and he knows it.

He looks up at me, as most men do, and I hear him swallow. He moves his hands away from Lola's waist and raises them in the air.

"Sorry, friend," he stammers. "Didn't know she was yours. You should tell her to be more careful. It's dangerous for a girl in her state to be wandering the streets at night."

I take a step forward, the snow squelching under my boot. My jaw clenches as my eyes burn with ire. "I don't like you, and I don't want you in my town, so if I see you again, I'm going to shove my fist down your throat and drag you out of here by your intestines. Do you understand me?"

The man gulps. He's shaking, but it has nothing to do with the cold. "Sure. Whatever, man. My bad."

I snarl. "Now get the fuck out."

The three men back away before turning on their heels and heading in the opposite direction.

I hear a giggle and Lola's fingers curl around my hand. "That's a dollar for the jar, Henry. Hey. What are you doing here?"

My thumping heart slows in my chest, and I see colors besides red again. I turn to Lola and close my hand around her fingers without a second thought.

"Are you okay?" I ask, my breath turning to smoke in the air.

"Sure am!" she laughs, and I can smell the candied booze drifting from her blue, trembling lips. "Are you out tonight too?"

"You texted me," I say, "to come and pick you up?"

Lola rolls her tongue in her mouth. "No I didn't. I texted Lucas."

I reach into the pocket of my coat and pull out my phone, then show her the text.

Lola strains her eyes to make out the letters, and when she's processed the information, her mouth falls open. "Oh my gosh! I'm so sorry!"

I return my phone to my pocket and scratch the back of my head. Fuck. I should have replied. Of course she didn't mean to text you, idiot. But what if I hadn't come? Would Lucas have gotten here in time? I don't even want to think about what could have happened if I wasn't here. No. I don't regret hauling ass here at all. Lola is safe now, and that's all that matters.

"It's fine," I reply. "I'm glad you texted me."

Lola raises an eyebrow and gives a cheeky grin. "You are?"

I gesture to the trio of predators who appear long gone. "I scared those guys away."

Lola looks around. "What guys?"

I glance over my shoulder. "There were guys here harassing you."

Lola frowns. "I don't remember any guys."

"Well, luckily I got here in time, so now you don't have to worry about picking them from a lineup down at the station."

Lola giggles and face plants into my chest. "You're so weird, Henry."

My body fills with warmth as she leans against me and I find my hand drifting to her hair, brushing it from her face.

"You're freezing. Let me get you home," I whisper.

She hums her agreement and I guide her to the car, opening the passenger door and delicately placing her inside. She lays limp in the seat, her arms splayed either side of her, her legs twisted. I take hold of the seat belt and stretch it across her chest, her nose brushing my bristled cheek as I pass her face. I can smell her bubblegum scent, her breath warm against my neck. I click the belt, and it takes all my strength not to linger over her.

"Thanks, boss," she yawns, kicking off her shoes.

Her words snap me from the spell. Fuck. That's right. I'm her boss. What a fucking creep. I jump back, somehow forgetting I'm six-foot-six, and bang my head on the roof.

"Fuck!" I howl, cupping the back of my head in my hands.

"Swear jar," Lola mutters as she falls asleep.

That damn jar is going to cost me a fortune. I stand up from the car, ducking down this time, and as I watch Lola snoring, puffing her hair with every exhale, I think it might not be the worst way to go broke.

I walk around to the driver's door, nursing the oncoming bump on the back of my head, and jump inside. As soon as the engine's on, I crank up the heat.

"How's that?" I ask, but all I get in reply are snorts and wheezes.

I grin and hit the gas. The entire drive to Lola's house, I find it hard to focus on the road. I can see her out of the corner of my eye, and I fight the urge to turn and look at her. When I catch sight of her white-paneled townhouse, it's not a moment too soon. I pull into the driveway and trudge through the snow to the passenger's side. I open the door and let out a deep, thoughtful breath. This is going to be the tricky part. I need to get her awake.

"Lola," I say softly, nudging her shoulder.

Just more snorts and wheezes.

"Lola. Wake up."

"No! How about you clean up the cat vomit for a change!" she blurts. Lola lunges forward but barely gets a couple of inches before the seatbelt snaps her back to the seat.

I jerk back, startled, but mindful of my head this time. Surely that's woken her up. I lean close and can't believe it when I find her eyes still firmly shut.

I grumble. Well, she can't stay here all night. I lean over and unclip the seatbelt, and as soon as it's not holding her, she flops forward like a rag doll. I gasp and quickly catch her before she bangs her head on the dashboard. She goes limp in my arms like a sack of grain. I bend low enough to get one arm around her back, the other under her knees, before scooping her up and out of the car. I stand up without a hiccup. I could carry her for miles without breaking a sweat. But when she nuzzles into my neck, my knees go weak and I feel utterly powerless. There's her smell again, and I'm entranced by the way she's licking her dry lips as she sleeps.

Enough, I tell myself, shaking these ridiculous thoughts from my head. Even if there's a chance I'm more than a boss to her, Lola being drunk and asleep in my arms is not the time to explore those possibilities. I resolve to get up those stairs, bang on her front door and hand Lola off to whoever answers.

The first part's easy. Then, with arms full of Lola, I angle myself where I can awkwardly thump on the door with my elbow. After sleeping through cracking my skull on the roof, yelling in her face and hauling her from the car, Lola's brown eyes flutter open and she stares at me hazily.

"Where are we?" she mumbles.

"Your front door," I reply. "Just waiting for someone to answer."

"My keys are in my bag," she says, rubbing her dry lips together.

"Okay. I'll have to put you down to get them."

"Don't," she blurts. Her hand slides up my neck and along my jaw until she's cupping my face. The warmth of her touch sends blood surging hot through my veins and, for a minute, it feels like my heart is going to burst through my chest. "Never let me go, Henry," she murmurs.

She pulls my face down, brings my lips to her lips, and I don't even try to stop her. She tastes just how I imagined she would. Warm, sweet, and safe. As if this is exactly where I am supposed to be. In Lake Mistletoe, with Lola Nixon in my arms and her soft mouth on mine.

Suddenly, the door opens, and my stunned, wide eyes lock on Lucas. He looks just as startled, but judging by the grin tugging at the corner of his mouth, he finds the situation a little more amusing than I do. Lola is still holding my face, oblivious to the fact her brother is standing right there.

I gently pry her from my mouth. "Lola. Lucas is here."

She pouts and her pursed lips search for me as I pull back.

"Wakey wakey little trollop," Lucas chuckles. "No kissing the boss now, you hear?"

Lola's eyes flicker open and she gives me a dopey smile. "You're the best boss in the universe, Henry."

"Cool. Please remember that when you're suing me for sexual harassment in the morning," I mumble gruffly. My cheeks flush red, and I'm not exactly sure what I'm supposed to do with her, so I awkwardly hand Lola off to her brother like a casserole dish. She's barely in his arms two seconds before she's asleep again.

"Don't worry," Lucas sighs. "She won't remember a thing in the morning."

I exhale. Thank god, I think to myself.

"But I'll remind her over breakfast," Lucas adds with a grin. "Night, Henry." He spins around, knocking the door shut with his foot.

I stand there for a minute, trying to comprehend the events of the last hour. Was this all just a fever dream? Am I still at home with my feet on Goldie and Janie screaming in my ear? Shit. I wish that was true. I wish I wasn't standing here trying to understand how the best thing that's ever happened to me should have never happened in the first place. But fuck... I would live that mistake a million times over if it meant being able to kiss Lola again.

5

Lola

Oh my god. My head is killing me. I feel like I've been hit by a train, after falling from a plane which collided mid air with a helicopter that had been shot down by an alien spaceship. Why do I bother drinking? I bounce off the walls after too many cranberry GoGo juices. Who was I to think I could have a couple of glasses of wine and not become violently hungover? Alcohol and I do not mix, like oil and some other liquid-ish substance that oil doesn't mix with.

I prop myself up on my elbows, blinking my eyes until the haze clears. I recognize my sunflower comforter and pink polka-dot curtains. Good. At least I got home. But how? I furrow my brow as if it helps me think better. Then it comes to me. Lucas... and speaking of my brother, I could really use some aspirin. I'm hoping signaling him with our twin mind powers will mean I don't have to scream his name out loud. Unfortunately, the powers were more of a cool thing I wish we had rather than a reality. So screaming it is.

"Lucas," I call groggily. My head throbs and I close my eyes to stop the room from spinning. "Lucas. Are you there?"

I hear footsteps down the hall and breathe a sigh of relief when the door swings open and Lucas pokes his head in.

"Morning, sunshine," he greets.

I shut my eyes tight as the sound of his voice reverberates through my skull like I'm at a death-metal concert. "Can we bring it down a decibel, please?"

Lucas grins, then runs into my room at full speed and leaps onto my bed, executing a perfect frog splash on my legs.

I hiss and reach for my legs. "Lucas!" I yell, which only makes my head pound more.

He laughs and bobs up and down on my mattress. "Didn't just stick to the Gogo juices, then? You're such a lightweight, Lola."

My eyes are still closed as I draw circles on my temples. "Thanks for the feedback, Lucas. Now, can you please get me some aspirin?"

He slaps my knee and my eyes flash open, but before I can yell at him again, I see him pointing to my bedside table where there's a glass of water, a little plate of crackers and a jar of aspirin. Such a thoughtful act would be touching if it didn't feel like my brain was pudding leaking out of my ears.

"And Lottie called this morning. Your car's all fixed. Dad and I went to pick it up while you were up here snoring like an eighty-year-old man."

I flop across my bed and fumble my way to the bedside table, then grab the aspirin and pop off the lid. I slap-shoot two into my mouth and chase them with the water before I lay back down and pull my covers up to my neck.

"Thanks, Lucas. You're the best. Getting my car, my aspirin, picking me up last night."

Lucas taps my foot, gently this time, before rocking to his feet. "Anytime, sis. Anytime." He wanders to the door, but before he leaves, he looks at me over his shoulder. "Oh, there's just one thing."

I'm only willing to open one eye. "What's that?"

Lucas grins. "I didn't pick you up."

I shrug. "Dad?"

Lucas shakes his head, his grin sliding higher up his bristled cheeks. The situation calls for both eyes open, and I suffer through my cracking headache enough to lean over the bed and grab my bag. I dig around inside until I find my phone and scroll through my messages. My mind goes blank. Nothing between my ears but a vast white void of eerie silence. My absolute horror at realizing what I've done sobers me up real quick and gets rid of my headache swifter than an entire barrel of aspirin.

"I sent a text to Henry..."

Lucas chuckles. "Yeah, you did."

I gulp and look up at my brother. "And he picked me up?"

"Yep," Lucas replies.

I swallow again, but these lumps in my throat keep coming back. "That's fine, right? I mean, it was obviously a mistake. I'm sure Henry gets I was drunk and confused. It won't be weird."

Lucas folds his arms over his chest. "I don't think so. I mean, yeah, he's your boss, but he's also your friend, and you needed help. No reason giving you a ride home from a bar would be weird."

I smile and feel a weight lift from my chest as the lump in my throat clears.

Lucas pinches his chin between his fingers. "Although... you shoving your tongue down his throat might make things a little awkward."

My jaw drops as Lucas' words replay in my head. "What?"

He can barely stifle his grin, clenching his bottom lip between his teeth just to keep from laughing. "He was such a gentleman, Lola. Picked you up in the middle of the night, drove you home, he even carried you out of the car to the front door."

My heart skips like a broken record, and I feel a smile bloom on my lips. "He carried me?"

"Oh yeah," Lucas replies. "And I open the door just in time to see you playing tonsil hockey with the Mayhem goalie on our porch."

I bury my face in my hands. "Oh my god. This can't be happening." I peer at Lucas through the gaps in my fingers. "Are you sure?"

His expression is pensive. "I haven't had a girlfriend since moving home, but yeah, I'm pretty sure I know an open-lipped, full-tongue kiss when I see one."

"Full tongue!" I whimper.

Lucas nods. "Oh yeah. You looked like Jabba the Hutt when he's getting choked out by Leia."

"That's a great reference," I sob. I fall back onto my bed and pull my covers over my head before letting out a muffled scream.

"Don't go back to sleep now," Lucas says. "You start work soon."

"Yes, thank you, Lucas," I snap.

I hear the door close and scream into my covers even louder. How could I let this happen? Henry's number is nowhere near Lucas'. I would have had to search for his name! Was it some subconscious thing? Did I want Henry to pick me up last night? Did I accidentally do it on purpose? Jesus, Lola. How desperate can you get!

I prepare to scream one more time, when a notion flashes in my mind... he came. He didn't leave me standing there or text back to ask if I had the right number. He didn't contact Dad.

I called. He came.

Does that mean... he cares... like... cares, cares? I slide down my comforter and stare wide-eyed at the ceiling. Could Hangry Henry, who notoriously cares about nothing, care about me?

Then common sense slaps across me like a cold wet mop. He's your boss, Lola. Of course, he wouldn't leave you to freeze to death on the sidewalk. Stop daydreaming that there's more to it. Reality rips me back into the hard truth of it all. Henry was just being a decent boss, and I've got to be at work in an hour.

I kick off my comforter and clench my jaw. There's still the minor complication of the kiss, a kiss which apparently used an obscene amount of tongue, but maybe we're both so traumatized that we'll just pretend it never happened. Yes. Nothing wrong with a little denial if it saves you from an awkward conversation.

Then, abruptly, my delusion resurfaces and my toes curl. If I have to suffer through the embarrassment and pretend the kiss didn't happen, I wish I could at least remember what kissing Henry felt like. I'd still want to beat myself to death with a string of Italian sausages, but at least I'd die knowing if his lips tasted as wonderful as they did in my dreams.

I feel my core tighten, which is like a foghorn telling me it's time to get up and get in the shower. My mind's a mess. I can't think straight. I shampoo twice and completely miss my knees when I shave my legs. I skip breakfast and head straight out the door, ignoring anything Lucas is yelling at me when I pass him and Dad in the living room. Then I'm in my yellow Mini Cooper car, and it's good to have my lemon slice back, even if she is driving me to my doom. I spy the fluffy cat with the stethoscope, my heart racing a million miles an hour while I park my car in the lot out the back.

I look around. Henry's not here yet. Good. I'll open up, crank the heat as usual, and be delightful for the rest of the day. Everything will be completely normal. I unlock the clinic door and spin the dial on the thermostat to a balmy eight-five. I feed the kittens and clap excitedly when Brian takes a spot at the bowl without coaxing. I check on Comet, who looks to be recovering well from his surgery. His eyes are bright and he demolishes his breakfast while his tail wags furiously behind him. I bet he can't wait to see Alice.

I let out a deep breath when I leave the overnight room. We have two dogs and their owners in the waiting room, and I sign them in with a bright smile, letting them know Dr. Gallagher should be here soon. It feels like any other day. What was I so worried about? Everything is going so well this morning. I'm sure there won't be any awkwardness between me and Henry at all. I just need to be a grownup and act professional. After all, this is a workplace.

I hear the jingle of the bell over the door and look up from my desk to see Henry walking in. He glances at me from beneath his heavy brow, his hands deep in his pockets, his lips stretched in a straight line. I take a pile of papers from my tray and tap them on the desk, then beam a smile at Henry.

"Morning, Lola," he grumbles as he walks toward me, and that's when my mouth falls open.

"I'm so sorry, Henry! I don't know what I was thinking! I didn't mean to text you. I was trying to text Lucas, and I know your names aren't similar at all. Maybe my thumb slipped, or maybe I was thinking about you when I was texting." My eyes widen and my body stiffens. "Not that I think about you or anything like that. I'm just saying I meant to text Lucas and I'm so sorry."

When my mouth finally closes, Henry comes over to the desk with his hands up, his eyes darting about the waiting room, observing the patient's curious stares.

"It's fine, Lola. No harm done. Now if you can send through my first patient, please."

I nod and look at the computer, but then my mouth opens again. "I'm just so embarrassed."

"It's fine, Lola."

"What I did was completely inappropriate."

"Can you just send my patient in?"

"I didn't mean to kiss you!"

The color drains from Henry's face and his shoulders slump. I feel every pair of eyes in the waiting room ogling me, and not only the two-legged ones. The dogs are just as invested, sitting tall and straight with their ears pointed to the sky.

Henry moves closer to my desk and leans over me, his jaw clenched. "Lola. Enough."

I'm trembling. His voice is deep and etched with ire. I've heard it before, but it's never been directed at me. My stomach knots. "I'm sorry, I..."

Henry shakes his head. "Please. Just stop talking. It was a mistake. Can we just get on with it?"

I don't understand why he's talking to me like this, so short and detached, almost like I'm a stranger. But he's only doing what I'm asking. Acting like the kiss never happened, and that's what I want. Isn't it? Then why does it feel like my heart's been tossed in a blender and set to smush?

Suddenly the door flies open and the blast of frigid air forces a collective shudder from the people in the waiting room. It also draws Henry's attention away from me, which is a blessing. I don't know how long I could have sat under his glare before bursting into tears.

The door shuts with a thwack behind Sophie, bundled up in a coat and scarf, her hand tapping anxiously against her handbag. Her eyes fix on me, and she scurries across the waiting room straight to my desk.

"Hey, Henry," she says, paying him only a passing glance. "Lola, can we talk?"

I gulp and look at Henry, who avoids my eye contact. "Sorry, Sophie, I'm working."

"No. You should go. I think a little air would be good for you," Henry says.

My throat tightens. "But I..."

"Go grab a coffee or something. I can handle things here."

My chin drops. He's pushing me away, and it might as well be off a cliff. "Okay. Did you want me to grab you a Red Bull before I go?"

Henry reaches over me and grabs the file on top of the pile without blinking, before standing up straight and flicking through the papers inside, not looking at me once. "I can do it myself."

I plead with myself not to cry while Sophie tugs on my hand, oblivious to the fact my heart is breaking.

"Come on," she says.

I force my legs to walk, moving around my desk to join Sophie.

Henry looks up from the file in his hand. "Dave and Ginger?" he asks a rotund man holding the lead of a red-and-white patterned English Bulldog. "Follow me," he says, when the man nods in reply.

He turns his back and heads into the exam room, and like an idiot I keep staring, hopeful that at any minute he'll look at me and that'll somehow make everything less horrible. But he doesn't, and I'm staring at the door long after he's closed it.

"Lola, are you okay?" Sophie asks.

She sweeps my hair away from my eye and I sniff back a tear before it can give me away.

"Fine," I blurt, straightening my shoulders. "So what's happened? Is everything alright?" She furrows her brow at me, and I know she can tell something's off. I squeeze her hand for reassurance. "Seriously. I'm fine."

"Okay," she replies, but I know she's still not convinced. "Let's go to the cafe next door."

I grab my coat as we leave the clinic, and I take a leaf out of Henry's book, not looking back.

The Chilly Bean Bistro is just a few doors down. It's getting colder every day leading up to Christmas, and even the short walk between the buildings has me shivering. We get inside the cute little cafe and the rich aroma of freshly ground coffee beans fills my nose. The lights are warm and dim, casting a cozy amber glow on the wooden booths and worn brick walls adorned with vintage coffee-inspired art. The hum of conversation melds seamlessly with the rhythmic sounds of the espresso machine and the gentle clinking of ceramic against the old wooden counter.

Sophie and I grab a booth near the back, and we're only seated a minute before a red-haired server is standing beside us with her pen and notepad.

"Morning. What can I get you?"

Sophie smiles. "Hey Tamara. How are you?"

Tamara exhales. "I'm good. Thanks for asking. How about you?"

Sophie sighs. "Nothing a black coffee won't fix."

"No problem, and for you?" she asks me.

I'd normally take my time ordering the perfect drink combination. One for hydration. One for yumminess. But I'm struggling to find a purpose in anything right now. So just go for the default.

"A glass of lemon water and a cranberry GoGo in the box, please."

Tamara jots it all down on her notepad, finishing with a thumping full stop and a bright smile. "Sure thing. I'll get that to you right away."

Sophie and I watch her head to the counter.

"I still can't believe what my brother put that poor girl through," Sophie says.

"Yeah, well. Life sucks that way sometimes," I mumble.

Sophie's head jerks. "Okay..., who are you and what have you done with Lola?"

I want to tell her everything, hoping that the word-vomit makes me feel better. But if Henry and I are pretending it never happened, spilling my guts to Sophie seems like the opposite of what I should be doing, and Henry is mad enough at me as it is.

"Enough about Lola. Why did you drag me out of work?" I say, forcing a smile.

Sophie exhales, putting her elbows on the table and bridging her fingers before sitting her chin glumly on top. "Remember that adorable folk band with the violins and the cello who were going to play at the wedding?"

I nod excitedly. "Do I remember them? I helped you pick The Whimsys. They're great!"

"Well, The Whimsys apparently love a good seafood buffet. Food poisoning. All five of them. Their manager called Finn this morning. They won't be able to perform."

"Oh no, Sophie!" I gush, gripping her elbow. "Can you get someone else at such short notice?"

"Finn's on it," she replies. "He says the manager has a couple of other bands that might be available, but because the wedding is so close to Christmas, most of them are already booked or not working the holidays." There's a sparkle in her brown eyes, and I watch an idea bloom on her face. "Why don't you sing at my wedding?"

My heart stops dead in my chest for the second time this morning. "I would love to help, Sophie, but I don't perform anymore."

Her glow fades as quickly as it arrived. "I know. I shouldn't have asked. Can I just say that Dylan is a piece of shit for doing this to you?"

I nod. "I think all of you made that point very clear last night."

"Hey, speaking of last night," Sophie says. "Did you get home alright? Lucas didn't take too long?"

I gulp and tuck my hair behind my ears. "Nope. He was there in a jiffy."

"Good," Sophie nods. "How long is he in town this time, anyway?"

"Just to bartend at the wedding," I reply. "Last I heard, he's heading to Macaroy Beach after that."

Sophie grins. "He's still gorgeous. Those eyes."

I cringe, not only because she's talking about my brother, but because our eyes are the same color. Tamara returns to our booth and places our drinks on the table.

"You guys going to the game?" she asks. "Supposed to be a good one. There's been some Blaze supporters making trouble around town the last couple of days. I hope the Mayhem brings it to them tonight."

A cheeky grin slips onto Sophie's face and her cheeks flush. "When it's close to game day, Tom can't keep his hands off me. I don't need a calendar."

I screw up my face. "TMI, Soph."

Tamara laughs. "Good to know. Have a great day."

Tamara heads back to the counter. Sophie takes one sip of coffee and the stress seems to melt off her shoulders immediately. She slaps her lips together, then looks at me over the rim of her cup.

"Thanks for popping out. I know I've been a lot lately. Henry seemed really cool about it. Must be nice being the only person in town he's remotely kind to."

I poke my straw into my Gogo box and slurp the cranberry juice. "Not anymore."

"Oh please," Sophie scoffs. "You know what I think, Lola? I think it's great that Sean has found Lexie, and Blake has found Charlotte, and even though I'm pretty sure it's a sign of the apocalypse, I'm happy that Finn and Daisy are together too. But I always thought it would be you and Henry before any of them."

I gulp, trying not to meet her eyes in case I give myself away. "Why?"

"Because Henry doesn't play well with others. On and off the ice, and I swear to God I've only seen the man smile a handful of times."

"So?" I grumble.

Sophie grins. "He was looking at you every one of those times, Lola."

My eyes widen and my cheeks cave in as I suck the last drop of juice from the box until the cardboard shrivels up.

"You had to know that," Sophie laughs.

Maybe I do, and maybe I don't. But I'm in no hurry to go back to the clinic and find out. I search for Tamara at the counter, and wave when I catch her eye. "Another round of Gogos, please," I call.

6

Henry

I pull into the parking lot, and I can't remember driving here. It's called highway hypnosis, when all sense of time and thought mysteriously vanishes. You arrive safe and sound at your destination, but with no memory of the journey. It's usually because part of your brain is so focused on something else, the rest sets to autopilot, and I know exactly what's got me so distracted. Lola. I can't stop thinking about Lola. Of how coldly I treated her, of the things I said, of how soft her lips felt when she kissed me.

I didn't know it would sting like a kick to the nuts when she said she didn't mean to kiss me. But hey, maybe I'm just the stupid fucking idiot who thought an awkward smooch from a drunken girl in the middle of the night meant something. My jaw clenches when I recall the sadness in her eyes this morning. If there's one thing I never wanted, it was to cause Lola even an ounce of pain. I'd rather get beaten within an inch of my life than go on knowing I'm responsible for her unhappiness.

My eyes narrow on the arena and I grit my teeth. If I'm lucky, maybe one of these Blaze pussies will drum up the courage to scrap with me tonight. Shit. Maybe I'll just stand there and take the first hit. I fucking deserve it.

I climb out of my car and get a blast of cold air to the face. That's a good start. I grab my gear from the back and trudge through the snow to the arena, barging the door open with my shoulder. The ticket takers wave me past while the food vendors set up shop.

I love the smell of the ice before a game. When I left Rockford, I wasn't sure if I'd get to play hockey again, so when the opportunity to take over a clinic in Lake Mistletoe came up, I jumped at the chance. This part of the north has the strongest teams in the league. I'd barely unloaded my boxes from the rental truck before I grabbed my gear and headed to the arena for try outs. I wasn't surprised when I made the cut. I'm fucking good at what I do, and I carried my university team to three regional titles. It took a while for the guys to warm up to me. I can be a little... abrasive, and I'm not a big talker. But now that we're friends, they think my stoicism means they can unload all their fucking problems on me and I'll listen quietly.

I've been the sounding board for Sean pining for Lexie, Blake's fuck boy antics, Finn's bitching about Daisy, and Tom's wedding panic attacks, and all it's done is reaffirm to me what I thought about relationships. They're doomed from the start. All that heat and passion that launches them into the stratosphere, well guess what, those flames die out, and before you know it you're crashing back to earth and scattered across the ocean. I watched it happen to my parents. I watched Dad break Mom's heart over and over again, and even though I thought I was a better man than him, the way I treated Lola this morning tells me I'm on track to be just as big of an asshole.

I pass the rink and head for the changing rooms, but when I turn the corner I'm blindsided by the last person I expected. She's got my same brown hair and brown eyes. She's tall too, but all us Gallaghers are. We're almost carbon copies, though I'm sure she's grateful not to have the stubble.

"Stella," I mutter.

She throws her arms around my shoulders and I hook her waist. She smells like Rockford, like sunshine and endless meadows of wildflowers.

"Hey Grizz," she replies.

That's been my nickname since I was a kid, carried right through to my university years. I hate it because Dad was the one who gave it to me.

"Janie told me you took off. What are you doing here?"

"You talked to her?" Stella rolls her eyes. "I can't deal with her. She's impossible."

"That may be," I sigh, knowing firsthand how intense Janie is. "But she's running things now, so you've got to fall in line."

Stella tugs at my collar. "Can't you just come home?"

I exhale. "I hope you didn't come all this way just to ask me that, little sister."

She closes one eye and squints the other at me. "Maybe."

I drop my gear on the ground and dig my fists into my hips. "No. I can't come home. Not this year."

Stella's chin drops. "Dad's got us all on a tight leash with you away. We're doing so much at the ranch. There's no time for anything else. Having issues with the Brewers as well. It's getting pretty bad."

I shake my head and wave my hands, trying to block it all out. "I can't, Stella. Why doesn't anybody get it? That place almost killed me, and you're saying you can't make it through one Christmas? You know how things were getting with Mom and Dad. I had to get away."

"Yeah, well, that's great for you Grizz," she snaps. "But what about the rest of us? What about me?"

I swallow the lump in my throat and grip her shoulders. "Leave then if you have to."

Stella shakes her head. "Dad will never let us go. Not now that you're gone. He canceled my cards the second he knew I'd taken off. Lucky I already bought a round trip."

"Oh," I say, patting my jacket pockets. "If it's money, you need..."

Stella's face sours. "Of course not. You think I came all the way to this tiny freezing town for money? I came because I hoped seeing me would kick some sense into you. Remind you that you belong at home on the ranch with your family."

"And take the pressure off you three so you don't have to work as hard, right?"

The words fall out of my mouth before I can stop them.

Stella shakes her head, her glower thick with loathing. "You're right. I shouldn't have come. Sorry for interrupting this cute little life you've created."

She storms past me and I grab her by the elbow, but Gallagher's are built different. She shrugs me off like I weigh ninety pounds.

"Stella. Wait," I call.

She doesn't turn. Not once. She heads straight for the door with her head down and ears pinned back, and then she's gone. That's another thing about the Gallaghers. We're stubborn, proud and stupid to a fault. I can feel my blood pumping fast and hot through my veins. How is it I keep sticking my foot in my mouth and hurting the people I care about? I grab my bag and throw it over my shoulder, then charge through the locker-room doors.

The guys are laughing and bantering as I pass by, but they fall silent when I hurl my bag into my locker, the impact rattling like thunder.

They exchange looks, and Finn stands from the bench. "Hey, Big H. You okay?"

I snarl. "I'm not Big H. I'm not Grizz. I'm just fucking Henry, alright?"

Finn raises his hands like they're white flags. "Yeah, sure man. Henry."

I grab a fistful of shirt at the back of my neck and yank it over my head before rolling it into a ball and pitching it at my locker as well. It hits with a thud.

"What's your fucking problem?" Blake says, his arms folded across his bare chest as he leans against his locker.

I narrow my eyes on the pompous prick. "What's your fucking problem?" I spit. I'll take any excuse to get into a scrap right now, so if Blake pushes me I'm wiping the floor with him.

"Alright, both of you shut the fuck up," Finn moans. "How about you save that cock-swinging for the Blaze, huh?"

Sean laces his pants and gives Blake a disciplinary slap across the chest. "Sounds good, Cap."

Blake exhales, drops his chin and nods. "You got it, Cap."

I dig into my bag and pull out my gear, dumping it on the bench. "Well, let's stop fucking around and get out there then."

When we're laced into our battle gear, Finn stands on the bench and addresses his warriors, like he does every Friday night. Normally his words stir something in my gut, making me want to play as hard as I can, to go out there and wreck myself for the team if I have to. But tonight it's just hollow noise. My eyes burn red, and all I can see in the flurry of my anger is Lola and Stella, and how I hurt both of them today. All I want to do is get on that ice and piss someone off enough they kick my teeth in. Anything would be better than what I'm feeling right now.

The team huddles up and we start our cheer, our deep grunts booming in unison as we stomp our feet on the cold concrete. Each chant gets us more worked up, like we're man-eating sharks and the Blaze's blood is in the water. Then on the final cheer we howl, "Mayhem!"

We barge through the locker-room doors, shoving and slapping the back of each other's helmets, the air thick with a primal energy that makes me feel ten feet tall, fucking bullet proof, and hard as a rock. The Mayhem banners flap in the rafters: the snow leopard wearing a red mask with slash marks across its face. The Blaze banner hangs on the opposite side of the rink: a puck engulfed in a ball of fire. We hit our bench and take our seats, and I glare across the ice, wondering which of these motherfuckers I'm going to have the pleasure of sending to the hospital tonight.

Then, my eyes widen when I spy him. Merry Christmas to me. I recognize the asshole from outside Big Red's wearing the 72 jersey. The one who thought he could put his hands on Lola and live. He's sitting on the Blaze bench, and he's clocked me as well, but he doesn't seem as pleased to see me. I promised him I'd kick his ass if I ever saw him again. I'm a man who keeps his promises.

The arena pulses with energy as the Mayhem take the ice. At the start of third period, the score's tied, and the Blaze aggressively push forward. Mayhem's giving it everything we've got, but the breakout play we need evades us.

Suddenly, a scuffle erupts in front of the net. I see 72 cross-checking Blake as they battle for position. The referee's arm goes up, calling a penalty for interference. But before the whistle can blow, 72 shoves Blake into the boards. Blake stands his ground, and I can hear them slinging fuck yous between chirps. Then 72 shoves again and I see Blake's patience wearing thin. He takes a step forward, and the men eye each other up, fixed in a death stare, waiting to see who breaks first. As 72 draws back a fist, he's so focused on Blake he doesn't see me flank him from the left.

I put all my weight behind my shoulder, barging him into the boards like a rag doll. He lets out a low grunt when his body thuds into the hard plastic. Just before he slides down the wall and hits the ice, I catch him by the collar of his jersey. But it's not because of some moment of regret. I want to have him upright so I can see his eyes when I drive my fist into his chin.

The hit sends him back into the boards. He wobbles in a daze, still on his legs, but nobody's home. I draw my fist back behind my shoulder and fire another punch. This one connects with 72's mouth, and his head almost spins a hundred-and-eighty degrees. I feel a sting around my knuckles and notice a gash and some blood. I must have caught his teeth.

The Mayhem fans erupt into a mix of gasps and cheers, while the Blaze supporters leap to their feet, booing and turning their thumbs down. The referee's whistle shrills through the chaos, and he points a finger at me as the guys hook me by my arms and drag me away from 72 crumpled on the ice, making room for his teammates to take care of him.

"Henry," Finn snaps as he skates alongside me to the bench. "What was that? Do you know him?"

I say nothing. I'm so blinded by my rage that I won't make any sense anyway. No point wasting time looking at the ref. I know I'm out for the rest of the game. I skate off the ice, past the bench, and head straight for the locker room.

7

Lola

I watch Henry storm away from the rink and I can't believe what just happened. The girls can't believe it either. What do you think he said? Who is he? That was pretty hot... . I'm too worried about Henry to add to the conversation. I'm quick to my feet and the girls look at up at me.

"Where are you going?" Lexie asks.

"Bathroom," I say blankly.

They scoot in their knees and I shuffle past them, and when they're not looking, I head down the stairs instead of up, my eyes set on the locker room. My stomach knots tighter with each step I take down the white corridor, which suddenly feels ten miles long. I see the Mayhem logo on a pair of swinging doors and, judging by their sway, Henry busted through them not long ago. I stand before the doors, a lump the size of my fist lodged in my throat, and my hands are shaking when I push them open.

"Get the fuck out," Henry roars. "I don't want to talk about it."

I freeze, swallowing the lump with a loud gulp. Henry has his back to me, leaning over his locker with his jersey balled up in his fist. I lose all sense of time when I see the pronounced muscles of his back, each ripple and ridge of smooth, olive skin daring me to touch. His powerful shoulders form sweeping arcs, leading down to a V-shaped taper that accentuates their width. I imagine my arms wrapped around those shoulders, my fingers tangled in his hair, my legs wrapped around his waist.

"Lola. Sorry. I thought you were one of the guys."

I snap from my trance and dig my hands into my pockets before they try to touch him. "I wanted to see if you were okay. I saw the fight."

Henry still has his back to me, with his head turned to look over his shoulder. "Yeah, I'm fine. It was a stupid move when the game's this close. I couldn't control myself."

"Did you know him?" I ask. "It seemed really intense."

He exhales, and his eyes soften. "No. Don't know him."

Henry turns, and it takes all my willpower not to stare at his barreled chest dusted with dark hair dampened by sweat. I look at the wall, but take a moment to glimpse his toned stomach. I'm only human, after all. I hear him wince, so turn back, and notice him inspecting a bloody gash across his knuckles.

"Oh my goodness!" I rush over to him and snatch his fist into my hands. "Did he bite you?"

"No. His teeth just got in the way of my fist," Henry replies.

He's leaning over me, so close that my shoulder digs into his chest and his head hangs just above my ear. I shiver, too scared to look up in case our eyes meet and his dark gaze sees straight through me.

"We need some bandages and iodine. This could get infected," I mutter anxiously.

I feel his nose brush against my hair and the rumble from his throat sends a hot rush through my core.

"Lola," he breathes, and it's enough to turn the tingle into a lightning bolt. "I'm sorry about the way I treated you in the clinic. It was childish and stupid. I just couldn't face up to the truth."

I gulp and slowly tilt my head upwards to find his eyes and just as I feared, they pierce me like a needle straight through my heart. "What truth?"

His thumb brushes my hand. "That I wanted you to mean it."

His words steal the breath from my lungs. "Henry..."

He stops me, slipping his fist from my grip. "I know it's ridiculous. You don't even remember. Fuck. I feel like a moron."

I don't mention the swear jar this time. I want him to unleash his feelings on me. I want to know he feels the same way I do.

My hand traces the pronounced curve of his left pec before sliding onto his shoulder. "It might not have been the way I imagined our first kiss happening, but at least I finally had the guts to show you how I feel, Henry. It only took a prosecco or five."

His cut hand moves to my face, his taped fingers brushing the hair from my eyes. "Does that mean there'll be a second kiss?"

My heart races and my chest heaves with breath when a teasing tingle sweeps through my center. Henry leans toward me and our eyes close as our lips inch closer. When they collide, it feels like my entire body is on fire. His breaths are heavy and deep against my mouth, as if he'll die if he doesn't inhale me. My fingers tangle in his hair and he stoops over, just enough to scoop his hands under my backside and lift me up. I feel weightless in his arms as he holds me tightly against him, our tongues slipping into each other's mouths with teasing, flicking motions.

I feel him moving and realize he's walking us toward the wall on the other side of the room. I feel the brick against my back, and he eases me back to the ground, brushing his nose against my hard nipple as he brings me down. He kisses me again, harder and deeper, and his hand finds its way under my shirt, claiming my breast and kneading the flesh.

I moan into his mouth as his other hand traces the waistband of my jeans and I gasp when I feel the buttons pop open one at a time. Henry's kisses trail to my neck while his hand slips between my skin and the rigid denim, fingers inching toward my aching crevice. When he finds my clit, I moan louder, rolling my hips as he rubs so gently it's torture. My body shivers against him, my core burns for him, desperate for his touch, deeper, harder, faster. God. I've never wanted to be fucked so bad in my life.

The sound of loud, terse banter from the corridor startles us, forcing us apart. My fingers rush for my jeans, swiftly doing up each button while Henry adjusts the massive hard-on bulging against his pants. He looks at me, and I can see a million words balancing on the tip of his tongue, waiting to be spoken, but when the locker room doors swing open, we walk to opposite sides of the room with our backs turned, trying our best to make out nothing happened.

Finn eyes me curiously as he leads in the Mayhem, and judging by the looks on the guys' faces, the game didn't end well.

"Lola," Finn says. "What are you doing back here?"

Henry leans on his locker. "She just came to check on me."

Blake throws his helmet into his locker. "Well, you better have broken something. We lost."

"He was defending you," I snap.

Blake exhales. "No offense, Lola, but I didn't ask for his fucking help."

Henry is back on his feet, the bench screeching against the ground when he shoves it back. "Don't talk to her like that."

Finn pinches the bridge of his nose. "Jesus Christ, what the hell is wrong with you guys today?" He turns to me and tries to soften the stress painted across his reddened face. "This isn't a great time, Lola."

I nod, shrinking into myself when I realize I shouldn't be here, especially now. This is the Mayhem's first loss of the season. "I'm sorry. I'll go."

I feel Henry's eyes watch me until I leave and the trip back through the corridor is the longest walk of my life. By the time I clear the doors into the arena, the crowd is filing out, and it's quieter than I've ever heard. I look up to where I was sitting and see the girls have gone. I dig into my pocket, retrieve my phone, and see a message from Sophie.

SOPHIE: Hey. Everything okay? You never came back?

LOLA: Everything's fine. Just got caught up. I'll see you later.

I return my phone to my pocket and look around the deserted arena. We normally go to Big Red's after a game, but I imagine the Blaze will celebrate pretty hard tonight. Besides, the only person I'm interested in seeing is commiserating with his teammates, so I might as well head home for the night.

I walk through the arena, dodging hot-dog wrappers and empty beer cups, and head out the front doors into the parking lot. Fresh snow falls from above, dusting every surface with glittering white. I weave my way around the cars maneuvering through exiting traffic, and even beneath a layer of snow I can spot my little lemon car a few rows down.

I fumble the door open and hurry inside, rubbing my hands while starting the engine and mashing the heat button until dry air blasts my face. As I wait for the feeling to return to my fingers, my stomach rumbles so loudly you'd think a demon from another dimension was trying to break through into our world. I could really go for an unnecessarily large tub of cheese balls. They always hit the spot when I'm hungry or horny, and thanks to Henry, I'm a little of both. I wriggle my toes in my boots and hit the gas.

Mistletoe Market is on the main street. I glance at the clock on my dashboard. Nine pm. Does it close at 9 or 9.30? I can never remember. I push my foot a little harder on the gas pedal, just in case. The bright lights of the market beam like an alien spacecraft and the flickering i in the

Mistletoe sign always bothers me. Luckily, the game draws all the attention on a Friday night, so there are plenty of parking spaces. I take one as close as I can to the door, then literally sprint inside. The snow's coming down harder, and it feels like the temperature's taken a sharp drop.

I march purposefully through the aisles with their unforgiving lighting, the freshly mopped floor squeaking under my boots, while All I Want For Christmas Is You hums over the speakers. I find the cheese balls stacked in a pyramid at the end of the snack aisle, and even though I'm tempted to Jenga one from the middle, I sensibly take a tub from the top.

"I hope that's not your dinner," a haughty voice questions, and I need zero guesses as to who the culprit is.

I push a smile past my teeth. "Oh hi, Mrs. Bearenstein. No, not dinner."

She turns up her nose, unconvinced. "That's all sugar and fat."

"Don't forget the delicious orange dust!" I laugh lightly, but Mrs. Bearenstein doesn't find it funny. I doubt she finds anything funny. Probably never laughed her entire life. Poor thing.

I take a sneaky peek in her trolley, and though I'm not surprised by the towering tins of cat food, I didn't take her for a microwave dinner kind of lady. The way she acts, I assumed she was having caviar and champagne every night. Do you have those things together? But it's an assortment of single-serve roast meals and pasta bakes. My peak obviously isn't sneaky enough because she moves her trolley forward to get my attention.

"So, how are you?" I ask to cut the silence.

"Good. And you? Still singing to kittens?"

"Every chance I get," I reply. She just stares at me, and I roll my tongue in my cheek while rocking on the balls of my feet. "Anyway... nice seeing you."

As I spin on my heels and head in the other direction, I can't think of a bigger lie I've ever told. I loiter in the cookie aisle, wondering just how far I want to push my commitment to a week of no sugar, while hoping to avoid bumping into the delightful Mrs. Bearenstein again. I decide that a packet of shortbread isn't the end of the world and head for the registers, managing to check out and get to the exit without crossing Mrs. Bearenstein's path again. But my luck runs out when I find her standing outside.

Her hands are heavy with paper grocery bags and she's shivering, even with her long tweed coat. She's looking around, glancing between the sky and sidewalk.

I think about going the other way, but she catches sight of me.

"Hi again," I say, feigning a smile. "Everything okay?" She rolls her eyes and I wish I hadn't asked.

"Of course it is," she replies curtly, as she continues to check the sky.

"It's snowing pretty hard," I say. "Do you need help to take your groceries to your car?"

"Not that it's any of your business, but I do not have a car," she snaps. "I walk."

Now I'm looking at the sky with her as the snow comes down heavier. "It's probably not a good idea to walk home in this." I fight the words dangling from the tip of my tongue, but they unfortunately fall to their doom. "I can give you a ride home."

She cocks a pencil thin eyebrow at me. "Pardon?"

"Mrs. Bearenstein, you can't walk home. Let me drive you. My car's right there." I gesture to my Mini Cooper and she turns up her nose, which is rich coming from someone apparently car-less. She doesn't reply, but my conscience won't let me leave without asking one more time. "What do you say?"

She slaps her lips together, and checks the sky one more time, as if hoping for a miracle. I know I am. Then she turns back to me and lets out a deep breath that takes forever.

"Very well; 252 Maple."

I wriggle my keys out of my pocket. "Yep. I know the one. You live across the street from my friend Blake."

She scowls as if she's caught the scent of rotten eggs. "Oh. Yes. Blake. I'm not surprised to hear he's a friend of yours. Ghastly young man. Girls coming and going at all hours, and always barely dressed. Him as much as them."

I laugh. "Sounds about right. Probably not too much of that recently, though."

Her stiff shoulders ease and she nods. "It has just been the one lately. She's a nice girl. Did a wonderful job on my conservatory."

"Charlotte," I say with a smile. "Yeah. She's the best." I feel the cold nibble at my neck. I'm eager to get home to my electric blanket and these cheese balls. I gesture to my car. "Shall we?"

Mrs. Bearenstein hoists up her bags and takes a step. I try to carry one for her but, as expected, she brushes me away and carries on to the car. She's spritely for an old lady, and I have to quickstep to beat her to the trunk. I pop it open and she loads her groceries, and I need to hustle again to open the passenger door for her. She slides in and immediately grumbles her disdain.

"A little snug in here, isn't it?"

I don't reply. Instead, I feign a smile, which I'm getting pretty good at, close the door and head to the driver's side. I start the engine, grip the wheel and hit the gas. The sooner I drop Mrs. Bearenstein off, the better.

"Do pay attention to the speed limit. I have no desire to die this evening," she sighs, her eyes judging every inch of the interior, seemingly offended by my fluffy dice dangling from the rear-view mirror.

I frown and ease off the gas. "Sure thing, Mrs. Bearenstein."

We arrive at 252 Maple and not a moment too soon. When I park in her driveway, I glance across the street to see if Blake is back, but it's pitch black lights out over there. I imagine they'll be hitting Big Red's tonight to mourn their loss. Maybe I should have popped in after all. I'd take a hundred smug, raucous Blaze supporters over a single Mrs. Bearenstein any day, and I'm not opposed to Henry and I finishing what we started. The memory of his thick, rough fingers rubbing me has me feeling feral.

I climb out of the car and pop the trunk, and this time I get to the bags before she does, scooping them all up into my arms.

"My eggs!" she shrieks.

"Don't worry. They're fine. I'm excellent with eggs," I say.

She furrows her brow and shakes her head. "Such a strange girl."

"I try," I reply. I power walk down her drive and along her path, then up the stairs to her front porch. Quickness is key if I'm to survive this.

I wait for her to toddle along in slow motion, stopping to check a loose paving stone at the bottom of the steps. I bounce impatiently. I'm sure she's doing this on purpose. Eventually she loses interest in the stone and climbs the steps, fishing her house keys out of her purse when she reaches the door. I notice it's just as dark inside as Blake's house.

"Any one home?" I ask curiously.

She pushes the key into the lock. "No." The door opens and I feel something brush my legs, followed by a long, high-pitched cry. "Well, apart from Anastasia."

"Hi kitty," I gush as she weaves around my ankles.

"You can just leave the bags there," Mrs. Bearenstein says. I watch in awe as she taps the hall table and Anastasia's ears prick up. She leaps onto the table in a single bound then, with another jump, ends up in Mrs. Bearenstein's waiting arms. "I missed you too, my darling."

I put the bags down on the hall table and the first thing she does is open the egg carton. I watch her expression and smile brightly when she doesn't look mad.

"See. Told you."

"That'll be all," she sighs, then closes the door in my face, leaving me freezing on her dark porch.

I should be mad, grumpy at least, at the way she treats me, but I think there's more to Mrs. Bearenstein than she lets on. An elderly lady, shopping TV dinners for one at 9pm on a Friday night, coming home to a big empty house. That doesn't sound nice at all. In fact, I feel bad for her.

I think about knocking, even though I'm ninety percent sure it'll result in another door in the face. In the end I don't. Maybe because I'm chicken or just too tired, but for whatever reason, my hand slips away from the door and I head for my car.

8

Henry

We spend over an hour in the locker room going over the game. The guys never once put the blame on me, but I know that my stupid decision cost us the win. I appreciate their loyalty and support. Once we've cooled down a little and changed, we decide to drink away our sorrows at Big Red's, even if there's a chance the Blaze will be there celebrating. All's fair in sport after all, but before we leave, the guys ask if I can control my temper. I say yes. The last thing I need is to get into a bar fight. I've got Tom's wedding coming up, as well as important surgeries scheduled at the clinic, and I'm not missing a Mayhem game because I get injured or arrested, that's for fucking certain.

We head to Big Red's and, as expected, it's packed. There's a line out the door, but the bouncer, Chaz, lets us in without a hassle. Inside it's standing room only and shoulder to shoulder as we weave through sweaty bodies on our way to the bar.

The air is thick with the smell of beer and fried food, and I can barely hear the businessman on the karaoke machine over the chatter, wearing his tie around his bald head like he's Cobra Kai. We take over a row of stools, and we've barely been sitting for two minutes before an enormous cheer sounds off across the bar. Blaze. Blaze. Blaze. The chant starts slowly, but soon builds momentum before finally erupting in a war cry. I see 72 among them, and even with a busted jaw and front tooth missing, he's still better off than we are.

I grit my teeth and Tom slaps my shoulder, as if to remind me of my promise. I grunt indifferently in reply.

Sean orders us a round and we get to work drinking as much as we can to forget about the loss, as well as numbing ourselves to the Blaze's celebrations a few feet away. When the guys break into a discussion about next week's game, I think about Lola, and not just because of how good she felt on my fingers. She's a constant in my head, to the point I can barely function like a normal person, but when my mind is clouded and I'm angry and I need a touchstone to keep me sane, Lola makes it feel like everything will be okay.

But just when I think I'm a respectable gentleman, the sound of her moaning into my mouth while I draw circles around her clit has me hard as a rock. I tug at my jeans to give my dick some space. But if anything can kill my hard on, it's getting shoved in the shoulder by some idiot with a death wish.

"Do you mind?" I snarl, looking over my shoulder. I've never seen this asshole in my life. Tall and skinny, with long, dirty-blond hair knotted into a bun at the back of his head. He's wearing an oversized muscle shirt over his lean frame and a pair of black jeans ripped at the knees.

"Sorry, man. Didn't see you there," he laughs, and I know for a fact that's fucking impossible. I'm taller than everyone in this bar.

He loses interest in me almost immediately, and grabs Tom by the shoulder. My eyes narrow as I place my beer on the bar, and I need to remind myself again of my promise.

"Tom, is that you?" he says.

Tom swings around, and he takes a second or two to process the guy's face. Eventually he smiles, which I guess means I don't have to drag this guy out of here by his man bun.

"Dylan. Holy shit, it's been a while." Tom taps the guys on the back. "Look who it is."

They all spin on their stools to get a look, and I find their responses interesting. I may not have known my teammates for long, but I can tell when something's off. They discreetly exchange looks, and there are no handshakes or embraces, just polite smiles and nods. They know who this guy is, but they don't fucking like him.

"Dylan," Finn says, the only one to stand up and extend a hand, "what are you doing in town?"

Rather than shake, Dylan gives him a low five. "You should know, bro. You hired me."

Finn's eyebrows knit together. "Sorry, man, I don't know what you mean."

"I got a call from my manager. You need a band for a wedding because the last guys ate some bad clams or something?" He unfurls his arms and grins. "Well, here I am!"

Tom's eyes widen. "My wedding? You're playing my wedding?"

"Holy shit!" Dylan laughs. "It's yours? I'm a little upset I wasn't invited, but hey, guess I'm here now, right?"

Tom knocks back his half mug of beer in one gulp, then digs into his pocket and retrieves his phone. "I'll be right back. I have to call Sophie."

"Oh wow, you're marrying Sophie?" Dylan says. "You're still together after all this time? How cool. Boring. But cool."

Tom's jaw clenches as he walks away with his phone to his ear. Finn's scratching the back of his head, while Sean and Blake watch on.

"Sorry, so you're the replacement band?"

"Yeah, man," Dylan confirms. "The Thornz."

Sean furrows his brow. "Wasn't that your high school band's name?"

"Nah," Dylan chuckles. "This is Thornz with no E and a Z at the end. Totally different."

Blake looks over at me. "His last name is Thorne," he explains with an eye roll. "And when he sang with Lola back in the day, they called themselves The Thornes."

My blood boils when I make the connection. "You're that Dylan?"

He places his hands flat on his chest. "The one and only. I don't think we've met."

I rise to my feet, if only to show him how much wider and taller than him I am. "Henry Gallagher."

When he goes for another low five, I grab his hand and squeeze until he winces. He squirms until he gets loose.

"Hell of a handshake you have there," he says.

I say nothing, and just lean over him, looking down as he withers in my shadow.

"So, do you still sing folk music, like you did with Lola?" Blake asks, but his blasé body language says he doesn't really care.

Dylan screws up his face and vehemently shakes his head. "God no. I hated that crap, but when you're trying to get laid you pretend to like anything, right?"

I grit my teeth and feel my hand tighten into a fist.

"It's rock now. A little nineties grunge when the mood strikes."

Sean nods. "Sounds fun, man. Is it just you or... ?"

"Nah, we're a whole band!" Dylan replies. He lifts onto his toes to look over the crowd. "In fact, I'll introduce you to our star right now. Savannah!"

With my height I might as well be sitting in a crow's nest. I see a girl with the shaggy blonde hair weaving her way through the bar toward us, heavy dark makeup around her eyes, and lips painted bright red. When she reaches Dylan, she hooks her arm around his neck.

"I was looking for you!" she says.

"Sorry, babe. Just bumped into some old friends... and this guy... what was it?"

"Henry," I snarl.

Dylan gulps and I see his throat tremble. "Right. Henry... anyway... we're playing my buddy Tom's wedding."

"That's amazing! I've always wanted to meet Dylan's friends," Savannah gushes. She seems like a nice girl, so my fist loosens and I sit back down. "Babe, I'm just going to the bathroom. I don't feel well. I'll be right back," she says as she rushes off.

"She's nice," Blake says.

"Well, don't get any ideas," Dylan jokes. "She's all mine."

Blake leans back in his chair. "That's not me anymore. There's only one woman in my life now, and she's all I want and need."

Dylan's jaw drops. "Really? I never thought I'd see the day that Blake Ward settled down. You were my role model, man!"

Fuck, that's sad. I can't listen to this guy talk anymore. Every word that comes out of his mouth is cringe-worthy bullshit.

Dylan leans forward and talks to us out the side of his mouth. "Savannah and me have been together a while, and she's great, but my feet are getting a little itchy, if you know what I mean."

Sean shakes his head. "Can't say I do."

"You know," Dylan pushes, "I don't think I'm the kind of guy that can be held down to one girl. Especially as a musician. I mean, girls just throw themselves at me. That's how I met Savannah. She's got that face and that body, and then I heard her sing and I knew I needed her to be my lead singer."

Blake sniggers. "Didn't end too well for Lola though, did it?"

Dylan shrugs. "What can I say? The heart wants what the heart wants." He smirks. "Besides, Savannah's better than Lola at a lot of things, if you catch my drift."

I'm on my feet again and in Dylan's face. His eyes widen and he takes a step back, his frame crumpling. I feel Finn's hand on my chest, pulling me back.

"Enough," he scolds. "Remember?"

I can hear the exhaustion in his voice, having to put up with my bullshit temper. There's not many people I'd back down for, especially over a piece of shit like this guy. But Finn has earned my respect. So have the others, even Blake. So I step back.

When Dylan feels safe again, his shoulders straighten and his face burns red. "Who the fuck is this guy?"

Sean sips his beer. "Oh him? That's Henry."

"I'm Lola's boyfriend!" I bark.

Finn, Blake and Sean fall silent, their jaws practically on the ground as they gawk at me. I replay the moment in my head. I had to say something. I can't hit him. Even though I'm dying to knock that smug grin off his face, and the way he's talking about Lola is unacceptable. He needs to know that she is wanted and desired and claimed. By me. The massive motherfucker who can rip him to pieces any time he chooses. As long as I don't have to vaccinate any kittens that day, of course.

"Her boyfriend?" Dylan gulps. "Shit. Sorry man. If I'd known, I wouldn't have said anything."

"How about you just never say anything ever," I growl.

Dylan nods. "Yeah. Got it. I'm gonna get going. I guess I'll see you at the wedding."

Blake and Sean are trying to stifle their laughs, hiding behind their mugs of beer.

Finn's chewing his lip awkwardly. "Yeah. See you then, I guess."

Dylan vanishes into the crowd, glancing over his shoulder now and then to lock eyes with me, and I'm fixed on him until I see him leave.

"What the hell?" Blake laughs. "Where did that come from?"

"You're not with Lola, right?" Sean asks. "Lexie would have told me if you were."

I shake my head. "No. We're not together. I just didn't like the way he was talking about her. I had to shut him up."

Finn grins. "Well, mission accomplished. Dylan's always been full of shit, running his mouth about everything, ever since high school. Lola liked him though, so we cut him a break. I never understood what she saw in him."

"Yeah, you're definitely an upgrade," Blake chuckles, raising his mug to me.

I ruffle my hair and chide myself now that I realize what I've done. "Lola doesn't need to know about this, right?"

"Not from me," Sean says, then he points behind me. "But we're not the ones you need to worry about."

I turn and see Tom with his phone still at his ear. I didn't even know he'd come back. He's talking so low I can barely hear him, but I can hear Sophie squealing on the other end. He did what!

Blake exhales. "Well, that takes care of that. The whole town will be calling you Lola's boyfriend by breakfast."

Shit. He's not wrong. This will spread like wildfire through the girls. Do I text Lola to explain before she gets it second hand? No. That's embarrassing. Guess I have to move towns again.

Finn slaps my back. "Let me get you another drink, man."

I nod my appreciation as I stare at the checkerboard floor. I really know how to keep getting myself into trouble, don't I? But you know the weirdest part? Saying I was Lola's boyfriend felt like the most natural thing in the world, and saying the words out loud made me happy. I forgot about Janie and Stella and the ranch, about 72, about losing the game and letting my team down. I even wanted to punch Dylan ten percent less.

My head was full of Lola, the ray of sunshine that always manages to breakthrough this rain cloud that follows me, and I wonder what my life would be like if she truly was mine.

9

Lola

My eyes are barely open five minutes before my phone vibrates across my nightstand. With only one eye open, I grab it before it falls to the floor. I hold my phone over my face and take a second to focus. Fifteen missed calls and a bunch-load of texts since last night. I was so exhausted. I just climbed into bed, streamed some Netflix and demolished the entire tub of cheese balls, which is clear by the layer of orange dust on my comforter. They're all from Sophie. What did I miss? Probably another wedding disaster.

I answer the call before I miss that one too, but I'm still groggy and half asleep.

"Soph? Is everything okay?"

"Where have you been?" she squeals.

The glass-shattering pitch of her voice is enough to wake me up. "I've been at home sleeping. Why?"

"So much happened last night," Sophie states. "I don't even know where to start."

"How about the beginning?" I yawn.

"Yes. Right. So." I hear her suck in a deep breath and brace myself. "The management company Finn deals with found a replacement band. Apparently the only one that's available to perform at a Christmas wedding."

"That's great news," I say, smacking my lips together. I stop myself from asking if spamming my phone all night was necessary for this update.

"Yeah, kind of. It's Dylan's band."

Suddenly, I'm completely awake. I bolt upright in my bed. "What?"

Her voice gets softer. "Tom was in the bar last night with the guys and Dylan showed up. I've already called Finn. He says he had no idea, that the management company didn't give him any names, just that they only had one band available. I'm so sorry, Lola."

My mind goes blank. It's taken all the resilience I have to stop thinking about Dylan. He was my first love, my high school sweetheart. I honestly thought it was going to be him and me forever. Maybe even us having a Christmas wedding with all our friends some day. But that was before he decided I wasn't exciting enough, or spontaneous enough, or just plain good enough. I thought I was over him. I thought I had dealt with being dumped for someone else, and gotten to a better place. But judging by how my heart is stinging like it's been jabbed with a hot poker, I'm not sure anymore.

Then the realization hits me. If Dylan's here with his band, that means she's here too. Savannah, and that means they're both going to be at Sophie's wedding... and so am I... alone.

Normally I would let this stuff wash over me, like water off a duck's back. That's what I'm known for, after all. Looking on the bright side. The high of knowing everyone around me is happy makes me happy, even if it's hard sometimes. But I don't let that show. I never want to be the reason for somebody's bad day, and I'm not going to start now.

"It's fine, Sophie."

"No, it's not," she says. "I'll get Finn to cancel the band. I'll find someone else."

"There is no one else," I laugh lightly, disguising my worry. "You get married next week."

"I'll get a DJ," she blurts.

I frown. "Sophie, you've been planning this day since we graduated high school. Is a guy wearing a headset and shutter shades blasting Pitbull on your dream board?"

"Oh god... ," she mutters.

"It's no big deal. He's a talented musician, and I hear this new band of his is great. It's not like I have to talk to him or be anywhere near him. Besides, I don't even think about Dylan anymore."

"Really?" Sophie asks, and there's a plea in her voice, as if she's desperate for me to say yes.

"Really, really," I reply, hoping my forced smile makes my voice seem lighter. "Totally over him."

She exhales, and even through the phone I feel the weight lift from her shoulders. "Okay. If you're sure?"

"I'm ridiculously sure."

"Okay, then. Thank you, Lola."

"Sure," I reply.

"Now for the next thing."

"There's more?" I say nervously. What's next? Is the priest the boy who ripped the head off my Barbie when I was five?

Sophie giggles. "You're never going to guess what Henry did last night."

Just the sound of his name sends electric shivers through every nerve in my body. My mind flashes to last night in the locker room, remembering his rippled, taut skin and the sweat that trickled from the back of his neck and down his chest. The way he picked me up like it was nothing, and how boldly he took control.

"Lola, are you there?"

"Mhmmm," I hum, stirring from my daydream. "What about Henry?"

"So Dylan shows up at Big Red's last night, and he comes up to the guys to say hello. Don't worry, Tom says they were appropriately dickish to him on your behalf."

I laugh. "Okay."

"Anyway, apparently he says some really rude stuff. Tom wouldn't go into the details, but it got Henry really riled up. Next thing you know, Henry's on his feet, and Dylan is terrified."

I smile. Does it make me a bad person to find that image delightfully satisfying?

"Then Dylan is like, Who the fuck is this?" Sophie says, dropping her voice to a deep grumble that makes me giggle. "And Henry is like... I'm her boyfriend."

I throw my hand over my mouth and my legs jut out, causing my comforter to fly in the air and shower me in orange cheese ball dust. "No... he did not," I gasp.

"Oh yeah. He did, and apparently Dylan left straight away."

I brush the cheese-ball flakes off my face and chew on my bottom lip, my belly doing backflips. "Why would he say that?"

"Lola," Sophie says, "you know why."

My phone vibrates in my hand, and I look at the screen to find my alarm sounding.

"I have to get to work," I say. "I'll talk to you later."

"Sure," Sophie replies. "Say hello to Dr. Gallagher for me."

"Shut up," I laugh as I end the call.

I'm out of bed like a rocket, rummaging through a pile of laundry in the corner to find my work clothes. I love my job, but there's another reason I'm excited to get to the clinic this morning. Between our first mess of a kiss, our hot romp in the locker room, and now his boyfriend proclamation, I finally buy in to everything Sophie has been saying. Henry cares about me, and I'm not going to waste any time telling him I feel the same way.

I'm dressed and out the door in a flash, tying my hair in a low pony on my way to the car. The lemon and I fly through the streets, the sun glaring off the mounds of fresh, fallen snow. My stomach somersaults when I see the fluffy cat with the stethoscope above the clinic, and I'm so excited to get inside that my askew parking job could be called less than desirable for anyone else who wants a spot. I notice Henry's car is already in the lot, which is odd. I'm normally always first in. Maybe he's excited to see me too?

I head for the door and lean into the wood with my shoulder, already pulling my coat off before I'm even inside. I can't shift the wide smile across my face. "Morning, Henry," I beam.

Then my heart sinks when I see him standing in front of my desk with Krista, her arm draped over his shoulder, their lips dangerously close to kissing.

Henry gulps when he sees me, taking a step away from Krista, his eyes on the floor. "Lola. Good morning."

Krista looks me up and down. "Oh, hello, Lola. Nice to see you again."

"Yeah. Same here," I reply, but it's clear we're both lying.

Henry finally lifts his guilty eyes to meet mine, his heavy brow hanging low, like a kid caught with his hand in the cookie jar. "I'm going to check on the kittens," he says, turning on his heels and making for the overnight room.

"I'll call you," Krista calls to him over her shoulder, and he replies with a half-hearted wave before disappearing behind the door.

Krista walks toward me, her heels clacking on the tile floor. She's so pretty that I assume many girls are intimidated by her. But she's mean and shallow, two traits that have never made me envious of someone. Her lovely features are just misdirection, and if what happened with Dylan taught me anything, it was never to be fooled again.

"You look surprised to see me?" Krista says.

"It's just been a while since you've come to the clinic," I reply.

"Well, after our little talk the other night, I felt like I just had to see Henry. I should thank you. You really made me realize what I'm missing out on."

I keep my face stern, my shoulders straight, and don't let her words affect me. "Gee, Krista. I'm so glad I could help."

I notice she's wriggling her fingers, and I'm not sure why. But when I take a closer look, I spot the diamond ring, and it hits me like a brick. Suddenly the wall I've built doesn't feel as strong. She sees I notice the ring, but of course she does. That was her intention.

"Does that mean you're back together?" I ask, holding back the lump in my throat.

Krista shakes her head. "No. Not yet. Henry says he needs some time to think. For now, I'm just making sure it still fits." She holds out her hand to give me a closeup view. "Like a glove," she grins. "See you soon."

She breezes past me, through the waiting room and out the door, and even though I didn't crack, it feels as if she came out of that encounter as the winner. When she's gone, I take slow steps toward the overnight room, pushing the door slightly open and peering inside. Henry is on his haunches, scratching Brian under the chin while the rest of The Backstreet Boys munch down on breakfast. They're our only guests this morning, with Comet returning home to a very excited Alice yesterday.

He glimpses me in the corner of his eye and swings around, rising to his feet. "Hey," he says.

I wave, then nervously tuck the hair that's escaped my ponytail behind my ears. "So, you and Krista... ?"

"Are not a thing," he interrupts abruptly. "I want you to know that, straight off the bat."

I frown. "She doesn't seem to see it that way, and you two looked pretty cozy."

He shakes his head vehemently. "She just showed up and blindsided me. Nothing happened before you walked through the door, and nothing's going to happen after."

"You've got history," I say. "That can be difficult." I should know. Even though I tell myself over and over that Dylan doesn't even exist in my universe, I think about him more than I should. He has this hold over me, over my memories and my past. Maybe he always will. He still bothers me enough to have me nervous about the wedding, that's for sure.

"Like with Dylan," Henry says.

It's as if he's reading my mind. I nod. "Yeah. I heard about last night. Thanks for defending my honor. Being my boyfriend, though? That's a lot."

He shrugs. "Seemed to work."

"You didn't have to," I laugh lightly.

"Yes, I did," Henry says, his voice deep and sharp at the edges. "I didn't like the things he was saying."

I gulp. I don't even want to imagine what those things were. My wall's already a little worse for wear today. I don't think it could take much more.

"Thanks, but you know he's going to be at the wedding, right? He'll know straight away that it wasn't true when he sees me flying solo while you're there with Krista." I shudder just thinking about it.

"I'm not going to be there with Krista," Henry says. He scratches the back of his head. "If we're going to keep this up, maybe I should be there with you."

My eyebrows crawl up my forehead. "What?"

He shrugs, and it's always surreal seeing the biggest, toughest guy on the ice get shy and awkward around me. It's a side of him not many people get to see.

"It's just for a day, right? Let's go together."

"Are you sure?" I ask. Now I'm the one blushing. "You won't be embarrassed?"

He shakes his head, his eyes glazed over in pure disbelief. "Are you fucking serious? Embarrassed? To be with you?"

My cheeks burn red and my skin tingles. "Swear jar."

He reaches into his back pocket and retrieves his wallet, pulling out a dollar note, but I hold up a hand to stop him. "How about we put this toward our little project?"

He looks at me, bemused.

"Well, if we're going to be a couple for a day, we should probably act like one. Why don't we go on a date tonight?" I give him a second to pick his jaw up off the floor. "It can be a fact-finding adventure. An opportunity to get to know each other better. What do you say?"

He gulps, and I think he's sweating. "I say, yes."

I clap my hands together. "Okay. Great." I look at him over my shoulder before I leave the room. "Thanks, Henry. This is really nice of you."

Now I'm sure he's sweating as he wipes his brow on the sleeve of his white coat. "Yeah. No problem. It'll be fun." His voice cracks like a twelve-year-old boy and he hurries to clear his throat. "I mean. It'll be fun," he repeats, this voice decidedly lower the second time around.

"Red Bull?" I ask.

"Sure," he replies.

I nod and head to the lunchroom, and I can't stop smiling. I've never looked forward to a date as much in my life. Even if it is a fake one.

10

Henry

Considering this isn't a real date, I'm pretty fucking nervous. It took forever to choose what to wear and I've never messed with my hair this much in my life, and are my fingernails always this gross? These are things I didn't bother worrying about before. But suddenly it all feels incredibly vital. I want to look good for Lola. I want her to see that I tried. Fake date or not.

I head over to her house to pick her up, my knee jiggling uncontrollably the whole way. When I arrive and knock on the door, Lucas answers, munching on the most loaded ham-salad sandwich I've ever seen.

"Hello again," he muffles, a lettuce leaf escaping the confines of the bread and dropping onto the floor. "You here for Lola then?"

I nod. My palms are sweating. Do palms normally sweat?

"Lola!" Lucas yells from the corner of his mouth. "Your boss is here."

"Don't say it like that," I grumble, rolling my eyes.

Lucas laughs, showing far too much chewed sandwich in his open mouth. "I'm just fucking with you."

Lola appears behind him, peeking around his shoulder, her dark eyes framed with long lashes and a dusting of gold glitter. It's dark outside, in the middle of winter, but she looks as if she's spent a day in the sun. Her skin glows, luminous and warm. My eyes fall to her full glossy lips, and the urge to kiss her is hard to hold back. But my thoughts wander further and stronger when I see what she's wearing. The gold dress leaves nothing to the imagination, tight over every single curve, low cut enough that the rounded tops of her breasts spill slightly over the edges, and so short that her smooth thighs are on display.

I panic when I feel my cock lengthen and press against the fabric of my pants. The last thing I want is for Lucas to clock my hard-on. Normally I can control myself pretty well, but she looks so fucking good. This fake date could ruin me if I'm not careful. If Lola keeps looking like that, I might have no choice but to make it real.

I'm so busy staring at her, I don't notice she's staring at me, too. "You look... amazing," I breathe.

She smiles, her eyes gleaming. "You too."

I glance at myself and shrug. "Really?"

She nods. "Really, really."

Then whatever moment we were sharing turns to shit when Lucas playfully hooks her around the neck and ruffles her hair. "You two kids have a great time," he says.

"Lucas!" she shrieks, pushing him away and following up with a slap across his chest that makes the loudest thwack I've heard, and I've heard a lot of thwacks. "Don't be such a dork."

She checks her hair in a mirror by the door, but she looks perfect to me no matter what state her hair is in. "Do you want to head out?" I ask.

She glares at Lucas, but her expression softens when she turns to me. "Definitely."

When Lola walks, it's as if she's gliding. There's a lightness to her step, like she doesn't have a worry in the world, and I wish I could see things the way she does. Even now, with this beautiful, special woman by my side, my family, my responsibility, my team are always there bearing down on my shoulders, a constant pressure that I can never get away from, and I know they're responsible for the rain cloud that follows me. I know this is what keeps me from going all in with Lola. But not tonight. Tonight is about me and the girl of my dreams. She gets my full attention.

I open the passenger door for her and she shuffles inside. I try not to stare too long at her legs when she folds them, quickly closing the door to save myself from temptation. I jump in the driver's side and we head toward main street. Lola and I agree on Big Red's, because she likes the music and I like the wings. We pull into the parking lot and it's quieter than it has been the last few days. The Blaze and their supporters have taken their victory and thankfully left Lake Mistletoe, and if you're a Mayhem fan you're probably at home mourning. The upside is that Lola and I get a great table and a relaxed vibe to enjoy each other's company.

The server comes to take our drinks order, and I'm not beating around the bush. I order two servings of wings and a beer to get me started.

Lola pours over the menu for as long as expected. I don't mind waiting. It gives me longer to look at her, her tongue rolling in her cheek as she decides, her fingertips grazing her collar bone. I've never wanted to touch someone as much in my life. She smiles when she finally puts down the menu.

"I'll get tuna on rye with dill and mayonnaise, a tall glass of water with a slice of cucumber, and a GoGo juice."

The server nods as she scribbles on her pad. "What kind of Gogo?"

"Cranberry," I answer before she can. "In the box with the straw."

The server frowns. "Okay. Coming right up."

Lola grins her approval. "Great start." She leans into her hand, squinting her eyes at me while she ponders. "And your favorites are Red Bull and beer?"

"Those are everybody's favorites," I say.

"Okay then," Lola says, accepting the challenge. "A hot chocolate made with real milk chocolate, not powder, and white mini-marshmallows, served scorching hot."

My head jerks and I can't help but crack a smile. "That's eerily correct."

"I'm observant," she replies.

"I didn't like hot chocolate before I came to Lake Mistletoe," I say. "Not really hot chocolate weather in Rockford."

"Okay, let's go with that," Lola starts. "You were born and bred in Rockford Valley. Your family owns a ranch there, mainly dealing in cattle. Parents are married. H.T. and Darla, but I've got no clue what H.T. stands for. You're the oldest of four. Two sisters, Janie and Stella and a brother named... ," she bites her lip as she thinks, and it's adorable, "Rob," she blurts.

I narrow my eyes and nod. "Okay. Not bad. My turn." I rub my hands together. I love a challenge too. "Lola Nixon, born in Lake Mistletoe. Twin brother, name Lucas, kind of dick. Father is Tony. Teaches English at Mistletoe High. Mother is Robyn, does hair and makeup and is currently on a movie set in... ," I pause and furrow my brow as if that'll help me remember. I see Lola's lips part, and I quickly raise a finger. "Shush!" I say. "I know this." At last it comes to me and I beam a proud smile. "Hawaii."

She giggles and nods. "Is that it?"

I slap my hand on the table so hard that it startles her. "And Lottie is your aunt... father's side."

"I'm impressed," she sighs, leaning back in her chair. "Seems we already know each other well, although I'm pretty sure no one's going to be quizzing us on our family tree. This is for a wedding, not a green card."

"You want something tougher?" I ask.

She leans back, and when her tongue rolls over her bottom lip, it sends shivers down my spine. "Go ahead," she replies.

I gaze into her dark eyes, pushing past the Lola that she shows everyone else, searching for the Lola she truly wants to be seen, and when her eyes glimmer, I know I've found her.

"You hate the cold, but you love the snow. You're a fan of salads and tuna, but can eat an entire tub of cheese balls at the speed of light. You always order two drinks. One for hydration. One for yumminess."

She gulps, and the quiver in her throat makes my heart race. "Too easy," she mutters.

I laugh lightly. "Okay. You cry whenever you see a lost pet flyer. You call me Hangry Henry when I get on your nerves. You wish your mother didn't travel so much for work. You're sad that your dad is allergic to cats because you want one so badly." I take a breath. "You don't sing in public anymore. You do everything you can to make others happy, even if you're sad. You hand out second chances like candy at Halloween, and you're the most genuine person I've ever met."

Lola releases a long, trembling breath as she gazes at me. "Anything else?"

I cock an eyebrow. "You want more?"

She reaches across the table and clasps my hand. "I think I do."

The door swings open, and I might not have noticed if it wasn't so quiet, but I turn when the icy wind drifts inside. Dylan and Savannah walk in, shaking off the layer of snow they've collected before hanging their jackets on the coat rack. I look back at Lola, hoping she hasn't clocked them yet, but she's already staring in their direction. Her hand still rests on top of mine, so I flip it over so I can link our fingers. Mine are big and wide, almost too large to lace with her tiny digits. But the warmth catches her attention and she drags her eyes away from her ex and his new girlfriend.

"You going to be okay?" I ask.

She gives an unsteady nod, like she's trying to convince herself with each bob of her head. "Yeah. This is perfect. He'll see us here together, like a couple."

My brow droops. There's a nervousness in her voice, and where once I thought words like fake and pretend were all a part of the game we were playing, suddenly they feel real. Have I read this thing all wrong? Am I actually just the guy she's using to make her ex jealous?

Dylan spots us too. He slings his arm around Savannah's waist as they walk over to our table, and I feel Lola's grip tighten.

"Hey," Dylan says.

He runs his fingers through his hair and it's the first time I notice his hands are covered with tattoos. It's actually the first time I notice the variety of differences between the two of us. It makes me wonder if I'm even Lola's type.

"Hi," Lola replies, and I barely recognize her voice. I can't tell if it's nerves, or just the way she talks to him. She turns her attention to Savannah and smiles. "I'm Lola."

"Savannah," she says, offering a handshake.

Lola uses her free hand, while squeezing mine even tighter than before.

Dylan nods his chin at me, and I do the same in reply. "I met your new guy last night," he says.

"He told me," Lola says. "Sorry about that. Henry can get pretty protective."

"Geez, I wouldn't mind Dylan getting like that sometimes," Savannah says, nudging him in the stomach. "We play some pretty shady gigs now and then." She laughs, looking at Dylan for a response, but his eyes are locked on Lola and it gets my blood boiling. "Babe," Savannah says, a croak in her voice.

He nods. "Yeah, sure, babe. Whatever you say."

Lola and Dylan continue their stare, and I'm starting to feel a little like a prop. It's not until the server arrives with our food and drinks that they break their gaze.

"We'll leave you to it," Dylan says. "Don't want to interrupt your meal."

"Much obliged," I grumble tersely, snatching a wing from the lattice basket and stripping the meat from the bone with one chomp.

"Maybe we can catch up while I'm in town?" Dylan asks, and I glimpse Lola's chin drop.

"Yeah. Maybe," she replies.

I can't help but be disappointed that she didn't flat out deny him. I guess I am just the fake date.

Okay. If that's what Lola needs.

When Dylan and Savannah are far enough away, her blasé facade falls away, and she's Lola again, wide-eyed and giddy.

"That couldn't have gone any better," she gushes. Her hand slips from mine to take hold of her tuna sandwich, and another thing I've just learned about Lola is she has the bite force of a T-Rex.

I gnaw the chicken wing to the bone before discarding it to the basket, and I wonder if Lola can tell how confused I am. "It did?"

When she swallows the huge bite, her whole body animates. "Yeah. Don't you think he looked bothered?"

"And that's what we want, right?"

She cocks an eyebrow at me. "Yeah. Isn't it?"

I'm grateful when the bar owner, Skeet, who is neither big nor red, takes the stage and grabs hold of the microphone.

"Evening folks," he says, as a burly guy hauls the karaoke machine onto the stage behind him. "It's eight o'clock and you know what the means."

"Big Red's karaoke party!" the twenty-odd patrons cry out in unison. Lola and I give a little clap, and I'm startled when a line forms at the side of the stage.

"Did you know about this?" I ask.

She nods. "Oh, yeah. Open mic Saturday is always a big deal. I like to come and listen sometimes."

I sip my beer. "I guess that's something else I know about you now."

The first performers step onto the stage, and I'm not surprised when the microphone gets handed to Dylan. This motherfucker is everywhere lately, and I'm getting sick of seeing his face. He picks up a second microphone and hands it to Savannah.

"Hey Lake Mistletoe," he says. "It's great being back in my hometown."

"I don't think an intro is necessary," I grumble. That gets a giggle out of Lola, but she's still fixated on what's happening on stage.

"I'd like to introduce you to my girl, Savannah. The most beautiful woman and talented singer I've ever known."

Savannah bows and blushes, then does a twirl that sends her skirt of layered scarfs spinning.

I'm almost afraid to look at Lola's reaction, because I know for sure if she's crying I'll be on the stage in five seconds with my foot up Dylan's scrawny ass. When I finally have the guts to check, there are no tears. I should have known. She's too strong for that. But the sadness paints her face in dark blue and waves of gray. It can't be easy when your ex-boyfriend introduces your replacement to a room full of people, then follows that up with telling them how much better they are than you.

She may not be crying, but I think I'm still going to go put my foot up his ass.

"Anyway, here's a song I wrote, and you can find this on our EP, The Thornz."

"He kept the name... ," Lola says.

I take another swig of my beer, anything to dull the urge to charge that stage. "Apparently."

Dylan clears his throat before taking hold of Savannah's hand, and they fall under the spell of each other's romantic gaze.

She was starlight, and I was the moon.
But daylight came and took her too soon.
So I waited in that place where we used to go,
Where the wind whistles, and the bright lights glow.
Our place in the snow, our place on the hill.

Those colors of sadness fade altogether, and now Lola is pale white. She stares blankly at the stage, her eyes glazing over with a liquid shimmer.

"I wrote that," she mutters. "That's my song."

Savannah lifts the mic to her lips to sing her verse.

Our place in the snow, our place on the hill
Even if you wander, I'll love you still
I'll wait right here, day and night until
You make your way back to our hill

Lola's eyes well with tears, and I don't know how, but she holds them back. I clench my jaw and snap to my feet, then pin back my ears and charge for the stage. I'm only a few steps away when Dylan and Savannah stop singing and the bar breaks into applause.

"That's The Thornz," Dylan squeezes in before the microphone is yanked from his grip.

By the time I get to the stage they've walked down the other side, and I find myself standing awkwardly beside not-Big-Red.

"There's a line, big fella," Skeet laughs. "But if you insist."

He pushes the microphone into my hand and I freeze. What the fuck? The bar falls silent, and I can feel every pair of eyes fixed on me.

The burly guy next to the machine nudges my shoulder. "What song?"

I gulp and stare blankly at him, then I whisper, "I'd like to go now, please."

He scratches his head. "Who sings that?"

"Yeah. Go Henry!"

I turn at the sound of my name and see Lola on her feet. She's smiling, glowing again. Apparently, my impending humiliation is just what the doctor ordered. Shit. Why not? Lola deserves a little happiness. I look back at the karaoke master.

"Josh Turner. Hit it."

He gives a salute, then punches some numbers into the computer. I'm terrified at first, with my heart beating a hundred miles an hour and sweat pouring down my back, but as soon as the guitar intro hits, I'm back home on the ranch with a cold beer, swaying on the swing chair in the early evening.

Baby lock the door and turn the lights down low

Put some music on that's soft and slow

Baby we ain't got no place to go

I hope you understand

Lola's jaw drops. She's on her feet, clapping her hands in time, her hips swaying left to right, and I must not be complete shit because everyone else starts clapping too.

I've been thinking about this all day long

Never felt a feeling quite this strong

I can't believe how much it turns me on

Just to be your man

My left foot taps, and I can't remember when it started, but I'm snapping my fingers too. By the time I get to the end of the song, everyone's on their feet and singing along. The embarrassment has withered to nothing, and it seems silly I was nervous in the first place. I sing the last note and the backing music fades out. I take a bow and hand back the mic, getting a round of applause from the bar patrons and a nod of approval from not-Big-Red.

I walk down the steps from the stage and join Lola at the table.

"Josh Turner. Really?"

A smirk pulls at the corner of my mouth. "He's the best." I glimpse Dylan heading for the door, dragging Savannah behind him. "He doesn't look happy," I say.

"Who cares about him?" Lola says, taking the wing from my fingers before I can get it to my mouth. "Do you want to get out of here?"

"What did you have in mind?" I ask.

She exhales, a dreamy ease taking over her face. "Just a place on the hill, I know."

11

Lola

I wrote that song about Chestnut Hill. There's a spot right at the top where you can see all of Lake Mistletoe, and at night time, when the lights are glittering and the giant Christmas tree in the middle of the lake is all lit up, it's about the most beautiful thing in the world.

Henry drives us up there, and we pass the Northwellian on the way. I can make out the white tent behind the old building, and picture it draped in fairy lights, filled with our friends and family. I wonder what my wedding will be like one day. It used to be Dylan I saw standing at the end of the aisle, but now it's someone else. Someone tall and grumpy, who I imagine will look amazing in a tux.

I glance over at Henry in the driver's seat, his eyes fixed on the road as he navigates the weaving path that leads to the top of the hill. His waves of dark brown hair fall over his brow, hanging loose and shaggy around his sharp jawline, and I can't look at his lips without remembering that night in the locker room, and how they felt on my neck. I wanted him that night. Like I want him right now. It's time to stop denying that.

We reach my favorite spot on the hill, and Henry parks close to the edge. The snowfall ceases long enough to give us a clear night sky packed full of stars. Just as I hoped, Lake Mistletoe sparkles before us, from the blinking lights on the Christmas tree to the lit-up strip of main street.

"This is what your song was about?" Henry asks.

"Yep," I sigh. "He changed some of the he's and she's, but I wrote it about watching the stars on Chestnut Hill."

"With him," Henry says, his voice somber.

"Once," I reply, leaning back into the headrest, then turning my face toward him. "But not anymore."

Henry lifts his chin. "Who do you want to watch the stars with now?"

"I think you know."

I reach out and take hold of Henry's huge hand and pull him toward me, resting his palm on my upper thigh. I can feel him shiver as his eyes scour every inch of me. His breathing gets louder, rumbling deep in his chest, and soon I feel his fingers curve around my flesh and squeeze.

"I can't stop thinking about you," he says. "And not just since the night I picked you up from the bar. Before that. From the first day you walked into the clinic." I cup his face, then run my fingers through his hair and he closes his eyes, leaning into my touch. "But I'm scared, Lola. I don't know what kind of boyfriend I'd make. My parents are a train wreck, hurting each other over and over again. I'm a miserable bastard, just like my father." He inhales. "I don't want to hurt you. I'd rather die than be the one who dims the light that glows inside you. The world needs that light. I need that light."

I lift his chin, and he opens his eyes to look at me. "Well, first off, your dad sounds great," I say lightly. A smile cracks on his face. A smile just for me. "I'm in no hurry to get hurt either. It's well documented that I don't bounce back from breakups very well. But I don't think this is about what either of us wants. We need each other, Henry. We fit."

"Yeah. We do," he says.

He leans over, taking my face into his hands and drawing me to him, but he doesn't kiss me straight away. Instead, he drags his nose along my jawline, his lips grazing my neck. His breath sends shivers through me, an exquisite warmth radiating through my center. I feel his other hand grip my thigh, his fingers inching higher until they peek under my dress. I close my eyes and let out a deep breath, my entire body trembling beneath his touch. My heart races when his searching fingers find my panties and brush against my crevice. Just the thought of him touching me there gets me wet, and a moan escapes my lips.

At last he kisses me, pressing his lips against my throat. With each kiss, his hunger for me intensifies. He turns my face so I'm looking at the roof of the car, then buries his lips deeper in my neck, and with each kiss his fingers creep closer to exactly where I want them to be. They find the top of my panties, and slowly slip inside the fabric, inching down until they find my slick folds. He traces my crease with a gentle finesse I don't expect from someone so large, and though I feel a desperate need for him to tear at my clothes and take me like I know he can, the unexpected tenderness of his touch has me melting into the chair.

Then he whispers in my ear, and I lose my breath. "Open your legs for me."

I bite my lip and nod before widening my legs for him. He wastes no time sliding his fingers between my folds, his thumb drawing firm circles around my clit while he continues to kiss behind my ear.

"How does that feel?" he asks.

My eyes roll back in my head as he quickens his motion. "Good," I murmur.

"Just good?" he growls as he dips a finger inside me.

I gasp, and my legs splay wider in response. "Amazing," I groan.

His kisses trail down my neck to my shoulders, then my collar bone, hungry and desperate until he reaches the mound of my breasts. He opens his mouth wide, devouring my skin, his breaths heavy and guttural. He slides a second finger inside me and I whimper as he dips his digits in and out while his thumb rolls over my swelling clit. Henry buries his face in my cleavage, lapping at the skin as his fingers move faster, and I get wetter with every excruciatingly delicious plunge.

I reach out and find his leg, trailing my fingers up the inside of his thigh and it's not long before I feel the long, hard mass halfway down his pant leg. I take a second to comprehend just how big it is as I grip its outline and stroke him firmly up and down. I hear a soft grunt from his lips as his tongue probes beneath the top of my dress, so I stroke harder. He responds by pushing his fingers deeper inside me. I feel my muscles tighten around him as my orgasm builds, heat surging from my center, filling my belly and my chest, numbing my senses for a split second before reigniting them with ripples of thrilling pleasure.

I cry out, throwing my head back against the headrest, my mouth wide open as my hand tightens around his cock. It's been so long since I've cum that hard, and I want to feel it again. Now. I find Henry's belt and fumble with the clasp until it slides off, then I pinch the zip and drag it all the way down, revealing the gorgeous sight of Henry's enormous girth pitching a tent in his boxers.

I press my hand against his chest, pushing him back into the driver's seat. His hand slips free from my panties, and he watches intently as I hook the waistband of his boxers and pull them down. His swollen, purple tip catches the fabric, but springs back up once his boxers are off. I bite my lip as I study the ridges and veins, and appreciate the share size of it. I expected Henry to be big, but this is the most magnificent cock I've ever seen.

I smile and lean over, hovering just above the head before laying a soft kiss. Henry groans as I taste a drop of precum pearling at the tip. I look up at him, his face overcome with bliss, his eyes glazed and dreamy.

"I want you inside me," I say.

Suddenly he's alert and nodding eagerly. He lunges forward to the glove box and yanks it open with such force I think he's going to break the thing off. Henry searches through the junk inside, his face growing more frustrated the longer it takes.

"Shit," he groans.

I grin, reaching into my handbag at my feet and pulling out a condom. "Looking for one of these?" I try not to giggle at how relieved he looks. "You can't leave it up to a man to cover all the bases." I push him back down in his seat and lean over to him. "Even one as hot as you," I whisper before kissing him. I pull out the condom and line it up over his tip before easing it down his shaft, all the way to the base.

Henry's dark eyes fix on my every move, and he's looking at me as if I'm the only person in the world.

"Come here," he demands.

I smile, climbing over the handbrake and straddling him. Henry takes hold of my ass and squeezes as I lean forward to kiss him. We kiss deep and long, our tongues exploring each other's mouths. I feel his fingers move to my back and find the zipper of my dress. He pulls it down, then grips the straps, easing them over my shoulders and down my arms until I'm topless before him. Henry gazes at my breasts, taking in every curve and every freckle. His hands slide up my back, gripping me under my shoulder blades and pulling me forward until his mouth finds my nipple.

A surge of pleasure fills my body and dulls my senses to everything else. I put my hands on his shoulders and moan softly as he trails his kisses along my chest to my other breast, lavishing it with the same attention. The flicks of his tongue invoke a fresh need within me, and soon my folds are slick as my core tightens again. I lift my dress so it sits on my hips and grind against him, his tip grazing back and forth against my entrance. He utters deep, sexy groans each time I flirt with his cock, while his tongue laps greedily at my nipple.

Suddenly, he grips my hips, and I gasp. "Sit on my cock. Now, Lola."

My heart thumps hard in my chest, and the way he's talking has my pussy wetter than I thought was possible. He keeps a tight hold on my hips, but I'm the one who pulls my panties to the side and lowers myself onto him. I bite my lip, moaning with every inch that I bury inside me, each ridge sending a gorgeous surge of ecstasy through my nerves. God. He's so big.

"That's it," he growls, kneading my hips in his hands. "Almost there." He throws his head back when I finally nestle at his base and grind against him. "Yes. That's it."

I roll my hips slow at first, and now Henry guides me, lifting me up and down his cock, our eyes locked on each other, our mouths open and gasping for air. Soon our pace quickens, and I slide over him with ease. I ride faster and harder, and Henry thrusts against me, meeting me as I come down on him, pushing himself deeper inside me. His grip tightens on my hips, his fingers digging into my skin. I groan as I feel my orgasm building once more, and when he sees my response, he lunges forward with his mouth, licking at my nipple while he thrusts harder into me.

"Oh, fuck!" I scream, slamming my hands against the roof of the car, and my muscles clamp around his cock as I cum.

"That's so good," he groans. Henry pulls me down, holding me tightly against his chest so my ass is in the air. He buries himself deep inside me, then pulls out almost to the edge of his tip before plunging once more. "You feel so good," he whispers in my ear. "So fucking good." He moves faster, sliding in and out of my swollen entrance, his growls intensifying with each thrust. "I'm cumming," he groans. "Fuck."

He brings me down on his cock, all the way to the base, and holds me there as he growls into my ear. Our chests press against each other, and I feel our hearts beating in unison, our breaths ebbing and flowing as one. Henry cups my face and kisses me, sighing the last of his orgasm into my mouth.

"You owe a dollar to the swear jar," he chuckles lazily.

"You too," I reply, gazing at him with a dopey grin.

"How about we skip the swear jar and get some cranberry Gogo's instead?"

I laugh and kiss him again. "Sounds like a plan."

I ease myself off him and into the passenger seat, and straighten out my dress while he cleans himself up. This may have started as a fake date, but in this car, on this hill, beneath the moon and stars and high above the lights of Lake Mistletoe, being with Henry is the realest me I've ever felt.

12

Henry

I feel like my face is going to crack. It's not used to smiling this much. I normally reserve this kind of mouth action for christenings or the lady at the laundromat who does my shirts. She's nicer if I smile. But this smile is all because of Lola. She's drawn it out of me, found something no one else could and bought it into the light. I don't think I could be grumpy even if I tried.

I'm here solo on a Sunday to tidy up some charts for next week, and feed The Backstreet Boys, of course. The buggers are getting bigger, and we won't be able to keep them here much longer. We can't have five full grown cats waltzing around the place.

I cock a curious eyebrow when I hear the bell jingle over the door and peek my head out of the overnight room to see who it is. My heart hopes that it's Lola, but I know she's with Sophie and her friends today, doing last-minute prep for the wedding. Still. Nothing wrong with wishful thinking. The image of her riding me, bathed in moonlight is burned into my brain. I see it whenever I close my eyes. It makes me never want to open them.

I'm not thrilled when I see Krista standing in the waiting room, but it's a conversation I need to have. Problem is, I thought we were already through. When she ended things, I'll admit, I was glad that it was over. I don't know how my dumb ass even got into that situation. Being engaged to someone I barely liked, let alone loved. But that's my fault. Not hers. I should have been honest with her. Now that I have Lola, everything's different. I've never been so sure of something in my life, and I'm not going to waste another second pretending. I want to spend every minute being with my sweet Lola. My perfect fit.

Krista waves to catch my attention and I join her in the waiting room. "Morning. What are you doing here?"

She smiles. "I was driving past and saw your car. I thought maybe we could get some lunch? Talk things over."

I take a deep breath and shake my head. "I don't think so, Krista. I'm not interested in getting back together. I'm sorry."

She doesn't wear shock well, her jaw gaping as if she's never been told no before. "You can't mean that. You are I are perfect for each other."

I fold my arms over my chest. "Are we? Why?"

"We're both medical professionals," she blurts, her lips pursed as she thinks. "We both like animals."

"You hate animals," I sigh. "You call my dogs rambunctious demon spawn, when they're a pair of geriatrics who sleep all day."

"The theater?" she says, grasping at straws.

"I went once with you and slept the whole time," I reply.

She frowns. "Well, I know you hate karaoke."

I grit my teeth. "Actually, I think I might like it." I exhale and sweep my hair off my brow. "We don't have anything in common Krista. Having similar jobs doesn't make us perfect for each other, and I don't want to spend my life sleeping through the things you love, and you shouldn't either."

Krista frowns. "I do hate hockey."

"I know you do."

She rolls her shoulders, and a weight seems to lift from them, as if she understands what I'm saying and finally agrees. "Well, okay then." She wriggles the engagement ring off her finger and holds it out to me.

"No. That was a gift. You should keep it," I say.

"To be honest, I was hoping for something a little bigger," she replies, pushing the ring into my hand. She stares at me sternly, but slowly a smile creeps onto her lips, followed by a laugh. "I'm joking, Henry. Do me a favor and put it on someone who gets you. Maybe that little elf who runs around here singing to cats, I hear?"

I nod. "Lola."

"Yes. Lola." Krista pulls her bag tightly over her shoulder. "Goodbye."

She gives me one last smile before she heads out into the snow, the bell over the door jingling after she's gone. I look at the ring in the palm of my hand, rolling my thumb over the more than adequate-sized diamond. My chest fills with warmth, thinking that maybe I'll buy one of these for Lola one day. One that she'll wear for the rest of her life.

I walk into my office and tuck the ring away in my bag. My phone vibrates in my pocket and I'm quick to pull it out. A text from Mrs. Bearenstein. What the fuck does this woman want on a Sunday? I scroll through the message.

MRS BEARENSTEIN: I am in need of more medicine for Anastasia. Please bring to 252 Maple. Regards. M. Bearenstein.

I roll my eyes. I'm not exactly tech savvy, but I know you don't sign off a text message.

Maple is on my way home. I suppose there's no harm in swinging by and dropping off some pills for Anastasia. Maybe then she won't come into the clinic next week, but she probably will. I rummage through the cupboards in my office until I find what I need, grabbing a dozen tiny blue capsules and sealing them in a little white plastic bottle.

I tuck them into my bag and lock up the clinic, braving a blast of cold air to get to my car in the lot. I drive out to Maple, and I know Mrs. Bearenstein is right across the street from Blake. I pull into the driveway, then climb out of the car with the bottle in my hand while doing my best not to go ass-up on the slippery pavers. When I get to the door, I tap the little gold knocker, then wait for what seems forever. Is she even home? It's so quiet. Eventually, the door creaks open.

Mrs. Bearenstein peeks out from inside, and when she sees it's me, she opens the door a little wider. "Oh, Dr. Gallagher. Thank god you've come." She moves aside from the doorway, and I stand there, not sure what I'm supposed to do. "Well, are you coming in?" she asks.

My head jerks with surprise. "Am I supposed to come in?"

She rolls her eyes. "I need you to look at Anastasia."

I let out a deep breath as I walk into the house. "Mrs. Bearenstein, I'm not working today. I just came to drop off her pills."

She closes the door behind me, ignoring everything I'm saying. "It will only take a second, doctor. Please. This way."

She walks through an arch into a side room, and I follow under duress. The house feels old and faded, with dark, patterned wallpaper and hardwood floors scattered with faded, tasseled rugs. It's cold in here, and so quiet that my breaths are the loudest thing I can hear. It seems such a big place for just her, and I'm about to say this when I pass a beautiful old oak sideboard with carved doors and beading on the panels.

Photo frames cover the surface, so many that I can barely see the varnished wood beneath. There's an older man, about Mrs. Bearenstein's age. One where he's fishing off a pier, another where he's putting the star on a Christmas tree. Going by the crimson wallpaper in the background, it was in this very room. Then there's a picture where he's holding Mrs. Bearenstein around the waist and they're blowing out birthday candles. It's hard to recognize her at first. She looks happy. Another collection of photos tells a story spanning years. A baby who becomes a toddler, then a boy into a teen with braces, until he's finally a man. Then he's joined by a pretty blond woman, with a baby of their own. But this story is shorter. In fact, that's the only photo I can see of the man and his family.

My curiosity is piqued. I don't know any of these people. I've definitely not seen them around Lake Mistletoe. After I've fallen behind, Mrs. Bearenstein comes back to find me.

"Now, now. This way," she says.

But I'm far too intrigued to not ask questions. "Mrs. Bearenstein, is this your family?"

She sighs. "Yes. It is."

"But I've never seen them. Do they live here in Lake Mistletoe? Is that your husband?"

"Yes," she replies. "You moved to Lake Mistletoe after he passed."

I stand upright. "I'm sorry to hear that."

She shrugs her shoulders. "Cancer. But at least it was quick. Not everyone is so lucky." She points to the other photos. "And that's my son Andrew, his wife Melissa, and my granddaughter Rianna. They're still alive, if that's what you wanted to know. But they don't live in Lake Mistletoe. They moved right after Rianna was born. I don't see them anymore. Their choice. Not mine. Now, follow me. Kitchen is this way."

She leads the way, flicking on lights as she goes and I follow close behind.

"Why are we going to the kitchen? I thought I was taking a look at Anastasia."

"Oh, I'm sure she's fine," Mrs Bearenstein states. "She's pottering around here somewhere. Cup of tea?"

We walk into the kitchen, and she's quick to put the kettle on.

"Mrs. Bearenstein, I don't really have time for a cup of tea."

"Nonsense, always time for tea."

She opens a cupboard and I immediately notice a tower of white pill bottles, the kind that the clinic uses, like the one in my pocket. They're unopened, and there's got to be several months' worth. For someone so desperate to get medicine for Anastasia, shouldn't they be empty? She catches me looking and swiftly closes the cupboard.

"On second thoughts, you should get going now."

I'm still processing the last few minutes, but I nod. "Okay. Sure." I reach into my pocket and retrieve Anastasia's prescription, placing it on the countertop. "Have a pleasant weekend Mrs. Bearenstein."

She turns her back on me, continuing to make herself a cup of tea, but apparently now I'm not invited. "I'll see myself out," I mumble awkwardly.

I retrace my steps, taking a last look at the photos, before making my way to the front door. I walk outside and close the door behind me, but my hand lingers on the handle. Considering I was keen to get away moments ago, I'm reluctant to take another step. Something didn't feel right in there. She's all alone, with no family, and I think she's coming to the clinic just for somebody to talk to. But what do I say? What do I do? Is this any of my business? I head to my car and once I'm inside, I pull out my phone and call Lola.

When she answers, I can barely hear her voice. The girls are laughing so much.

"What's up?" she asks.

"I just had the weirdest encounter with Mrs. Bearenstein," I say. "She asked me to come over to her place to drop off pills for her cat, but she's still got a bunch of them in her kitchen cabinet. It's like she wanted me to come over just to keep her company."

"Similar thing with me at the supermarket!" Lola exclaims. "Stacks of single serve TV dinners. She's all alone in that house. We should do something about it."

I cock an eyebrow. "Like put her in a home or... ?"

"No!" Lola laughs. "Like figure out a way she's not so lonely at Christmas."

"Good luck with that Christmas miracle," I scoff. "Anyway, I... ," I look up from my feet to the big bay window at the front of Mrs. Bearenstein's house and find her standing right there, glaring at me. "Fuck, gotta go," I blurt, tossing the phone into the backseat and starting the engine.

I feign a smile and give a polite wave before reversing down the drive and getting out of there as fast as I can.

13

Lola

I can't believe it's finally Sophie's wedding day!

We spent all yesterday getting manicures and pedicures, and getting our faces scraped of anything dry or fuzzy. I feel smooth as a newborn from head to toe! I had a blast with my girls, treating Sophie like a queen on the eve of one of the most special days of her life. But between mimosas and stray-hair plucking, all I could think about was Henry. His hands, his arms, his mouth... and that gift from the gods that he carries around in his pants all day. My knees wobble just picturing it. I can't shift my smile, and these butterflies in my stomach seem to be taking up permanent residence. I'll be arriving at the Northwellian soon. The bridesmaids are going ahead early, then Sophie will come in the limo, and I can't wait to see Henry again.

I'm bunched into the backseat with Lexie and Charlotte, our heads peeking out from behind the puffy tulle skirts of our blush-pink dresses. The neck line is a plunging V, and it cinches tight at the waist, which makes the layers of tulle look amazing on my hips. Thank god we talked Sophie out of the ruffled collars. Daisy left even earlier than us. She's actually working today at the wedding, but has her dress ready to go for the ceremony. Lucas will be there too, tending bar and hitting on anything that moves, if I know my brother. Problem is, he's so good at it he tends to get what he wants. I'm looking forward to the day he meets his match.

We pull up at the front doors of the Northwellian and it's a hive of activity. There are rows of people carrying flowers and trays and dishes into the hotel. The sun's out today, and the snow has eased to a minor dusting. It's still frosty though, so as soon as the three of us are out of the car, we sprint into the foyer of the hotel.

The walls are dressed with elegant garlands, their golden ribbons intertwined with twinkling lights. There are wreaths around every archway, and bushels of bright red holly in every corner. Sophie really lucked out getting this place. It's going to make for the most beautiful wedding. As we walk down the corridor, I immediately recognize Dylan coming the other way, clutching a guitar in his hand. He sees me too, and his slumped shoulders straighten. I think maybe we'll walk past each other without a word, but he stops and waves.

"Hey."

Lexie and Charlotte look at me, and they don't need to speak to let me know they're there if I need them.

"I'll catch up," I say.

Neither of them seems pleased by the idea, but they nod and carry on down the wide corridor, leaving Dylan and me alone. He's slicked back his dirty-blond hair, his black shirt unbuttoned right down to his belly button, with sleeves rolled up to his elbows. An assortment of silver chains hang low around his neck, while his wrists are stacked with layers of leather bracelets. When we were singing folk music at birthdays and christenings, he wore beige cardigans and baggy jeans. Looks like he changed everything when he switched genres. Including the girlfriend.

"Hey," I reply.

He gazes at me wide eyed, scanning me from the tip of my satin-pink heels to the crown of blush flower buds woven into my hair at the top of my head.

"You look beautiful," he says breathlessly.

I used to cherish when he would say things like that to me, but now it's just a passing compliment, not words that send my heart racing.

"You look great too," I say because it seems like the polite thing to do, although I'm not a fan of the necklaces. He looks a little frazzled, scratching the back of his neck and tapping his finger methodically against the neck of the guitar. "Are you okay?" I ask.

"You don't want to know," he sighs.

The urge to make sure everyone around me is happy is stronger than even I realize when I reply, "Of course I do." Something so kind and civil to the man who ripped my heart out and stomped it into the ground.

"Savannah and me are going through some things. Feels like we're growing apart, you know?"

"I actually know first hand," I reply with a wobbly frown.

He slaps his forehead, then clenches his bottom lip between his teeth. "I really am an idiot. Aren't I?"

"Yeah. Kinda," I say, a light laugh following my reply.

He tilts his head to the side. "You hear people say it all the time, but you don't truly understand until it happens to you."

"Until what happens?"

"When you don't know what you've got until it's gone."

My heart thuds, but not because I'm swooning. I feel as if I've walked into a trap. "Dylan, I..."

"Just let me speak," he pleads. "Please? Then I'll never talk to you again."

I nod, and I can't help but feel this is a consequence of Henry, my not-so-fake boyfriend.

"Thank you," he says, steepling his fingers. "When you're young, you make some stupid decisions, Lola, and no one knows that better than me. I should never have left Lake Mistletoe, and I should never have left you. I've felt a giant void in me since I did and I thought Savannah would fill it. But she hasn't. She doesn't get me like you get me, and when we sing, it's soulless. Not like how you and me sound together."

My eyes narrow bitterly. "Dylan, I haven't had the courage to sing since you dumped me by text from another city, and you two seemed to harmonize just fine when you performed my song the other night and called it your own."

He leans the guitar against the wall and takes a step forward, gripping me by the wrists. "Lola, listen. There's an audition coming up next month, and it sounds like the real deal. They like everything about me, but they're not looking for rock. They want something more authentic, more small town, and they want original songs. This could be our chance."

I wrench my wrists free, take a step back, and glower at him with disgust. "Chance at what?"

"A chance at us, Lola," he says. "A chance at love, a chance at success, the things we always talked about."

I shake my head vehemently. "You talked about them. I was happy here in Lake Mistletoe with you. You were the one who needed more." I exhale. "And now I don't need you."

Dylan chews on his bottom lip. "Why? Because you're with that yeti now? And when did good ol' boys become your type?"

I try to stifle my laugh but it bursts from my mouth in a spurt, much to Dylan's chagrin. "Really? That's all you've got?"

"I don't have to put up with this," Dylan snaps. "Stay here in Mistletoe to grow old and do nothing if that's what you want. But just remember, you turned down a hell of an opportunity because you can't let shit go."

Heavy steps sound behind me, and a shadow lengthens across the floor. "Is there a problem here?"

I know his deep, rolling voice. I hear it in my ear whenever I close my eyes. Henry strides up to us dressed in a navy blue suit, accented with a blush tie and pocket square. His hair is slicked back, his facial hair neatly trimmed, and his dark eyes fix on Dylan with pure disdain.

I link my arm with him. "No problem. Right Dylan?"

He nods. "Right. Just saying hello."

"Good," Henry growls, as I fall under his gaze. "I don't want to have to fold you in half and mail you back to wherever the fuck it is you live. Not on my friend's special day." He strides forward, towering over Dylan, then reaches out and roughly adjusts the collar of his shirt. "Besides, who would play the song for their first dance?"

"Yeah. Sure. Whatever man," Dylan grumbles. He picks up his guitar from against the wall and takes several backward steps before turning on his heels and heading down the hallway.

Henry returns to me with the cheeky grin he puts on only for me. "How did that rate on the fake boyfriend meter?"

I stand on my tiptoes. Despite that, I'm only a fraction of his size. I reach up, looping my arms around his neck and he bends his knees so I don't look so ridiculous.

"I don't want you to be my fake boyfriend," I say, my eyes fixed on his. "I want you to be my boyfriend, boyfriend."

"Really?" Henry asks.

"Really, really," I reply.

"I want that too," he says.

He leans down and kisses me, and his warmth fills my body in an instant. Henry's hands find my waist, and when our lips press together I lose all sense of time. All I know is that right here, right now, I'm with Henry, and there's nowhere else in the world I would rather be.

"And what's this?" Sean chuckles as he, Blake and Finn approach us wearing the same navy suits. "You're really trying to sell this boyfriend thing, huh?"

"I don't think he's that good an actor," Blake sighs. "There's probably something to it."

Finn frowns. "This town is too damned small."

We head down the hall just as cars begin pulling up the hill and guests file into the hotel. In the main dining room Daisy has prepared a massive grazing table that stretches the length of the dance floor, covered in meats and breads and fruit and vegetables.

"That's a damn fine salami flower," Sean remarks as we walk along the table, grabbing at whatever takes our fancy.

The hall fills up quickly with friends and family. I can't believe how many people are here. Finn mingles, talking to guests and checking with the wait staff, but mostly he's cozying up in a corner whispering god knows what in Daisy's ear. Sean and Lexie are slow dancing on the dance floor, even though Dylan and The Thornz are doing an upbeat pop cover, and not surprisingly, Blake and Charlotte are at the bar, already on their fifth row of tequila shots. They'll drink their way through Tom and Sophie's tab in no time.

Not long ago I might have been standing here by myself, or perhaps I would have been so lonely and my self esteem so low that I would have accepted Dylan's offer. I grip Henry's hand and he looks down at me and smiles. The smile he keeps just for me. The smile that lets me know it's not my job to make everyone happy anymore. Just him, and that's enough.

"Ladies and gentleman," Finn calls, taking a break from Daisy's arms to address the guests. "If you'll follow me outside, it's time for the ceremony to begin."

The guests move outside, passing beneath a long white awning that leads to the wedding tent on the edge of Chestnut Hill. We help Daisy change into her wedding dress, which is made harder by her micromanaging the dinner staff at the same time. When we pop the last hairpin into place, and she screams at the top of her lungs, "Let's make this perfect people!", it's time for us to take our positions.

The guests are seated when we arrive, and we wait at the end of the awning for everything to be just right. The bridesmaids and groomsmen partner up in a line, us holding our little bouquets of ivory roses framed by sprigs of baby's breath and bound with a soft blue ribbon, while the guys clasp their hands.

When the piano starts we know it's time. I shiver with nerves, and it's not even my wedding! But I'm also terrified of falling over and ruining everything. I count my steps in my head and try not to stare at my feet as we walk down the aisle. I see Tom waiting at the end, and realize my nerves are minuscule compared to his. His hands are clasped tightly together, his bottom lip clenched between his teeth. I always find it such a stark contrast when I get glimpses of these big mean hockey players caught so vulnerable.

When we reach the simple yet elegant arch, adorned with garlands of white roses and evergreen, our lines veer in opposite directions. The groomsmen join Tom, shaking his hand as they pass him in single file, while the bridesmaids take our positions to the left of the celebrant, waiting for Sophie to arrive.

As soft strains of the music fill the air, all eyes turn toward the end of the aisle. There, in a halo of soft light, Sophie appears like a vision of a winter princess. Her wedding gown cascades in layers of pristine white satin, and the delicate lace appliqué on the bodice mirrors frosty filigree, framing her collarbones. In her hands Sophie holds a bouquet of ivory roses, delicate and pure, with silvery eucalyptus leaves adding a frosty shimmer, and bound with the same wintry blue ribbon as the bridesmaids' bouquets.

Sophie, radiant and poised, walks down the aisle, arm in arm with Blake. Her eyes lock onto Tom's with an unwavering certainty and Tom stands equally mesmerized. Sophie joins us at the arch, while Blake moves into line with the groomsmen, and as I stand by her side beneath the expansive white tent adorned with gossamer drapes, the air fills with a serene hush while snowflakes pirouette outside.

Tom and Sophie hold hands, and I promise myself not to burst into tears with how beautiful they both look. As they exchange vows their promises echo like sweet melodies, reaching every corner of the tent. Sophie, her voice steady and filled with emotion, promises to weather life's storms together. Tom, his gaze never leaving hers, vows to be her unwavering anchor, a partner through the good and the bad.

As the ceremony draws to a close, the couple seal their vows with a kiss, and cheers erupt like a chorus of joy. The groomsmen applaud, slapping Tom's back as he lifts Sophie into the air. Now that it's over, I have permission to burst into tears. I feel better when I see Lexie and Charlotte doing the same. Even Daisy's eyes look wetter than usual.

When Tom finally puts Sophie down, we pounce on her, wrapping her in a tangle of arms and bouquets, eucalyptus and petals flying everywhere.

"You look so beautiful!" we scream, blubbering like we're doing a re-watch of The Notebook.

"Thank you!" Sophie sobs, her face glowing, her cheeks blushing red. "I'm married!"

We cheer one last time as the guests applaud, and now I'm starving. I wonder if Daisy has some cheese balls out the back.

We all make our way back inside the hotel and pass through the two giant wooden doors into the dining hall. It's like the rehearsal dinner, but with all the trimmings. A warm draping of twinkling lights, fresh snow powdering the glass dome ceiling overhead, and the tiered chandelier dangling above, its prisms catching the golden sparkles of light.

We're seated at the bride and groom's table up front, which is dressed in crisp white linens and mixed winter blooms; white roses, red amaryllis, and wild sprigs of evergreen. Tall candles stand proudly in the center, their flames flickering romantically.

When dinner is served, The Thornz take to the stage. I glance up from my meal now and then, when I'm not giggling with my friends or making moon eyes at Henry on the other side of the table, and see Dylan singing with everything he has. Even watching him with eyes wide awake now, he is a talented performer, and the notes that drift from his lips still give me goosebumps. But I've performed enough myself to know when there's a weird vibe on stage. His body language is all wrong, turned away from Savannah, singing about her, rather than to her. Savannah's just as uncomfortable, her voice struggling to hit the notes, her eyes pleading at Dylan.

Suddenly she bursts into tears, right there on the stage. The microphone falls from her hand and hits the ground with a thud, a screech of feedback piercing the thrum of the guests' chatter. They stop and stare as she runs from the stage, her face buried in her hands.

"Oh my god," Sophie gasps. "Is she okay?"

"I don't know," I reply, watching as she hurries through the doors and out of sight. "Maybe I should go check."

Sophie grabs my hand. "Now what's he doing?"

I look up just as Dylan follows suit, leaping off the stage and running after Savannah.

Charlotte sips her wine. "Well, that was dramatic."

Sophie looks at me, panic-stricken. "But the dance. Tom and I have to have our first dance. How do we dance if no one's singing?"

"The band's still there," I say, searching for a solution. "Won't they do?"

"No. It's not our song," Sophie whimpers. She grips her dinner knife until her knuckles turn white. "That son of a bitch. I should have just gotten a DJ."

"Me and Lola will sing," a voice says from the groom's side of the table, and although I recognize Henry's voice, I have to do a double take to be sure he is the one suggesting such a ridiculous thing.

"No, we won't," I scoff, almost choking on the most delicious piece of asparagus I've ever eaten.

"Fine. I'll sing then. You come be my emotional support."

"What is happening?" Blake asks, his eyebrows halfway up his forehead.

"I think Henry's going to sing," Sean replies.

Finn shakes his head in disbelief. "Like... with his mouth?"

Henry doesn't pay them any attention, standing from his chair and tossing his napkin onto the table. He holds his hand out to me.

"Come on," he says. "I need you."

I smile, my cheeks blushing as pink as my dress. How can I say no to that? I stand up and take his hand and we walk to the stage. The guests are in a flurry, trying to figure out what's going on as Henry picks up the microphone, giving it a couple of taps to get their attention.

"Well, hey everyone," he coughs, clearing his throat. "Welcome to Tom and Sophie's wedding."

The guests instinctively clap, but it's clear by their stunned faces they have no idea what's going on.

"The Thornz are having some technical difficulties," Henry explains, "so Lola and I will be taking over, and making sure our good friends, Tom and Sophie, have the first dance they always dreamed of."

"Don't oversell it," I whisper through gritted teeth.

Henry grins and covers the microphone with his hand. "What's the song?" he asks.

I whisper in his ear, and he cocks an eyebrow. "Are you fucking serious?" he says, his hand slipping from the microphone and streaming his question over the speaker.

The guests gasp and I look over at Sophie, burying her face in her hands as Tom comforts her. I slap Henry's arm and take a step backwards to tell the band what song to play, then I snatch the microphone from Henry's hand.

"Please welcome Tom and Sophie to the dance floor," I say, clapping my hands, and slowly the guests join in.

Tom stands from the table and extends his hand to Sophie. She braces herself, then accepts, and he leads her to the dance floor, her flowing gown seeming to float on air. Tom puts a hand on her waist and clasps her hand, holding it against her chest, and a blushing smile blooms onto Sophie's face. She rests her hand on his shoulder and leans into him. As he lays a kiss on her forehead, the band begins to play, and then, for the first time in forever, for a reason I can only assume is love, I sing.

You are my fire
The one desire
Believe when I say
I want it that way
But we are two worlds apart
Can't reach to your heart
When you say

That I want it that way

Sophie's face lights up when she looks at me over Tom's shoulder, the worry melting away from her. The guests applaud, then join the happy couple on the dance floor. When it's time for the chorus, I turn to Henry, and he gives me a knowing nod.

Tell me why, he sings deeply.

And I giggle through the words when I follow with,

Ain't nothin' but a heartache

Tell me why

Ain't nothin' but a mistake

Tell me why

I never wanna hear you say I want it that way

The guests applaud when we sing the last chord, and Henry and I bow before our adoring fans. My body fills with warmth, and I didn't realize how much I missed singing. Why did I let Dylan take something so special away from me? I grip Henry's hand and he leans down, kissing my cheek.

"You were amazing," he gushes. "I want to hear you sing every day from now on."

That's when I know in my heart I've made the right decision. Everything I lost, Henry just gave back, times a million.

14
Henry

I'm dancing with Lola and she feels perfect in my arms. She's gazing up at me, her eyes glazed over with this dreamy glow, like I'm the only one here. I hope she can see I feel the same way. But we're surrounded by a sea of people, and they're the only ones keeping me from slipping her out of this pink dress and kissing every inch of her body. Just the thought has me hard as a rock.

"Do you want to get out of here?" I ask, unable to keep my cool any longer.

She nods without hesitating. "Your place?"

I reach into my pocket and pull out a Northwellian key card.

"I had something else in mind," I reply.

I cup her face and kiss her parted lips, taking my time tasting her while our tongues tangle. I take her by the hand, slipping through the crowded dance floor and out the doors, hoping no one notices us sneaking out early. We laugh when we make it unseen into the hallway, and I take her by the waist, walking her back until she's against the wall where I kiss her again with all the passion I've been restraining since I saw her this morning.

"Dylan!" a voice calls out, wrenching Lola and me apart.

I wipe her lipstick from my mouth and look further down the corridor. Savannah's standing at the entrance of the hotel, her hands clasped behind her head as she sobs, staring out into the snow.

Lola takes off, leaving me to chase after her. This is one of those times I wish she could have just walked away. When it comes to Lola, I'm selfish and greedy and I want her all to myself. But she wouldn't be my Lola if she were any other way. She needs to know that Savannah is alright.

"Hey," she says, and Savannah turns, her eyes red from crying, her mascara running in streams down her cheeks.

"He's gone. Can you believe it? He's gone."

Lola offers a sympathetic smile. "Yeah. I can believe it."

Savannah drops her chin. "Worse part is, I knew it was coming."

Lola nods. "He's a runner, always has been. I'm sorry you had to find out this way."

Savannah grits her teeth and her eyes flash with rage. "Well, running out on me is one thing, but if he thinks he's dodging his responsibilities, then he's got another thing coming."

Lola's eyes bulge when Savannah places a hand on her belly, and although I take a little longer to put the pieces together, I'm just as stunned when I figure it out.

Lola throws her arms around Dylan's girlfriend in a way that only Lola would. Savannah freezes in place, and it's clear she can't comprehend why Lola would do such a thing, but slowly her hands circle Lola's waist and she rests her head on her shoulder. Next thing I know, she's crying again, and the chances of me getting Lola into the hotel room in the near future are dwindling.

"You need to come back to the reception," Lola says. "Have something to eat."

Savannah wipes her tears on the back of her hand and shakes her head vehemently. "I couldn't."

"Sure you could," Lola laughs lightly. "Everyone in that room hates Dylan, so you'll be in great company. I'll introduce you to my friends."

Savannah gulps, sniffing away the last of her tears. "Really?"

"Really, really," Lola replies. "Come on."

She puts her arm around Savannah, and they walk back toward the hall. "Just a sec," she whispers as she passes me, but I know how Lola's seconds work.

Much to my disappointment we're back in the hall, and Lola has taken Savannah over to the bride and groom table. From the bar across the room, I watch her as she explains the situation, her arms in the air, and her face twisted with disgust. Likewise, the girls are just as horrified and, before you know it, they've taken Savannah under their wing.

Lucas puts a beer down on the bar in front of me. "Lola collected another stray?"

"That's one way to put it," I sigh, picking up the glass and taking a sip. I look at Lucas over my shoulder. "I hear you're not hanging around. Heading to Macaroy Beach?"

He grabs the towel over his shoulder and starts wiping down a glass. "Great weather. Beach side bars. Football. Sounds like paradise. I'm sick of freezing my ass off around here."

"Lola's going to miss you," I say.

Lucas grins from the corner of his mouth. "I'll come if she ever needs me. She knows that. Just take good care of her so I don't have to come back and beat your ass." There's an awkward pause, until at last Lucas laughs, pointing a finger at me. "Got ya."

I shuffle uncomfortably and force a choking chuckle from my throat. "Yeah. Funny."

Then abruptly Lucas' laugh vanishes, and he glares at me, his lips in a straight line. "No but seriously, hurt my sister and I will fuck you up, big boy."

I roll my shoulders. "You're like Lola, but evil, do you know that?"

He smiles. "That's us. Twinning."

I finish the rest of my beer and put the glass down on the bar.

"Another?" Lucas asks.

I raise my hand and shake my head. "Nope. I'm good. I'll catch up with you later."

He winks. "Have a good one."

I walk away, adding a little speed to my stride. I've checked some of the biggest, toughest bastards in the league, and been head-butted by one or two as well, but Lucas Nixon scares the living shit out of me, and I get angsty being anywhere near that kind of crazy.

As the night gets on, I decide I've allowed everyone the pleasure of Lola's company long enough. I want to finish what we started, because if I don't get inside her again soon I might explode, but while I'm looking over guests' heads trying to find her, I feel her little fingers walk up my back before gripping my shoulders and spinning me around.

"There are you," I groan, taking her by the waist and pulling her against me. "Is Savannah okay?"

"Oh yeah, she's one of the girls now. Nothing bonds women faster than dirt-bag exes."

"So," I drawl, rolling my tongue in my cheek. "Does that mean I have you to myself now?"

She nods. "And what exactly do you want to do with me?"

A sly grin slips onto my lips, and I lean down, pressing my brow to hers. "So many nasty things. But I want to start with getting my face under that dress."

I feel her shiver under my touch, her tongue sliding between her lips. "What are we waiting for?"

I take Lola's hand and lead her once more through the dining hall, but this time, we're not stopping for anyone. Wayne Gretzky could be in that corridor and I would have no problem politely telling him to fuck off.

I guide her into the elevator and hit the button for the fourth floor, but I can't wait until we get to the room. As soon as the doors close, I take her wrists and pin her to the wall before leaning over her to devour her with my kiss. She inhales sharply, her body writhing as my tongue dips deep into her mouth. I groan. She tastes so fucking good. But not here. No. I want her in that hotel room where I can do whatever I want for as long as I want, undisturbed.

The elevator dings and the doors slide open, revealing an older couple waiting to go down. Lola and I spring apart. She stifles her laugh behind her hand while I try to adjust my massive erection without making it too obvious.

"Evening," I say, tipping my head.

They narrow their eyes and glare at us, and it's clear they know exactly what's going on.

I take Lola's hand and we leave the elevator, quickening our pace to get down the hall and away from the couple as soon as possible. I check the key card in my pocket. Room 202. I scan each door we pass, conscious of my cock trying to bust its way out of my pants.

Lola drapes herself over my shoulder, nibbling at my neck as I read the numbers. When I see 202 I can't get the key card in the slot quick enough, and when the door opens Lola and I tumble in laughing.

I slam the door behind us, stalking her as she walks toward the bedroom. I shrug off my jacket, then yank off my tie, my eyes fixed on her hips as they sway back and forth in front of me. We reach the bedroom, the floor-to-ceiling windows looking out over Lake Mistletoe as the moon rises high in a sky full of stars.

Lola looks at me and smiles. "Is this our place on the hill?"

My blood races as I bury a hand in her hair, cupping her face behind her ear. "Yes, baby. Forever. You and me."

I pull her hungrily into my kiss, and I can't believe how good she tastes. Her pillowy lips, her sweet tongue, the way she sighs when I kiss her deep and hard. She fumbles with my shirt buttons, getting the top few undone before I stop her.

"What?" she murmurs.

"Nothing," I growl, my hands on her hips as I guide her backward. "I want you on this wall. Now."

Her back presses against the wall and she gasps, then giggles.

"Just like the locker room," she says.

"That's right," I reply. "But this time, no one is going to interrupt us. This time I'm going to taste you."

Lola gulps as I kiss her cheek, then her neck, then trail my kisses down the soft crease of her cleavage until I drop before her on my knees. I lift the layers of tulle, poking my head underneath, and Lola giggles and squirms. It's like a pink cavern under here, and when my eyes adjust I'm faced with Lola's creamy thighs and the stunning sight of her white, lace panties. I let out a deep breath before taking her by the hips and pushing my face to her mound. Then I inhale, savoring her intoxicating scent. When I nuzzle my nose along her folds I hear her moan, and it's not long before her panties dampen. I let my tongue flick at the fabric, getting a small taste of what's coming.

"Fuck, you smell good," I growl.

I can't wait any longer. I need her in my mouth right now. I hook the waistband of her panties with my fingers and ease them down her thighs until they fall at her ankles. I tug them free from her feet and toss them aside before I take one of those gorgeous thighs and drape it over my shoulder.

Lola opens before me, and gazing at her perfect pink pussy puts me in a trance. I lean forward, my tongue sliding between her slick folds, and Lola responds with a long whimper. I feel her hands on my head through the tulle skirt, and her body tenses as I work my tongue deeper between her legs, skimming over her entrance, before finding her swollen pearl.

Lola gasps when I lick her there, her hips rolling against my face as I flick my tongue. I feel her muscles tightening, but I don't only want her to cum on my face, but my fingers as well. I take two fingers and slide them up and down her slippery crease until they're nice and wet before slipping them inside her. Again Lola gasps, her body stiffening against the wall, her muscles gripping my fingers, and I don't think I could get them out if I tried.

I work my fingers in and out of her tight pussy, licking at her clit as I go, drawing circles with my tongue. Lola writhes on my face while my fingers move faster in and out, until at last she explodes, crying out in a long, pained moan.

I emerge from beneath the tulle and rise to meet her. She looks so fucking beautiful, standing limp against the wall, her eyes half closed, exhausted and gorgeous, and ready to be fucked. I undo my belt and unzip my trousers, just enough to free my cock, but leave my pants sitting on my hips, and this time I'm prepared. I reach into my pocket and retrieve a condom, tear open the packaging, then slip it over my achingly hard dick.

Lola's eyes flutter open and she gazes up at me. "That was so good Henry," she mutters.

I press up against her, digging my hands under the tulle until I find her ass, then scoop her into the air. She gasps as I adjust her, wrapping her legs above my hips. I line my swollen head up with her entrance, but before I bury myself inside her, I gaze into her eyes.

"I'm so glad to be here with you tonight Lola," I mutter.

She looks at me and smiles. "Me too."

I lean forward, pressing my lips to hers, soft and tender, and then slowly I ease my cock inside her. Her eyes close and scrunch up tight, as she squeals into my mouth.

"Shhhh," I whisper, kissing her bottom lip. "That's so good."

I push deeper, burying myself in her warm pussy an inch at a time until I'm flat against her. Lola throws her head back, her face twisted in blissful agony.

"That's so good, baby," I whisper, kissing her throat. I begin slowly, making sure she enjoys each ridge of my shaft and when she opens for me, I quicken my pace. I hold her ass tight in my hands, gripping her smooth skin as I thrust. She bangs against the wall with each pound, but that's not what I want. I take a step back so I'm holding her in midair, lifting her up and down so she bounces on my cock.

Lola wraps her arms around my neck, her eyes rolling back in her head as I plunge deeper and harder with every thrust.

"You feel so good," I growl. "Too fucking good."

I feel my orgasm swell inside me, higher and higher until I can't fucking hold it a second longer. I clench my jaw and throw back my head as my cock explodes inside her, and I fill the condom with my hot, sticky seed. My chest heaves for breath, and I'm panting when she leans forward to kiss me so soft that our lips barely touch. With what strength I have left, I walk her over to the bed and lay her down before collapsing beside her.

My chest hair is damp with sweat and my muscles throb as if I've played a doubleheader. Lola holds her hand up, and I reach out to lace my fingers with hers.

"See how perfect it fits," she mutters, as we bathe in the moonlight streaming through the window.

"Perfect," I murmur. "Hey. Lola."

"Yeah," she says.

"Thanks for being my date to Tom and Sophie's wedding. I had a great time."

Lola laughs, closing her fingers around mine. "Really?"

I bring her hand to my lips and kiss every knuckle. "Really, really."

15

Lola

The days since the Tom and Sophie's wedding passed in the blink of an eye. I guess time really does fly when you're having fun, and Henry and I have been having plenty. Now it's Christmas morning, and it's hard to get out of bed when Henry is lying next to me. Not only does he have more wattage than an electric blanket, but there's no other place I'd rather be than in his arms while his fingertips draw circles on my back. Plus, his bed is massive. It's some kind of gel core, thermacool, memory foam, independent pocket spring, Swiss space mattress. But life has other plans for me today.

My phone rings and I reluctantly roll out of Henry's embrace and grab it from the nightstand. I see Lexie's name and answer the call.

"Hey, what's up?" I ask.

"Oh, my god!" she shrieks. "Are you with Henry?"

I glance over my shoulder at the devastatingly hot man lying shirtless beside me, his hands clasped behind his head, his shaggy hair hanging over his eyes.

"Yeah. He's here," I smirk.

"Can you guys come to my place? Like now?"

There's a desperation in her voice, enough to make me want to sit up. "Sure. What's wrong?"

Henry gets worried too when he sees my reaction and curls around my back to listen to the conversation.

"Something's wrong with Polly. Can you get here quick?"

"Yes. Totally. See you soon."

I end the call, then scooch off the bed and bolt to my feet. I'm wearing one of Henry's t-shirts, which hangs to my knees. "Come on. Get your stuff."

Henry groans and rolls his eyes. "Babe, it's Christmas morning. I'm off the clock."

I frown, grab one of his hypoallergenic foam pillows and slap him across the face with it. He doesn't even budge, and where it was supposed to piss him off, it's had the opposite effect. He's grinning at me, licking his lips, his eyes wandering over my body.

"Enough," I laugh, pointing a stern finger at him. "Get up. Lexie needs us."

Henry throws back the blanket, his black trunks taut against the outline of his firm bulge, and the thighs, my god, the thighs. Like tree trunks. I'm suddenly hypnotized. Where did we need to go again? Luckily, I snap from my daze and shake my head vigorously to get back on track. I point the finger again. "No."

Henry laughs as I rush out of the room, for Lexie's sake as well as mine. I grab my pile of clothes .crumpled on his bedroom floor, and duck into the bathroom to have a lightning fast shower. When I don't smell like I've been rolling around swapping fluids all night, and my hair isn't sticking straight up, I emerge from the bathroom to find Henry still in his underwear, his jeans and shirt bundled up in his arms as he waits near the door.

"You're not ready?" I say.

"I'm waiting for the shower!" he replies.

I shake my head. "Oh no, there's no time for that. We've got to go. Get dressed."

He frowns. "Oh, so you get to wash off the sex smell, but I don't?"

My shoulders heave when I let out a deep breath. I walk to his dresser and fumble around the limited products he owns until I find a can of body spray called Fuel Injection. I pop the cap and dowse him, starting at the top of his head and ending at his feet. I let out a choking cough when I'm done. This stuff smells just like it says it does, and I can feel it burning my eyes and stinging the back of my throat.

"There," I gag. "Like roses."

Henry shakes his head and grumbles. "Fine. Let me get dressed."

I stand there watching like a perv as he pulls his jeans up, and there's something about the way he buckles his belt, his big, rough hands sliding the leather beneath his toned stomach dusted with dark hair, that gets me weak in the knees. He pulls his shirt over his head and cocks an eyebrow when he sees me staring.

"Enjoying the show?"

A lazy grin spreads over my face as I slink toward him, holding his waist and feeling the ripples of muscle tensing beneath his shirt. "I'm looking forward to enjoying it for a very long time."

He leans down and kisses me, his fingers tangling in my damp hair as he brushes it away from my face, and just when I think it might be time to go back to bed, my phone buzzes in my pocket. I drag myself away to check, and it's a message from Lexie.

LEXIE: Hey. Are you guys far away?

I gulp and slap Henry hard against his chest. He winces and laughs.

"What was that for?"

"Stop messing around," I snap, gathering up my hair and slinging it into a ponytail. "We have to go now!"

We hustle down the stairs and out into the bracing cold. It's eerily quiet this morning, the sun bright and glaring against the overnight snowfall. It's ridiculously early to be motivated and everyone is probably inside, bundled up, unwrapping Christmas presents in their PJs and slippers. My Christmas eve was spent with Henry, tangled on his couch, watching Hallmark movies whenever we came up for air. Lucas headed to Macaroy Beach right after the wedding, and Henry and I are having lunch with Dad this afternoon.

We're in the car and down the street in minutes, and I do this thing where I rock back and forth as if that makes the car go faster. It drives Henry crazy, but not as much as when I throw an are we there yet? at him.

We pull into Lexie's driveway and I'm out the door and up the porch before Henry's even put the car in park. While I'm banging on the front door, he calmly walks to the trunk to get his medical bag, then passes the passenger side to close the door I left wide open. He's casually climbing the stairs to join me when Lexie peeks her head out.

"Thank god!" she gasps, grabbing me by my sleeve and dragging me inside. She points to the living room where Polly is mewling, lying on a raised red-velvet cat bed with a mattress that looks better than mine. "She's been like that all morning."

I look around and see that her parents are nowhere in sight. "Where's Stan and Beth?"

"They're visiting friends, and Mom's not answering her phone. I'm cat sitting." She rubs her temples and scrunches up her face. "Why does this shit always happen on my watch?"

Henry pats her shoulder awkwardly. "I'm sure Polly's fine." He brushes past us and heads into the living room, dropping to his knees beside Polly and opening his bag.

Lexie huddles behind me, peeking over my shoulder. "I can't look. I did exactly what they told me to do."

Suddenly, the door bursts open and Sean tumbles inside wearing nothing but a puffer jacket over a pair of festive red silk boxers and unlaced snow boots.

"Okay," he pants, his arms bundled with supplies. "I've got Tylenol, bandages and a hot water bottle."

I raise a curious eyebrow. "Because... ?"

He tips his chin toward the living room. "Polly."

I turn to Lexie and she's smiling through gritted teeth.

"I didn't know what to do! You were taking so long!"

I sigh and pat Sean's hand. "Good try, champ. But let's leave this to Henry."

Sean keels over and exhales a deep breath. "Oh, thank god."

I stand on my tiptoes for a better look. "How's it going in there?"

Henry chuckles. "She's not sick. Just uncomfortable. But that happens when you're about to give birth."

"What!" Lexie screeches. "How? She's not allowed outside." A notion flashes across her face. "The Christmas party... ." She looks at Sean. "That nativity scene by the school. When she was giving up her goodies to that ginger cat!"

"Wasn't that only a few weeks ago?" Henry asks, and when Lexie nods in response, he shakes his head. "She's been pregnant longer than that. A cat pregnancy is around nine weeks."

"I knew it!" Lexie blurts, clenching her fist. "I can't wait to tell our mom. We'll see who the favorite is now." She freezes when she realizes what she's said and clears her throat. "I mean my mom. I said my mom."

Henry stands up and turns toward us. "We'll need some towels and warm blankets. Make sure she has food and water, and her litter box close by. But apart from that, we just leave her to it."

"Really?" Lexie asks.

"Really, really," Henry replies, shooting me a subtle smile. "She knows what to do. But if you get concerned, just give me a call."

"Oh god," Lexie groans. "What are we going to do with a bunch of kittens around here? I know Mom and Dad will want to keep them all, too."

Sean puts his arm around her waist and pulls her against him, and when he bumps her with his hip, it draws out a smile. "You'll be moving in with me soon anyway, right? Your parents will love the company. It can get pretty lonely in a house all by yourself."

An idea blossoms in my mind, and I can't wait to share it with Henry.

"If Polly's okay, do you mind if we slip away? We've got something we need to do," I say.

Henry furrows his brow. "We do?" Slowly, his confusion morphs into a sly grin. "Oh, we do?"

I sigh. "No. Not that."

"Sure," Lexie replies. "Just keep your phone on. If this gets sticky, I'm calling you immediately."

I give Lexie a hug, and then once again I'm waving my arms at Henry, telling him to hurry, and I glimpse Sean offering him a sympathetic smile as we leave. When we're back in the car, he looks over at me as he buckles his seat belt.

"So, where are we going now?"

"The clinic, then Mrs. Bearenstein's house," I state.

"Mrs. Bearenstein's house? Why would we want to go there?"

"Trust me," I say.

Henry sighs and starts the engine. "Okay."

We head to the clinic and duck inside, collecting a special Christmas surprise and some supplies to go with it. Then we're back in the car and off to Mrs. Bearenstein's house. When we arrive, it's as if no one is home. No lights and no movement. Henry grabs a large box out of the trunk and follows me up the stairs. I take a breath and knock on the door, and after a while, it creaks open.

Mrs. Bearenstein peeks her head out and looks confused to see us. I don't blame her. I'm a little unsure too.

"Merry Christmas," I say brightly.

Her expression doesn't change, but now it's tinged with annoyance. "Can I help you?"

I didn't expect her to wheel out the welcome wagon, so I get straight to the point. I know she likes that.

"You see, Henry and I have got a problem I'm hoping you might be able to help us with."

"You need my help?" she asks, opening the door a smidge wider.

I step aside and let Henry come forward with the box in his arms. He puts it on the doorstep and pulls back the flaps of cardboard. Mrs. Bearenstein looks inside and her eyes glisten as her face flushes with a rosy color. The quiet morning air fills with the sound of The Backstreet Boys meowing, standing on their back legs trying to climb their way out of the box.

"They're pretty cute, right?" I laugh lightly.

Her head tilts up, and her expression shifts back to a scowl. "And what is this exactly?"

I keep smiling, even though she's trying to push me away. I get this woman now. I understand her, and despite the way she acts, I know she doesn't want to be lonely anymore.

"They're getting bigger, and I don't want them to be stuck in the clinic over Christmas, not when they're ready to find their forever home." I look down at them. "I think they're lonely."

Mrs. Bearenstein's eyes widen and she swallows a lump in her throat. "You do?"

I nod. "I was kind of hoping you might take them in?"

She freezes, and I don't think I've ever seen her speechless before.

"I mean, I could put an ad up at the clinic for foster homes..."

"Oh, don't be ridiculous, you silly girl," Mrs. Bearenstein snaps. She tips her chin at Henry. "Bring them inside straight away before they freeze out there."

"Oh. Right," Henry stammers. He swiftly picks up the box and Mrs. Bearenstein opens the door all the way.

"Into the living room, on the piano." Henry does as he's told and I follow him, glancing at my feet when I feel something warm weaving around my ankles.

"Merry Christmas, Anastasia," I say as she purrs. "Looks like you're going to have some new friends for the holidays."

Henry walks into the living room and puts the box down on the piano in front of the big bay window.

"I've got some food and toys in the car. I'll go grab them for you," he says.

Mrs. Bearenstein waves him away. "No need for any of that, Dr. Gallagher. I have more than enough for these poor things right here." She looks at me. "If you needed help, you should have come to me immediately, Lola. What were you thinking?"

I stifle my grin, nodding and turning down my eyes so I look sorrowful about the whole thing. "You're right. Thank you so much for doing this. Dr. Gallagher and I are so grateful."

Her expression is still stern as she peeks into the box, and after a few minutes she looks back at us over her shoulder, apparently surprised we're still here.

"Well? Was there something else?"

Henry and I exchanged stunned looks.

"No," we stutter in unison.

"Then show yourselves out. We're just fine."

Henry and I nod, then collide awkwardly when he goes left and I go right as we try to get out of the house as quick as possible.

"Merry Christmas," I say once more as Henry drags me into the hallway.

"Oh, Lola," Mrs. Bearenstein calls when I'm halfway out the door.

I scurry back and peek around the wall into the living room. "Yes?"

A smile smooths onto her face, deepening the creases in her pale skin. "Merry Christmas."

My chest fills with warmth. I smile back, then head outside to meet Henry on the porch, closing the door behind me. As we head to the car, I glance through the bay window just as Anastasia leaps onto the piano to inspect the contents of the box. I watch as Mrs. Bearenstein lifts Brian into her arms, her face glowing as she nuzzles her nose to his, and when he licks her cheek she laughs.

When I turn back to the car, Henry is standing on the driver's side, looking at me over the roof.

"Well, look at you. Creating Christmas miracles."

I sigh. "It's hard work, you know, being this outstanding. Now that the wedding's over and Christmas is done, I'm looking forward to a nice, long rest before next year."

Henry cocks an eyebrow. "Why? What's happening next year?"

I shrug as I open the passenger door. "I don't know yet. But I can't wait to find out."

Epilogue

Henry - Three Years Later

It's a week out from Christmas, and the house is in absolute fucking chaos.

"Do you know where Cheeseball's little jumper is?" Lola calls from the other room.

I tug at my collar, sweat dripping down the back of my neck. Since Lola moved in, it's like a Turkish bathhouse every day in here. I've got a duffle bag open on the couch and I'm throwing in an assortment of rubber chew toys and fuzzy mice with bells on their tails. "No. I can't find Goldie's squeaky chicken. Have you seen it?"

"It's in the studio. I'll grab it," Lola replies.

Goldie and that damn chicken. Since we used the swear jar money to convert the basement into a recording studio for Lola, he's always taking his toys down there.

"Do you know where the glass food bowls are?" Lola calls.

I frown. "Just grab the plastic ones under the kitchen sink."

"The glass ones are classier," Lola calls. "I don't think Meredith allows plastic in her house."

I put a plastic Ziploc bag with Bomb's arthritis pills in the duffle just as Lola scurries into the living room, her arms overflowing with sweaters, treats, and the glass bowls she was looking for.

Anyone else might think we were packing for our kids, and technically we are. Our two dogs, Bombay and Goldberg, and our ginger cat, Cheeseball, son of the infamous feline tramp, Polly.

Lola doesn't think twice when she dumps the items into the bag, which I've meticulously packed.

"There," she pants with her hands on her hips. "I think that's it."

I put my thumb and finger between my lips and blow a high-pitched whistle, and Bomb and Goldie patter into the living room straight away. They wag their tails excitedly, their tongues hanging out their mouths. I drop to my haunches and give them both a rough scratch under their chins.

"That's my boys," I grunt at them. "Ready for a holiday with Meredith?" Their tails wag harder, thumping the couch like a drum. "Yes, you love Meredith, don't you?" I look up at Lola. "Did you catch Cheeseball?"

She screws up her face. "He's a slippery little sucker. He was here a minute ago."

I sigh, then click my tongue and snap my fingers. "Puss, puss. Here, puss."

The curtain billows, and an orange barrel of fluff leaps off the windowsill and minces toward me. Lola folds her arms over her chest, looking decidedly cross as Cheeseball purrs and slides against my leg. I pick him up and tuck him under my arm, giving his ears a good scratch.

"Well, that's not fair. You're a professional," Lola whines.

She holds out the cat carrier and I put him inside, then snap the door closed.

"Alright. We're all set." The gravity of what we're about to do hits me, and I feel a little unbalanced on my feet, but Lola's is always nearby to anchor me.

"It'll be fine," she says softly, entwining her arm with mine and leaning into my shoulder. "We'll do it together."

Her words sink in and chase away the doubt. "Together."

We grab the duffle and our suitcases and load it all into the car, then come back for our fur babies. Bomb and Goldie can't wait to get going, dragging me to the car as I struggle to keep hold of their leads. When they're in the back, Lola locks up the house and climbs in the passenger side with the cat carrier and Cheeseball on her lap.

I jump in the driver's seat and start the engine. I take one last deep breath, then I exhale my lingering hesitation before throwing the car into drive and heading for 252 Maple.

When we pull up, the driveway is full, and I have to park on the street. The old house is covered with Christmas lights, the twinkling bulbs cascading like a waterfall. Bushy green garlands speckled with red holly hang from the eaves and in the front yard a giant glass snowman in a top hat greets us.

Lola and I grab the duffle and unload our pets, then head for the front door. We can hear music and laughing as we climb the stairs onto the porch, and I don't have time to tap the gold knocker before the door flies open. A little girl, around five years old, sprints past me, followed by a smaller boy lumbering along after her.

"Rianna. Wait!" he grizzles, his little legs unable to keep pace.

"Come back inside!" a voice calls. "It's too cold out there."

Lola and I turn and smile at Mrs. Bearenstein in the doorway.

"Merry Christmas, Meredith," I say.

Her face beams, a twinkle in her sky-blue eyes. "Merry Christmas you two. Happy holidays."

The girl, Rianna, comes running back up the porch, frustrating the boy even more when he has to awkwardly turn to follow her. Rianna grabs hold of Meredith's hand.

"Grandma. Can we have desert now?"

"Well, it's 9am, I can't see why not," she replies. "Go tell your father I said you could."

"Yay," she squeals.

"And take your brother with you," Meredith adds.

Rianna frowns. "Fine. Hurry, Colin."

The little boy smiles, grunting and stomping his tiny feet across the porch to join his sister.

"He's getting so big!" Lola gushes.

Meredith nods, an immovable smile painted on her lips. "Isn't it time the pair of you started thinking about a family?"

Lola's eyes bulge and she shakes her head. "Please. These three run us ragged as it is!"

"Speaking of my angels," Meredith coos. "Hello, Bomb. Hello, Goldie. Hello, Cheeseball."

The dog's tails are off again, whipping back and forth like window wipers. Lola hands Meredith the cat carrier, and the orange menace lets out a soft cry. Immediately, I hear the gentle padded trot of an army of cats, as Anastasia and The Backstreet Boys appear from every side. Meredith flips the latch and Cheeseball leaps from the carrier and onto the floor, joining the gaggle of felines.

"Are you sure they won't be too much?" Lola asks.

Meredith waves away her concerns. "Of course not. The more the merrier." She reaches out and relieves me of the leads, and Bomb and Goldie patter into the house, seating themselves on either side of her. "Now you two go and have a lovely trip. I'll see you when you get back."

"Mom," a man calls from down the hall, dodging the train of cats scampering past him. "Did you say the kids could have desert?"

"I'll be right there," Meredith replies with a cheeky grin. "Safe travels."

We wave goodbye as the door closes, and I know without a doubt that my babies are in expert hands. Meredith has become one of our closest friends. To be honest, I don't know what we'd do without her sometimes, and all it took was someone making an effort to bring some sunshine into her life. I look over at Lola, her hair half up, half down, pinned back with a pair of glittery red hair clips. I lean down and kiss her, her lips soft and cherry flavored from her lip gloss.

"What was that for?" she giggles.

"For being you," I sigh.

She blushes and playfully slaps my chest. "Come on. We'll miss our flight."

We head to the car, and the next stop is the airport. Once we've checked our bags and passed through security, we make it on board with only minutes to spare. My stomach churns when we take off, but I know it's got nothing to do with us being in the air. I'm not nervous about flying. Even with all Lola's support, I'm more worried about what's waiting for us when we land.

Lola notices immediately, but she always does. Says she can tell something's wrong by my aura.

"You're tense," she says.

"My head's a mess," I grumble. "I can't think straight. It's just noise."

Lola leans over the armrest. "Sounds like you need something to help you relax."

I lie back in my seat. "Any ideas?"

Lola grins, and her eyes dart to the bathroom behind us.

I cock an eyebrow. "Are you serious?"

She unclips her seat belt and stands up, shuffling past me into the aisle. I watch her walk back toward the stall, and the last thing I see is her biting her lip before she closes the door behind her.

I gulp and grip the armrests, my cock already rock hard and suffocating in my jeans. Is she fucking serious? I lick my lips as I figure out whether I should go back there, but it takes less than a second to decide. Of course I'm fucking going. I try to unclip my seatbelt, but it won't budge. In the end, I'm wrestling with it, breaking into a sweat before I finally get it off.

I stand up and run a hand through my hair, doing my best to look calm and collected on the outside, when all I can think about is Lola's tight pussy wrapped around my cock. I make it to the bathroom and stand there as the flight attendant walks past me.

"Are you alright, sir?" she asks with a bright smile.

"Yep," I cough, my eyes on the floor. "Just ah, stretching my legs."

"Okay, sir. But you'll need to get back to your seat shortly."

I nod. "Absolutely. Thank you."

She turns her back on me, making her way down the aisle, and I take the opportunity to open the door and duck into the bathroom like the Flash.

Lola's leaning against the sink, giggling into her hand. "What took you so long?"

She parts her thighs, and the sight of her creamy skin has me feral. "We land soon," I say, my voice rumbling from the back of my throat. I undo my belt and slowly drag down the zip of my jeans.

Lola clenches her bottom lip between her teeth, reaching out and grabbing me by the waistband of my boxers, dragging me toward her. "Then we better not waste any time," she whispers.

A growl escapes my throat when I lift her onto the sink and slide between her legs. It's a tight fit in here, and I can't have my girl as wide as I'd like, but as long as I get inside her, I don't care. I bury my mouth in her neck, planting firm kisses upon her quivering skin. She finds her way into my boxers, and I groan when she grasps my cock with both hands.

"You're already hard," she whispers.

"I'm always hard when I'm with you. You're so fucking hot," I breathe into her neck.

She strokes me good, rolling her thumb over my swollen head, drawing a pearl of pre-cum to the surface. Fuck. I could just stay here all day, kissing my beautiful Lola, inhaling her intoxicating scent while she jerks my cock. But we don't have time for that. I'm going to have to take her now. Hard and quick.

I lift her skirt up to her hips, and with such easy access, I wonder if she had this planned along. I drag my fingers up her thighs until I feel her panties, then hook my fingers under the lace and pull them to the side. She's already so wet, and I rub a teasing thumb over her clit. Lola groans, writhing against me, and when I rub a little harder, she cries out.

I swiftly cover her mouth with my hand and shake my head, staring down at her as my eyes darken. "I'm going to give you every inch of me, baby, but you have to be quiet. Promise?"

Her eyes glass over and she nods, mumbling into my hand. I push her legs open a little wider, then with my free hand, I grip my cock at the base, lining it up with her slick entrance. Lola's on the pill now, and since she's mine and I'm hers, we don't use condoms anymore, which is useful for fucking in airplane bathrooms.

I waste no time and plunge inside of her, and Lola's eyes roll while she whimpers into my hand. I find my pace, thrusting in and out, slamming a little harder each time I enter her. I worry I'm being too rough, but she reaches out and grabs my hips, digging her nails into my skin as she pulls me deeper inside. It doesn't take long before I feel her muscles clench, and the choke hold she has on my dick makes me want to cum sooner.

"I'm going to cum, baby," I whisper. "And I'm not going to waste a fucking drop. Do you understand?" She nods, her body trembling as I thrust again. "That's good. That's so fucking good."

I feel my cock lengthen as my orgasm builds, and now I'm the one moaning loudly. With one hand Lola reaches inside my mouth and clamps hold of my jaw, dragging my face closer to hers, then covers my mouth completely with the other, just as my seed spills in thick ropes into the warmth of her pussy.

I release a low, guttural roar, falling against her, spent and happy, and we laugh softly together.

"Feel relaxed now?" she asks.

"If relaxed means I can't feel my legs. Then yeah, I'm pretty fucking relaxed," I chuckle.

I take a step back and do up my jeans while Lola shimmies off the sink and fixes her skirt.

"I'll go first," she giggles, slapping a kiss on my check before she slithers out of the stall.

I wait a few seconds before it's my turn to leave, but when I open the door, the attendant from earlier is standing right there.

She frowns. "Still stretching your legs, sir?"

She glances at my jeans, and that's when I notice my zip is down. I swiftly yank it back up.

"Ah, yep. All stretched. Thanks."

She looks down her nose at me, then carries on down the aisle. My cheeks burn red as I hurry back to my seat. Hopefully, I won't see her for the rest of the flight. I get in my chair and Lola is on her phone, her mouth wide open and her eyes bright and bursting with excitement.

"What is it?" I ask, craning my neck to find she's reading emails.

"My agent sold Starlight," she squeals through clenched teeth.

"That's amazing, Lola!" I cheer, leaning over to kiss her cheek. "Do you know who to?"

Her cheeks puff, and her face turns bright red, and for a second I worry she might explode.

"Hollie Arrow!" she screams, causing every passenger in our row to turn around and stare. "Hollie Arrow is going to sing one of my songs!"

"I'm so proud of you," I say, gripping her tiny hands in mine. She tries to catch her breath, her eyes welling with tears of pure joy. "Do you need to call your agent when we land?"

She shakes her head, dabbing at the tears that escaped the corners of her eyes. "Nope. I can do that later. When we land, we're focusing on you."

I furrow my brow. "But Lola. This is so much more important."

She shakes her head vehemently. "No, it's not. You are much more important, and this is something we need to put right."

I exhale. "You're right. Thank you."

When the plane touches down, I'm not as nervous as I once was, but that's probably helped by the happy ending I got in the bathroom. Lola and

I deboard and walk across the small tarmac to the terminal, where a large sign reads Welcome to Rockford Valley - Heart of the Southeast.

The weather today is doing its own little welcome dance for me. The sun peeks through scattered clouds, casting warm beams that make me squint. A light breeze carries whispers of the life I used to live here, and I swear the air has that sweet scent of honeysuckle I'd almost forgotten.

When we reach the terminal and the automatic doors slide open, I recognize each of the faces staring back at me. Janie, Rob and Stella tip their Stetsons at me, Janie and Rob in jeans and flannel shirts like they've just stepped off the ranch, while Stella wears a yellow sundress that sways at her knees and a pair of cowboy boots. My Mom's smile is brighter and prettier than I remember, with her straw-blonde hair in long layers over her shoulders, and it's not until her eyes well with tears that I realize how much I missed her.

But it's the towering, broad-shouldered man in the black shirt and jeans who approaches me first, his shaggy brown hair thick with dust beneath his black Stetson. His hands are deep in his pockets, and I catch the scent of his chewing tobacco in the corner of his mouth.

"Welcome home, Grizz," he says, his voice just as deep as mine.

I nod my head to greet him. "Dad." I look beside me and grip Lola's hand. "This is Lola. My girlfriend."

She smiles and the room lights up like it always does. "Nice to meet you."

Dad tips up the brim of his hat. "Nice to meet you too, miss."

He turns his attention back to me, and our eyes lock in a stare thick with questions and uncertainty.

He strokes his stubbled chin. "We got a lot to talk about. Don't we, son?"

I nod. "I reckon we do."

He exhales, his eyes drifting to look at the endless Rockford Valley sky. "Why don't we head back to the ranch? Grab something to eat and a couple of beers and talk then? Your mom's made a special dinner just for you and your lady."

I squeeze Lola's hand and my nerves ease when I feel her squeeze back. "Sure. Let's do that."

Dad walks away, which gives the rest of my family the all clear to pounce upon Lola and me, hugging and kissing and fussing like crazy.

My mom and sisters pull Lola aside while I talk to Rob, but I hear them asking her a million questions.

How do you put up with him?

You're brave to want to take that sourpuss on.

Don't his moods drive you crazy?

Lola looks over at me wide eyed in the commotion. I always thought she was the most beautiful girl in Lake Mistletoe, but the way the Rockford Valley sun shines on her flawless skin makes me think her light follows her wherever she goes, and I want to be at her side for the rest of our lives so I can soak up some of that glow. But that means having to leave things behind. The sun can't shine fiercely if there's always a rain cloud hovering overhead. So maybe I'll leave the Grinch back in Mistletoe and spend my life being Lola's sunshine, too.

THE END

www.ingramcontent.com/pod-product-compliance
Lightning Source LLC
Chambersburg PA
CBHW051549250626
47157CB00001B/234